EDWARD TRENCOM'S NOSE

EDWARD TRENCOM'S NOSE

A Novel of History, Dark Intrigue and Cheese

GILES MILTON

LARGE PRINT

Oxford

First published in Great Britain 2007
by
Macmillan, an imprint of Pan Macmillan Ltd.

Published in Large Print 2007 by ISIS Publishing Ltd.,
7 Centremead, Osney Mead, Oxford OX2 0ES
by arrangement with
Pan Macmillan Ltd.

British Library Cataloguing in Publication Data
Milton, Giles
    Edward Trencom's nose. – Large print ed.
    1. Cheesemakers – Virginia – Fiction
    2. Heredity, Human – Fiction
    3. Nose – Fiction
    4. Humorous stories
    5. Large type books
    I. Title
    823.9'2 [F]

ISBN 978–0–7531–7838–6 (hb)
ISBN 978–0–7531–7839–3 (pb)

Printed and bound in Great Britain by
T. J. International Ltd., Padstow, Cornwall

For Alex B.

The longest of beards

"Throw up your chin a moment, so that I may catch the profile of your face better. Yes, that's the d'Urberville nose and chin — a little debased."

Thomas Hardy, *Tess of the d'Urbervilles*

But when from a long-distant past nothing subsists, after the people are dead, after the things are broken and scattered, taste and smell alone, more fragile but more enduring, more immaterial, more persistent, more faithful, remain poised a long time, like souls, remembering, waiting, hoping, amid the ruins of all the rest; and bear unflinchingly, in the tiny and almost impalpable drop of their essence, the vast structure of recollection.

Marcel Proust, *Remembrance of Things Past*

PROLOGUE

16 July 1969

When Edward finally stirred from his sleep, he found himself in a room that he thought he recognized. He rolled over; opened one eye. Yes, yes, just as he had hoped. Satisfied that he was indeed in familiar territory, he pulled up the blanket and allowed himself to drift gently back into the world of sleep.

He was caught in that blissful state of non-being that lies somewhere between slumber and wakefulness. He was aware of his legs, but only as weights. He could feel his hands but only their warmth. Yet his nose was alert to the fact that something in the here and now — in this very bedroom — was causing him a most agreeable, most delectable sensation. Yes, indeed. His nose was twitching and tingling as it detected a smell — a smell of cheese that was pleasantly familiar.

For more than two months, Edward had lain in a palsied state in his bedroom at Number 22, Sunnyhill Road. He remembered nothing of being brought back to England. The boat journey to Italy, the plane trip home — the details were cloudy and intangible, as if they belonged to the world of dreams. Although he had been wide awake throughout the trip, his glazed expression had reflected the absolute vacancy of his inner head. The monks of Mount Athos had at first thought that he had suffered from some sort of stroke — that he was beyond redemption. A few of them said that he was afflicted by delusion and pride — that sins had gripped his mind in much the same way as demons can possess men's souls.

Edward had still been delirious when Elizabeth brought him back to Streatham and tucked him up in the comfort of his own bed. He did not seem to recognize his wife. He had not even known he was home. He didn't speak; he spent much of his time asleep. It was as if his very lifeblood had been plunged into a hibernant state and that nothing but the warmth of summer would rouse him from his slumbers.

The doctors diagnosed that he was suffering from the severe aftershock that (they said) often followed a trauma. Their only prescription was sleep and rest. Complete relaxation — that was what Edward Trencom most needed.

Now, seven weeks after being helped into the marital bed, Edward's slowly ticking brain was stirred by a smell that he was sure he recognized. "Yes!" Sniff, sniff. "Yes — yes!" He could feel his nasal passages clearing themselves. There was a tingle in his olfactory bulb. His head seemed filled with the thick scent of goats, milk-sheds and wild smilax. "Oh — mmn — yes!" And then, quite without warning (and preceded by a long loud yawn), a single word popped out of Edward's mouth: "touloumotyri". And as he said this, his nose twitched for a second time, his eyes sprang open and he found himself sitting bolt upright in his own bedroom

4

with his wife sitting next to him. She was once again holding a thick slice of touloumotyri under his nose, in the hope that some flicker of recognition — something deep in the recesses of his memory — would shake him out of his slumber.

Without saying another word, Edward took the cheese from Elizabeth's fingers and sniffed it again. It seemed to cast a spell over his body, like a wilting flower that is put into a vase of fresh, cold water. It was as if the cheese itself was re-invigorating him — clawing him back into the world. He could feel saliva welling in his mouth. He found himself having to swallow. And his belly, of which he had not been aware for weeks, was suddenly shot through with pangs of hunger. He could feel the cavernous emptiness within.

He popped the cheese onto his tongue and savoured the ripe tang. And then, unable to control himself any longer, he squashed the creamy cheese against the back of his front teeth, forcing it through the gaps with his tongue.

"Ah, yes," he said in a low voice. "That's touloumotyri all right. It's one of Teodoro's — and it's a September cheese, definitely a September cheese."

He savoured the taste for a moment longer, detecting the subtle aftertaste of the fiery tsipouro that Teodoro used to wash the rind. And then — suddenly — Edward became consciously aware of Elizabeth's presence. Until now, he had been so lost in his world that he hadn't even noticed the fact that she was sitting on the bed, less than two feet away.

He looked her up and down in a detached sort of way, as if he was still not sure if he really was awake. But, as it gradually dawned on him that he was, and that Elizabeth was indeed sitting on the bed, his eyes began to focus on something unexpected.

"What's happened to you?" he said abruptly. "You've changed — you look different."

Elizabeth smiled and smoothed her blouse over her tummy. "Yes," she said, feeling a prickle of excitement course over her body. "Edward, darling — I'm pregnant. We're going to have a baby — and you — you're going to be a father."

There was a long pause as Edward's brain continued to process the several unexpected facts that had occurred in the last minute. So it was true, then. He *was* awake. He really *was* sitting in his own bedroom — and his wife, Elizabeth . . .

There was a break in his thoughts as he was sidetracked into examining the altered shape of his wife. Hmm — she looks rather good. Yes, and I've always liked her in that blouse and — how strange! Did she just say that she's pregnant?

"But how?" he asked with a look of complete stupefaction. "When? Why didn't you tell me before?"

"Ssh!" soothed Elizabeth. "Don't think too much. Lie back on the bed. You're still very weak."

"But . . ." Edward settled into the soft pillows and pondered. His mind led him back to the last scene that he could remember with any clarity. It seemed so vivid, so absolutely real. And yet, well, it also seemed so very far away. It was almost as if he had been awoken with a start and his mind had not yet shaken off the images of his slumber. He suddenly recalled Father Seraphim's words — how the abbot had told Edward that it was time for him to rally to the cause. He pulled himself up again and looked at Elizabeth.

"They were all there, Elizabeth, *all* of them. I saw them laid out in their coffins. I was shown their skeletons. And then —"

"Don't worry yourself about that now," said Elizabeth. "There were many people who helped us home — we both had a very lucky escape. I think the demons are in the past."

Edward leaned over his wife in order to cut himself another slice of cheese. He felt desperately hungry.

"And here's the strangest thing," he said. "My nose is back on form. It's back to normal — in tip-top condition. I can smell everything. And not just the touloumotyri."

"So where do we go from here?" asked Elizabeth. "What happens now?"

"I must reopen Trencoms," said Edward. "That's a certainty. And we shall have a party — in honour of dear Mr George. Where would we be without Mr George? We'll invite everyone we know — except for Monsieur d'Autun — and we'll feast on your gratin dauphinois. But before we do any of that, Mrs Cheese, I think that we have some catching up to do. You know, it's been a long, long time . . ."

Elizabeth smiled and lay back on the bed. "Come here, Mr Cheese," she said playfully. "Let me have a look at you."

And at exactly the moment when she planted her first proper kiss on the lips of her newly restored husband, Mrs Hanson at Number 47 peered into their bedroom from her house across the street.

"Good gracious," she said as she twitched back the curtain. "It looks as if Mr Trencom is at long last on the mend."

PART ONE

CHAPTER
ONE

3 September 1666

Humphrey Trencom rolled over and sniffed at the air. He was caught in that blissful state of non-being that lies somewhere between slumber and wakefulness. He was aware of his legs but only as weights. He could feel his hands but only their warmth. Yet his vigilant nose was already alert to the fact that something in the here and now — in this very chamber — was not quite right.

In the time it took to trigger an alarm in his somnolent brain, Humphrey allowed his thoughts to drift back to the world of sleep. He had been dreaming of roasted capons and honeyed parsnips, of succulent woodcock and jellied eels. His sleepy reverie had transported him to the great banqueting hall of Whitehall Palace, where he was the seating partner of King Charles II. His brain had failed to register that this was as unlikely as it was improbable. Instead, it was once again focusing itself upon the long oak trestle that seemed to stretch to the furthest end of the room.

In the dream-filled orbit of Humphrey's head, the tabletop was laden with partridge pies, pomegranate pastries and quince conserves. There were castors of pepper and gallipots of oils, pitchers of chocolate and posnets of sauce. At the centrepiece of this display was a great tower of English cheeses — more than twenty different varieties that were stacked up on a decorative pewter platter. Humphrey himself had supplied all the cheeses for this morphean banquet and he was about to proffer his expert advice to the monarch, who was currently seated on his right.

"And which," asked the king with uncommon familiarity, "do you particularly recommend we try?"

Humphrey's favourite had long been the smoked Norfolk tynwood. Gingerly and with great care, he eased it from the base of the tower, causing the pile to wobble slightly. Then, after showing it to the king, he sliced a thick wedge from the tynwood round. He noticed that the pock-marked rind was coated in a thin film of ash that imparted an oaky softness to the lemony flesh of the cheese. Humphrey put it to his nose and inhaled deeply. Ah, yes — there was a tangible richness to the scent. The smell of bonfires and woodsmoke was working its way deep into his consciousness, causing his still-sleeping mouth to dribble with saliva.

It was at exactly this point in the dream that his conscious nose flashed a message of alarm to his not-quite-conscious brain. And just a second or two later, an abruptly awoken Humphrey realized that not everything was quite as it should be on this hot late-summer's morning.

The smell of smoke had not come from the slice of Norfolk tynwood; rather, it was drifting in through the casement window — invisible to the eye but altogether present in the sensitive nostrils of Humphrey Trencom.

"Mercy!" he said to himself as he sat bolt upright in bed. "Something is most certainly amiss." He straightened his nightcap, which had slipped over his eyes, and swung his legs over the side of the bed. As he did so, he noticed that the room was infused with a dull orange glow. With a growing sense of alarm, he climbed the four steps up to the high leaded window that had a view over much of the city.

The sight that greeted his eyes was so shocking and unexpected that he had to clutch at the woodwork to stop himself from reeling. "Oh, Lord," he said. "Oh, my good Lord." As far as he could see, from St Giles's in the north to Thames Street in the west, the entire city of London was aflame. Canning Street was a sheet of fire; the Exchange was a mass of burning timber. Botolph's Wharf was ablaze. Even some of the dwellings on London Bridge appeared to be smouldering from within.

It took Humphrey approximately three seconds to comprehend the scale of the disaster and a further two seconds to realize that his own life was quite possibly in grave danger. The parish of St Agatha, less than a hundred yards from his home, was consumed by fire. The Golden Cocke was sending out a funnel of sparks; the Fox and Grapes was a smoking ruin. Humphrey peered through the pall of smoke and realized that the pitched leaded roof of old St Paul's, which he could just make out, seemed to be a molten torrent. Liquid metal was pouring from the gargoyles and splashing onto the ground below.

He raced down the back stairs and out onto the lane. The air was a soupy mixture of acrid smoke — much stronger and more pungent than it had been in his own chamber. Humphrey could smell pitch and tar and burning brimstone.

Foster Lane was crowded with people — women, squealing babies, maids and soldiers. Broken furniture lay strewn across the cobbles. Carts and wagons were blocking the street.

"What in the devil's name is happening?" roared Humphrey to a passing soldier. "Where should we go?"

"The whole city is afire," came the reply. "Get yourself down to the riverside."

As soon as he realized that escape was still open to him, and that his own life was therefore not in imminent danger, Humphrey's thoughts became desperately focused on his shop.

"My cheeses," he thought. "What shall I do with my cheeses?"

Several options flashed through his mind. He could load them onto a wagon. He could pay people to carry them to the waterfront. He could try hauling them down into the cellars. But when he stared down the lane and saw it choked with people, he realized that none of these was realistic. London was on fire and no one would help to save his cheese.

The flames were growing dangerously close. The very air had been heated to a furnace and flames and squibs were dropping from the heavens. King Street and Milk

Street were now ablaze and several dwellings on Lothbury were burning fiercely. It was only a matter of time before the wall of fire would reach Trencoms.

When the flames did arrive, they came in a relentless wave. They latched themselves onto the corner shop — Mr George's, the vintner — grasping at the woodwork before tearing off the roof. Humphrey watched, horrified yet fascinated, as the gable end detached itself from the building and crashed to the ground in an explosion of flame. The Olde Bear was the next to be consumed; the flames — fuelled by tuns of brandy in the cellars — made short shrift of the wattle walls. They then tore through Number 12 and the Olde Supply Store before sniffing hungrily at the parch-dry facade of Trencoms cheese shop.

Humphrey moved as close as he dared to the flames, observing with detached horror the impending ruination of his life. The heat was intense — a pulsing, scalding blast — yet he seemed incapable of fleeing until he had witnessed with his own eyes the destruction of his livelihood.

The flames licked at the wooden timbers as if they wished to sniff and taste the cheeses before taking their first big lunge. The ancient beams, which had been set into the ground more than two centuries earlier, were as dry as an old corpse. London had not seen rain for more than three months and the parched surface of the timber was charred in seconds. Then, all at once, the entire front of the shop burst spectacularly into flame.

The little windowpanes held out valiantly against the rush of heat, but only for a few more seconds.

Humphrey could not tell which melted first — the lead or the glass — but he noticed that the famous Trencoms shopfront, bought at a cost of more than twenty guineas, fell from its casement in a dramatic molten collapse. Moments later, the darting tops of the flames began filtering inside the ground floor of the building, sniffing out anything that might be combustible.

Humphrey was standing dangerously close to the fire — he was less than thirty yards from the shop. In spite of the heat, which was roasting his cheeses, he remained rooted to the spot, watching in detached horror as the flames located their first victim. A large pile of prize Suffolk gilden was displayed on a tabletop close to the window. For the previous few minutes, it had been shielded from the worst of the heat by the thin, leaded window. Now, with that gone, it bore the full force of the flames.

Its surface turned shiny as it began to melt. Then, ever so slowly, its innards started to liquefy. The pile shrank slightly as its solid structure softened. The top cheese oozed into the one below and that, in turn, melted into the large round at the bottom.

Small bubbles appeared on the surface. It began to blister and splutter. And then, all at once, its gooey underbelly began to drip to the floor. The hard rinds still held out defiantly against the fearsome heat. But, deprived of their inner organs, the cheeses soon puckered and collapsed in on themselves. Humphrey's gildens were transformed into a runny puddle.

The flames were encouraged by the ease of their success and pushed themselves deeper inside the building. As the heat intensified, more and more cheeses began subsiding into waxy lumps. They lost their rigidity. Their edges softened. And then — finally — they were slowly unclotted by the flames. The charworths leached into the bridgeworths; the stiltons mingled with the blues.

In the midst of this oozy catastrophe, the noble parmesan alone held its shape and form. For more than five minutes it stood proud against the relentless onslaught of fire and flame. But, seemingly disheartened by the surrounding doom, its rotund belly began to shrink and buckle.

For more than two months, this 50 lb drum had brought pleasure and delight to Trencoms' regulars. Now, its rheumy innards were drip-drip-dripping to the floor.

Humphrey knew that when the inside of the shop reached a certain temperature, all of the surviving cheeses would spontaneously combust. He only had to wait a few seconds longer before this sorry moment came to pass. As the bells of St Mary's knelled the seventh hour — the last time they would ever ring — Trencoms cheese shop exploded into a fireball.

Humphrey watched in a mixture of awe and horror. He had already resigned himself to the loss of his shop and had also grasped that this spelled the end of his livelihood. And yet, amid this scene of utter devastation, he took pride in the fact that his cheeses were putting on a far more ostentatious display than all the other burning buildings. The tavern had disappeared in a squib of flame. The Olde Supply Store had burned long and slow. But his cheeses were proving theatrical to the last. Molten, dripping and turned to liquid oil, they now transformed the shop into a spectacular furnace of fire.

It was as Humphrey watched this operatic finale that his nose once again started to twitch. This time, his brain responded in seconds. Ah, yes! His cheeses — his beloved family of cheeses — were giving him one final burst of pleasure. Amid the stench of burning timber, pitch, dust and ash, there was the all-pervasive aroma of molten cheese. Humphrey could identify no one variety in the pungent concoction of smells. Instead, his nose was infused with a powerful miscellany of scents — one quite unlike anything he had smelled before.

He looked around him and was suddenly gripped by panic. He realized that he was now entirely alone and almost encircled by a wall of flame. He had been so enrapt in watching the cheese-fuelled flames that he had quite failed to notice that the fire had spread southwards and eastwards, tearing its way along the length of Lawrence Lane. The air was heated almost to roasting point and Humphrey could feel his wedding ring burning his skin.

"Great God!" he thought. "Where's everyone gone? I must get out — I must get myself to the river."

He allowed himself one final glance at the still-burning corpse of what had only recently been Trencoms cheese shop before turning on his heels and fleeing down the lane, stumbling over charred timbers and mounds of fallen masonry.

18

His mind was focused absolutely on saving his own skin and it was not until he at last reached the waterfront that he began to assess his predicament with a degree of clarity. As he did so, his thoughts performed several somersaults before turning in a most unexpected direction. He began to ask himself if the fire was the sign that his mother, in her characteristically cryptic fashion, had told him to one day expect. She had always insisted that the Trencom family was awaiting some sort of signal from the heavens and that when it came he would not fail but to notice it.

"Watch out for it, Humphrey," she had said to him when he was still a young boy, "and seize the moment. The sign will mark your destiny and it will also mark the destiny of the Trencoms. Yes, it will betoken good tidings for our family for generation upon generation."

As a small boy, Humphrey had often asked his mother to tell him more, but she would only ever offer him one of her customary monologues. "All the noble courts of Europe once sought our blood," she would say with a vigorous nod of her head. "Oh, yes. And we could have married into some of the very greatest dynasties. Tsar Ivan the Terrible proposed to Irene, your great-great-great-grandmother. And King Gustavus II Adolphus of Sweden offered one of your aunts the city of Lutzen in Saxony as her dowry."

The youthful Humphrey had listened entranced to his mother's litany of royal names and houses. He had heard these stories so many times that he knew, almost to the word, what was coming next.

"Here it comes — here it comes," he would think to himself, mimicking in his head his mother's strange accent. "And *I* could have married Prince Christian IV of Denmark, Norway and the Lofoten Islands."

"And *I*," she said right on cue, "could have married the Holy Roman Emperor himself — yes, indeed — Ferdinand III. But I didn't like the cut of his moustache."

Humphrey had involuntarily gulped when he realized that the well-worn script had suddenly acquired a new and most illustrious personality.

"*Really*, mother?" he had said. "Are you sure it wasn't Prince Christian IV — of Denmark, Norway and the Lofoten Islands?"

"Aye," had been her answer as she spat in the dust. "Him as well. I could have married them all. But I — we — didn't want to mix our blood with such *inferiors*."

"Then why," Humphrey had asked tentatively, "did you marry my father?"

There was a long pause as his mother, Zoe, looked dreamily at the cob and timber dwelling that had been her home for the last ten years.

"I fell in love," she had replied, wiping her eyes on her kirtle. "And I knew that together we could produce the son who would reclaim our patrimony. That's you, Humphrey. And when I saw your nose — when I saw that you had inherited *my* nose — I felt sure that it was only a question of time. We had left our homeland in a

20

welter of fire and flame — and a welter of fire and flame would surely send us back there again."

What exactly had his mother meant by these words? Humphrey had never known for certain, but now, as he turned his head towards the burning skyline, he quickly convinced himself that the fire was the mysterious portent of which she had spoken. To his way of thinking, the flames that had destroyed his shop heralded something of the utmost importance.

"Why, of course," he thought, with a tingling sense of excitement. "'Tis certainly the sign of which she spoke. This *must* be the sign. It has at long last come to pass, just as she promised it would."

No sooner had Humphrey concluded that the fire was a message from on high than he found a rush of ideas swift-footing themselves through the overheated chambers of his brain. Within a very short space of time, and in absolute disregard of either practicality or logic, he decided upon a dramatic and quite unexpected course of action.

"I shall go to Constantinople," he said to himself with a vigorous nod of his head. "Yes, indeed. That's surely what my mother wanted me to do. I shall put these charred ruins into the capable hands of brother John and seek my destiny in Constantinople."

And so he would. But little did he know that in following the sign and making his voyage, Humphrey was to spark a most catastrophic train of events — one that would not reach its nemesis until the spring of 1969, precisely 303 years and nine generations after his hasty and unexpected departure. It would fall to a certain Edward Trencom, a direct descendant of the precipitate Humphrey, to deal with the terrible consequences of his decision.

CHAPTER
TWO

January 1969

The guide clapped her hands and let slip an impatient cough. She was anxious to start the tour. "Excuse me — ladies and gentlemen. Ahem — if you're ready. Could I ask you — ahem."

The little group fell silent and she began.

"First of all," she said, "let me welcome you all to the tour. It'll last about forty minutes and if anyone has any questions, well, please don't hesitate to ask.

"Now — where shall we begin? Trencoms, as you can see, is housed in a most unusual building. The exterior facade is quintessentially Georgian — red brick, three storeys and finely proportioned — the sort of house in which, Mr Trencom once remarked, many of Jane Austen's characters might have been very much at home.

"Take a look at the fan light over the door. It's original. Look, too, at the sash windows. Most of them still retain their eighteenth-century glass. Yes, sir, you're right, it *is* very unusual in London — and for that we must thank Mr Albert Trencom. He boarded up the windows on the day that World War Two broke out — much to the amusement of the neighbouring shopkeepers — and the panels were not removed until Armistice Day.

"Above the main door, which has been dark green for more than a century, you'll notice the sort of wrought-iron sign that was once a familiar sight all over London. *Trencoms, 1662.* That was, of course, the year in which the shop first opened its doors.

"Yes, sir — you have a question. Ah, yes — so what *did* happen to the original Trencoms? Well, the first shop no longer exists. It was burned to the ground in the Great Fire of 1666 — completely destroyed. It had only been open for four years when it suffered its first great catastrophe."

The guide shuffled on her feet for a moment and stared briefly at the ground. "Perhaps I should point out," she said, "that the fire was not the only disaster Trencoms has suffered in its long history. It's strange. You see, almost every generation has had to face some accident or other." She lingered over the word *accident*, as if she wished to hint at something more sinister. "You could almost say that Trencoms is in some way — cursed."

The guide had managed to get everyone's attention with this last comment and, in the dramatic silence that followed, she took the opportunity to crack a well-worn joke — one she knew would make everyone laugh.

"Well," she said, "let's hope that it doesn't suffer another disaster in the course of the next forty minutes."

24

As the group duly let out a collective chuckle, the guide acknowledged their enjoyment with a knowing nod of her head and pressed on with the tour.

"Now then, just a couple of other things to add. Notice the royal insignia and those three magical words, 'by royal appointment'. I'm sure that some of you will have seen this on other shops during your stay in London — yes? Hmm? I can see that some of you are nodding.

"Well, I can assure you that a 'royal appointment' is indeed a great honour. Trencoms was awarded this status during the reign of Queen Victoria, who was particularly partial to Mr Henry Trencom's double-aged double gloucester. Prince Albert, incidentally, preferred the salty gewurtskäse, from northern Bavaria. We had someone on the tour the other day, a German businessman, who actually came from the village where gewurtskäse is made."

She paused for a moment in order to acknowledge a new arrival to the group. "Good morning, good morning," she said with characteristic jollity, motioning with her hand to draw the man closer. "Please come and join us. A holiday, is it? Tell us your name. And *do* tell us where you're from. I always like to know what countries I've had on my tours."

The man looked distinctly uneasy, as if this was the last thing he was expecting to be asked. "Er — Greece. I'm from Greece." He spoke hesitantly, in a voice that was heavily accented. "The name's Papadrianos. Andreas Papadrianos," he said, extending his hand. "From Salonika."

"Ah, good — good," said the guide. "We haven't had a Greek on the tour for many a month. A little word of advice — once we're inside, do try a slice of Mr Trencom's haloumi. Delicious, it really is. You won't find better outside Greece and that's a guarantee."

She smiled and asked the man another question.

"Business or pleasure?"

"I beg your pardon?" said Mr Papadrianos.

"Are you here for business or pleasure?" repeated the guide, who was speaking rather more slowly than usual on account of the fact that she was addressing a foreigner.

"Business," snapped the man, who was clearly annoyed at having to reveal anything about himself. "I'm here on — *personal* business."

"I see, I see," said the guide, who took this as a sign that her nosiness was once again getting the better of her. "Well now, ladies and gentlemen — and Mr Papa-what's-it — if you're ready, we can enter the shop. I'd ask those of you who have cameras to switch off the flashes as they have been known to interfere with the growth of the mould of the cheeses."

With that little caution and with one last glance at the facade, the group was ready to enter the oldest, finest and most famous cheese shop in London.

The first and most immediate sensation on first entering Trencoms was the extraordinary smell. The pungent odour of cheese permeated the air, as if the very walls and ceiling were built of great slabs of creamy-white emmental. Whenever customers and tour guides first walked through the door, the smell of cheese momentarily stopped them in their tracks. It was not unpleasant — not at all — but it took more than a minute for one's nostrils to adapt to such an abrupt change.

The air was at its foggiest and most fusty in the early morning, when the shop had just been opened. It was as if, all night long, the mouldering cheeses had been exhaling in their sleep — yawning, sighing and respiring stale cheesy odours. The Trencoms had long been convinced that, in the depth of their slumber, the stiltons burped and the roquefort broke wind. And why not? After all, every single cheese in Trencoms was a living being — a dense and vibrant clump of greeny-bluey-creamy bacteria.

The family had long ago discovered that many of the cheeses underwent a mysterious transformation during the hours of darkness. They would arrive in the morning to discover that the bell-shaped clochettes — which had been unripe just a few hours earlier — had acquired a new and greenish patina of mould. They would find that some of the couhé-veracs had miraculously divested themselves of their chestnut-leaf wrappers, as if they were petticoats or negligees to be wantonly dropped to the floor.

Many a Trencom had amused himself with thoughts of what really went on in the noctural world of cheese. Did the tommes make advances on the picodons? Did the gaperons woo the willowy buchettes? Whatever antics took place during the hours when Trencoms was closed — and no one could ever be entirely sure — the cheeses managed to imbue the shop with a distinctive, if ambiguous, morning odour — the sort of pleasant-unpleasant smell that occasionally finds itself trapped under the duvet of young lovers.

"Good morning, Mr Trencom," said the guide as she entered the shop. "And how are you this morning?"

"Ah, good morning indeed, Mrs Williamson," he replied, smiling at everyone on the tour. "Yes, yes — I'm tickety-boo, just tickety-boo." This was nothing short of the truth. Mr Edward Trencom, the proprietor of Trencoms — the tenth generation of the family to occupy this position — was in the finest possible fettle. He gave his belly a hearty slap and then polished his nose with the corner of his apron. A couple of people in the group sniggered when they heard him speak and several others exchanged glances when they noticed the curious shape of Mr Trencom's nose. But the better mannered managed to keep their composure.

"Here we go, Mrs Williamson — a slice of pencarreg to perk you up for the morning." The guide blushed ever so slightly and popped it into her mouth.

"And if that doesn't bring you out in goose pimples," chuckled Mr Trencom, "then we'll have to prescribe a large chunk of Burgundian clacbitou." Mrs Williamson smiled, the tour group laughed and Mr Trencom wished everyone a most agreeable visit.

The shop had a green and cream chequered marble floor. During the day, the tiles were scattered with sawdust, rendering it treacherous to anyone foolish enough to enter Trencoms wearing the sort of high heels that were popular with typists and office secretaries in the late 1960s.

Along both walls there were long marble counters topped with glass and brass frames. These allowed customers to view the cheeses on display — a tiny fraction of what was stored in the cellars — while at the same time protecting them from any contact with the breath, or wandering fingers, of Trencoms' clientele. Each cheese sat upon its own handmade straw mat, which had been imported from the Carmargue since the late 1870s. These were neutral in colour and odour, allowing the cheeses to breathe, but not imparting any unwanted flavour.

The shop's interior dated from 1873 — the first and only time when Trencoms had been redecorated. Two Victorian fans — installed in that year — still turned slowly in the ceiling, clicking slightly on every fourth rotation. They churned the air with heavy monotony, mingling all the individual odours into one. If you stood directly below the fans and held your head at approximately forty-five degrees, there was something about the way in which the air circulated that forced the smell deep into your nose. Yet if you stood at the end of the counter, the result was very different — light, fragrant and almost musty. It had long been a tradition among the Trencom proprietors to stand in four different spots each morning and allow the smell to permeate their nostrils. They liked to see how many individual cheeses they could identify in the pungent cocktail.

The walls of the shop were lined with rectangular tiles whose creamy colour matched the sticky inside of a ripe maroilles. Three shelves stood above the counter; each was stacked with rare bottled cheeses from the Peloponnese which were preserved in piquant olive oil. Behind each counter there was a ripe, ready-to-eat epoisses and a mug containing teaspoons. Tour groups were always greeted with a spoonful of epoisses and a warm personal welcome. Americans were particularly keen to meet the descendant of a family that had "been in cheese" for more than three centuries.

"And now," said Mrs Williamson, "if you're ready? We shall descend into the crypt."

It was as the tour group was clambering down the wooden stepladder and into the cellars that something rather peculiar happened — something that was to cast a shadow over the rest of Edward Trencom's day. The Greek newcomer to the group hung back from everyone else as if, out of politeness, he intended to be the last to descend the ladder. But no sooner had everyone else disappeared from view than he made his way back into the shop and hurried over to Mr Trencom.

"They know about you," he whispered. "Everything. And you are in grave danger. They've been watching you for at least a week, perhaps more. Even now they are monitoring you."

Edward Trencom was so completely taken aback at being addressed in such a manner — and by a complete stranger — that his immediate reaction was to rub his nose with great vigour, something that he always did when he was nervous or perturbed. He then fixed his eyes upon the man in a way that suggested he was wondering, firstly, if he had heard him correctly and secondly, if he should eject him from the shop.

"I do beg your pardon," he said in a tone that retained its customary politeness but was somewhat firmer and more insistent than he would ever use on his regular customers. "Can we help you in any way? Were you after any particular cheese?"

"I cannot tell you any more," continued Mr Papadrianos, who was completely oblivious to Edward's response. "But even now, you — we — are being watched."

As he said this, he motioned towards the street outside. Edward swung his gaze across to the large glazed window and was startled by what he saw. A very tall man — who looked just as Greek as the stranger standing before him — was peering in through the window. Yes, staring straight towards him. As their two sets of eyes met — and connected — the stranger outside suddenly bowed his head and scurried off down the street.

"I can't talk now," said the man standing before Edward. "But watch your back — and be cautious. We need you. All our hopes are pinned on you, Mr Trencom, all our hopes. I'll be back to tell you more. I can't say when, but I will be back. That much I can promise." And with that said and done, Mr Papadrianos gave a wave of his hand and made a hasty exit from the shop.

"Well, I'll be blowed," said Edward to himself as he reflected on the peculiar scene that had just taken place. "That is quite the strangest thing that has happened to me since . . ." His mind was briefly sidetracked into thinking about the last strange thing that had happened to him. Unable to recollect anything at all, he let out a series of indignant tuts before returning to the matter in hand. "Now then," he thought, "what on earth was that all about? *What* did he say? 'We need you. All our hopes are pinned on you.' Well, well, really! I've never heard such a preposterous piece of nonsense in all my life."

As he replayed the scene in his head — and allowed himself a little smile — he popped a slice of creamy caussedou into his mouth.

"Oh, no, no, no," Edward said aloud as he squashed the cheese against the roof of his mouth. "It doesn't taste quite right. Not at all. Indeed, one could even argue that it tastes as if it's gone off."

CHAPTER
THREE

Edward Trencom was in possession of a quite extraordinary nose. It was long, aquiline and marked by a prominent yet perfectly formed circular bump over the bridge. He had studied the architecture of his nose for much of his adult life and never tired of examining its curious shape. He was not a vain man — not at all. Aside from his habit of slipping on a fresh apron every morning, and being a stickler for cleanliness, he had scarcely a care in the world about his external appearance. It was rather an act of idle curiosity — speculation, if you will — that caused him regularly to check his nose in one of the many mirrors that adorned the walls of Trencoms.

There was a time when he felt it was modelled in the perpendicular style so beloved by England's cathedral builders. But no. Such a conclusion denied the very complexities that gave his nose its charm. For the bump over the bridge lent a dash of Byzantine excitement to its structure.

After years of reading and researching, measuring and anatomizing, Edward had reached a few definite conclusions. "My nose," he decided, "combines sensuality" (the bump) "with authority" (the straightness) "in a perfect blend of Greek and Roman." Yes. Edward Trencom was in possession of a truly Graeco-Roman nose: one that adhered to Sapphic concepts of beauty yet overlaid them with a strict Virgilian sense of duty.

Although the Trencoms had been in possession of their hereditary appendage for many hundreds of years, it had not always been so finely shaped. The earliest generations of the family had been born with noses that lacked any hint of the traits and characteristics that would one day become their most distinguishing hallmark. There had been no oriental bump. The bridge had none of the Roman straightness. The fine Greek facade had yet to be erected. Those early noses were the product of inbreeding and poor nourishment — malformed and born out of Saxon pillage and rape, bred on offal and turnips, smashed by blunderbusses, broken in ale-house brawls, subjected to the stench of the slaughterhouse, frozen in winter and abused by centuries of over-strong cider and ale. Incest had contributed to the skewed tip. Violent sword fights had left their scars. And although the owners of these noses would eventually dress themselves in elegantly slashed doublets, the flaccid red nostrils would reveal them to be in an advanced stage of deterioration. Capillaries would rupture and wiry hairs protrude from each nostril.

It was not until the mid-seventeenth century that the family suddenly found that an extraordinary nose had been thrust upon it. In or around 1637, a certain Humphrey Trencom was born with an appendage that was clearly out of the ordinary. It was uncommonly long and aquiline and particularly notable on account of a large bony dome that appeared almost to hang suspended above the bridge. No Trencom had ever been born with such an extraordinary-shaped nose and it was clear to the gaggle of family members crowing around the birthing bed that this particular specimen had come lock, stock and two fine barrels from the newborn Humphrey's mother, the exhausted but deliriously happy Zoe. She, in turn, had acquired the nose from her father, from whom it could be traced back into antiquity, through fathers and mothers and occasionally aunts and cousins as well. There was no obvious logic as to how and when the nose would appear, yet it was present — proud and immutable — in every generation.

By the time Humphrey was born, his mother was the only surviving member of the family to bear such a nose and she breathed a very heavy sigh of relief — and made the sign of the cross three times — when she saw that Humphrey was in possession of the family patrimony. She had performed her duty with perfect timing and others would duly follow suit in the decades and centuries to come. Ever since the birth of Humphrey, each generation managed to produce at least one offspring — usually, but by no means always, the firstborn son — who possessed a nose of formidable shape and sensitivity.

There were times, of course, when it lost a little of its magnificence. Its structure had become temporarily debased during the Regency period and a daguerreotype of old Henry Trencom revealed the dome above the bridge to have listed sharply to the left. But such architectural catastrophes never lasted for long. By the late nineteenth century, the nose was back on form. Edward's grandfather was so proud of his specimen that he underlined its qualities with a luxuriant moustache. Edward's father had also been blessed with a fine exemplum — one which turned a lustrous pink whenever he drank his evening glass of porter.

When still a young boy, Edward had quizzed his uncle about the family nose. "Uncle Harry," he had asked, "who first gave us our nose?"

His uncle had shot him a steely look and given an even sterner reply. "That subject is strictly forbidden in this household," he said with a shake of his head. "These noses have been the making of our family and they have also been our downfall."

He paused for a moment in order to wipe his dewy eyes with his lavender-coloured kerchief. He thought of Peregrine Trencom — Edward's father — and a tear rolled down his cheek. He thought of George Trencom — Edward's grandfather — and a second tear splashed to the floor.

"But what do you mean?" persisted Edward. "You must tell me more."

"God gave you your nose," replied Harold, "and so you must use it. But never ask questions about it. And never go in search of its origins. Never, never, never. From this time forth, Edward, your nose is a subject that is strictly forbidden in this household."

And that — for more than thirty years — was that.

CHAPTER
FOUR

Cheese had been in the Trencom family blood for even longer than they had possessed their extraordinary noses. The fifteenth-century *Boke of Nurture*, written by the court physician John Russell, was the first to speak of the ful-some properties of the trencom round — a hard, aged cheese made from cows' milk. "The trencom rounde," wrote Russell, "wille a stomache kepe in the botom open." Just a few years after these lines were written, Fulke Regis, Bishop of Exeter, presented half a hundredweight to King Henry VIII.

From this moment on, the Trencoms never looked back. Their cheeses were trumpeted in both the 1596 *Haven of Health* and the encyclopaedic *Booke of Goodnesse*. And, in 1662, their fortunes took an even more dramatic upward turn. The finely nosed Humphrey Trencom sold a large parcel of the patrimonial farmland in Dorset's Piddle Valley and headed to London. He founded Trencoms in the heart of the city and quickly established a reputation for quality.

Humphrey had a singular ability to detect and buy the most fragrant cheeses and he was soon granted the honour of supplying the court of King Charles II. It was most unfortunate that the Great Fire should destroy the shop and that the mercurial Humphrey should make the terrible mistake of allowing his nose to lead him to Constantinople. But other members of the Trencom family managed to rebuild the business and re-establish themselves as the leading cheese merchants of London.

The few decades that saw them transformed from farmers to merchants coincided with the remarkable transformation in the morphology of their faces, as well as a dramatic change in the sensitivity of their newly acquired appendage. Their noses had an extraordinary ability to discern the composition, maturity and quality of a cheese. And ever since that time, the family nose had sniffed, whiffed, judged and tested the great cheeses of the world, from camemberts and chèvres to saint nectaires and saint paulins.

Their reputation hinged fairly and squarely upon their noses. For generation after generation, the menfolk of the family relied on this finely tuned organ to tell them good from bad and fair from foul. Their nose was both defence and prosecution, judge and jury, and it was only when the combined talent of two nostrils had confirmed that a cheese was exceptional that it was sold to the ladies and gentlemen of the city.

The Trencoms did not consider themselves shop-keepers, nor would they have described themselves as purveyors of fine cheeses. A purveyor, they argued, merely buys a product at a low cost and sells it for profit — a hawker or pedlar on a grand scale. No. The

Trencoms had always viewed themselves as connoisseurs and experts, judges and hierophants whose role in life was, as the sagacious Thomas Trencom had once remarked, to separate the curds from the whey. Just as a priest prays for the souls of his flock, so the Trencoms were custodians of their clients' palates. Their shop was a breath of fresh air in the mouldering and rather smelly world of cheese.

The family had long believed that a nose could only be truly refined by withholding the object of desire. From grandfather to grandson and from generation to generation, every Trencom had spent six long years in the company of cheese before being allowed to taste it. Thus it had always been and thus it was with the young Edward.

No one in the family could remember why six years had to pass. It was, perhaps, because it took six years for Provençal cachaille to reach maturity. Or it may have been because the most exquisite cantal was made with milk from six-year-old cows. Whatever the reason, it came to pass that Edward first tasted cheese on the occasion of his twenty-second birthday. He arrived at Trencoms at a little after 8.00a.m., as was his custom. He sniffed at the frowzy air and took a long inhalation of breath. Then, glancing down, he noticed that his hands were trembling. He could scarcely contain his excitement.

He clambered down the stepladder into the cellars and checked the air for a second time that morning. As he did so, he was greeted by his uncle, Harold, who had cared for Edward since he was ten years old. Harold was in the process of tapping and wrapping a small selection of cheeses.

"Ah — at last — here you are," said Harold, as he popped up from behind a precariously balanced tower of Savoyard tomme. "Edward — many happy returns. I only wish your father was still alive. He would have been proud to have been here today."

Harold paused for a moment as he wiped a film of damp mould from a mature tomme du Mont Cenis. Then, with great care, he rubbed the mould into his moustache and inhaled deeply. "Ah, yes," he said in a low murmur, "a truly rumbustious cheese."

Edward nodded in agreement as he detected the glacial freshness of an Alpine breeze. Then, a few moment's later, he found himself sniffing at freshly scythed meadows. There was the hint of crushed cowslip, the fragile scent of gentian.

Five seconds had passed.

Then ten.

"A tomme," asserted Edward, "but from where?"

"Wait," was Harold's reply. "Be patient."

And just as he spoke these words, there was another wave of scent, this time warmer and more homely. Edward smelled the body sweat of cows and the thick odour of the milking shed.

"Of course — it's tomme du Mont Cenis," said Edward with a confident smile. "Straight from the Rhone Alps. You can almost smell" — he gave a theatrical sniff — "the imminent arrival of snow."

Harold congratulated Edward and ushered him over to a corner of the cellar where he had prepared a birthday parcel bound in thick brown paper. Its contents came as no surprise to Edward, for he was well versed in the Trencom tradition. Even so, he ripped through the wrapping with growing excitement. Inside, sure enough, was exactly what he had expected: one epoisses, one whole stilton, and three farm-produced chèvres wrapped in copper coloured chestnut leaves. He was finally going to taste them.

Slowly, gently, he pulled back the covers on the stilton to reveal a sight more beautiful than any he had seen in his life. She was complete perfection. Cloaked in brown-grey mould, firm yet sensual, she had the finest crust he had ever seen.

"Can I open her?" exclaimed Edward. He was hot and flushed and his fingers had once again begun to tremble.

"Yes," said his uncle. "But you know the rule. Clear all the other cheeses out of the way. You must allow each individual specimen to breathe."

Edward hastily moved the other cheeses and returned to the stilton. He removed the thin muslin and allowed it to fall gently to the floor. He then stood back for a moment to admire her extraordinary skin before bringing his nose up close to a small crack in the surface. Then, gingerly, he reached for his knife and positioned it inside the crack. Pausing for a second, he thrust it deep into the stilton's heart. Suddenly there was an explosion of scents and smells that sent Edward reeling backwards. There was the odour of damp churches and enclosed vaults, mushrooms and waxed wood.

Harry watched as Edward separated the two halves of the round. He, too, was shaking, excited at the effect the cheese was having on Edward and exhilarated at the prospect of tasting a smear of the rich blue mould.

"Stop," said Harry as he moved nearer to the stilton. He wiped his finger over the moist surface then frotted it carefully into his moustache, introducing a second scent to his bristly upper lip. "Oh, yes! Smell, smell — what can you tell me about this cheese? Can you tell me when it was made? Can you identify the farm? Do you know the cow?"

Edward inhaled deeply, urging the scent into the furthest reaches of his olfactory bulb. His nose seemed to be growing, expanding, as it allowed the stilton's odour to brush past millions of hairs and pores. Within seconds Edward felt himself transformed: he could smell the cheese in his throat, his mouth, his lungs, his entire body. He was tingling all over; he felt light-headed. There was no doubting that this was a veritable giant among stiltons.

"It was . . ." said Edward as he momentarily lifted his nose away from the cheese, "it was made on St Cuthbert's farm — the one next to the church in Colston Bassett." He sniffed again. "It's certainly an August cheese. Yes, I'd guess at 28th August — late afternoon. But the cow? That's tricky."

"Yes, indeed," agreed Uncle Harry, "tricky-dicky."

Edward paused for a second as he sniffed the cheese again. "It's not Buttercup — it's too creamy for her. And I don't believe it's Daisy or Cowslip. Did the milk come from Wittgenstein?"

"A hole in one!" exclaimed Harold with a smile. "A veritable hole in one! Welcome to Trencoms, Edward. You are, without doubt, in possession of the finest Trencom nose in generations."

He smiled, but it was an anxious and rather nervous smile. "And I hope to God," he said under his breath, "that it doesn't inflict on you the same terrible curse as it did" — he paused in order to dab his eyes — "on all of the others."

Edward's nostrils became ever more refined as the years unfolded. It was not long before a single whiff was all he required to detect the exact provenance of any of the world's great cheeses. He became a Master Cheesemonger at the precocious age of twenty-four and then went on to become a Maître de Fromage. He received a gold medal from Heidelberg's Milchprodukte Institut, and was made an honorary member of the board of the Accademia del Formaggio in Rome. A year later he received his greatest honour when he was made Life President of the Most Worshipful Company of Cheese Connoisseurs.

He wrote four specialist books on cheese (all of which received ecstatic reviews from the critics) before embarking on his greatest project: his twelve-volume *Encyclopaedia of Cheese*. When published in 1967, the *Daily Telegraph* heralded it as the most important cheese book ever written. *The Times* was even more effusive, labelling Trencom "the Edward Gibbon of the cheese world".

Such praise did not leave Edward resting on his laurels — indeed, it had quite the reverse effect. Inspired to even greater heights, he envisioned writing a monumental *History of Cheese* — a book that was to follow the evolution of cheese from Neolithic times to the present day, ending with a chapter on the history of Trencoms. It was to be dedicated to "the noble epoisses", which Edward had long considered to be the finest cheese in the world.

CHAPTER
FIVE

21 January 1969

Tuesday, 21 January began like any other day. At 8.31 a.m., Edward unlocked the door to Trencoms and stepped briskly into the shop. He blew his nose, checked the temperature, and sniffed at the air.

"Hmm," he thought to himself. "To think that it's still January. Why, today is unseasonably warm."

He made his way to the back of the shop, pausing briefly as he passed underneath the twirling fans. Then, satisfied that the air smelled as rich as ever, he cut himself a thick slice of chèvre from the Nièvre and held it to his nose.

"Ah — yes," he said to himself. "What a way to start the day!"

After savouring the fragrance of goats and the mild bitterness of the rind, he set to work, unpacking boxes and carrying cheeses upstairs. Then, at exactly 9 a.m., shortly after the arrival of Mr George, his senior assistant, he unbolted the inner lock of Trencoms' front door and swung the sign from "closed" to "open".

At 9.11 a.m., the first customer arrived and bought a large slice of Normandy brie. At 9.32 a.m., Mr Jançek the Polish chemist bought a 4 oz pot of creamy edelpilzkase. Edward was pleased to see that Mr George was in the process of carefully arranging a new delivery of neufchatel, sniffing at each individual cheese before placing it on its mat. Where would he be without Mr George? He was a thoroughly dependable type who knew exactly what needed to be done. "A safe pair of hands," mused Edward as he wiped his own on a muslin towel. "A very safe pair of hands." If anything was ever to go wrong, one would want a Mr George right behind one in order to put it right again.

Mr George was a good deal older than Edward and had faithfully served in Trencoms since the time of Uncle Harold. He had always spent long hours in the shop and, ever since the death of his dear wife, had seemed keen to work six days a week rather than the customary five. Truth was, he was a somewhat lonely figure (though by no means a sad one) and enjoyed the gentle camaraderie of working in the shop.

The two men rarely spoke of the late Mrs George, for neither of them liked to touch on personal matters. Edward had never been invited to Mr George's house and Mr George had never been to Edward's; that was just as it should be. Nor did it strike either of them as remotely odd that they had referred to themselves as "Mr" for so long that they'd almost forgotten each other's first names. Just moments earlier, Edward had found himself scratching his head in frustration as he'd tried to recall Mr George's Christian name. It had gone clean out of his head and it was only when he sold Mr Jançek the piece of edelpilzkase that he remembered it was Edwin.

The sudden remembrance of this set off a chain of associations in Edward's brain cells. The historically minded ones latched themselves on to another Edwin, the Saxon king of Northumbria, whose reign had long been a source of interest to Edward. He surprised himself by recalling that King Edwin had married the enchanting Princess Aethelburh of Kent — and surprised himself even more when he found himself wondering, with a bemused inner smile, if Mrs George had been called Aethelburh.

"What a strange and inappropriate thought," he mumbled in a low voice, and was in the process of admonishing himself when something caused him to look outside into the street. To his surprise, and immense disquiet, he realized that he was being watched. Yes, he was being watched by the same tall Greek man that he had first sighted a couple of days earlier. The man was peering into the shop and appeared to be studying Edward's every movement. But no sooner had their eyes met than the man spun round, turned his back to the window and hurried off down the street.

"Can you hold the fort for a moment, Mr George?" said Edward. "There's something I urgently need to check." And without waiting for an answer, he stepped outside and looked to the left and right.

It was almost fifty yards to the end of the street and yet the man had already disappeared. Edward sniffed at the air and immediately picked up his scent.

"Thank heavens," he thought. "This is going to be easy. He's been smoking that revolting Balkan tobacco."

He set off down the street and turned left at the end, following the trail of scent. In the distance, he spied his quarry heading down King Street. "Where can he be going?" thought Edward. "And, more to the point, who the devil is he?"

The man was walking extremely fast, obliging Edward — whose legs were somewhat shorter — to break into an occasional jog. Yet still he fell behind and by the time he reached the junction with Gresham Street, there was no sign of him.

Edward sniffed again at the air and took two deep inhalations of breath. "Ah, yes", he said to himself. He could still detect a faint aroma of old tobacco.

He turned right into Gresham Street and once again caught sight of the man as he dashed along the pavement — he was now about fifty yards in front. "How odd," thought Edward, with growing disquiet. "I'm sure that *he* should be following *me*, and yet here I am tracking him."

He was alarmed by the morning's strange turn of events yet he couldn't help but feel a tingle of excitement. As he hurried through the city streets, he imagined himself in a detective story in which he was tracking down the villain. Just a few days earlier he had been reading Harry Barnsley's *Ten Chimes Before Midnight*, in which there was a chase just like this. Detective Jim Moorhouse had dashed through the city streets in pursuit of a secret agent and he, too, had been helped by the smell of cigarette smoke. The only difference was that in Barnsley's book, the city had been Moscow and Detective Moorhouse had ended up in the arms of a female double agent.

Edward glanced at his watch and saw that it was almost 10.30a.m. "I'll give myself twenty minutes," he thought. "If I haven't caught up with him by then, well — I oughtn't to leave Mr George all alone for any longer than that. Unless, of course, there's a female double agent waiting for me."

The man in front turned suddenly into Old Jewry and quickened his pace still further. When he reached the end of this street, he turned a sharp right into Cheapside. Edward was by now so puzzled that he stopped in his tracks for a second. "He seems to be going round in circles," he thought. "At this rate, he really will end up chasing me."

But no. The man veered left into Queen Street — where Edward's oldest friend Richard Barcley had his offices — and began walking much more slowly. He took a quick glance over his shoulder, as if to ensure that Edward was out of sight, then reached for his keys and opened the door to Number 14. By the time Edward turned into Queen Street a few seconds later, the man had disappeared from view.

"Gone," said Edward to himself. "He must have gone into one of the buildings. Right opposite Richard's office."

He followed the rapidly vanishing scent along the street until he reached the door to Number 14. "And this," said Edward to himself, "is where he's gone to."

He stared at the plain wooden door for a moment or two before glancing at the plaque on the wall. It read "Christos Makarezos and Sons, Piraeus".

"So he *is* Greek," thought Edward as he rubbed the end of his nose. "At least I know that much. I wonder if Richard knows him."

He thought about calling on his friend, but a quick glance at his watch reminded him that he ought to get back to Trencoms.

As he retraced his steps to the shop, and recalled the strange man who had approached him two days earlier, he felt a wave of goose pimples spread over his body. He was shivering and sweating at the same time, partly from exertion and partly from fear.

"Could it be that the man from the tour group really *was* trying to warn me about something?" he thought. "Could it be that someone really is spying on me?" And as Edward thought these thoughts, it dawned on him that perhaps his life really was in danger.

But from whom, and why, he had absolutely no idea.

CHAPTER
SIX

Before plunging any deeper into the terrible fate that was to befall Edward, we must first make the acquaintance of the Trencom wives. The womenfolk had long been the heart and lifeblood of this extraordinary family. It was they who provided the Trencoms with their sensitivity and their souls; they who breastfed their offspring and first gave them milk. Indeed, it is certainly true to say that were it not for the women — or one woman in particular — the Trencom males would never have acquired their magnificent noses.

For centuries, the Trencom men had joshed that their women distinguished themselves in one of two fields. They were either childbearers (like Dorothea, wife to Joshua Trencom), or cheese-makers (like Caroline, wife to Emmanuel Trencom). The childbearers were — according to received male wisdom — treble-chinned, of rounded girth and adorned with ample bosoms. Jovial and with a tendency to guffaw, they generally died young but happy after bearing enormous numbers of children.

The cheese-makers, by contrast, were said to be wiry, bony and in possession of chests so flat that even the tightest corset (with whalebone upthrusts) failed to introduce any hillock or dimmock to the barren plains of their upper bodies. They had shrew-like eyes and sharpish noses, unnaturally small ears and uncommonly pointed chins. They were devoted and hard-working folk, and their husbands would have one believe that they had spent the greater part of the eighteenth and nineteenth centuries compiling notes on cheeses with a pince-nez clipped to their noses.

There were grains of truth in all of this, yet the men had never really understood the essence of their wives. A tendency towards dullardness, overlaid with an unfortunate streak of superciliousness, rendered them incapable of seeing the wood for the trees. And there were times — entire generations — when they didn't even see the trees.

When Caroline Trencom went into labour for the sixteenth time, she survived the pains of childbirth by delving into the depths of that much-mocked voluminous belly and finding there an inner strength that was quite lacking in the Trencom men. And when Dorothea gave her vexatious husband a violent arm jab to the belly, winding him so badly that he couldn't eat a morsel for fully three days, she demonstrably proved to herself and her adoptive family that she had her own internal powerhouse.

The Trencom women knew — though never admitted — that they had the upper hand. They would assemble at the frequent family gatherings aware that their only obvious bond was conjugal: viz. they were all married to Trencoms. Yet they had among themselves a complicity of behaviour and camaraderie that made them feel very much at home in one another's company. Like sheafers in a meadow, they worked as a team — and the cut and thrust of their conversation followed a tidy and intuitive pattern that, in most people, would develop only after years of shared intimacy.

"Our menfolk are like mice," joked Claire Trencom at one family gathering, while the men were guttling grog.

"And we," added Theodora, "are the cats to play with them."

"I pounce," said Eliza. "And he jumps," rejoined Grace.

"I snooze," laughed Katherine. "And he comes out from the wainscot," added Anne.

"And when I want my milk," purred the ribald Bertha-Louise, "then I'll 'ave myself away with 'im."

The Trencom men often joked that they changed their taste in women with every generation, a pattern that had stood them in good stead since the seventeenth century. They would choose a childbearer if they were in need of children to work in the shop and a cheese-maker if they were short on supplies.

By the nineteenth century this see-saw pattern had become the unwritten rule of the family; when Henry Trencom chose a lumbering childbearer in 1835 (and fathered twenty-two offspring), it was both inevitable and necessary that his eldest son, Emmanuel, would choose a skinny, bony cheese-maker.

But such self-regulation was unable to survive the pressures of the modern age. When Edward's grandfather married a large-bosomed cheese-maker, tradition could be seen to be on the slide. When she went on to catch brucellosis — a disease more prevalent amongst dairy herds than young women — it was feared that the two types of wives had become inextricably confused.

Edward threw yet more spanners in the works by marrying a slight woman who had never made cheese. Elizabeth — for it is high time we made her acquaintance — was a pale and rather delicate woman whom Edward met in the spring of 1957.

She gave the outward impression of having rather more defences than most women of her age and it was true to say that she sometimes appeared demure in the company of men. This was not due to nerves — nothing could have been further from the truth — but because of a certain self-imposed reserve. Elizabeth had an absolute abhorrence of impinging on other people's territory. Indeed, there was a side to her that was peculiarly English — not in the patriotic sense of flag-waving and hymn-singing and cabbage that's been boiled for so long that it's no longer green. It was more the fact that she valued more than anything else in the world the much underrated virtue of respecting one another's space.

She fully understood why commuters on the train to London liked to hide behind the vast acreage of *The Times*. After all, she thought, didn't everyone have the right to a few snatched moments on the way to work, simply enjoying the privacy of their own company? She, too, took the train into town each morning and was visibly angry when Mrs Powell from Number 7 would sit next to her and chatter, chatter, chatter. "And then *she* said, so *I* said, but *she* said . . ." and so on and so forth until Elizabeth had very little option but to close her book and take part in a conversation that was neither stimulating, nor informative, nor of any interest to anyone except Mrs Powell herself.

"It drives me to distraction," she remarked to a friend she met up with after work. "I cannot abide people who thrust themselves upon you like that. Next time, I shall tell her that much as I would like to help her out of her predicament, I am a very bad listener at that hour of the morning."

And so she did, with a quite remarkable effect. On the following day, Mrs Powell clambered into a different carriage of the 8.23 a.m. to Victoria and spent the next fifteen minutes assaulting the ears of one of the other commuting neighbours who lived on the same street.

On the day that Edward first met Elizabeth, she was dressed in her most conventional clothes. These included a Burberry skirt, pleated blouse and shoes that would have been sensible almost everywhere except on the beach of a tropical island. Other men might not have given her a second glance — yet for Edward, it was the very attributes of primness and apparent shyness that enabled him to be more at ease in her company than he usually felt when talking to young ladies. Little matter that he had completely misread

Elizabeth's outward reserve. It would be many years before he discovered that it actually concealed a fathomless pool of what in those days was usually referred to as "spunk" — a spunk that placed her in a very similar (though rather less bawdy) basket to the Trencom women who had preceded her.

In Elizabeth's case, her adamantine core had without a doubt been inherited from her mother — a curious woman who, though no less quietly spoken than her daughter, was in her own way as formidable as a Victorian great aunt. She had spent her late twenties nursing the war-tortured victims of the battlefront and had often headed to work with a very young Elizabeth in tow. Elizabeth's formative years had thus been spent in the company of men whose minds had been curdled by the horrors of war.

She remembered it all so well; they would cry aloud, scream, whimper and sink for comfort into her mother's ample bosom as if they were suckling babes in search of milk. Her mother had once said, "When everyone else is losing their head, that's precisely the moment when you most need to keep yours."

Elizabeth, aged ten or thereabouts, had asked her mother *how* one kept one's head — a particularly apposite question since she'd just been reading a storybook about Marie-Antoinette. "Just remember these men," her mother had replied. "And take them with you wherever you go. It's no use the blind leading the blind."

Edward first glimpsed Elizabeth in Throgmorton Street and though he didn't normally give women a second glance, on this occasion he remembered being struck by her pretty nose and sensitive face. She had the complexion of a ripe bethmale, a cheese of which he was uncommonly fond.

Some days later — quite by coincidence — he found himself face to face with this very same woman. He had left Trencoms at lunchtime and, as was his custom, bought himself two sandwiches at Mrs O'Casey's. After eating them on a bench in the little garden at the corner of Love Lane, he retraced his steps to Gresham Street and then struck out eastwards until he reached the door of Percy's, Dealers in Fine and Antiquarian Coins. Such a visit was by no means unusual: as we shall discover, Edward had a fine collection of antiquarian coins.

To the uninitiated, Percy's was a daunting place to visit. It was never sullied by browsers, for the first floor "showroom" could only be accessed by climbing a formal staircase that was draped in rich crimson. Edward was no stranger here, yet he felt inexplicably nervous as he began to climb the stairs on this particular day.

"What *is* wrong with me?" he wondered.

And then, out of the corner of one eye, he realized exactly what was wrong. It was she. The girl he had seen in the street. There, sitting behind the counter and twisting her hair into a tidy chignon.

At this point, it is worth pausing for a moment to explain that Edward was not overly adept in the art of wooing. He had never "known" a woman (in the biblical sense) and nor had he ever felt particularly attracted to the female of the species.

It was not that he had inclinations towards his own sex — not at all. It was just that, well, given the choice between an uncertain evening in the company of a young lady and a few hours spent with a male friend, he would certainly have plumped for the latter.

So that when it came to pass that on 9 March 1957 he came face to face with Elizabeth — and felt a joyous little hopscotch in his heart — he was not entirely sure how to react.

"What is *she* doing here?" thought Edward. But before he had any time to consider the matter — or, indeed, to regain his composure — he found himself facing quite the most enchanting smile he had ever seen.

"What are *you* doing here?" he blurted, before realizing what he had said. "I mean — how did you? Where? How? You see — we've met before."

"I'm not sure we have met," she said sweetly, as she flashed her bluish-grey eyes in a manner that was not entirely innocent. It suggested a hint of coquettishness on her part — a feminine playfulness that would have caused heart spasms and angina in the usual (elderly) male clientele of Percy's.

"I'm Elizabeth Merson," she added. "And you must be Mr Trencom. I've heard a lot about you."

"Trenc — Me?" said Edward with growing astonishment. "But how . . .?"

"Oh, come now, you can't be that surprised", she said with an enchanting smile. "Or are you just being modest? You are, are you not, Edward Trencom? The famous author of *All the World's a Cheese?*"

"Er, yes, yes — but — yes." And for the first time in his life, Edward was completely lost for words.

In the time that it took him to pull himself together, he lifted his gaze to the topmost corner of the room. He noticed that high on the ceiling, balanced precariously on the stucco cornice, sat the cherub-like figure of Cupid.

"Funny," thought Edward. "I've never noticed him before. Not in all the times I've come here."

Edward had been a Percy's regular ever since his first visit in 1950. Long before Elizabeth had applied for a temporary job, he had returned each week to add to his increasingly splendid collection of Roman coins. He had begun by collecting one coin from the reign of each emperor, from Augustus in 27 BC to Anastasius in the sixth century. The denomination of the coin did not matter and nor did the place in which it was minted. All Edward looked for was the finest imperial portrait he could afford.

Within months, he had built up a sizeable collection. Searching in antique shops, lesser-known auction houses, and the roguish dealers of Villiers Street, he had soon acquired coins depicting Augustus, Tiberius, Nero and Caligula. A week later he added Claudius and Domitian. Next he bought Caracalla and Lucius Verus. And one Saturday, while browsing at an antique fair, he paid £1 2s 4d for a bagful of bronze containing coins of the usurping Emperors Valerian, Gallienus and

Saloninus. Less than a week later, he bought more than a dozen Byzantine coins, one of which had a fabulous portrait of the hawkish Michael Palaiologos. Henceforth, Edward expanded his collection to encompass the emperors and despots of Constantinople.

But here we must pause for a moment and return to that spring day in 1957 when Edward and Elizabeth first met.

"I'm in a state of some confusion," he murmured to Elizabeth, when he had at long last composed himself. "You see, I'm currently searching for a coin bearing the portrait of the Emperor Diocletian, but I cannot for the life of me remember if it was he or Carasius who first issued the bronze follis." And he suddenly realized with a start that he no longer cared two hoots who first issued the bronze follis. It was of absolutely no importance whatsoever.

Elizabeth's face offered sympathy but there was little she could do to help. She had been working at Percy's for just three weeks and knew nothing of the currency of the later Roman Empire.

"I really can't help, I'm afraid," she said. "But would it be useful to look at some coins? I've got Diocle . . . Diocletian's trays here by my knees."

"Your knees," said Edward, his voicing trailing off into a whisper. "Yes — I'd love to look at your knees."

No sooner had he realized what he had said than he felt a sharp stabbing pain in his back. Elizabeth, too, felt a similar pain. As both of them rubbed the affected spot, and she smiled inwardly, Edward's gaze returned to the stucco cornice, where the cherub-like Cupid was still smiling on the scene below. "Strange," thought Edward. "I could have sworn that he had an arrow in his bow."

Their courtship was brief but enjoyable, with many an evening spent tasting cheeses in the private vaults of Trencoms. Edward was besotted with Elizabeth — so much so that he even told Mr George of his intention to propose to her. Mr George congratulated him wholeheartedly and said, with a mist in his eye, that when Elizabeth wore her fawn raincoat she reminded him of the young Mrs George.

Elizabeth was no less enamoured of Edward, savouring his eccentricity, his zest for life and his idiosyncrasies. "I love his passion," she told a friend who couldn't quite see why anyone would want to marry someone who seemed old beyond their years.

"*You* might not have noticed it," said Elizabeth defensively, "but he's full of passion. He's got a passion for cheese, a passion for coins, a passion for history. He speaks of everything with such enjoyment. He might not be fashionable" — she stressed the word fashionable with more than a passing hint of disdain — "but at least he's sincere."

Two months later, Edward and Elizabeth were married in St Margaret's Church, Chichester, Elizabeth's home town. The two of them were now set to embark on a journey that would take them into hitherto undiscovered pastures.

CHAPTER
SEVEN

We must probe a little more deeply into the private lives of Mr and Mrs Trencom in order to shed light on a marital relationship that was curious, touching and soon to be stretched to near-breaking point by two strange Greek men whom neither of them had ever met.

Their wedding took place on 22 May 1957 — an afternoon event that was followed by a long and joyful reception. By 10p.m., the last of the guests had departed and the bridesmaids were safely tucked up in bed. The vicar, who was only now beginning to realize that he had drunk rather more than was his custom, was trying to remember if he had been unduly familiar with Elizabeth Trencom's mother.

The clock struck the hour with a timorous chime, as if to signal the fact that this was Edward and Elizabeth's first night together. They were both, if the truth be known, a trifle nervous about what was going to happen next. For each of them knew that today — tonight — within the next half an hour — they must surely perform the act of *coitus penetratus*.

The venue for this momentous event is of little importance. (It was, for the record, the White Hart

Hotel in Chichester.) The exact time when it occurred is of similar inconsequence. But the actual scenario is worthy of further study. In room 14 of the White Hart Hotel, Mrs Trencom could be seen standing in front of a full-length mirror wondering how on earth she would ever manage to unbutton her blasted wedding dress.

"Edward, my dearest," she said in a voice that sounded surprisingly assured, "would you — could you — undo my buttons?"

Edward glanced up from the *Country Life* he had been studying rather too purposefully and strode over to his wife of a few hours. Then, with fumbling fingers, he slowly began to unfasten the buttons that led from Mrs Trencom's pretty neck all the way down to her curvaceous bottom. And here was the strange thing. As he did this, Edward could feel a peculiar stirring in his loins. There was a tingling sensation. His blood began to race. And he suddenly realized that he was very soon going to find himself in a terribly embarrassing predicament, right here in front of his new wife.

Neither Edward nor Elizabeth had any experience in matters of the flesh. They had cuddled a lot during their courtship and on two or three occasions they had kissed each other in the cellars of Trencoms. During one of these embraces, Edward even put his hand on Elizabeth's bottom. But it had crossed neither his mind nor hers to discuss what might happen on their wedding night — and they had certainly never seen each other without clothes. In fact, Edward had never seen a naked woman and Elizabeth had never seen a naked man. It was probably the thought of seeing Mrs

Trencom naked — coupled with the sight of her shapely back — that was causing parts of Edward to stir from their customary slumber.

It is important to note at this point, lest we paint a too unfavourable portrait of our hero, that this was not Edward's first erection. He would often awake in the early morning to find his appendage (he was never quite sure what to call it) pointing due north instead of its customary due south. Yet on this particular occasion, both situation and sensation were altogether different. Edward could feel an uncontrollable tingling, an overwhelming urge, in those parts which he normally kept firmly out of his thoughts. To his horror, he realized that unless something dramatic happened — and happened fast — he would no longer be able to hide the rapidly growing bulge.

"Would you mind, darling, popping to the bathroom for a moment?" said Elizabeth. "While I finish getting undressed." It was with considerable relief that Edward went into the adjoining room, shut the door and doused his face and neck with cold water. Then, when everything down below was back to normal (and pointing due south, rather than a cockeyed north-north-west), he slipped out of his suit, shirt, trousers and pants and clambered into his cotton pyjamas.

"Ready, Edward," called a nervously excited Elizabeth from the bedroom. "It's safe to come out." And so Edward, with a sharp intake of breath and an involuntary shake of his head, stepped back into the bedroom and climbed slowly into bed.

★   ★   ★

It took a great deal of fumbling for Edward to get his thing into hers, but once he had done so he found that the experience was not altogether unpleasant. He kept his eyes firmly closed — he could not bear the thought that Elizabeth might see him in such an embarrassing position — and concentrated on what was going on down below. "This," he thought to himself after a couple of minutes, "is actually rather agreeable."

And what did Elizabeth Trencom make of it all? An aerial view of the marital bed would reveal her to be lying on her back, still wearing her full-length nightdress. Her legs were open a little and her arms were clutching tightly onto Edward's shoulders. Her eyes were closed — she could not bear the thought that Edward might see her in such an undignified position — and she was concentrating hard on the act that was being performed.

She was not particularly enjoying it, if she was completely honest. But at the same time she felt that, after all these years, this was the right time and place to be doing "it". And Edward was certainly the right man. She couldn't have borne the thought of being with someone smoothly confident and self-assured. No, she was happy that her new husband was as inexperienced as and, if anything, more nervous than her.

She also knew that it would all be over very soon. Edward's pace was quickening and the bed was beginning to squeak with alarming noise and regularity. And at the very moment when she let out an embarrassed "Ssshhh" — and with a final twang of the springs — it was indeed all over. Edward had finished his part of the act and the bed-springs returned to their customary positions. In the room below, the couple winked at each other. The couple next door looked at each other and smiled. And Mr and Mrs Trencom finally opened their eyes, relieved that they had — in their own, idiosyncratic and rather endearing way — lost their virginity to each other.

Henceforth they would make love once a week, on Sunday evenings, after they had eaten their roast dinner. The earth rarely moved for either of them and the act itself remained rather perfunctory. Yet they were a couple who were very much in love with each other and they both looked forward to their shared moments of intimacy. It never occurred to either of them that their regular Sunday night custom might one day be shaken up — indeed, utterly transformed — by the shades of Trencoms past.

CHAPTER
EIGHT

23 January 1969

The labyrinthine cellars of Trencoms had not existed when the store had first opened its doors. Indeed, it was not until the 1750s that a freak accident had led to their discovery. Samuel Trencom, a forefather of Edward, opened the shop one morning and discovered that the floor had collapsed in on itself. "Damnation and bother," he had said to himself. "This will require the services of Mr Joppell the mason." But Samuel's irritation had quickly given way to astonishment when he peered down the hole and saw a large cavity below the shop. He ran to fetch a ladder and descended down through the partially collapsed floor. And, to his immense surprise, he found himself in a series of large medieval chapels, all of them retaining their vaulted stone ceilings. They were partially filled with rubble and a couple of the doorways were almost blocked, yet it was still possible to crawl through all the interconnecting rooms.

Samuel was well known in the neighbourhood for his sangfroid, yet even his pulse had quickened as he descended into the medieval crypt. There, below his very shop, were six large chapels, each of which was accessed through the principal cellar.

"Heyday!" he said to himself. "This is most fortuitous."

The storage of cheese had been causing the Georgian Trencoms many sleepless nights and they had already been obliged to take leases on several local warehouses. Now, below their very own shop, they had a series of stone-lined cellars which were blessed with a constant year-round temperature and humidity. Samuel was not a devout man — indeed, he was constantly bemoaning the interminably long church services that were so popular in the 1750s — but on that very morning he took himself to the parish of St Lawrence Jewry on Gresham Street and left three silver shillings on the collection plate.

Samuel later discovered that the underground chapels had belonged to St Egbert's Cistercian abbey, which had once stood between what is now Gutter Lane and King Street. The abbey itself was razed to the ground during the Reformation; the church, refectory and all the outbuildings were demolished by King Henry VIII's band of vandals, thugs and plunderers. But the vast crypt of the abbey was lost in the rubble. Intact but buried, it was built over in the 1570s, whence it was soon forgotten. The site was destroyed once again during the Great Fire and by the time the area was redeveloped in the 1680s, everyone had quite forgotten that the chapels even existed.

Two centuries after Samuel's discovery, the crypt had become the organic heart of Trencoms. The staff who worked at the shop, and the tour groups who visited almost every day, entered through a large trapdoor at the rear of the shop. A steep wooden staircase led straight into the principal cellar, which contained more than 3,000 different cheeses.

These six chapels had been divided into geographical regions for longer than anyone cared to remember. When you reached the bottom of the stepladder you found yourself in the fertile pastures of the Nord-Pas-de-Calais, where the shelves were stacked with local *fermier* cheeses, such as the pungent saint-winoc and the brine-washed abbaye du mont des cats. From here, the main passage led through crates and racks towards Picardy and Burgundy and (eventually) the mountainous scrubland of the Haut-Languedoc. Here, the path divided and you had the choice of bearing either left or right. The left path led over the Pyrenees and into the mist-cloaked peaks of Euskadi, where the cheeses were as fresh and resinous as the pine-forested Basque slopes. If you followed this path into one of the larger side chapels, which was piled to the ceiling with crates, you would find yourself wandering southwards through Spain. It led onwards, across the Straits of Gibraltar, over the Atlas Mountains and into the dried goat's cheeses of the sub-Saharan scrub. Few of the Trencom family willingly chose this route, for they knew that it petered out among the okra-flavoured cheeses of Mauritania.

The other principal route wound its way towards the grassy slopes of the Jura, passed the moularens of Provence and the vachards of the Rhone. It then led high over the snowcovered Alps until the floor dipped suddenly and dramatically and you found yourself entering the warm valleys of Piedmont — an arrival that was heralded by the tangy smell of ripening gorgonzola. Again the path divided. One route led towards Naples and the great cheeses of the Italian south. The other headed east towards Macedonia, Thrace and the grassy plains of Anatolia. Once you crossed the Hellespont, you found yourself in the great cheese-making towns of Sivas, Erzincam and Erzurum. A few more paces brought you to some of the more remote provinces of eastern Persia. There were the hand-churned yoghurts of Bakhtaran; the Zoroastrian cheeses of Atashkade and Yazd. And further still, you headed northwards again to the acrid goat's curds so beloved by the Turkmen nomads. From here, you entered the hinterlands of the Trencoms storeroom — the blank vastness of Kazakhstan, the cities of Astrakhan, Chechnya, Tbilisi and Yerevan. Paths, alleys and gangways that wound through to the other little cellars led to every corner of the globe — to Asia, India, the Americas and Australasia.

And what of the great cheeses of the British Isles — the cheshires, the wensleydales and the stinking bishops? The Trencom family had never considered Britain to be a part of Europe. Separated by an iron grille and kept firmly behind lock and key, the cheeses of England, Wales and Scotland were housed together in one of the medieval side chapels.

The famous Trencom altar stood in the very heart of the principal crypt — a thick slab of Purbeck stone that rested on two chunky legs. Centuries earlier, this had been where the monks of St Egbert's Abbey had assembled to say their daily Mass. This was where they consecrated bread and wine. This was where their tonsured abbots had chanted dirges to their Lord. Albert of Wichbricht once celebrated the divine liturgy at this altar. St Branoc made a pilgrimage here in 1198. King Henry II heard Mass here before riding into Herefordshire to crush the barons' revolt.

Now, a very different worship took place at the altar. On this same slab of stone, cheeses were cut and smelled, examined and tasted. The monks of St Egbert's (several of whose bones lay beneath the floor) would have shot bolt upright in their graves if they could have seen what had happened in the intervening centuries. St Branoc would have cast his venomous snakes at the Trencoms, cursing them for their defilement. Abbot Henri of Clairvaux would have had them burned for heresy. Yet the Trencoms themselves saw nothing blasphemous in their actions. Quite the contrary. In cutting their cheese on the altar, in eating at the table of Christ, they saw themselves as custodians of a long and holy tradition.

Edward's working day could be broken down into constituent parts which seldom if ever changed. At 8.31 a.m., he would unlock the front door of Trencoms and step sharply into the shop. He would blow his nose and sniff at the cheeses. And then, after standing under the twirling fans, he would make his way down into the cellars.

His lunches, too, followed an unchanging pattern that suited both his temperament and his constitution. At 1p.m. sharp he would suggest that Mr George should take his break, knowing that he would return to the shop at 1.58p.m. Four minutes later — no more, no less — Edward himself would put on his overcoat, bid Mr George a cheery goodbye and step outside into the street.

But on 23 January 1969, two days after Edward's unexpected dash through the streets of the city, he found himself changing the habits of a lifetime. On any normal day, he would turn left into Mumford Court then left again into Milk Street. He would then join the queue outside Mrs O'Casey's. Regular as clockwork, he would buy himself two sandwiches (one ham, one egg — "Extra lettuce in the egg, please") before heading to the little garden at the corner of Love Lane. On this particular afternoon, however, Edward did not go to Mrs O'Casey's. True, he still sniffed the air in his customary way as he left Trencoms. Certainly, he examined the sky to check for gathering rain clouds. But instead of turning left as he stepped out of the shop, he turned right — away from Mrs O'Casey's — and struck out in the direction of Queen Street.

In his heart of hearts, Edward must have been aware that such a deviation from the norm could only presage ill. He must have known that Mr George would have been dismayed to see him turn right out of the shop. Yet he didn't falter in his decision, even though he had a frown on his face and a murmur in his heart.

Two remarkable things had happened to Edward over the previous forty-eight hours. The most disquieting of the two was the fact that Edward was now convinced he was being watched — watched by someone whose identity remained a complete mystery. This caused him considerable alarm and had constantly preyed on his mind, quite spoiling the enjoyment of his daily routine.

Now, something no less mysterious had occurred in the cellars of Trencoms. Edward had made a most startling discovery — a discovery so out of the ordinary that he felt sure his life was about to change forever. And although these two things were entirely uncon-nected — at least, they seemed to be unconnected — Edward couldn't help feeling that one, in some strange way, had led to the other.

His discovery in the Trencom crypt had taken him so completely by surprise that he had sneezed uncontrol-lably for the better part of three hours. And although the sneezes had eventually subsided, he found to his dismay that he had lost all powers of concentration. Whereas he normally looked forward to his mid-morning coffee break, today he had been itching for lunchtime. While he usually enjoyed chatting with Mr George about the action of bacteria on milk, such conversations suddenly seemed completely humdrum. Even the roquefort, the prince of cheeses, seemed to have lost its perfume on this particular morning. Some hidden anxiety — and Edward did not yet know what — was gnawing away inside his head.

He hurried down Lawrence Lane and began retracing his steps from two days earlier when he had followed the mysterious Greek man. He walked purposefully along King Street, as if looking for clues, then turned right into Gresham Street. After sniffing the air in Old Jewry and Cheapside, all the while sticking to the same side of the pavement as before, Edward found himself once again in Queen Street.

He paused for a second as he passed the offices of Christos Makarezos and Sons and looked up to the first floor to see if there was any sign of life. The curtains were drawn shut at both of the windows and yet he could see quite clearly that there was a light on in the room.

"Something to hide," thought Edward to himself. "Definitely something to hide." And he recalled how the puritan pastors of Amsterdam never used to draw their curtains, claiming that only sinners needed to close themselves off from the world.

He took one more look at the building before crossing the road. A few more steps brought him to Number 11, the offices of Barcley, Berkleigh and Barklee, Solicitors and Commissioners of Oaths. He strode up to the shiny black door with great purpose and, before pressing the bell, paused briefly to admire the profile of his nose in the polished brass plaque. He examined it carefully, allowing his index finger to slowly massage the finely crafted ridge. Then he smiled. Oh yes, yes, yes! Of all the uncertainties in the world, one thing was sure. He was, without doubt, in possession of a truly priceless treasure.

The bump brought him the greatest delight. It was hard. Solid. Bony. The sort of bump that would have caused vainer, vulgar folk considerable distress. Edward, by contrast, would have not have been too upset if the bump were ever so slightly larger.

"Fancy!" he said to himself with a smile. "What a fine nose you have, Edward Trencom." And as he lightly dusted his nostrils with a cream cotton handkerchief, he tried to remember the famous quotation about noses. How did it go? That the history of the world would have been utterly different if Cleopatra's nose had been shorter by half an inch. Was that it? Or was it longer by half an inch?

He knocked on the door with three loud raps. After a few seconds, he heard the sound of shuffling feet in the hallway, followed by the turning of a latch. The door opened and the secretary, Mrs Clarke, looked Edward up and down.

"Yes?" she enquired.

"I've come to see Mr Barcley," said Trencom as he shuffled his feet on the doorstep.

"Which particular Mr Barcley?" enquired Mrs Clarke. "Mr Barcley, Mr Berkleigh or Mr Barklee?"

"Mr Richard Barcley," said Edward. "One y and no i."

"I'm afraid he's not available at the moment," said Mrs Clarke, "but I can let him know you're here. Who shall I say would like to see him?"

"The name is Trencom," said Edward. "Perhaps you would be kind enough to tell him that I have something of the greatest importance to relay to him."

Mrs Clarke frowned and motioned him to step inside. "I'll see if he's available," she said.

Five minutes passed before an office door opened and Richard Barcley appeared clutching a half-empty mug of hot chocolate and a copy of the *Daily Telegraph*. He was a man for whom middle age had arrived with unseemly haste, as if it were anxious to wipe away any vestige of his once youthful frame. He was balding, dishevelled and with a rapidly spreading belly that clearly had designs on the last, as yet unused notch of his brown suede belt.

Richard had been born to be a solicitor. He was clever without being intelligent, smart without being wise, like the over-bright schoolboy who knows everything and yet somehow nothing. He could cite his logarithmic tables with impressive ease and could tell you all the stations (in order) on the Central line, Bakerloo line and Northern line.

"And," he would say with a pride that was just a whisker away from boasting, "I can generally finish the *Times* and *Telegraph* crosswords in under ten minutes." And so he could, but it would have been a trifle more impressive if he had kept this undeniable accomplishment to himself.

Despite his high IQ — and membership of MENSA — Barcley was somewhat deficient in the charm department. Like so many people who are aware of their own superiority, he had an unfortunate tendency to talk to others in a manner that suggested they were not quite on his high-frequency wavelength.

"But don't you see?" was one of his favourite phrases, often said with an exasperating sigh after the final "see". "It's quite clear to me," was another one — and was obviously intended to show that he felt it should have been quite clear to everyone else as well.

So why, it may be asked, did Edward like Richard so much? Even the most unprepossessing of people have qualities to balance the faults and Richard was no exception to this general rule. When his work colleague had been desperately ill, Richard had taken over his workload with admirable grace. And when his elderly neighbour had been robbed of her pension, he popped over every evening for more than a month to make sure that she was all right. In short, Barcley was a dependable and loyal friend — uncommonly loyal — and once he had formed a friendship he was in it for the duration.

"A friend in need," he liked to say, "is a friend indeed." Not the most original of saws, perhaps, but Richard had his own little twist which he would add with a flourish. After a theatrical pause he would say, "Did you know it was the Earl of Rochester who first coined that phrase?" Edward did, for he had been told it many times before, but he nodded with charitable goodwill nonetheless.

On this particular day, Barcley was not in the best of humours. His journey to work had been disrupted by a road closure in Sutton and his crossword had been ruined when his fountain pen had inexplicably voided a large globule of brilliant green ink. And just as he was about to slurp his first hot drink of the morning, he had jogged his elbow and spilt it all down his shirt and tie.

"Edward, old man," he said with a wan smile as he stepped out into the corridor. "If I'd known it was *you* waiting to see me, I'd have invited you in earlier. Mrs Clarke has a habit of matching the wrong names with the wrong faces then sending them to the wrong room."

"Well, on this occasion," said Edward as he settled himself into Barcley's office, "Mrs Clarke was one hundred per cent correct. Yes, yes — it's me all right. And what's more, I have a spot of news to tell you. Or, more accurately, I have two spots of news. One is very exciting indeed and I wanted you to be the first to know. The other is — well, to be honest, Richard, I'm hoping you might be able to help. You see, something rather strange has happened to me. Something that has left me feeling, well, uneasy."

He watched a large, plump bluebottle circle the lamp then zoom across to the window. It banged itself noisily against the glass then sped twice around the room and somersaulted over the armchair, before settling on the paperweight on Richard's desk.

"Before we go any further," said Richard with a detectable hint of weariness, "we must have something to drink. Would you like tea or coffee? If you want tea, I'll tell Mrs C you want coffee. If you want coffee, I'll get her to make you tea. If, on the other hand, you would care for a cold drink, I suggest you ask for hot chocolate. It's all very simple: Mrs Clarke invariably gives you the opposite of what you ask for.

"I think she's got dyslexia of the brain — and it gets worse every year. The only cure is a complete surgical removal of the head — Ha-ha! — but our dear old National Health Service claims it's too expensive."

Edward smiled and asked for a cup of coffee.

"Good. I'll have a coffee too," said Barcley, before shouting down the corridor for two cups of tea. "And Mrs Clarke," he said, as he winked at Edward, "this time we won't be needing any biscuits."

He settled back in his chair and faced his friend. "Now, old chap," he said, "what can I do you for? What are these spots of news?"

"Have you ever noticed anything strange about my face?" said Edward. "Have you ever looked at me and thought there was something, well, out of the ordinary about me?"

"In what particular sense, old chap?"

"Have you ever thought that your friend has a fine — an uncommonly splendid — nose?"

Richard shifted uncomfortably in his chair then looked at Edward's face. There was a certain truth in what he said. His friend did have a strange nose. Yes, a quite extraordinary nose.

"Fine? Yes. Splendid? Hmm, OK. But that's not to say, mind, that I'd want it myself."

"Take a look at my profile," said Edward, as he swivelled around in his chair to enable Barcley to make a closer inspection. "Look at the ridge of my nose — look how it begins to tilt downwards towards my mouth."

Richard stared at his friend with puzzled bemusement. Edward, his friend for more than twenty-two years, could be such a queer fellow at times.

"Now look at the bump. Examine it, Richard, examine it. Curious, don't you think? It's a perfect circle perched upon a perfect ridge. And what's more, Richard, it's shaped into a perfect dome."

Barcley noted that Edward had become so animated — excited — that his cheeks were infused with colour.

"Can't you see? It's totally unique. No one in the world has a nose like mine. It's one hundred per cent original."

Richard solemnly agreed with Edward. "It's a fine nose, old chap. A splendid nose. But I'm not sure there's a lot I can do about it. Unless, of course, it's locked in a legal dispute. Then, I suppose, we might be looking at some rich pickings."

He guffawed at his own joke and was rather disappointed to see that Edward was not even smiling.

"I've come to you precisely because you *can* do something about my nose. At any rate, you may be able to help. You see, I've unearthed something, Richard, of extraordinary importance. And I have a feeling that my life is about to change in a most fortuitous way."

Richard stared at his friend. Edward often behaved strangely, but on this particular afternoon he was excelling himself.

"So what *can* I do for you?" he had started to ask, but before he could finish his sentence he felt — he thought — he was certain . . .

But no.

The sneeze had suddenly subsided.

"Have you ever considered," said Edward, "the build-up to a sneeze?"

"Good God!" thought Richard, with a gathering sense of foreboding. "Next the old chap will be telling me he's psychic."

"It takes more than fourteen seconds for the body to produce a full-blown sneeze. There's the itching tickle in your lungs. The tingle in your eyes. And before you know it — a-a-a-tsch."

Richard begged Edward to stop. He drew his breath, covered his mouth and — with tears welling in his eyes — let rip a sneeze so loud that the very foundations of the building seemed to shake.

"Congratulations!" exclaimed Edward, "And right on cue. But let me get to the point. Yesterday — less than twenty-four hours ago — I was clambering down the stepladder in Trencoms when I also let out a violent sneeze. Just like yours. I hadn't sneezed like that since we last took delivery of a frühstückskäse and I sniffed at the air to see what was wrong. And do you know what happened? My nose twitched and tingled for a second time and my eyes filled with water. And once again I was overwhelmed by an extraordinarily forceful sneeze.

"And as I stood there wondering what had caused this unanticipated attack, I detected an unusual though not unpleasant smell filtering upwards from deep inside our cellars. It was unlike any cheese I'd come across in all my years at Trencoms. True, there was the dusty hint of the mistral that I've often detected at this time of the year. And there was also that faint scent of straw and lavender that's not uncommon in the goat's cheeses of the Languedoc. But there was none of the maturity or ripeness that is present in every single cheese that we stock."

Barcley raised his hand as if to stop his friend, but Edward was in full flow and scarcely even noticed.

"It had the briny tang of a chevrotin des aravis," he said, "but lacked its creamy richness. It had the saltiness of a bonde de gatine but without its lightly worn maturity. It was certainly an old smell — of that I could be certain. But it was not, I was sure, produced by any of the three thousand one hundred and twenty-six cheeses, yoghurts and fromages blancs that were being stored in the crypt."

Edward had been so excited and mystified by the smell that he had allowed his nose to track it down, following it down the alleys and walkways that led through the interconnecting cellars. He entered the fertile pastures of the Pas de Calais and followed the path all the way to the blue cheeses of the Jura. As he brushed past the crates of picadou, which were piled almost to the ceiling, he thought he could discern a whiff of fresh walnut.

But the smell had pulled him onwards, southwards, towards Piedmont and Lombardy and the majestic River Po. Here, however, the trail suddenly died and Edward found himself drawn towards one of the side cellars, which was filled with the mellow cheeses of Thrace. He pushed north-eastwards, towards Wallachia, Moldova and the cheese-producing towns of Transdneiper. But the smell once again petered out and he was drawn southwards towards the olive-marinaded cheeses of Istanbul.

"And here, Richard, the smell suddenly seemed to fill the air. It seemed to be pouring out from beneath the crates of cheeses we keep reserved for the Greek and Turkish restaurants of north London.

"Well, you can imagine my reaction — I was desperate to locate its source. I needed to know where it came from. I was in such haste that I knocked over two boxes, spilling their cheeses onto the floor. A third crashed into a stack of whey from Anatolia. It was only when I'd unstacked the tower of Turkish feta that I noticed the crate at the very bottom had split and come apart. And this was the source of the smell. It was filtering out of the crack in the wood."

Edward paused for a moment, anticipating that Barcley might have some questions. When none were forthcoming, he pressed on with his story.

"I crouched down to the floor and pushed my nose against the wood. And what did I smell? It was a strange concoction — leather, musty apples, vinegary cider. I detected musk and lilies, violets and myrrh. And as I unpacked the surrounding crates and shifted this one from the bottom of the pile, I realized that I had discovered something of uncommon interest."

"And what might that be?" asked Richard. He had noticed, as Edward was speaking, that the unseasonal thunderstorm had blown itself out and that brilliant winter sunlight was now streaming through the window. It struck the chrome-dial clock on the wall opposite his desk, scattering screaming shards of light across the four corners of the room.

"Ah-ha," said Edward. "That's a most pertinent question. It was most certainly not a cheese. Not a cheese at all. It was — are you ready? — the family records, or *some* of the family records, of the Trencoms. Of my ancestors. Yes, I had found a great box of family papers."

Richard raised an eyebrow and examined his index finger minutely, as if looking at it under a microscope. He then pushed it deep into his ear in order to track down and neutralize a most persistent itch. It was a habit — a rather unpleasant one — that tended to manifest itself whenever he was intrigued or excited. And he was, indeed, somewhat intrigued by what Edward told him. He realized that it might prove interesting after all.

"I had no idea what were they doing there. And I had no idea who put them there. In fact, I wasn't exactly sure what I'd found. The records seemed to be jumbled together. Whoever had placed them in the box had not sorted them into any particular order. But I soon realized that these old papers referred to my ancestors — yes, to all the Trencoms who had worked in the shop."

Barcley leaned forwards and tapped his pen three times on his desktop.

"And?" he said.

"And what?" asked Edward.

"Well, what *did* you find? What was in this box?"

"Birth certificates, baptismal records and notepads. There were census returns, a handful of old photographs. There was a book written by Humphrey Trencom — the founder of Trencoms — and a Victorian family Bible."

Edward paused for a second as he tried to remember what else he'd found.

"Oh yes, there was an edition of Byron's poems that contained several handwritten letters and any number of maps of the Ottoman Empire. There was even an old icon in the box, along with four or five books written in Greek."

"Hmm," said Richard, wondering where Edward's discovery was leading.

"And it dawned on me there and then," continued Edward, "that the contents of this box might well provide me with the opportunity to discover the truth about my nose."

Here, his voice dropped almost to a whisper.

"For more than three decades I've wondered who first bequeathed us this family heirloom. I could never ask my father, for he died when I was a boy. And I never met my grandfather. When, many years ago, I tried to ask my uncle about the Trencom nose, he forbade me from ever again mentioning the subject.

"Ever since I was a child, Richard, I've pondered over the strange shape and structure of my nose. I've wondered about its extraordinary sensitivity. All my life I've wanted to know how it entered the family.

"And now that I've unearthed these papers, well, I'm sure I'll be able to find out a great deal more. I'll be able to discover where we come from, Richard — and who I *really* am."

There was a long pause before Barcley spoke.

"Well," he said with a smile, "I'd caution you against getting too excited. You never know what you might find. My old father researched our family tree in the hope he'd find we were descended from Sir Launcelot Barkleigh, one of King Henry VIII's chancellors. He'd quite convinced himself that we were a branch of the same family and even began claiming that it was us Barcleys who'd instigated proceedings against Anne of Cleves.

"And do you know what he discovered? That we came from nothing more interesting than a long line of solicitors."

Barcley let slip a little snort and was surprised to see that Edward didn't share the joke. Indeed, his friend seemed suddenly agitated and had got up from his chair and walked over to the window.

"There's another thing," said Edward as he looked out across the street. "Something that *you* may be able to help me answer. That building over there — to whom does it belong? Is it an office? Or does someone live there?"

"What, Number 14?" asked Barcley, who got up from his desk in order to join his friend at the window. "Well, now — why do you ask about that all of a sudden? You're not going to tell me that it's got something to do with your family?"

Edward shook his head.

"That building has long been something of a mystery to Mrs Clarke and I. We've never quite discovered what goes on there. There are always people coming and going from there. Always a lot of activity."

"Activity?" queried Edward.

"Yes. Cars pulling up. Parcels being delivered. That sort of thing. And Mrs Clarke drove past late one evening, when Queen Street is always deserted, and noticed that all the lights in that building were still on."

"But whose offices are they? The plaque on the door suggests that it's some sort of family business from Piraeus."

"Yes, indeed — you *have* been doing your research. As far as I'm aware, it's a shipping company. Some sort of importexport business. But, tell me, why are you getting so worked up about Number Fourteen, Queen Street? I'm beginning to think it *has* got something to do with your family".

"No," said Edward. "Not at all. But —"

He stopped speaking for a moment as he wondered whether or not to tell his friend about the strange encounter he'd had with the man from the tour group. But he was concerned that it would all sound too odd. He didn't want Richard to think he'd lost his marbles.

He weighed up his options and then, with considerable reluctance, decided to spell out exactly what had happened over the previous two days. "It's like this," he said. "You may not believe me, Richard, but I have the distinct impression that I'm being watched. Indeed, it's more than an impression. I *know* that I'm being watched."

Edward told Barcley how the man on Mrs Williamson's tour had approached him and told him that his life was in danger.

"I'm not sure if I should believe him," continued Edward, "or dismiss him as somebody who's deranged. But one thing is sure, Richard. When he said I was being watched, he was indeed telling the truth. Someone *was* observing me — and that someone, whoever he is, has got something to do with this building here."

The two men looked back across the street towards Number 14. And as they did so, something happened that caused a chill to run through both men's spines. The curtains of the first floor window — which had been closed throughout the morning — momentarily parted. In the seconds that followed, Edward realized that he was being spied on by the very same man whom he had followed through the streets just two days earlier.

"Good God, Richard," said Edward. "That's him. That's him there. And he's looking straight at me."

PART TWO

CHAPTER
ONE

July 1942

Peregrine Trencom is clutching a wrinkled goatskin and trying to solve a most difficult conundrum. He is wondering if the creamy curd inside the skin is the most aromatic goat's cheese he has ever tasted. Or is it, perhaps, just a little too pungent? Although his nose is — sniff, sniff — thoroughly enjoying the salty tang of wild flowers, his brain is less convinced by the acrid stench of goats.

When Peregrine first held a piece of touloumotyri to his nose, he found it distinctly unpleasant. It had smelled very strongly of goats. But, after sniffing and eating it almost every day for eighteen months, the smell has started to grow on him. If he is ever to leave this remote mountain — and he has begun to have his doubts — he feels sure that he would soon start to pine for its overpowering smell.

"What a marvellous addition to Trencoms this would be," he thinks to himself. "Oh, yes — I could sell it in its goatskin." He lets out a little chuckle as he imagines one of his most loyal customers, Mrs Browning, collecting her daily skin of touloumotyri. "Here you are, madam," he would say to her in a clear voice, "your goatskin awaits."

Peregrine sighs gently as he thinks about Trencoms and then looks at his current home — a makeshift wooden shack perched six thousand feet above the Aegean. How his life has changed. He left London in the middle of the Blitz, having entrusted the running of the cheese shop to his younger brother, Harry. His departure had come as an unwelcome surprise to the family and was met with tears by his son, the nine-year-old Edward Trencom. "Why are you leaving, Papa?" the young lad had asked his father. "Why do you have to go now, when they're bombing us?"

Young Edward's sentiments had been shared by Peregrine's wife, Emily. She'd pleaded with him not to go and begged him to rethink. When this had had no effect, she'd snuggled close to him in bed and cooked him samsoe on toast for his breakfast. Why was he taking himself to Greece? she repeatedly asked herself. Why, oh why? He was following a whim — and a most selfish and dangerous one at that. She reminded him that it was just such a whim that had sent his father to an early grave. Oh, yes. Peregrine's own father had met with his death in pursuit of the selfsame obsession. Could he not see? Could he *really* be blind to the fact that history might repeat itself?

Peregrine had refused to listen to Emily's entreaties. "You don't understand the importance of my mission," he'd told her in an uncharacteristically pompous tone. "Can't you see, my dearest? The fate of an entire country rests upon my nose." He had paused for a moment at this point in the conversation in order to frot his moustache, a habit that manifested itself whenever he was nervous. Then, no less instinctively, he had pulled out a handkerchief and begun to polish his appendage. "Oh, yes, yes, darling — an entire country is awaiting this nose."

Emily had shrugged and scowled. The pink blotches on her cheeks betrayed her anger. "You Trencom men are all the same," she'd told him with weary resignation. "You're stubborn — and selfish. Your *blasted* nose, Perry, will be your downfall. And you'll leave me a widow."

Peregrine's voyage to Greece had been undertaken in the greatest secrecy. He'd switched ships on three occasions before being met as arranged in the bay of Theodoroi. From here, he had been ferried in a local fishing skiff to the secluded port of Dhafni, on the Athos peninsula, where his arrival was anxiously awaited by the National Byzantine Liberation Army.

This band of resistance fighters, known locally as the Eagle Brigade, had established themselves as protectors of Mount Athos in the spring of 1940. Their self-appointed role was to safeguard the twenty monasteries that were dotted around the peninsula and stall any attempt on the part of the German army to ransack their treasures. With the arrival of Peregrine Trencom, they had a new and most important duty to perform. They had become guardians of the hereditary Trencom nose.

The Eagle Brigade's leader was a loose-limbed bandit who answered to the name of Demetrios. He had spent so long living outside on the mountain that his face and hands had come to resemble Athos's crags and rock faces. Though not yet thirty, his eyes were lined with ravines and his chin was littered with the protruding boulders of weals and scabs. Even his clothes were at one with the elements. His patchwork jacket was within a whisker of becoming a living organism and in spring, if conditions were right, seedlings had been known to germinate in the seams of the cuffs and collar.

Demetrios had met Peregrine at Dhafni and escorted him, under the cover of darkness, up the steep slopes of Agion Oros, the Holy Mountain. As the two men had neared the summit, and Demetrios called out the password, Peregrine found himself being hailed by five other members of the brigade. They had been expecting him for almost a week and were overjoyed that he had at long last arrived in safety. "In Christ's name and in the name of Greece," said Artemios, one of the five, "you are welcome!"

It is almost noon on a torrid July day. On the islands far below, goats, farmers and fishermen are all moving at half speed. But up here, halfway between heaven and earth, there is a satisfying coolness to the air. Peregrine is seated among little clumps of wild smilax and staring at the scintillant Aegean, keeping watch for passing tugs and warships.

"Hmm," he says to himself as he holds another lump of touloumotyri up to his left nostril. "Funny — it doesn't smell as good today. Less goaty and more . . ."

And for the first time in almost eighteen months, Peregrine Trencom is unable to say of what, exactly, the cheese smelled.

He summons Artemios and is about to ask him to sniff the cheese when he suddenly becomes aware of something happening in the bay directly below. "Well, I'll be blowed," he says, and points downwards. Both men watch as a little landing craft is drawn up onto the shingle beach. It has eight men on board — all German soldiers — who appear to be heavily armed.

Artemios notices with alarm that they are making no secret of landing their weaponry. "You see," he says to Peregrine, "they know that we're watching them." It quickly becomes apparent that these intruders are intending to scale the peak, but instead of ascending the eastern flank, the easiest route, they appear to be double-backing around the furthest side of the mountain and taking the more treacherous western slope.

This causes considerable alarm among Peregrine's comrades-in-arms. The western flank offers numerous possibilities of shelter for anyone ascending the mountain and they all know that its rocky overhangs will make it hard for them to launch a counter-attack.

"Lord Jesus," whistles Konstantios to Demetrios. "They must have discovered he's here." He points to Peregrine. "Yes, yes, I have a terrible sense that they're coming after him."

"But how can they know?" asks Peregrine. "I could swear that no one saw me when I arrived."

"Possible," says Iannis. "But the swine have been keeping an eye on us up here. Father Panteleimon told me. And they've interrogated the monks at Grand Lavra. They've even been quizzing the Abbot of Stavronikita."

Peregrine shivers into the warm breeze and rubs his nose. It feels cold and damp. "Just as it should be," he thinks. "Just like a cat. And yet — how strange that the touloumotyri doesn't have any smell."

This thought for some reason reminds him of his wife and son and he wonders how they are getting on without him. What's young Edward doing right now? Perhaps he's helping in the shop? Peregrine is not a sentimental person, but he has been thinking about his son a great deal in recent weeks.

"Maybe I should have stayed at home. Perhaps I should have remained at Trencoms." He closes his eyes for a moment and dreams of samsoe on toast, of cauliflower cheese and gratin dauphinois. "No, no," he says to himself as he chews on his saliva. "Quite impossible." He thinks about all the extraordinary things he has been shown over the last four months and decides that he has been right to come to Athos.

"Besides," he says, "there's no going back now. Not after all the things that I've discovered. After all, this mountain is the only true home we have. Oh, yes indeed. This is where we Trencoms belong."

Peregrine's reverie is broken by Demetrios, who stokes the fire with his rifle butt before addressing his men. He orders them to fan out across the mountain, avoiding the gullies in the rock. "It will take them a good four hours to reach us," he says, "longer if they come up the ridge-back. If they follow the western scree, which is possible, they won't be here until nightfall. In the name of Christ, we'll kill them."

Demetrios orders Peregrine to stay in the lee of the peak, where an old Krupps machine gun has a magnificent sweep across the western slope of the mountain. "Only fire if they're close," warns Iannis. "Otherwise, you risk hitting us."

The men embrace, as they do whenever they go to fight. "*Kyrie eleison!*" they call to each other. "Lord have mercy and may God protect us." They cross themselves three times and pick up their guns. "Until tonight."

Within seconds, all six men have disappeared. Two head towards the southern spur. Two others make their way to the hideout on the eastern promontory, known as "the lair". Kostas and Iannis head straight down the western flank of the mountain, hoping to block the path of anyone coming up. Peregrine is left alone and he shifts himself closer to the machine gun.

An hour passes. And then another. At some point during the afternoon, Peregrine munches on some touloumotyri and realizes that the sun is now on the far side of the mountain. "Gracious," he says. "How did that happen? Did I fall asleep?"

A noise from below suddenly causes him to start. He hears a rock dislodge itself from the mountainside, then detects the clatter of metal striking on the ground. He freezes, rooted to the spot. It is not Demetrios or his men. They can't be back yet. Nor can it be a monk climbing up from one of the monasteries below. He would have given a warning. As Peregrine sits there, staring downwards, he feels a wave of goose pimples work their way up his arms and legs. For the first time he feels fear. Yes, he is truly afraid. Where are his comrades? Why did he agreed to stay here alone?

In absolute silence — and still shaking with fear — Peregrine shifts himself over to the machine gun. Then, still in silence, he swings the barrel of the gun in the direction of the sound he has just heard. He is sure there is someone there.

He notices a bank of clouds on the horizon. Strange, he thinks. The sky was brilliant blue just a few moments earlier. How can he have failed to notice such dark clouds? The wind stiffens. It suddenly feels chill. Peregrine curses the fact that he is not wearing more layers.

When the attack comes, it is sudden and furious. Peregrine notices a flash of movement on the grassy ledge below. One, two, three soldiers are creeping up — their guns trained on Peregrine. Automatically and quite without thinking, he squeezes the trigger on the machine gun. Tum-tum-tum-tum-tum-tum-tum-tum-tum-tum-tum-tum-tum-tum-tum-tum-tum-tum. It spits out an endless volley of shot, sending convulsions up Peregrine's arm and into the blades of his shoulders. Tum-tum-tum-tum-tum-tum-tum-tum-tum-tum-tum-tum-tum-tum-tum-tum-tum-tum.

He is just about to swing the gun around to a noise on his right when he feels a thud deep in his head. It is as if someone has struck his head with a hard rock. His eyes go blank. There is a blackness in his brain. In the space of what is less than two seconds, Peregrine Trencom passes from life to death.

He reels backwards, pushed off balance by the force of the shot. His back hits the edge of a rock, his head lands with a squelch on the cheese-filled goatskin. Consciousness leaves him with extraordinary speed. He has no time to think of his wife and son. The last vague stirrings of his mind register the pungent smell of goat's cheese and two German soldiers standing over his body. They look at his nose and smile. "*Das ist unser Mann!*" Peregrine Trencom is someone they have been hoping to kill for more than eighteen months. And now he lies dead.

CHAPTER
TWO

28 January 1969

On the fifth day after his lunchtime visit to Richard Barcley's office, Edward returned home from work rather earlier than was his custom. Although he had been shaken by the sight of the man staring at him from the building opposite, he had been reassured by the fact that three whole days had gone by without him so much as catching a glimpse of him. Yet still he felt uneasy. On two occasions he had dreamed that someone was chasing him through a maze of interconnecting streets and only the previous night he had woken in a cold sweat. He had been trapped in a nightmare in which a faceless spectre had its hands gripped tightly around his throat.

Each day at work, Edward hoped against hope that the man from the tour group would reappear. Again and again, he reflected on what the man had said, yet he could still make no sense of it whatsoever. "We need you. All our hopes are pinned on you." Why, why, why? And why on earth should he, Edward Trencom, who had never done anyone any harm (so far as he could recall) suddenly find himself in grave danger?

It was all most peculiar. He had even telephoned Mrs Williamson to ask if she could remember anything more about the man. "Not a great deal, Mr Trencom," said Mrs Williamson, who was most delighted that Edward had called her at home. "But I'd be more than happy to meet up for a cuppa if you like. I might be able to remember a few details if I put my mind to it."

"Oh, no, Mrs Williamson. I don't want to inconvenience you unduly."

"Oh, it's no trouble," interjected Mrs Williamson. "Really. No trouble at all."

"But do call me," continued Edward, "at Trencoms if you remember anything more."

He bid her good day and replaced the phone on the receiver. Within less than a minute, it rang.

"I do recall one thing," said Mrs Williamson. "He came from Salonika, yes, and he said he was here on business. I even remember asking him what sort of business, which seemed to annoy him."

"Why?" asked Edward. "What did he say?"

"He told me it was personal," said Mrs Williamson. "And I had the distinct impression, Mr Trencom, that he thought I was being nosey. I wasn't, of course. I just like to know."

"I know, I know," replied Edward. "You're just too friendly and kind, Mrs Williamson."

"Do you think so?" said a rather flustered voice at the other end of the phone. "It's Edith, by the way. Or Edie. Whichever you like best. I didn't realize that you were so, well, that you felt so . . ."

Edward was suddenly so alarmed by the implications of having phoned Mrs Williamson at home that he decided to terminate the conversation before she could take it any further.

"Well, good day," he said in a firm but friendly voice. "No doubt I'll see you on the next tour."

"Yes," said an emotional voice at the other end of the phone. "And I'll be looking forward to the cheeses that you select for me to try."

Edward's disquiet at the manner in which Mrs Williamson had spoken to him was matched by the uneasiness he felt when serving in Trencoms. He no longer felt any sense of pleasure or satisfaction when the shop bell jangled. Now, the sound of the bell spawned two conflicting emotions. There was the fear that it might herald the appearance of the mysterious man from Queen Street. And there was the hope, albeit faint, that the individual from the tour group might reappear in order to explain exactly what he had meant by his cryptic warning.

In such trying times, the presence of Mr George was a cheering one. Edward comforted himself with the thought that whatever else might happen in the world, there would always be Mr George. He had not revealed his anxieties to him — indeed, he had tried to press on as normal, unpacking cheeses and serving customers in the same cheery manner that had won him such a loyal clientele. Yet the intuitive Mr George had already noticed that something was not quite right. Each evening, he would arrive home and greet his cat with the words: "That Mr Trencom — he's got something on his mind."

The cat, Dubonnet, appeared to agree wholeheartedly. It nodded, miaowed twice and pawed at Mr George's left leg.

"Unless I'm very much mistaken, Dubonnet, history may well be about to repeat itself. Mark my words — he's going to fall headlong into the same trap as his father."

Mr George had never been entirely sure as to what this "trap" might be — and nor had he ever been able to fathom why Mr Trencom senior had left London in the middle of the war.

"But it cost him his life," he said with a sigh, "and I'm told that the 'trap' cost him *his* father's life as well."

Dubonnet once again agreed with everything Mr George said and pawed his leg with even greater vigour when his master reached for a tin of cat food.

"And I've brought you a special treat tonight," he said, stroking Dubonnet under the chin. "A lovely slice of vinney — just for the two of us. We'll share it for our tea. You'd like that, wouldn't you? Yes, you would! I know you would!"

He cut the vinney in two equal parts and popped one into Dubonnet's metal food bowl. The other he left on the kitchen worktop. He'd have it later in the evening, he thought. After his toad-in-the-hole.

Richard Barcley had not taken Edward's fears seriously at first. It all seemed so far-fetched and preposterous. But no sooner had he glimpsed the man opposite staring into his office than he realized that Edward had good cause to be concerned. There was indeed something strange about the man's appearance at the window and Barcley promised to keep a careful watch on the building. With uncharacteristic bravado, he even promised to tackle the man if and when he should appear in the street.

Shortly before leaving Barcley's office, Edward had asked his old friend whether or not he should tell Elizabeth about everything that had happened. Barcley thought for a moment before giving his considered opinion.

"Bad idea, old chap," he said. "You'll only worry her. And you wouldn't want to do that. Let's keep it" — he tapped his nose knowingly — "among ourselves. At least for the time being. Let's speak every day — keep each other posted on developments. And, by the way, one other thought . . ."

Edward looked expectantly towards his friend.

"For heaven's sake take care when you go home from work. Yes — make sure you're not being followed. The last thing you want is for them — *him* — to know where you live. After all, you most certainly wouldn't want to place Elizabeth in unnecessary danger."

Edward had not for one moment considered that the events that had occurred in the shop might spill over into his life at home. And yet Barcley was right. What if the man who was spying on him managed to find out where he lived? Taking heed of his friend's warning, Edward decided to break his routine whenever he left work.

"I'll take a different route to the station each day," he thought. "And I must try to leave home at different times each morning. *And* leave the shop at different times in the evening. Surely that'll be enough to throw them off my scent."

Thus it was that at 6.10p.m. on the twenty-eighth day of January — fully twenty minutes earlier than normal — Edward left Mr George in charge of locking up Trencoms (the first time he had ever entrusted the keys to him) and made his way home to Streatham.

He had not yet revealed to Elizabeth his fears of being watched and followed, but he had told her about his discovery of the family papers.

Elizabeth's reaction was curious and quite the opposite of what Edward was expecting.

"I'm not always sure that poking around in the past is a good idea," she said bluntly. "Some things in life are best left untouched. Unless, of course, you're properly equipped."

Edward was so surprised by what she said that he didn't even hear her last comment.

"But, Elizabeth, you know how much I want to find out these things. I know almost nothing about my father — and even less about my grandfather."

"But what you *do* know is hardly appealing," she said, glowering at him. "Think about it, Eddie. Your father — he abandoned his wife and young son, you — in the middle of wartime. It's — it's . . ." She thought for a moment, aware that she needed to choose her words with care. After all, Edward had never really come to terms with his father's disappearance. But then she thought better of it. No, now was not the moment to choose one's words with care.

"It was downright selfish of him. Leaving Emily like that. And you, for that matter. He must have been completely bound up in his own little story. I'm afraid I've got no sympathy for him. None whatsoever."

Edward was momentarily left speechless, he'd never heard Elizabeth talk quite so frankly. He conceded that she had a point — his father's behaviour *had* been strange. And his mother had certainly resented it for the rest of her life. But that only made him more curious to discover what had happened and he found it odd that this was something Elizabeth didn't seem to understand.

Later that evening, after he had finished the drying up, Edward looked again at one of the letters that he had found among the family papers. He had studied it a dozen or more times already but couldn't make any sense of it whatsoever. Far from providing any answers, it seemed to raise many more questions. The paper was of wartime quality and was stamped at the top with the smudged motif of a double-headed eagle. It was signed by a man named Demetrios, the leader of an organization that called itself the National Byzantine Liberation Army. Typed in poor English, and with the occasional word in Greek, it informed Edward's mother that her husband, Peregrine Trencom, had been killed in action.

On morning of 15 November, a group of Germans were sighted advancing up the west side of Agion

Oros. We go to engage them, leaving him [Peregrine] in safety on the top . . . We fight the enemy for two hours and killed them all. We did not know about a second group advancing up the western side of mountain. We know nothing until it is too late. Peregrine Trencom is shot as a hero while defending his position.

The letter concluded by informing Mrs Trencom that the National Byzantine Liberation Army was devastated by her husband's death. "If all Greece knew of this tragedy," said the letter, "then all Greece would mourn. But his death must remain strictly secret, for obvious reasons."

Edward put the letter back in its envelope. "Why, Elizabeth?" he asked. "Why *all* of Greece? What had my father done?"

Elizabeth looked up from her needlepoint. She was in the middle of sewing a large and rather artful platter of cheeses and was having a most awkward time with the mould of the roquefort. The blue cotton, she thought, was far too blue and the green cotton was definitely the wrong sort of green. Mould was so terribly difficult to get right.

"Was there nothing more about him in the box? Didn't your mother tell you anything about him before she died?"

Elizabeth put down her needle for a second and tried to place herself in Edward's shoes. "Surely you remember *something*? After all, you must have been — what — almost nine years old."

"I was," replied Edward. "And that's the strange thing. I don't remember anything at all. And you know what mother was like. She refused point blank to speak about him. She never said a word. I don't even know why my father went to Greece in the first place. He was forty-three years old — he had no need to fight — and yet he volunteered" — he stressed the word "volunteered" — "to abandon my mother and I. Why, Elizabeth, why?"

"Well, it beats me," she said, with a finality and apparent lack of interest that irritated Edward. But Elizabeth had not yet finished.

"To go off like that — I don't know — some men get so obsessed with things that they lose all sense of proportion. They can't see" — she trawled her brain for a suitable metaphor — "the darkness from the night. As I said before, he must have been a very selfish man. And, frankly, I'm *very* glad you don't take after him."

Edward fell silent for a moment. He leaned back in his chair and allowed his mind to wander. Just supposing, well, what if he'd *had* to go to Greece? Could he have been on some sort of special assignment? "You know what?" pondered Edward, who was by now thinking aloud. "Perhaps he was working for the secret service. Perhaps that's why his name could never be mentioned at home."

"I hardly think so," said Elizabeth in an uncharacteristically scornful tone. "You'd have found out after the war. Remember what Marjory told us? *Her* mother received a whole dossier of information when the war was finally over." And with those words — and a quick slurp of Earl Grey — Elizabeth turned her attentions back to the needlepoint roquefort.

But Edward was unable to switch off quite so easily. He put the letter down on the coffee table and stared blankly at the ceiling. "Greece, Greece, Greece," he said to himself. "What is it about Greece? My father died in Greece. The man on the tour group was Greek. And the stranger I followed through the streets was also Greek."

The more Edward thought about it, the more he convinced himself that he was not alone in knowing about his discovery of the Trencom family papers.

CHAPTER
THREE

29 January 1969

On the following morning, Edward awoke rather earlier than usual and got dressed without having a bath.

"My, you're in a hurry this morning," said Elizabeth, who normally got out of bed before her husband. She was even more taken aback when she glanced over to the alarm clock. "*Edward*," she said. "It's not even half past six."

"I know, I know," said Edward. "But I need to get into town early today. There's a mountain of cheeses to be sorted and stacked and we've also got to do the monthly stocktaking."

"Well, I *am* surprised at you, Mr Cheese," replied Elizabeth with an early-morning yawn. "I hope this up-with-the-birds is going to be the exception and not the rule. I know you. Once you develop your habits, you don't easily break them. Now, do you want me to come downstairs? I suppose I should get up as well."

Edward shook his head and headed down to the kitchen, where he ate a hurried breakfast. Instead of making Welsh rabbit, which required the grill to heat up, he ate a slice of bread and a large hunk of cheese.

"Not nearly so good as when it's cooked," he thought as he glanced at his watch. "But it's gained me ten minutes. Should be able to make the two minutes past seven train if I hurry."

After taking three more sips of tea, he rushed back upstairs to say goodbye to Elizabeth. "I'll try to be back earlier this evening," he said. "Assuming all goes well at the shop."

"Well, I hope you're not going to come back any later," she replied with a smile, "or I'll begin to think you've got yourself a fancy woman."

"I have," said Edward with a cheery grin. "And she's called Elizabeth Trencom."

It was 6.50a.m. when Edward stepped out of the front door. The morning was as sharp as a blade and the lawn had been bleached with hoar frost. Edward gulped at the air in order to cleanse his lungs. But as he did so, he froze with fear. The air did not have the usual chill, metallic palate of a biting winter's morning. Instead, it carried the unmistakable aroma of Balkan tobacco. The smell was not at all strong — indeed, most mortals would not have detected its presence at all — but to Edward's finely tuned nostrils, it had infiltrated the neutral air with as much subtlety as a clumsy-footed intruder in someone's locked and bolted home.

He was so taken aback by the smell — and so horrified — that he involuntarily clutched at the front door porch and stared vacantly at the carved woodwork. His eyes focused themselves on a large and uncommonly plump earwig that was clambering down the drainpipe. It stopped for a moment and seemed to wave its forceps in his general direction. Then, without so much as a by-your-leave, it popped into a crack in the pipe.

Edward sniffed at the air for a second and third time. He knew that there was no hope of sighting the person who had been smoking the tobacco. From the faintness of the scent, he surmised that the man must have left more than an hour ago.

"That means," thought Edward, "that he knows where I live. And it also means that I must have been followed home last night. And yet I could have sworn that no one was shadowing me."

These two thoughts troubled him deeply. He asked himself if he could possibly leave Elizabeth in the house all by herself. After all, she might also be in danger. "What if he should come back?" pondered Edward. "What if he does something to her?"

He was half-tempted to remain at home, he even thought of calling the police. But he quickly realized that neither option was practical or satisfactory. "The police will simply laugh at me if I tell them I'm being followed by a foreigner whose identity is a mystery. And, frankly, I wouldn't blame them."

He also decided against staying at home, since he would have to tell Elizabeth everything that had so far happened — something that he was not yet ready to do.

"Best to go to work," he thought with a sigh. "Press on as normal. One should never give into these sorts of things."

112

In spite of his resolution and brave words, it was an anxious and decidedly nervous Edward Trencom who made his way to work on that bitter February morning.

He arrived at Trencoms at a little before eight o'clock and unlocked the main door of the shop. As he stepped inside, he immediately sniffed at the air in order to catch that first fusty scent, unsullied by the influx of fresh air from outside.

"Ah, yes — lovely." He could most certainly smell the Burgundian epoisses over and above all the other odours and perfumes. "You were up to your antics again last night," joshed Edward with a knowing chuckle. He wagged his forefinger in the general direction of Burgundy. "Oh, yes, indeed. Now then — don't tell me, don't tell me. You've been out gallivanting with the soumaintrain."

It was a busy morning in the cheese shop and there was a steady stream of people right through until lunchtime. At one point, a couple of young ladies entered the shop and asked for directions to Bister and Brown, the publishers.

"Good gracious," whispered Edward to Mr George as they both peered over the counter. "They look like they've forgotten to put on their skirts." The two of them chuckled and Edward allowed himself the luxury of imagining Elizabeth in such an outfit.

"Well, why ever not?" he thought. "It's the way things are going."

Customers continued to come into the shop throughout lunchtime and Edward grew increasingly frustrated that today, of all days, was so busy. He was desperate to retire to the cellars in order to continue searching through the rest of the family papers yet he had to wait until almost 2.20p.m. before he could finally take his break.

"Mr George," he asked, "would you mind holding the fort for a few minutes longer today? I've got some paperwork I really must see to downstairs."

"As you wish, Mr Trencom," said Mr George. "Though I might need to call on your services if we get very busy."

He hesitated for a moment, wondering whether he dared ask what paperwork needed to be done. It wasn't really his business — paperwork wasn't his department — yet there was something about Mr Trencom's manner that had aroused his suspicions.

"Is it your family papers, Mr Trencom? Have you found anything interesting?"

"Oh, no, no," replied Edward. "Nothing that will change the world. And — no — this is paperwork for the shop. Order forms, invoices — you know, that sort of thing."

"Ah, right, right," responded Mr George. "Then in that case I'll try not to disturb. Happy paperwork!"

When Edward at long last descended into the cellars, something happened to him that was so strange, so out of the ordinary, that we must pause for a minute to examine it in more detail. He had long been accustomed to stopping on the fourth tread from the bottom of the stepladder and allowing himself a long, deep inhalation of breath. On any normal day, the odour was enough to start him salivating. Edward's nose would first of all detect the cheeses closest to hand — the thenays, saint benoîts and barbereys — before picking up far more subtle overtones in the stagnant air. Was that a whiff of pepato? Could he smell the malevolent Alpine robiola? Was that hint of earthenware emanating from the kareishes of Egypt?

It was with such expectations in mind that Edward Trencom descended into the cellars and sniffed at the air as he reached the fourth step from the bottom. He sniffed; he snuzzled; he inhaled; he swallowed. But here is the strange thing. There was nothing there. No scent. No perfume. No odour. *Rien de rien.*

"Tum-tum," said Edward to himself. "Most disconcerting."

He tried again, gently tapping at his nose in the manner that some elderly gentlemen tap at their watches. Still nothing.

Edward now became seriously alarmed. "Well, I'm blowed," he said. "What in the devil's name is happening?"

It was as he prepared to inhale for a third time that his nose began to twitch. It tingled. It grew warm. And as Edward sucked deep on the thick air, he was relieved to discover that his sense of smell had recovered. Suddenly — like a rush of air — he could smell the sour odour of Irish taith. "Oh, thank heavens," he said. "Thank gracious heavens."

Edward made his way over to the crate of family papers and lifted them onto the altar. After pausing for a moment to sniff the air once again, he cleared the limestone slab of the Auvergne chèvres that he had been tasting on the previous evening.

"The altar will do very nicely for the records," he thought. "Very nicely indeed."

So far, Edward had only taken a cursory glance at most of the books and papers in the box. He had removed the few items that pertained to his father, along with those that referred to his grandfather. Now, he lifted everything out of the crate and sorted the papers into neat piles, generation by generation. On top of each, wherever possible, he placed a portrait of the person concerned. "In that way," he thought, "I can put a name to a face."

Each time he removed an item from the box, he felt a little tingle of excitement pulse through his body. "They're all here," he murmured under his breath. "Every single one of them."

The documents had a pleasing scent — it was reminiscent of old country churches — and Edward placed each new item under his nose and inhaled deeply. He noted that several of the records smelled strongly of incense — unquestionably myrrh — as if they had sat for a long while in a monastic chapel.

He was surprised to discover that there was a great deal more information about the earlier generations than there was about his immediate forebears. There were only two or three items relating to his grandfather, George, and yet there was a great file of letters and papers referring to Humphrey Trencom, who appeared to have died at some point in the late seventeenth century. Several items seemed to have no obvious connection to anyone in his family. The icon, for example. To whom had that belonged? And who had owned the books published in Greek? Edward was not aware that any of his ancestors had been linguists. The most perplexing item was a copperplate engraving of a man with cruel eyes and a forked beard. His head was wrapped in a voluminous cloth turban and he looked oriental, perhaps Turkish. The man's nose was the most striking element in the portrait: it was long, aquiline and marked by a prominent yet perfectly formed circular bump over the bridge. Edward's hand instinctively reached for his own nose as he studied the engraving. "My God," he whispered under his breath. "How odd. Whoever this is has got exactly the same nose as me."

Edward was so surprised by the portrait that he did not hear Mr George descend into the cellars in order to ask for a hand in the shop. "Mr Trenc —" he began, but stopped himself in mid-sentence. "Hmm — paperwork, was it?" he said to himself. "Order forms and invoices." He shook his head in an admonishing manner and then turned in his tracks and quietly clambered back up the ladder. "Oh, well. I'm glad there's one of us who's got his head firmly screwed on."

He turned to the growing queue and slapped his hands together as if to announce that he was ready for action. "Now, ladies, who was next to be served?"

Edward was a methodical chap and decided to work his way backwards in chronological order through the stack of documents. There were nine generations in total and they spanned fully three centuries. A few of the items seemed to be even older. The engraving could easily have dated from the sixteenth century, while the icon looked as if it had been painted in the Middle Ages.

He popped a whole chèvre into his mouth before reaching for the pile of documents that referred to his grandfather, George Trencom. Edward had never met George, who died long before he was born, and his name had been scarcely ever mentioned at home. Edward had clear memories of asking, when still a young boy, about his grandfather.

"Ah, him," his mother had sniffed. "A fool — and a selfish one at that. Like all of the Trencoms."

"But *why?*" Edward had asked.

"Never you mind about your grandfather," replied Emily. "And never you mind about your father. In this world, you must never dwell on the past."

And that was that. Edward, aged eleven, was none the wiser as to the character, personality, life or looks of his paternal grandfather, who he knew not as "Grandpa", or as "Granddad George", but only as George Trencom.

Now, at long last, he found himself holding a photograph bearing George Trencom's autograph. It depicted a handsome young man dressed in that combination of frock coat and check trousers that was so fashionable in the London of the late 1890s. Edward smiled when he saw that his grandfather was standing in front of Trencoms — the shop's facade was instantly recognizable — and holding what appeared to be a large crate of German weisslackerkäse. "Of course, of course," said Edward to himself. "That was the Prince of Wales's favourite cheese." When Prince Edward had finally ascended to the throne after half a lifetime of waiting, Trencoms had supplied the weisslackerkäse for the coronation festivities.

The most pleasing element in the photograph of George Trencom was the fact that he had the very same nose as Edward himself. "Ah, yes, yes," thought Edward. "And his conk is every bit as fine as mine. Indeed, it's a mirror image."

He flipped the photograph over and saw that someone had written George Trencom's dates on the back. Born 1869, died September 1922."

"Heavens — my father must have been quite young when George died," thought Edward. "Very young indeed. Strange how history repeats itself."

He put down the photograph and flicked through the other papers and documents. There seemed to be very little information about his grandfather, yet the few items that *did* refer to him were most curious. Two of them were yellowing newspaper reports, one of which was written in Arabic while the other was in Greek. Edward would never have known that they pertained to his grandfather had it not been for the fact that both of the cuttings carried photographs of George Trencom. He was standing in front of a large basilica and was accompanied by what appeared to be a Greek priest. In the margin of the Greek paper, written in English, was the single word, Smyrna.

"How very odd," thought Edward. "What on earth was he doing *there*?"

He looked at the date of the newspaper, which was printed in Roman script: 12 September 1922. "If I'm not mistaken" — and he checked the photograph to make sure that he was not — "that was the very month in which he died."

No sooner had he realized this than he felt an icy chill run all the way through his body, from his toenails to his knees and thence to his hips and his neck. His fingers turned numb. So did his arms. And he even felt a wave of goose pimples on his nose, something that had never happened to him before.

"George Trencom," thought Edward, "Grandpa George, must have died in Smyrna, the second member of the family to have died abroad. And that is something — indeed — that I find most peculiar."

"Peculiar?" said Barcley later that evening. "It's not *that* peculiar. Lots of families have ancestors who died abroad. It's interesting, I concede that much. But it's not peculiar — not unless you want it to be peculiar."

Edward emitted a weary sigh. He and Richard never did quite see eye to eye on certain things and family history was clearly going to be one of them.

"It's like collecting coins," explained Edward. "I'm sure you can't understand my excitement when I acquire a coin depicting an emperor that I've never owned before. But, well, don't you see how satisfying it can be? When I first bought a denarius of the Emperor Olybrius, why, it cheered me up for days on end. Olybrius reigned for just four months — *four months!*

— and I'd been looking for one of his coins for almost a decade.

"And, well, it's much the same with these family papers. Every time I open up the box, I get a little shiver running up my spine."

"But why?" asked Richard with a strange chortling noise. "I mean, you haven't found a single answer yet. In fact, there are far more gaps in your family history than there are facts."

"You've put your finger on the button," said Edward. "It's the gaps that I love. You've seen my coin collection — you've seen my Roman coins laid out in their trays. One slot for each emperor. Well, it's the gaps that make it all so exciting. The missing ones. You see — the day will come when I'll fill those gaps."

He paused for a second, wondering if he would ever manage to convey his passion to Richard.

"There were a hundred and five Roman emperors, if you exclude the usurpers, and ninety-one Byzantine emperors. That's a total of one hundred and ninety-six. I've already got eighty-six coins of the former and sixty-two of the Byzantines. That leaves just forty-eight gaps! But those gaps, Richard. I dream of them. They follow me around, day and night!

"The time I managed to acquire a coin depicting the Emperor Manuel II Palaiologos — I swear it was one of the happiest moments of my life. I bought it on Villiers Street in the Saturday coin market. And do you know why it made me so happy? Emperor Manuel came to London in 1400. And he spent Christmas with King Henry IV at Eltham Palace. And I, for the very modest

121

sum of one pound and three shillings, became the proud owner of a coin depicting this very man. If that's not history coming alive, then I don't know what is."

"The pleasures of the chase," said Richard with a wry smile. "It's like my legal cases, I suppose. Except that I get paid at the end of it, whereas you have to spend money to fill your gaps."

"I used to be interested only in Roman emperors," continued Edward, who was only half-listening to his friend. "Nero, Caligula, Hadrian. But these days I'm increasingly drawn to the Byzantines. And do you know why? It's because they're harder to find. Ever since Elizabeth left Percy's, I've had problems tracking them down. And that takes us back to the gaps. The day I manage to acquire a coin of Constantine XI Palaiologos, the last Byzantine emperor, will be a very happy one indeed."

"Except that you will have filled the gap," responded Richard, quick as a flash.

"True," smiled Edward. "A gap will have gone. But now, what with all these family papers, I've got plenty of other gaps to pursue. Dozens, in fact. And I fully intend to pursue them, Richard, I really do."

"Oh, I believe you all right," retorted Richard. "And it's actually starting to concern me."

CHAPTER
FOUR

9 September 1922

The terrace of the Hotel Bristol is crowded with people
— American sailors, Armenian merchants, Jews, Turks
and British consular officials. Signor Orlando, the
Italian librettist, can be seen sipping a glass of sweet
black coffee. Monsieur Dupont, the piano-maker from
Marseilles, is smoking his afternoon hookah. And the
figure seated at the far end of the terrace — why, it is
none other than George Trencom, of Trencoms cheese
shop in London. What on earth is he doing in the
Ottoman Levantine city of Smyrna, on a cloudless
autumn day in 1922?

"The situation is desperate," he whispers to his table
companion, a bearded individual who is dressed in the
garb of a Greek Orthodox metropolitan. "All is lost —
all hope is gone. You do realize? It's only a matter of
time before everything implodes."

The metropolitan nods in agreement though, in
truth, he is lost in his own thoughts. "*Kyrie eleison*," he
says after a long silence. "The end — the end." He
pauses again and sips his lemon water before speaking
further. "Yes, yes — it marks the end of your dreams,
Georgios, and the end of mine as well. And I fear that

we've reached a turning point — yes — one that spells the end of all Greece's aspirations. Avarice and pride — these are the sins of the Greek nation."

George rubs his elbow as he listens to Metropolitan Chrysostomos. A jagged shard of shrapnel is lodged close to the bone and causes the nerves to twitch in a most unpleasant fashion. "This blasted arm," he mutters to himself before explaining to Chrysostomos, "from a Turkish shell — *whoosh* — it got me right here. I was hit at Afyonkarahisar."

Just five days earlier, George and his Greek comrades had been in combat against the Turkish army close to Ushak, some one hundred and forty miles east of Smyrna. The division with which he was serving had been hoping to break through the Turkish flank and head for Constantinople. The men had spent their evenings carousing after a string of victories and discussing how they were going to enter the city. One of them, a cocksure colonel named Teodoro, had proposed that George should ride into Constantinople on horseback; ride in on a white charger, mimicking Sultan Mehmet the Conqueror's entrance into the city on that terrible day in 1453. "You must be the first to enter Constantinople," said Colonel Teodoro. "With God's blessing, you *have* to be the first."

The colonel's suggestion had raised wild hurrahs from his men and George had managed to further increase the volume and tempo by proposing a toast to the recapture of the city from the infidels. But their confidence and morale had soon been shattered. The entire Greek army, which had for so long looked invincible, had been devastated by the forces of Mustafa Kemal, who had orchestrated a lightning, twinpronged attack. The few survivors had fled towards the coastal town of Smyrna.

George had been fortunate to have arrived there first. He'd found a city that was oblivious to its impending doom. The casino was open as normal. The quay was crowded with porters and stevedores loading sticky figs onto waiting cargo vessels. Greek shipping patriarchs were dining in the Hotel d'Angleterre; the English residents in Bournabat continued to drink gin and bitters; the little American community was in the midst of arranging the autumn season of tea dances at the YMCA.

George pops a cube of local tulum into his mouth. Instead of chewing it, as is his custom, he squashes it slowly with his tongue. He can feel it squelching through the gaps in his teeth and sticking itself to his gums. "Hmm," he says to himself with a frown. "It doesn't taste quite so good today. No, it's got quite a different flavour." As he thinks this thought, he glances towards the sea. His sensitive nose has alerted his brain to the fact that something untoward is happening on the quayside, less than three hundred yards from where he is seated. Yes, a terrible stench is being carried on the breeze and it brings with it a story of misery and despair. Hundreds, perhaps thousands, of wounded Greek soldiers are pouring into Smyrna from the interior of the country. They are stumbling, shuffling, bent almost in two by the weight of their packs. Their gaunt faces and blank expressions speak of extreme suffering. Some are leaning on their comrades for support. Others are dragging one foot after the other, struggling to reach the docks of Smyrna where they hope to find refuge.

The metropolitan lets out a low whistle as he watches a wounded rifleman collapse in pain. "I never thought it possible," he says. "I thought victory was ours."

He swings his gaze back to the quayside, which holds the attention of everyone on the terrace of the Hotel Bristol, and watches anxiously as an ever-increasing number of soldiers shuffle their way along the seafront.

"The Turks will not dare enter the city," whispers the metropolitan. "Not with all these foreigners here." He points towards the harbour, which is playing host to more than two dozen foreign warships. George counts eleven British ships, five French cruisers and several Italian minesweepers. There are also three American destroyers, the largest of which had arrived late the previous evening and is now anchored next to the Standard Oil terminal at the northern end of the quay.

"I hope you're right, Father," says George Trencom. "I hope to God you're right." But even as he speaks these words, it becomes apparent that the situation is about to deteriorate still further.

All eyes at the Hotel Bristol are transfixed on the furthest end of the quay, where a most disquieting scene is unfolding. It is so disturbing that Metropolitan Chrysostomos involuntarily stands up and makes the sign of the cross. The infamous Turkish cavalry, commanded by Murcelle Pasha, can be seen riding along the harbour front. They sit erect in their saddles and wear high black fezzes emblazoned with the crescent and star. In their right hands, each horseman is clutching a polished curved scimitar. They shout "Victory! Victory!" as they ride, then give themselves a rousing cheer.

"In the name of all that is holy," says the metropolitan, who once again crosses himself, "it has indeed come to pass."

More than two thousand Turkish troops flood into Smyrna during the course of the afternoon. They are greeted as heroes and liberators by the Turkish minority living in the upper part of town, but elsewhere in Smyrna the mood has changed to one of foreboding. Scores of Armenians have been butchered in cold blood and several hundred shops have been looted. George Trencom watches in silence as the wealthiest Greek families board their pleasure craft and slip quietly out of the harbour. Those left behind have spent their time cleaning their weapons and preparing for the worst.

At exactly 3.22p.m., General Noureddin, the newly appointed commander of Smyrna, sends an order that Metropolitan Chrysostomos should come to his headquarters. The metropolitan knows that he has little option but to obey and he heads to the general's office, accompanied by Mr George Trencom, who has offered to act as his dragoman. Although the two men have a Turkish military escort, they have considerable difficulty reaching the portal of the building, for an ugly mob has gathered to jeer at the Greek metropolitan. As he comes into sight, they hurl scraps of rubbish and small stones.

Chrysostomos enters the general's impromptu headquarters and extends his hand to greet Noureddin, a man he has met on several previous occasions. He congratulates him on his victory and asks him to show magnanimity towards the vanquished. Noureddin refuses his hand, gives him a disdainful sneer and then spits in his face. "You are a dead man," he says coldly, "and so are your people. Now get out. My people have some old scores to settle." He utters not a word to George Trencom, although his flickering eyes betray the signs of recognition. "Is it really him?" he asks of his chief lieutenant. "Have we so easily lured him into our lair?"

The lieutenant nods and says, "Just look at his nose — it could hardly be anyone else."

Metropolitan Chrysostomos and George Trencom turn to leave the general's office and head back downstairs towards the entrance hall. Before stepping outside, they exchange glances and look warily at the mob. Chrysostomos instinctively makes the sign of the cross and mutters a prayer. "Only God can save us now," he says.

As the two men reach the bottom step, General Noureddin makes an appearance on the balcony of his headquarters. He addresses the mob in fiery language, giving them carte blanche to act as they wish. "Treat the dogs as they deserve to be treated," he says, "and most especially this one." He points at George Trencom, making an unambiguous throatslitting gesture before calmly heading back inside. As he closes the doors to the balcony, the crowd surges forward and grabs Chrysostomos by the beard. George Trencom tries to defend his friend but, as he does so, he is stabbed in the neck by one of the mob. He falls to the ground in shock, clutching the gaping wound with his hand.

His last sight before losing consciousness is the murder of the metropolitan. Chrysostomos's throat is slit and his eyes are gouged out with knives. The mob then cuts off his beard with a razor.

The crowd's fury is assuaged by the killing and they soon begin to disperse. A couple of men remain behind to string up the corpses from a lamp-post. They place a placard round each man's neck — a placard that is written in Turkish, Greek and Armenian. Its message consists of just three words: "Constantinople is Turkish."

CHAPTER
FIVE

7 February 1969

Edward had not been at work for long when the shop bell tinkled and the door burst open. He sprang to his feet in a mixture of panic and alarm but was quickly reassured when he saw a familiar figure enter the shop.

"Richard," he exclaimed. "You put the fear of God into me. What a surprise! What brings you here again?" And before he had a chance to finish his question, he realized *exactly* why his friend had come. "You've got some news," he said in an urgent tone of voice. "You've filled a gap? What have you discovered?"

"Calm down, old chap," said Barcley, smiling at his friend's impatience. "I'll tell you everything — only, well, I must admit, there's not a great deal to tell."

"But you've found out who he is?"

"No," said Richard. "I haven't found out who *he* is. But I have discovered that something strange took place at Number Fourteen yesterday. Something that I witnessed with my very own eyes."

"What? What?" said Edward. "Come on — tell me."

Richard paused. "Well, perhaps we should go downstairs. Into the cellars. This isn't the most appropriate place."

"Spot on," said Edward, who walked over to the top of the stepladder and called down to Mr George to ask if he could serve in the shop for a few minutes.

"At the double," responded Mr George, whose appearance at the top of the ladder was masked by the two large boxes of camembert he was carrying. "Ah, hello, Mr Barcley," he said in a friendly voice. "Long time, no see. To what do we owe this pleasure? Is it cheese or personal?"

Richard smiled. "I need to borrow Edward for a moment," he said. "Just for a moment, mind. Can you stand guard? Keep the home fires burning?"

Once Richard and Edward were down in the cellars, Edward was desperate to know every detail of what had happened. "Well," said Richard, "there really isn't a great deal to tell. But for what it's worth . . ."

He described how he had been standing at the window of his office on the previous evening at about 5.30p.m. "The curtains of the building opposite were open," he said, "and I could see directly into the room. There had been no one in there all day, as far as I was aware, but now — not long before I was due to pack up — I saw three men enter the room. It was hard to make out exactly what was taking place, for the sunlight was reflecting off the windows. But I'm convinced that one of those three men was the same person who was staring at us just the other day."

"What was he doing?" asked Edward. "And the other two — what were *they* doing?"

"Well, it was clear they were having an argument. In fact, they were having an almighty row. Two of the men seemed to be shouting at the third. And at one point, they grabbed the lapels of his jacket."

"And then?" asked Edward.

"And then, unfortunately, they saw me standing at the window. And then it was curtains. They closed them, I mean."

Edward let out a long sigh. "And that's it?" he asked. "There's nothing more?"

"No," said Barcley. "I mean, yes. There is something more. There's something very much more. In fact, there's this."

He pulled an envelope from the inner pocket of his jacket and waved it at Edward, rather as if he was displaying a trump card.

"What have you got there?" said Edward. "What is it?"

"When I got to work yesterday", explained Richard, "this was waiting for me. It had been pushed through the letter box and left on the mat. Mrs Clarke picked it up when she arrived in the morning."

"Well?" said an increasingly impatient Edward. "What does it say?"

"Not a great deal," said Barcley. "In fact, not very much at all. But it's no less interesting for all that. Listen to this. It says: 'Please be kind enough to meet me on Friday, 21 February, at noon, at the junction of Throgmorton Street and Old Broad Street. I have something of the utmost importance to tell you — something that needs to be relayed to your friend. I cannot, for reasons that I am unable to explain here and now, meet with you before this date.' "

132

"And that's it?" asked Edward as he flipped over the sheet of paper.

"And that," replied Richard, "is indeed it. Nothing more, nothing less."

"So what now?" asked Edward with a long, exasperated sigh. "That's two weeks away. Will you go? No — you can't. You can't put yourself in danger because of me. No, Richard, I shall go. *I* will meet him that Friday."

"No," said Barcley firmly. "*You* can't go. It's quite clear that you are the one that's in danger. Someone, for reasons as yet unknown, wants to do you harm. And you're already an easy enough target without going to this rendezvous. No, no, Edward. I shall go."

Richard picked up a small piece of gorgonzola and pressed it to his nostrils.

"Wow, Edward, that's a pungent one. It's a bit too early in the day for that. And now," he said, glancing at his watch, "if you don't mind, I need to get on my way. Dear Mrs Clarke will be worrying herself senseless about me. Look after yourself, old chap. I'll keep you posted about any developments."

And with that, Richard Barcley headed across the cellar towards the stepladder and disappeared upwards into the shop.

CHAPTER
SIX

Edward Trencom had long held that there were two types of people in life. One type, which included his good self, could only make sense of the present by constantly referring to the past. "It's like a fine stilton," he would say. "Unless you can compare it with its predecessors, how on earth can you pass judgement?"

The second type — of which Richard Barcley was an outstanding example — cared nothing for old objects. For him, the past was only useful if it provided the answer to a cross-word clue or a put-down quip to an over-smart client.

One had only to cast an eye over the decor of their respective houses to realize that there was more than a grain of truth in Edward's little theory. Barcley's house was furnished with functional chairs and tables that had been bought from Arding & Hobbs with little effort and less thought. Edward's home, by contrast, was cluttered with old armchairs and side-boards that had been acquired from junk shops and auctions over the previous twelve years of married life. His Sedgefield dining room table (circa 1890) had come from Pringles of Honiton. His East India tea chest, which still smelled pleasingly of jasmine, had been bought at Dobson

Antiques in Tower Street. Although Edward had never kept an inventory of the things he had bought, he could remember where each item of furniture came from and the price that he had paid.

Recalling these facts brought him nearly as much pleasure as the thought that generations of people like him had already enjoyed the objects that filled the rooms of Number 22 Sunnyhill Road. Every time Edward relaxed in his Windsor settle, he recalled how he had bought it for £2 4s — a veritable bargain. He was the first to admit that there was nothing especially noteworthy about the chair. The headrest was unadorned and the legs were less ostentatious than on many Windsor chairs he had seen. Yet the oak had acquired the deep patina of old boots over the years and there were grooves in the arms where generations of elbows had rubbed and rested. When Edward sat in the chair, he would sniff at the newly applied wax (which itself smelled of antiques), emit a satisfied sigh and think of all the people who had enjoyed the warmth of its moulded back.

He had many other favourites as well. Some years ago, he had bought a Royal Doulton coronation mug of King Edward VIII — a most unusual item, given that the king had abdicated before he was crowned. Edward derived pleasure from simply looking at the mug, not so much because of its value (it was not actually worth a great deal), but because it was such an oddity. It was on a par with the eighteenth-century minke whale rib that hung above the fireplace.

All these objects paled into insignificance when compared to the family papers that Edward had discovered in the cellars of Trencoms. It was not just the fact that he had unearthed a crate of old objects — itself a cause of considerable contentment — but the fact that each and every item in the box had a direct bearing on his own life.

On the evening of 7 February, Edward spent more than an hour pondering over the records that referred to his grandfather. He quickly realized that there was frustratingly little information about George. Aside from the photograph, there were the two newspaper articles and six or seven maps of the Ottoman Empire. And that was all.

Edward was about to pack up the papers and retire to bed when he noticed a handwritten letter tucked inside the fold of one of the maps. With tremulous hands, he unfolded the notepaper and, scanning his eyes to the bottom, realized that it was a letter from George to his wife, Alice:

Dearest Alice,

All our hopes are at an end. All our dreams have been in vain. My last letter came from Afyonkarahisar, where I was wounded in the elbow by shrapnel. We had hopes of breaking through the enemy lines and my comrades in arms were talking of me being the first to ride into Constantinople — and on a white charger, too! But we have now been beaten back to Ushak (from where I write this letter) and our forces are in poor shape. In two days, I shall head for Smyrna, from where I shall try to find myself passage home.

How is Trencoms? How is Peregrine? How are you? I regret this whole foolish business — which I am now abandoning for ever — and ask for you, my dearest, to accept my sincere apologies.

With all my love and affection,

George

Edward read the letter a second and then a third time. He was still no clearer as to its meaning and studied it line by line in the hope that it would all fall into place. He scratched at his nose — a habit he had developed at a very tender age — and stared blankly at the ceiling. "And on a white charger," said Edward to himself for the umpteenth time. "Why a white charger? That's what I find so bizarre."

Edward was still troubled by these questions on the following morning when, at a little after nine o'clock, he pushed open the newly installed swing doors of Southwark's municipal public library. He sat himself down at the third desk on the right — his usual — and was about to open a book when he spied a familiar face on the far side of the library. "Ah-ha," he thought to himself, "here's someone on hand to help and he's coming right this way. Hello, Herbert!"

Herbert Potinger was the chief librarian at Southwark's municipal public library, as well as being a friend and close neighbour of Edward. Amateur historian, model railway enthusiast, vegetarian and

137

lover of Greek, Herbert (a bachelor) was a singularly English fellow — the sort of chap (he was definitely a "chap") who spent two weeks each summer under the grey skies of Broadstairs, sheltered behind a windbreaker, devouring the comedies of Aristophanes. He was obsessed with all things Greek, particularly medieval and modern Greek, and had acquired for Southwark library an impressive collection of recently republished Byzantine chronicles (cost: £48 5s 2d) and the complete works of Kostis Palamas (cost: £13 6s), all of them generously paid for by the borough's taxpayers.

Herbert and Edward shared many things in common — a love of history, old coins and foreign cheeses — and, not least (though they did not know it), a certain unfamiliarity with their own bodies. In Herbert's case this was, perhaps, understandable, for to see him naked was to witness something that was not easily forgotten. He was not, of course, in the habit of removing his clothes in the very public environment of the municipal borough library. Indeed, none of the regulars had ever seen their chief librarian in the way that Nature had apparently intended. But Edward had — once, on a weekend outing to the Tooting lido — and it had left such an impression on him that he could not fail to remember it every time he saw Herbert.

His naked friend was indeed quite a sight. It had nothing to do with his xylophone of protruding ribs, nor his small but perfectly rounded pot belly. Rather, it was because the pallid and otherwise slight figure of Herbert Potinger was uncommonly, unnaturally hirsute.

His nether regions — which had never yet seen action — were covered in a tangled mass of orangey-ginger hair. So, too, was his head. It was adorned with a corona of ginger curls that reached a full three inches above the highest point of his head.

Edward gave a cheery smile as Herbert approached, noticing as he did so that his ginger eyebrows seemed to have lengthened by fully quarter of an inch since the two of them last met. "He should trim them," thought Edward to himself. "Or at least his barber should."

Herbert was not aware of the many strange things that had happened to Edward over the previous few days, but he *did* know all about his friend's discovery of his family papers. He also knew that Edward was having difficulty in translating the newspaper cuttings that referred to his grandfather and had offered to lend a hand. Now, two days later, he had come up with some answers.

"Thank *goodness* for the *Annual Register*," whispered Herbert to Edward. "Wherever would we be without the *Annual Register?*"

"The *Annual Register* — the *Annual Register*," repeated Edward. "No, I'm not quite sure I understand what you mean."

"Ssh! You *must* keep your voice down," hissed Herbert as he propelled his finger to his lips. Then, after looking all around the reading room to make sure no one had been disturbed, he produced a small green volume that had been nestling in the comfort of his armpit.

"Here we go: the *Annual Register*. It tells us what was going on in the world each year. And this" — he

139

held up the spine so that Edward could see it clearly —
"is the volume for 1922."

"And?" said Edward.

"And," replied Herbert, "I may just have a few
answers as to why your grandfather was in Turkey —
yes, answers. But I'm afraid I must warn you that each
answer seems to raise several more questions. Now, let's
move into my office, where we can talk more freely."

Edward noticed that Herbert's desk was piled high
with books and pamphlets and he wondered if his
friend had been here all night studying *Annual
Registers*.

"The history is clear enough," said Herbert. "At the
end of the First World War, Turkey was forced to sign
the Treaty of Sèvres — a complete humiliation, as I'm
sure you know. In effect, it dismantled the Ottoman
Empire. Syria was to become independent. Armenia
too. And large parts of Turkey, including Smyrna, were
to be handed to Greece."

"Right," said Edward, who suddenly felt uncommonly hot. It was stuffy in Herbert's office and quite
airless. There was a stale odour of fried mushrooms, the
lingering after-effects of Herbert's breakfast, and a
quite unpleasant smell of cheap instant coffee. "How
can he work in such an environment?" thought
Edward, never for a moment considering that some
people would find working in an airless and perennially
pungent cheese shop beyond the pale.

"Well," continued Herbert, who had failed to notice
the twitch in Edward's nose, "for a while, all went
swimmingly for the Greeks. Their army marched

inland, deep into Turkey, and won a string of victories over their historic enemy. But they were to meet their match in a certain Mustafa Kemal."

"Ataturk?" asked Edward.

"Indeed," confirmed Herbert, "and his forces swept back through the Greek areas of Turkey." He paused for a moment and dropped his voice to a whisper. "A common thug, Edward, an out-and-out criminal. I can't think why the Turks revere him so much."

Edward was concerned that Herbert would launch into one of his lengthy monologues and sought to forestall him with a question.

"But what puzzles me," he said, "is this obsession with Greece. Why on earth would George Trencom have been fighting with the Greeks? Remember, Herbert, he was leaving a very prosperous cheese shop in order to go abroad, and he was also leaving his wife and son — my own father. If it hadn't been for my great-uncle, Trencoms might well have been forced to close."

"I must confess," said Herbert, "I don't know all the answers. But I've got a hunch. Listen: the defeated Greek armies retreated to Smyrna, on the coast, where they thought they'd be safe. And your grandfather was there in September 1922 — we know that for certain — at absolutely the critical moment.

"Now, you've assumed all along that he was *fighting* with the Greeks, and I agree that it does sound like it from his letter. But I've come to a rather different conclusion. I think he was actually a reporter — yes, indeed — and working for a newspaper."

Edward shot his friend a sceptical look.

"Ah, ah," continued Herbert, who sensed that Edward was about to interject. "Before you say anything, Edward, you know he wouldn't have been the only amateur reporting on the war. There was John Grimble, who later became foreign editor of *The Times*. And there was also that famous chap — oh, you know — what's his name? *The Old Man and the* —"

"Hemingway?"

"Yes, Hemingway. He was there as well. I think your grandfather was a reporter like Hemingway."

Edward breathed out deeply and accidentally let slip a little snort.

"No, no, Herbert. Impossible! George Trencom was a cheese merchant, not a journalist. And besides, answer me this. Why did the troops want him to be the first to ride into Constantinople? And why on a white charger? Eh?"

"Ah, well," replied a visibly excited Herbert, who could scarcely restrain himself from delivering his coup de grâce. "You see, if you accept my theory, everything makes sense. You must understand that the British newspapers had been on Turkey's side throughout the course of the war with Greece. Oh, yes. But when news of the massacres reached London, opinion suddenly changed. Overnight, the great British public was clamouring for a Greek victory."

"And?" said Edward.

"Well, just imagine," said Herbert, "imagine the coup of a journalist — a newspaperman — being first into Constantinople. After all, it remained the goal, the ultimate prize, of the Greek army. And imagine how dramatic it would be if that same reporter entered the city on a white charger, in the style of Mehmet the Conqueror. It would have been right up the *Daily Telegraph's* street, that's for sure."

Herbert had become so animated that his cheeks, which were normally of a pallor that only redheads can truly attain, suddenly sprouted little blotches of red. The last time Edward had seen his friend so excited was the day he had bought A. C. Glenny's rare 1824 edition of Aristophanes' *Frogs*.

"Well, it's a good theory," he said. "Full marks for that. But have you seen George Trencom's name in any of the newssheets from the time? I doubt it. And nor does it tie up with why my father also seems to have been fighting with the Greeks."

"True," admitted Herbert, "that *is* strange."

"And another thing," said Edward. "My grandfather never made it home so I presume he must have died in Smyrna."

"Ah, yes," replied Herbert, "and that's what these newspaper clippings are about. Apparently — and this *is* queer — your George Trencom died trying to defend this chap here. Some sort of Greek bishop."

Edward stretched back in his chair and let out a loud whistle.

"Ssh!" said Herbert. "*Please* try to remember where you are."

Edward picked up one of the two newspaper cuttings and looked at it closely. It was quite uncanny, he thought, how closely he resembled his grandfather. The same eyes. The same shaped face. And above all, yes, above all, the same nose. He held the clipping away from his face, in order to put some distance between himself and the photograph. "Yes," he said, "it is the very image of my nose." Next, he held the cutting close to his face right next to his skin, so that his nose and that of George Trencom were touching at the tip. And it was at exactly this moment, when the two noses came into contact, that Edward felt an electrifying tingle — like a shiver or goose pimples — travel at high speed across the surface of his body. The little hairs on his arms pricked themselves up and the nerves in his shoulders involuntarily twitched. There was no doubt in Edward's mind. George Trencom's nose, photographed more than forty years earlier, was warm to the touch.

More cynical observers would point out that the clipping had been lying in a little pool of sunlight. They might also have noticed that Edward had been clutching it with his hot and clammy hands. But to his own way of thinking such explanations were not at all satisfactory. He had always known that the Trencom nose had preternatural powers and now he had confirmation of this fact.

"I think George is part of a much bigger story," he said. "I have this feeling that — well, it's hard to put a finger on it — but I'm convinced my uncle was right all along. There *is* something fishy about the Trencom nose, something strange about its origins. There's a portrait I found in the box of papers — it must be at least four hundred years old — and whoever it represents has got exactly the same nose as me. That's proof enough that it's been in the family for many centuries. I wouldn't be surprised to discover that he, too, died because of his nose. And his son. And his grandson. And all of them — all of them — right down to my own father and grandfather."

Herbert shot Edward a sceptical look.

"Can't you see?" continued Edward. "They knew something. There was clearly some hidden goal that —"

"That cost them their lives," interrupted Herbert. "That much is true. Take care, Edward, take care. You may be playing with fire."

"It *did* cost them their lives," said Edward, "but it's not going to cost me mine! Unless, of course, I die of frustration. No, seriously, *they* were all engaged in wartime activities. My father died in a German ambush. And my grandfather was killed at the end of a particularly bloody war in Turkey. My circumstances are rather different. I can assure you that curiosity alone will not kill this particular Trencom cat."

"Well, I do hope you're right," said Herbert. "The past is a dangerous land."

"By the way," continued Edward, catching his thoughts. "I've got another question for you, on a different subject. Since you're my resident Greek expert, does the name Makarezos mean anything to you? It's a company in Queen Street."

"Makarezos?" repeated Herbert. "Well, I've not heard of the company in Queen Street. But I've most certainly heard of the name Makarezos. And I'm rather surprised that you haven't. Makarezos is one of the ruling junta in Greece. Nikolaos Makarezos, if I'm not mistaken. But whether or not he has any connection with your Makarezos in Queen Street, I'm afraid I have no idea. But what queer questions you ask," said Herbert. "Why on earth do you want to know?"

CHAPTER
SEVEN

10 February 1969

On a bright Monday afternoon in the second week of February, Edward Trencom could be found unpacking cheeses in the cellars of Trencoms. He was still wearing his customary smile but the deep frown on his forehead suggested that he was not feeling quite himself.

"What *is* wrong with me?" he said to himself. "I'm not feeling myself at all."

There is a group of illnesses known by the collective title of Munchausen's syndrome, in which people imagine themselves to be ill. There is another group in which people actually think themselves into being ill. And there are the illnesses which, for some unknown reason, are impossible to pin down; they leave their victims feeling not quite themselves, but in a way that they can neither understand nor explain.

"I don't feel particularly ill," thought Edward. "But I don't feel particularly right either. I simply don't feel myself."

In olden days, Edward's illness might have been ascribed to an imbalance of the humours — a preponderance of black bile, perhaps, or a sickly surge of a yellow phlegm. Such liquable instability led many a Renaissance gentleman to his doom.

Whether or not Edward had mismatched humours is difficult to ascertain, but what *is* certain is that he had become unbalanced — unbalanced like a kitchen scale that's got all the heaviest weights stacked in the little pan. He had become lopsided, wonky, lacking that essential equilibrium that keeps more fragile mortals vaguely on the straight and narrow. And this is a most dangerous state of affairs. We all know that a leaning clock ceases to tick. We know that an unbalanced machine can no longer function. Its cogs seize up. Its pistons shudder to a standstill.

So it was with Edward Trencom. It was not that he had completely ground to a halt — on any given weekday, he could still be found behind the counter at Trencoms. But he was most certainly out of sync, listing heavily to starboard in the turbulent waters of family genealogy.

He picked up a slice of Sussex slipcote and placed it to his nose. On any normal afternoon it would have smelled of thyme and rosehip, overlaid, perhaps, with a faint lemony tang. But on this particular day it smelled, well, what *did* it smell of?

"Lichen?" thought Edward. "Mushrooms? Peat?"

He placed it back on the mat and reached, instead, for a thick triangle of bauden, a recent arrival from the mountains of Bohemia. "Now this one should help me," thought Edward. "This one I know well."

But where was the scent of summer *alpage*? Where were the chill breezes of the ice-encrusted upper slopes?

Edward's disquiet was not helped by Mrs Toller, a Trencoms regular, who stepped into the shop just as Edward put down the bauden.

"Why, Mr Trencom," she said. "You don't look quite yourself today."

She looked around at the familiar display of cheeses and added under her breath, "and nor, for that matter, does your shop."

This much was true. The cheeses stood on their customary mats just as they had always done, yet they were not piled quite as high as they had been a few days earlier. The fans still twirled in the ceiling, yet they seemed to have developed a yawnful languidity over the preceding days. It was as if the air had grown thick and heavy; as if every turn required a monumental push and heave.

Mr George had done his level best to keep things ticking over, but there were limits to what he could do. He noted with alarm that cheeses had gone unordered and that stock was not being replaced. He had taken it upon himself to call up for more Danish havarti and had also telephoned the shop's supplier of Bavarian limburger. After more than a week without a delivery of Milanese grana lodigiana, he asked Mr Trencom if he should order some of that as well.

"Yes, yes, Mr George," replied Edward in a half-hearted, disconsolate sort of fashion. "And any others. We need to keep the supplies rolling in."

"But don't you prefer to do the ordering, Mr Trencom? That's always been your department."

"It has — it has. But if you don't mind lending a helping hand, it's a weight off my mind. We'll soon get the shop back to normal — that much is sure."

As Edward said these words, a strange thought went shooting through Mr George's head.

"If something should happen to Mr Trencom — why — there would be no one to take over the shop. He's the only one left."

Mr George studied Edward's behaviour over the days that followed and grew increasingly concerned that the end had already come. Edward had not done a single piece of stock-keeping since his discovery of the family papers more than a fortnight earlier. Nor did he take home his little parcel of cheeses at the end of each week. He had even given up going to Mrs O'Casey's for his midday sandwiches. On most days, he announced that he was heading to Southwark Municipal public library for an extended lunchtime period of research. This often lasted fully three hours and on at least one occasion occupied the whole of the afternoon. Yet the pursuit of his ancestors did not seem to make Edward any more stable — indeed, it had quite the reverse effect. The more he investigated the Trencom family documents, the more he knew that something was seriously awry.

Elizabeth had noticed with growing alarm the change in her husband. She was still in the dark as to many of the disturbing events that had happened to him over the previous days and was surprised that the discovery of his family papers should have had such an effect on

150

him. She was particularly concerned that it was also beginning to have an effect on their relationship. She felt that a distance had opened up between the two of them. It was only a little cleft at the moment, but one (if left unattended) that could easily become a gaping, dangerous, icy-jawed crevasse.

Edward always used to kiss Elizabeth on the cheek when he returned from work. Now, for several days in a row, he had neglected to do so. He used to tell her all the details of what had happened at Trencoms. Now, he showed little enthusiasm in talking about either the customers or the cheeses. Only when she asked him about his family research would he spark into life. He could happily chat for an hour or more about George and Peregrine Trencom.

"I have to do something," thought Elizabeth, clutching at a wine glass with such force that the stem snapped clean in two. "Otherwise, things will surely spiral out of control." She noticed that she'd cut her hand on the broken glass and wiped away the blood on the dishcloth. But it continued to well to the surface, so she ran it under the cold tap.

It was not confrontation she was seeking. No, she preferred to think of it as intervention. Only the other day she'd listened to a newscaster talking about the United Nations "intervening" in some trouble spot in the world. "Intervening" — that's exactly what she intended to do. Restore peace and harmony before the troubles took a turn for the worse.

She removed her hand from the water for a second, but no sooner had she done so than the blood began to flow once more. It bonded instantly with the water on her hand, like ink on blotting paper, making the cut look a hundred times worse than it actually was. She had heard of many a marriage going wrong precisely because of a breakdown of communication — she was thinking specifically of Michael and Susan Whitelock — and was determined that this would not happen to her relationship.

On the evening of 10 February, she and Edward were seated side by side in the comfort of their Streatham lounge. Elizabeth had just made herself a cup of fennel tea and was about to put the finishing touches to her needlepoint. Edward was re-reading a library copy of the *Annual Register* for 1922. But each of them was finding it hard to concentrate on the work in hand.

"I can see that it's interesting for him," thought Elizabeth, "but can it really be *that* interesting?"

"She simply doesn't understand," thought Edward, "and worst of all, she doesn't want to understand. She's unable to see what's at stake."

"Perhaps this is the evening when I should say something? Perhaps now's the time to discuss it?"

"If she raises it again, if she tells me once more to stop my research . . ."

"Edward," said Elizabeth, breaking the stillness of the room.

"Mmm?" replied Edward, without looking up from his book.

"Edward, please. Just stop for one second. We need to talk."

152

"Here we go," he thought. "I'm not sure I'm ready for this."

This once-happy couple had sat in this room almost every evening of their married life, with the exception of the times when Edward was away on his cheese-gathering trips. They were accustomed to spending the hours before bed chatting, reading books and discussing Edward's research about cheese. In all that time, Edward had never once wondered — how shall we put this? — not ever considered, how Elizabeth, his rather lovely wife, would look if she was sitting in her armchair, right there, completely naked.

But that was exactly what happened on this particular evening. In fact, it happened right now. His thoughts, his strange, erotic thoughts, suddenly ran away with him. Ran right away. Over the hills and far away.

Whether or not this was due to his current lopsidedness, it is impossible to say. Was it a result of his unbalanced humours? His wonky equilibrium? Even Edward himself could not pinpoint what *exactly* was going on inside the confused orbit of his head.

The scenario began like this. Elizabeth had just started to warn her husband that his interest in his origins was fast developing into an obsession. She'd already made the opening gambit when the following thing happened. Suddenly, and quite without warning, Edward whipped off his wife's shirt. Whoosh! It had gone.

"You're becoming so obsessed, darling. Yes, obsessed."

Zoom! Off came the shoes and tights. Elizabeth was now sitting there in bra and skirt and Edward was pondering over what to remove next.

"Tum —" he thought. "Take it slowly, Edward, take it slowly. Remember, she's not used to this."

"You remember what Marjory said? She said that —"

Vroom! Off came the skirt. Edward sat back in his armchair in order to survey his handiwork. He watched in delight as two pinkish-red spots appeared on Elizabeth's cheeks, a sure sign that she was agitated.

"Why," he thought, "she's even flushed."

"And another thing, Edward —"

Elizabeth was about to tell her husband another thing when — quick as a flash — he stripped her of her bra and panties. She was now completely naked and still doing her needlepoint. Strangely, it was that last detail that he found the most erotic of all.

"Edward? Are you listening?"

He was most definitely NOT. He was in his own world — a world that was filled with infinite possibilities.

"*Edward!*" She was really quite cross.

He blinked three times and looked at his wife. Damn and blast and bother. She was fully clothed.

"Yes, yes, yes," he said. "Let's go to bed."

"But Edward, dear," she replied in an anxious tone, "it's not even half past eight."

CHAPTER
EIGHT

25 March 1878

Emmanuel Trencom sniffs at the air and lets out a most voluminous sneeze. Then, feeling thoroughly relieved, he rubs his belly with unusual vigour. "The fact is," he says to himself, "I am hungry — oh, yes, indeed. Mr Emmanuel Trencom is ravenously hungry."

He massages his belly for a second time, as if to confirm that it really is empty. Then, pausing only to make a mental note of the fact that there are no customers in the shop — and none in the street outside — he reaches for his knife and cuts himself a thick wedge of Swedish vasterbotten. But before popping it into his mouth, he allows himself a moment or two of speculation. "Gad so!" he says. "What does one drink with a vasterbotten? A glass of porter? Or a large mug of negus?"

In the few seconds it takes him to find an answer to this most vexing of questions, we have just time to make a mental note of the physiognomy and disposition of Mr Emmanuel Trencom.

He is, without doubt, a man of contentment and good humour. He is happy with his work, delighted with his wife (the lovely Constance) and besotted with each and every one of his fifteen children. "Got to keep the little ones coming," he says to himself with a cheeky wink. "Ah, yes — we've got no choice in the matter."

Emmanuel's happiness is reflected in the rounded curve of his belly which, when wrapped in a muslin apron, gives the impression that his frame is encompassed in a gigantic smile. His face, too, is as round as a puncheon and adorned on each side with thickly sprouting mutton chops. The adipose belly and luxuriant whiskers are without doubt among Emmanuel Trencom's more distinguishing features, but it is his extraordinary nose that singles him out as a thoroughbred Trencom.

"My nose," he says, tapping it lightly with a fountain pen. "My nose." Long and aquiline, it is marked by a prominent yet perfectly formed circular bump over the bridge.

Emmanuel performs a heavy hop and skip as he moves along the counter in order to reach for a bottle of porter. "Oh, there's a drink for every cheese, tum-tum," he sings, "and a cheese for every drink." And, as he pours a splash of the thick brownish-red liquid into a pewter cup, he breaks out into the playful little ditty that he thought up himself.

"Oh, a porter for a pavé and a sherry for a sleight. A claret for a cantal and a toddy for a tomme. A julep for a jorbkase and a negus for a niolo. A gin for a gomost and a grog for a gruth. Champagne for a chacat and a cider for chaource. Oh, there's a drink for every cheese, tum-tum, and a cheese for every drink."

As he finishes his song, Emmanuel lifts the chunk of vasterbotten to his nose and inhales deeply. His quivering nostrils are anticipating the resinous aroma of Swedish pine and the muggy odour of damp hay. But his little nasal hairs are already recoiling in disgust. Something is not quite right with the cheese and Emmanuel instinctively pulls it away from his nose and examines it through his monocle. Then, satisfied that it looks just as it should, he places it back to his nostrils.

"Goodness gracious," he says out loud, "either this cheese is off — or it's my nose." He has quite forgotten his hunger and his empty belly has silenced its growl. Emmanuel has far more important matters to attend to; he is anxious to get to the bottom of this mystery.

He cuts a slice of mycella and holds it up to his nose. "Yes, yes," he says, "*that's* all right." But the German romadurkase smells distinctly bitter and the piora has a scent that is redolent of old roosters. "Well, I'll be blowed," says Emmanuel, as he takes a deep glug of porter. "Come on, old chap," he says to his nose, "pull yourself together —"

It is at exactly this moment in the nasal life of Emmanuel Trencom that the door to Trencoms opens with a clang-clang-ding-a-ling of the bell. He looks up and sees two unfamiliar faces.

"Afternoon, afternoon," he says with his customary good cheer. "And what can I do for you two gentlemen?"

As he asks this question, his brain is working over-fast. Somehow, and for some unknown reason, it is sensing danger. These two men are dark of hair, unshaven and dressed in the most eccentric clothes. One is wrapped in a double-breasted cape that is far too big for his frame. The other is wearing the sort of waistcoat that Emmanuel Trencom has not seen on the streets of London for many a year.

"They're foreigners," he thinks. "Yes, they most definitely look foreign."

This is confirmed when one of the men speaks. "We have a delivery of Turkish milhalic," he says.

Emmanuel pauses before replying. His brain is busily processing this information. The fact is, he cannot for the life of him remember ordering any milhalic. Normally, all his deliveries of Ottoman cheeses come through Mr Papadrianos of Albert Wharf, a Greek épicier from Constantinople. And — no — he could swear an oath on the Holy Bible that he hadn't ordered anything from Mr Papadrianos in recent weeks.

"Well, well," says a puzzled Emmanuel Trencom. "I must confess that this is strange indeed — there must be some sort of confusion — but, hey ho, you may as well bring it down into the cellars. Come along, gentlemen, follow me."

The two men don't say another word. They are staring at Emmanuel intently as he is speaking, as if they are trying to judge whether or not he is merely *playing* the fool. But no, they both decide simultaneously that he really *is* a fool. Yes, a fool and a buffoon.

As Emmanuel leads them towards the cellar trapdoor and pulls up the iron ring handle, one of the men whispers to the other in Turkish. "Look — his nose. It's him all right."

"*Allah*," murmurs the other. "*Allahu akbah*."

"Eh?" says Emmanuel, who overhears something of their chatter. "Did you ask me something?"

"No, no," replies one of the men. "We were just speaking about Mr Papadrianos. You know him well?"

"Ah, yes, Mr Papadrianos — a good man," says Emmanuel. "His family and mine have been friends for many a year."

Emmanuel has by now reached the bottom of the ladder and the two strangers are following him down. One of them reaches out his arms to take the crates of milhalic; the other lowers them gently down before starting to descend the ladder.

"Now, let me see — where do I want it?" Emmanuel asks himself. "Hmm, now, where's the best place to put it?"

He potters off among the stacks for a moment in order to search for a good place to deposit the cheese. "Ah, yes — here's a fine place," he says to himself as he glances back towards the two men. And it is at exactly this moment in the life of Emmanuel Trencom that his customary smile disappears for ever. For the sight that greets his eyes is so shocking — so absolutely terrifying — that he freezes to the spot. "Oh, no," he says. "Oh, not this — oh, no, oh, God."

"On the orders of the Sultan Abdul Hamid II, the Benificent," says one of the men, "and with the blessing of God the Merciful." Then, without another word, the two intruders advance towards their victim.

Emmanuel blunders backwards a step — and then a second — but his path is blocked by a large stack of

Corsican rustinu. He wants to turn — to run — to escape. But it is too late. There is nowhere to hide.

"Oh, my father!" he exclaims, not entirely sure if he's referring to the unfortunate Henry Trencom or the good Lord Himself.

His last sight is of two long daggers being lifted high above his head and then plunged deep into his neck. He feels a sharp pain and then tastes blood in his mouth. His tongue is encompassed with warm blood and he can no longer swallow. He remains on his feet for a few more seconds before, cloudy-eyed, his voluminous frame crashes to the ground. As he falls, so do three huge stacks of maroilles.

"Quick", says one of the assassins. "Let's go — we've done our day's work."

Two days later, somewhere between the hours of dusk and dawn, the corpulent corpse of Emmanuel Trencom is transported in secret to Albert Wharf. It is met by Yannokis Papadrianos, whose tears are genuine and freely flowing. "A gifted man," he thinks to himself, "who might yet have saved us." With the aid of his brother, the two Papadrianos men lift the bulky corpse by its legs and ease it into a full butt of brandy. Emmanuel sinks slowly into the liquid, head first, until his back bends slightly and his legs crumple over. Seconds later, he disappears below the surface. "And so farewell, dear friend," says Yannokis. "May you have a good final voyage."

With this said and done, the two brothers seal the cask and gently roll it along the quayside and on to the good ship *Vasilios*. Within a few hours, both vessel and barrel are sailing down the Thames Estuary, bound for the little Greek fishing port of Dhafni.

CHAPTER
NINE

12 February 1969

Four days after his conversation with Herbert Potinger, Edward Trencom did something so out of character that it was as if he had already gained some insight into the dark machinations of his forebears and was being drawn inch by inch towards the treacherous plates and faultlines of the Trencoms' genealogical tectonics.

The evening in question began prosaically enough: Edward returned home from work at a little after 7.15p.m. and, seemingly more cheerful than of late, greeted Elizabeth with an affectionate kiss on her left cheek and a second one — more tentative — on her lips.

"Evening, Mr Cheese," she replied with a smile. "And how was your day at the shop?"

Edward thought for a moment as he scratched his scalp. "Nothing to report," he replied in as nonchalant a manner as possible. "All quiet on the work front."

"Something must have happened," she said, willing him to recount at least *some* detail of his day. "Did you have a tour group in the shop? Was Mr George swept off his feet by Mrs Williamson? Did a herd of rhinos charge through the cellars?"

Her breezy tone belied the fact that she was more concerned about Edward than she had ever been. Only that morning, she had discovered that for more than a fortnight he had not so much as glanced at the manuscript of his *History of Cheese*. When she tried to broach the subject, he merely commented that he had given it to Mr George to make some corrections.

Elizabeth was rather more alarmed when she learned that Edward had completely lost his sense of smell on at least two occasions in the previous week. This was something that had never before happened. Even when he'd been suffering from the flu, which he'd caught from Mrs Tolworth the previous winter, he had retained some sense of smell. Elizabeth smiled as she recalled how Edward had managed to distinguish between a bleu de bassillac and bleu de laqueuille, even though his sinuses were so blocked that they left him with a sharp headache behind each eye. And then there was the small matter of the cauliflower cheese. That was no less troubling. On the previous evening, she had cooked him his favourite cauliflower cheese with a sauce made from Austrian bergkase and Swiss toggenburger. But Edward had picked at his plate like a young adolescent before declaring that he was not particularly hungry.

Elizabeth did her best to draw the poison out of her husband. Heavens, she tried sympathy: "I know it can't be easy for you"; persuasion: "I'm sure you'd feel better if you spoke about it"; affection: "You know I'm here for you if you need to talk." But Edward said nothing, causing Elizabeth no end of frustration. "It's a little hard," she thought, "to help somebody who doesn't want to help themselves."

But Edward was about to reveal that he very much knew how to help himself, although in a way that Elizabeth was not at all expecting. For years their lives between the sheets had been tender, conventional and bordering on the perfunctory. It was not that they did not enjoy making love — Elizabeth, in particular, took much pleasure from their moments of shared intimacy. If Edward had been in agreement, she would willingly have extended their Sunday sexual encounter to other evenings of the week and (had push come to shove) might even have purchased one of those intriguing manuals — invariably by a Dr Comfort or Professor Easy — which seemed to appear on the bookshop shelves with increasing frequency. She'd always longed to peek inside the covers and had come close, on occasions, to pulling one down from the shelf. But a hidden hand had always prevented her and she was mortified at the thought that the shop assistant might see her. Besides, what was the point? Edward would have been appalled at the idea that "such things" could be learned from a book.

"I suppose I've got nothing to complain about," thought Elizabeth. "Virginia once let slip that she hadn't — *done it* — for more than six months."

It may be asked why Edward and Elizabeth had no children. It was not because they didn't want children. Mrs Trencom had often remarked to Edward that "if it's *meant* to happen then it *will* happen". But so far it hadn't and — if the truth be known — Elizabeth, now thirty-five years of age, was desperate to have little Trencoms running around their Streatham home.

Edward's own views on children were more ambiguous. Yes (he thought), *it would* be good to have a family — keep the Trencom name going for another generation — but, well, — he already had quite enough on his plate, thank you very much. The shop, his books, the festivals. How on earth would he also have time to fit children into such a busy schedule? If they came, well, they came — and all well and good. But he had no intention of pressing too hard for children.

Such thoughts had remained unchanged in Edward's head for twelve long years — from the night of their wedding to the evening of 12 February 1969. It was on this very night that he suddenly displayed a most unusual desire, urge and need to have sexual intercourse — indeed, to procreate. And happily for him, this desire was simultaneously coupled with a full-blown realization that Elizabeth Trencom might well be — was — the most important woman in his life.

It was a little after 11 p.m. when they went upstairs to their bedroom. Elizabeth removed her skirt and top and, still dressed in bra and panties, searched around for her nightdress. She untied her hair and allowed it to fall over her shoulders, catching sight of herself in the full-length mirror that she'd only recently hung on the back of the door. She was not a vain woman and nor — by any stretch of the imagination — could she be described as a boastful one, yet she had to admit that she was pleasantly surprised by the sight that greeted her. Just a couple of days earlier, she'd been admiring (with a twinge of envy) the figures of models in the colour magazines on display in the reception area of her dentist's. "Perhaps I shouldn't have been envious after all," she thought with a smile as she turned a compete circle in front of the mirror.

Edward was rather less attentive to his wife's shape than Elizabeth herself. On any given evening, he would head into the bathroom while his wife prepared for bed. He would brush his teeth, go to the toilet and then take off his clothes and climb (somewhat clumsily) into his striped pyjamas. Then, after opening the bathroom door and taking four carefully measured strides to cross the bedroom, he would get into bed, kiss Elizabeth on one or other of her cheeks and pick up the book he was currently reading.

On this particular night, he brushed his teeth as normal. He went to the toilet as normal. He removed his clothes as normal. But instead of slipping into his pyjamas, which were hanging on the towel-rail, he strode out of the bathroom wearing not so much as a pair of pants and jumped into bed.

Mrs Trencom gulped with surprise and emitted a sound that could almost have been made by a squeaking floorboard. Not once, in all her years of married life, had she witnessed such unusual behaviour on the part of her Edward. He'd always been so modest about his body, so hesitant about showing his bits.

This opening act was to prove only the prelude to five acts of surprises on this extraordinary Wednesday night. For no sooner was Edward in bed than Elizabeth found herself being kissed with such vigour and enthusiasm that she couldn't help wondering if Edward *had* flicked through one of Dr Comfort's manuals. But this thought was soon overtaken by strange happenings under the eiderdown. Elizabeth emitted a ticklish giggle as she felt her belly button being nibbled, and laughed rather more nervously as she realized that the part of her that Edward referred to as "the tropics" was coming under sustained attack from what she could only assume was her husband's tongue. Edward had by now completely disappeared from view. Indeed, the writhing and falling of the eiderdown was the only indication that there were currently two occupants in the marital bed of Number 22 Sunnyhill Road.

Elizabeth closed her eyes and thought, not of England, but of the fact that tomorrow she had to pick up Edward's suit from the dry-cleaner's. That meant that today was Wednesday, which meant that it was not Sunday, which meant that events occurring somewhere to the south of her midriff were even more extraordinary than she had first thought. She had been close to abandoning herself to the pleasure of it all, and yet she now found herself quite unable to switch off. For at the very forefront of her mind, a shrill bell was emitting an alarm signal. She was suddenly back in reality — albeit a rather unusual reality — and wondering if Edward's uncharacteristic behaviour was in any way linked to all the other curious things that had occurred over the previous few days. "Where *is* it going to end?" she asked herself.

In the short term, it was to end in a most pleasurable fashion. In all their years of married life, Edward and

Elizabeth Trencom had always made love in what Dr Comfort and Professor Easy would have referred to as the missionary position. But on the night in question, when the time for coitus arrived, Elizabeth found herself being gently rolled onto her tummy. Then, after a lot of wriggling — and a most embarrassing squelching noise — she was pummelled with such gusto that she could do little else but chew vigorously on the goose-down pillow. And at the very moment when she let out her second squeak of the evening, the bells of St Stephens parish church chimed midnight. Seconds later, it was all over. The bed, the bedroom and the streets of Streatham fell silent. The bedsprings returned to their original positions and Elizabeth quietly rubbed her hand over the pillow in order to get rid of the tooth marks.

"My goodness," she thought to herself. "How and why did *that* happen?"

"If we really *do* want children," whispered Edward into his wife's ear, "then we'll have to practise long and hard."

Then he yawned, rolled over and fell asleep. Five whole hours were to pass before he once again ventured deep under the eiderdown.

CHAPTER
TEN

29 May 1853

Henry Trencom awakes with a start. Outside his window, the call to prayer is just beginning — a long, low wail that floats through the still morning air and sneaks its way in through the slatted wooden shutters. Henry rolls over, still thick with sleep, and pulls a bolster over his ears. "Blasted noise," he thinks. "Wretched, blasted noise."

He closes his eyes in a vain attempt to regain his dream but to no avail. His brain is already whirring like a waterwheel and there is absolutely nothing he can do to return to his previously morphic state.

On any other morning Henry would have guided his thoughts back through the events of the previous day. The boat trip across the Bosphorus; the tea dance in Pera; the magnificent reception he had been given by the bishop of the Fener quarter of Constantinople. But on this particular morning his only thoughts are of the coming day. For the hour has come; the hour that Henry has been awaiting for many years. It is for this very day that he left the lovely Mabel Trencom; left his son Emmanuel; left Trencoms cheese shop; left London and made his way to Constantinople, the City of Dreams, the Queen of the Bosphorus.

On the far side of the city, in the imperial Dolmabahce Palace, Sultan Abdul Mecit is also preparing for the day ahead. Unable to sleep (on account of the call to prayer), he has summoned three of his Circassian concubines to play the lute and sing for him. "Play until dawn breaks the sky," he tells them, "and sing to me like the birds." The ladies of the harem duly oblige, aware that the sultan will surely reward them with slipper money and costly jewels if pleased by their performance.

Shortly after sunrise, they are interrupted by Munejin Bashy, the court's chief astrologer, who is the bearer of good news. The conjunction of the planets foretells some unknown triumph in the course of the day's proceedings. "Yes, your worship," he says, falling to his knees. "This year's procession — this celebration of victory — is set to be the most magnificent of all."

The sultan lets out a long, low sigh. Courtly processions have always bored him and this one — to celebrate the capture of Constantinople from the infidel Nazarene in 1453 — is set to last for the course of the entire day.

"Four centuries have passed, master, since the greatest of all victories," says Munejin Bashy. "Praise be to Allah, the All-Merciful One."

Henry Trencom has discovered every detail of the route of the procession. It will begin at the Dolmabahce Sarayi, from where the sultan will be rowed in the imperial caique towards the lower quarter of the old city. He will then make his way on foot to the Gate of Salutation in the Topkapi Sarayi, where he will receive the congratulations of all the notables of his empire, along with expressions of praise from many foreign delegations.

"And it is there," says Henry to himself with a troubled expression, "that I myself shall meet him. Ah, yes, the Trencom family, too, will be offering their thanks — but in their own particular and idiosyncratic way."

The sultan's flotilla is the very picture of magnificence as it slips graciously down the Bosphorus. The imperial caique is adorned with gold lacquer that glints and twinkles in the May sunshine. The other boats are bedecked with a gaudy mishmash of streamers, baubles and pennants. As the fleet heads slowly towards the old city, cannon boom out from the palaces along the shoreline. "God grant the sultan many more victories," shout the crowd, which is standing ten deep on some parts of the waterfront. "God be with us — and may victory be with us for ever."

As the caique approaches the wharf of the Golden Horn, Sultan Abdul Mecit is helped up from his cushions as he prepares to disembark. First to greet him is Patriarch Vasilios, head of the city's Greek Christian community, who makes the customary deep prostration at the sultan's feet. Then, after being summoned to rise, he (somewhat wearily) presents Sultan Abdul Mecit with the keys to the city, symbolizing on behalf of all Christians his acceptance that the Byzantine Empire has been for ever defeated.

"May God have mercy on you," says the patriarch, "as your forefather, Suleiman, had mercy on us." As the sultan turns to leave for the Topkapi Sarayi, the patriarch adds a new, unscripted greeting. "And may God grant you," he says, "many years of life and health and prosperity."

The sultan nods his appreciation and summons his entourage. With a blast from a trumpet and the hollow roll of a kettledrum, his cortège proceeds on foot towards the Gate of Salutation.

Henry Trencom has been watching the proceedings from the high ground above the wharf. "Well, well," he says to himself. "He'll be there in a few minutes from now. Come on, Henry Trencom, better prepare yourself — it's now or never."

As he thinks these thoughts, he can feel a shiver of nerves run through his body, starting somewhere in the vicinity of his big toe and not coming to an end until it reaches the nape of his neck. When he glances at his arm, he notices that it is covered in goose pimples. "Oh, pull yourself together," he whispers to himself. "Come on, Henry Trencom — live up to yourself."

He thinks for a moment about his beloved Mabel and their children. "I'm sure that young Emmanuel is doing fine work in Trencoms. Ah, yes, Emmanuel — he's a one — and isn't he just blessed with one of the finest Trencom noses in generations?"

172

Henry touches his own nose as he says this and then polishes it with his kerchief. "It's this little chap," he thinks, as he carefully wipes the rim of each nostril, "that's brought me here."

Henry makes his way up past the imperial fishing pavilion towards the enclosed menagerie. He blinks in the bright sunlight then blinks again when he sees the long neck of a giraffe poking out from a little coppice. He is surprised to see so many people milling around inside the second courtyard of the palace. "No bad thing," he thinks. "It will make my life that much easier."

The fact that he is clearly not Turkish provokes very few curious stares from onlookers and passers-by. Many of the people flocking towards the Gate of Salutation are Europeans — representatives of large enterprises and corporations who have made their fortunes out of the extravagances of the sultan.

There is a burst of cannon-fire and another blast of the trumpet. "Ah-ha, here he comes," says Henry to himself with considerable excitement. "Come on, Henry Trencom, brace yourself."

Sultan Abdul Mecit is less than twenty yards away when Henry unfastens the top two buttons of his waistcoat and draws out a small German revolver. Displaying extraordinary calmness, he raises it up to shoulder height, checks his line of vision and aims directly at the sultan. He winces slightly as he prepares for the inevitable bang. But — c-c-click — there is no bang. "Bother and d — nation." The catch has jammed and the gun has not fired.

Henry squeezes the trigger for a second time and on this occasion there is a loud bang, followed by a second and a third retort. But they do not come from his own pistol. Two of the sultan's marksmen have been watching Henry Trencom's movements from the rooftop of the inner treasury and have hastily taken aim. Bang. Bang. Bang. Henry Trencom just has time to rub his nose for a final time before falling — dead — to the cobbles.

As the crowd let out a collective gasp of horror, Munejin Bashy, the court's chief astrologer, makes his way over to the sultan and whispers something in his ear. "Just as the heavens foretold," he says. "That must have been the triumph that was predicted by the planets. Now, at long last, your empire is finally safe."

CHAPTER
ELEVEN

14 February 1969

Edward knew that something was wrong, even before he put the key into the door of Trencoms. There was an unusual scent in the air — something that he did not recognize. He sniffed at the air — once, twice and a third time. "Strange," he said. "It's tobacco, all right. Definitely tobacco. But it's not that same Balkan tobacco. And nor' — sniff, sniff — is it English."

The scent was so faint and difficult to detect that Edward surmised that whoever had been smoking it had left at least four hours earlier. "And that means," he thought, "that they were here in the early hours of the morning."

He opened the door, stepped inside the shop and flicked on the fans. When he came to inhale his first gulp of fusty morning air, he got the shock of his life. That same scent — foreign tobacco — could be detected *inside* the shop. And that could only mean one thing. Someone had broken into Trencoms during the course of the night.

Edward was alarmed; so alarmed that he felt as if his blood was starting to congeal. He rushed back outside and examined the lock on the door. It showed no signs of having been tampered with and nor had the door been forced. He reentered the shop and looked around carefully. Apart from two couhé-veracs, which had shed their chestnut-leaf wrappers, everything else was exactly as he had left it on the previous evening.

"The cellars," thought Edward in a flash. "It must be the cellars."

He ran to the rear of the shop and descended the stepladder as fast as he could. Sniff, sniff. There it was again. That same scent of cigarettes, fainter than it had been upstairs, yet easily picked up by the sensitive nostrils of Edward Trencom.

He followed the trail of scent through Normandy and Burgundy until he found himself approaching the cheeses of the Massif Central. He sniffed again and immediately realized where it was leading him.

"Of course!" he murmured under his breath. "The altar — I should have known."

Edward had re-sorted the great stack of family papers shortly before he had left work on the previous evening. A stickler for order, he had once again placed the papers in neat little piles and made sure they were arranged chronologically. At first glance, they seemed to be exactly as he had left them. But when he examined them more closely, he noticed that one of the piles — Humphrey's — had been disturbed. Although none of the books and papers was missing, they were most certainly not in the same order in which they had been left.

"Someone," thought Edward, "has been down in these cellars. And someone has been rifling through these papers."

And so they had. And yet to Edward's eyes, they did not appear to have taken a single thing.

Elizabeth's fears that Edward had abandoned his monumental *History of Cheese* were to prove unfounded. Just two days after their unusual encounter between the sheets, Edward announced his decision to resume work on his book.

"Mr George has been through it with a toothcomb," he said. "He's done a sterling job."

"Did you really give it to Mr George?" asked Elizabeth. "I thought that was a joke."

"I wanted a second opinion — he's quite a reader, you know. And he loved the book. He felt that very little needed changing. One last push and it'll be there."

"Well, what did I say, my love?" replied Elizabeth, with the beginnings of an inner smile. "You wouldn't listen to *me*. If it's as well received as your *Encyclopaedia* — and sells as well — I suggest we take a proper holiday. You need a break — you've been under far too much pressure recently. We both have, and it's not good. Look what happened to the Pattersons — look how they ended up. He ran off to Cape Town in search of goodness only knows what, and she's completely fallen to pieces. The last time I saw her she told me that Desmond was living with a young Zulu girl."

"Well, if you were married to Sally Patterson . . ."

"Edward!" exclaimed Elizabeth. "Don't even think it."

Elizabeth was delighted by Edward's change of heart, for she felt sure it heralded an end to his uncharacteristic behaviour. "Now we can at long last get back to normal," she said to herself. But even as she had this thought, she found herself adding a little mental appendix to it. "Although I must say, I wouldn't complain if the events of the other evening were to be repeated."

What Elizabeth did not realize was that Edward had decided to abandon almost everything he had already written — some five or six years' work — and embark on a history of the Trencom family. It would recount the inexorable rise of the Trencoms from Humphrey Trencom, founder of the shop, up to the present day.

"*Dynasty*," said Edward with a note of triumph. "That's what I shall call it. The Americans will love it. I always thought cheese was the be-all and end-all of everything. But my family's far more interesting."

He had toyed with the idea of structuring his book in strictly chronological order, beginning with Humphrey and ending with himself. But the more he looked into his family papers, the more he became convinced that this was not the way to approach the subject.

"Of course it's not. Why didn't I see it before? It must be written *backwards*, as if it were a family tree. It must start with me and end with Humphrey Trencom. In that way, I can lead the reader back through time."

This thought put him in mind of a different title. "What about *Time's Arrow?*" he mused. "*Time's*

Arrow." *Time's Arrow.* But no — it sounded too like one of those dreadful Kingsley Amis novels. *Dynasty* was better.

"After all," he said to himself, "I've already got three mysterious deaths in the first three generations. And I wouldn't be at all surprised if I stumbled across more skeletons in the cupboard on the way."

What had surprised Edward most during his researches was the fact that of the four generations he had so far investigated, three of them had abandoned the shop at some point during their career. This was something that Edward had never been told. "How strange that Uncle Harry never mentioned it. How strange that he never told me anything."

He was only now beginning to realize that his uncle had concealed a great deal of other information as well — information that had a direct bearing on his own life.

"Uncle Harry must have known all the answers — he *must* have. Could it even have been he who hid the papers in the cellars?"

The more Edward thought about the records he had examined, the more frustrated he grew at the gaps in his knowledge. They no longer brought him any pleasure — rather, they left him with the disturbing feeling that someone was deliberately trying to conceal something. His father, grandfather and great-great-grandfather had all gone abroad in pursuit of some unknown goal, leaving Trencoms in the hands of a younger brother, nephew or cousin. "And what this goal was . . ." He tapped his fingers on his desk. "Well, it seems to have taken over their lives — each and every one of them — and required them to go to either Greece or Turkey."

The only exception to the rule was his great grandfather, Emmanuel Trencom, who had not travelled abroad — at least not when he was alive. Edward had taken some comfort in the fact that at least one of his ancestors had been able to override the family obsession. Yet it now transpired that he had been killed — murdered — in the cellars of the shop. This was something that no one had ever mentioned to Edward. "And why on earth was his body taken to Greece?" he asked out loud. "Why was he not buried in London?"

There was another peculiar fact that Edward had discovered in the course of his research. Shortly before each member of his family had left England, the fabric of the shop had suffered some sort of mishap. On a couple of occasions it had been so serious that it could quite conceivably have delivered a fatal blow to Trencoms, had it not been for the hasty intervention of builders and engineers. In Edward's father's case, the roof of one of the side chapels (the one that contained all the Swiss bellelay and Austrian schlosskase) had cracked open like a nut. At the time, Peregrine blamed it on the firebomb that landed on King Street in the summer of 1940. But Edward was not convinced. The Trencom chapels were each supported by six squat stone columns that were well-nigh indestructible.

"I just don't believe it," thought Edward. "Something else — something *other* — caused that chapel to break open."

180

Then there was the strange episode of the shop's facade. In 1921, just weeks before George Trencom set sail for Smyrna, the front of the shop had slumped more than two inches. Such was the fear that the building would collapse that all the neighbouring properties had to be hastily evacuated. George left for Turkey in spite of the problem and it was only through the diligence and quick thinking of his brother, Archibald, that the building was saved.

The cause was never properly determined. George himself had blamed the unseasonably dry weather which, he said, had caused the underlying London clay to dry and shrink. But even at the time his views were treated with suspicion. Mr Sampson of Sampson's Meats pointed out that no other building in the neighbourhood had been affected by the drought.

The shop had suffered similar vicissitudes under the stewardship of both Emmanuel and Henry Trencom. On one occasion, a part of the floor had subsided. On another, the ladder leading to the cellars had broken apart and very nearly caused the death of Henry.

Edward pondered over these "accidents" and wondered if there was something that linked them all together. He had his suspicions that there was. He didn't dare mention this to anyone else, for he knew it would sound quite ridiculous. Yet he had actually begun to convince himself that the shop was in some way alive. Yes — it was in some inexplicable way reacting to the decisions of its proprietors. His father had headed to Greece and the shop had almost split itself in two. His grandfather had gone to Turkey and the place had almost collapsed. "Can such things really happen?" asked Edward.

His conviction that they could — and did — was not quite as strange as might first appear. After all, he had long held that the cheeses inside his shop had a life of their own. To his own way of reasoning, this was unquestionably true. Cheeses had their own idiosyncrasies. He knew this for sure, because they played merry mischief whenever he was not there.

And since he accepted that the cheeses had a life of their own, then it was clearly possible that the building was also in some sort of way alive. Edward thought back to the moment when he had unlocked the door earlier that morning. The door had squeaked, the floor had creaked and the cellar had emitted a low, lazy sigh.

This building *is* alive, thought Edward. It's as sensitive as a taleggio. It's as highly strung as a moularen. When it's worried, it reacts. When it's concerned, it shrugs its shoulders. And if it thinks — yes — if it thinks that there's something wrong with the proprietor, something seriously wrong, then sure as I am Edward Trencom it lets it be known.

He popped a slice of cantal into his mouth and chewed vigorously. It tasted strangely bitter, as if the milk had soured before the cheese had even been made. He cut himself another slice, from a different cheese, and as he did so he was suddenly gripped by fear — a real and terrible realization that it could only be a matter of time before he, like each and every one of his ancestors, would also receive the sign.

PART THREE

CHAPTER
ONE

20 February 1969

At a little after 7p.m. on a warm, breezy evening, Edward and Elizabeth Trencom stepped outside their Streatham home at Number 22 Sunnyhill Road and climbed into a waiting London taxicab.

"You're looking very — delicious — my dear," said Edward to his wife. As he spoke these words, he gave her hand a little squeeze. Elizabeth, still unaccustomed to her husband displaying any overt signs of affection, was quite taken aback. "And you, Mr Cheese, look most — handsome," she said, inclining her head to take a better look at him. "Oh, yes — give me a hug. I want to gobble you up."

Edward and Elizabeth didn't normally take taxicabs since they considered them to be an unnecessary extravagance. But tonight was an exception to the rule. They were heading to the annual dinner of the Most Worshipful Company of Cheese Connoisseurs and the taxi was supplied free of charge to each of the seventy "connoisseurs".

"One of the perks of the job," said Edward to the driver with jaunty good humour. "Never refuse a kind offer."

The annual dinner was the highlight of the cheese year. All of the country's most prestigious producers and vendors of cheese were due to be in attendance as well as a handful from the continent. It was Edward's role, as Life President and Master of Ceremonies, to formally open the banquet. He had also agreed to give the closing address at the end of the cheese course.

There were two reasons why he always looked forward to this event. First, it enabled him to have confirmed (before the assembled company) that he had the finest nose in Great Britain. It was also an opportunity for him to receive the praises of many of the country's best producers of cheeses — praises that he accepted with grace and gratitude. "And my gratitude will be sincere," he said to Elizabeth as they headed up Borough High Street. "It really will."

And indeed it was. Edward took his role as Britain's leading cheese connoisseur extremely seriously and was delighted when his expertise was recognized by the various Masters of Cheese.

There was another reason why Edward took pride in their praises. He was not a vindictive man and nor did he take vicarious pleasure in watching others suffer. But he always felt a thrill of pleasure when the assembled company re-elected him as Cheese Merchant of the Year. For the last eleven years there had been a pretender to the throne — one Henri-Roland d'Autun — who was at that time the proprietor of d'Autun's cheese shop in St James's Street, Piccadilly. He was perennially jealous at being beaten into second place by

Trencoms (though he tried hard to conceal it) and that gave Edward an annual little puff of satisfaction.

"Evening, Mr Trencom," said the doorkeeper of the historic Cheese Hall, that imposing Jacobean refectory which stands close to the Guildhall in the City of London. "And you must be Mrs Trencom? A very good evening to you too, madam."

"Good evening, good evening," said Edward, addressing both the doorkeeper and a group of familiar faces standing in the panelled atrium. He made a friendly gesture at Mr Gresham of Colsham Farm, producer of a quite exceptional colsham blue. He shook hands with John and Mary Walstone, makers of ribblesdale original. And then he turned and saw . . . "Ah — Henri-Roland. Evening — and how's business?"

The sight of Maître d'Autun caused an inexplicable flicker of guilt in Edward Trencom. It was almost as if he was embarrassed to be sharing a room with him — embarrassed, not for his own sake, but because Edward (a sensitive soul) knew that his presence would certainly spoil the Frenchman's evening. He nonetheless offered his rival a conciliatory smile and greeted him with as much good humour as he could muster.

His self-conscious chirpiness was not matched by Henri-Roland d'Autun, for whom Edward Trencom represented an unsightly mould on the surface of an otherwise flawless chèvre. "Bonne soirée, monsieur," he said curtly, speaking with a Provençal accent so pungent you could almost smell the fields of purple lavender. "I 'ear that you "av" 'ad — ow shall we say? — your share of trrroubles *récemment*."

"Troubles?" replied a somewhat perplexed Mr Trencom. "And what troubles might these be?"

"Ah," replied Henri-Roland, whose turn it was to feel embarrassed. He suddenly realized that he was on the point of being unnecessarily rude. "Well — non. Please forgive me — I 'ad 'eard you were 'aving problems with hors d'oevreing stock." He paused again before adding, "You know, if we can ever — *assister* — please don't 'esitate to call upon our services. As you say in England, a trouble shared is a trouble doubled."

"Halved," corrected Edward. "A trouble shared is a trouble halved."

"Ah," said Henri. "Well — 'alved. But, Mr Trencom, don't cut off your ears to spite your face."

"What a horrible man," sighed Elizabeth as she and Edward moved away. "He never changes, does he? Now, let's go into the hall. Look, I can see Sir George calling us over." Mrs Trencom pushed open the glazed door and entered the Cheese Hall, closely followed by her husband.

The first thing one noticed was the magnificent hammerbeam roof which dated from the time of the hall's foundation. It spanned more than sixty feet and its heavy oak bosses were carved with representations of the country's most famous cheese. Although the roof dated from Jacobean times, most of the bosses were more recent (Victorian) additions. At the furthest end of the hall, on a raised dais, was the top table which (on this particular night) was laden with cheeses for the tasting. The other tables were arranged in three rows along the length of the hall. The centrepiece of each table was a large platter of cheeses from around the world, many of which had been supplied for tonight's dinner by Trencoms.

"Can you smell the touloumotyri?" whispered Edward with a suppressed chuckle. "It's completely invaded the room." He sniffed at the air and then wriggled his nose in a most idiosyncratic fashion. "You know what, Elizabeth? I said to myself before we left home that the touloumotyri would be the first cheese I'd smell on arriving. It smells so strongly of goats — it's so pungent — that I can't believe I only discovered it last month."

Edward was not the only one to comment on the touloumotyri. "Good grief, Trencom," said Sir George as he gave him a vigorous shake of the hand. "Where in devil's name did you find this stuff? It, well, to be honest, Trencom, it pongs."

"I'm not sure it should go by the name of cheese," chortled Christopher Grey, who was known to all and sundry as the producer of a very fine Lincolnshire goat's cheese. "It's more goat than cheese. Yes, a cheesy goat."

Edward smiled and held up his hands as if submitting to surrender. "I must admit," he said, "that it both smells and tastes of goats. Elizabeth has forbidden me from bringing it home. But some of our customers love it — especially the Greeks. Have you ever been to Artemis Restaurant? Close to Paddington Station? Well, they take three skins of the stuff each week. They tell me it's become one of their most popular cheeses."

The hall was steadily growing louder as more and more vendors and cheese-makers arrived. Elizabeth was surprised to see Mr George enter the hall.

"He's never been before," she whispered to her husband. "How did he get invited?"

"That was my doing," Edward smiled. "I thought it was high time. After all, he's my right hand these days."

Edward didn't notice his wife's frown, for he was too busy greeting all his friends and acquaintances. "Evening, Mrs Bassett. Your ardrahan is selling like hot cakes. Hello, Brian. We really must order some more of your toolhea. Ah, look, there's Heinrich Trautwein. Good evening, Herr Trautwein — very good to see you again. Yes, yes — it's selling well, indeed it is."

It was while Edward was chatting away in this manner that his eye was drawn to a face that he vaguely recognized on the far side of the room. It belonged to a slight, dark-haired individual who looked — to Edward's eyes — as if he came from somewhere in southern Europe. Spain? Yugoslavia? Greece? He was holding a large piece of touloumotyri between his thumb and index finger and examining carefully the texture of the cheese.

"Who's that?" said Edward to Elizabeth. "That man over there? I'm sure I recognize him."

"I've no idea," she replied. "Shall we go and find out?"

"You stay here for a minute," said Edward. "Go and chat with Mrs Bassett. I'll be right back."

And it was as he said these words that Edward got the surprise of his life. "My God!" he exclaimed to himself. "It's him — it's him — it's the man from the tour group."

Edward hurried over to the other side of the hall, neglecting to greet many familiar faces in his haste to talk to the man.

"We've met," he said breathlessly as he approached the stranger. "Edward Trencom of Trencoms."

"Yes, yes — I know exactly who you are," said the mystery man. "Indeed you are the only reason I am here. I must apologize for not coming back into your shop as I promised I would. But urgent business carried me back to Greece."

"And who, may I ask, *are* you?" said an anxious-looking Edward. "I've been desperate to find out — ever since you came into Trencoms."

"Papadrianos — Andreas Papadrianos — from Salonika. I've been admiring your touloumotyri. It's uncommonly good."

Edward was so delighted to meet someone who appreciated his touloumotyri that he momentarily forgot that he was at long last standing face to face with one of the two men who had occupied his every waking hour for the last two weeks.

"You're the first person tonight to tell me that," he said. "Although it's proving very popular with the Greeks in London. Perhaps you know Artemis Restaurant? They take several skins a week."

He checked himself in mid-sentence when he remembered to whom he was speaking. "But who *are* you?" he said. "And what on earth did you mean by your cryptic comments? And why am I in danger? I *am* being watched — yes, indeed, and by the very man you warned me about. And now my shop has been broken into. Someone managed to get inside in the middle of the night. But why?"

"But they didn't find what they wanted," interrupted Mr Papadrianos with a telling smile. "Because it's no longer in your hands — no. It was handed over to us more than quarter of a century ago."

"What was? And why? And who is 'us'?"

Mr Papadrianos raised his hand to stop Edward from asking anything more.

"Listen", he said. "There are many things you need to be told. And, believe me, I can understand why you have so many questions that you want answered. But you must be patient for just a little longer. I promise you that very soon you will learn everything you need to know. Within a few months, maybe less, we hope that all our plans will be in place. But I cannot answer your questions right now. If I did, your life would be in even greater danger."

"But I'm in danger enough already," blurted Edward, who was desperate to wring at least some information from the man. "I've told you — I'm being followed wherever I go, and I'm being watched."

"You are indeed," replied Mr Papadrianos. "You are indeed. But nothing will happen to you just yet. Of that, I am quite certain. They are simply keeping an eye on you. Trying to find out what you know. And this is precisely why it is better that you know nothing — at least for the moment."

Edward let out an exasperated sigh. "At least tell me this," he said. "Who is this man who is constantly in my shadow? Outside my shop — outside my home. Does the name Makarezos mean anything to you?"

Mr Papadrianos involuntarily twitched when Edward spoke this name. "How do you know what he's called?" he asked. "Who told you?"

Edward explained how he had followed the man to Queen Street, using his nose to guide him through the city.

"Your nose! Of course!" said Mr Papadrianos. "They wouldn't have thought of that — just as it was with your father."

"My father!" exclaimed Edward.

"And your grandfather. It is your nose that will save us all," said Mr Papadrianos. "You may not have been told this before, but you have the finest nose in generations."

Edward sighed once again. He was so frustrated that he felt he was going to implode.

"Listen to me," said Mr Papadrianos. "Within a short space of time, you will come to Greece. Your voyage will be arranged for you — every last detail. We will be in contact about the exact dates, as well as the place where you will be met. Then, and only then, will you learn everything. I can promise you that everything will be revealed. But until that moment, you must do nothing. Take care of yourself. Behave as normally as you can under such difficult circumstances. And — a word of advice. Stop researching your family history. It will do you no good. You will be told everything you need to know when you come to Greece."

"I will come to Greece?" repeated Edward blankly. His words were by now completely dislocated from his mind and thoughts, and Mr Papadrianos's assurances only served to confuse him still further. Hitherto, he had been annoyed at having information withheld from him and could feel the blood pulsing through his body. But now, all of a sudden, he blanched. He turned so pale, indeed, that Elizabeth — who glanced across to him from the far side of the room — was suddenly concerned. "Excuse me for one minute," she said to Mrs Bassett, as she headed off in the direction of her husband. "I'll be back in just a second."

In the time it took her to reach him, Edward had experienced a whole gamut of unusual sensations. He had felt strangely hot, as though a surge of warm liquid had percolated upwards through his body. Then, he had felt uncommonly cold — so cold, indeed, that goose pimples appeared on his arms and cheeks. He had felt dry in the mouth; then dizzy and strangely light-headed. He had felt sick, then suddenly hungry. He felt detached from his surroundings, utterly divorced from the hall and the people. He could hear the incessant chatter — the voices and the conversation — but it was all a babble and a blur. It was as if he was not quite here; not quite in the room. It was as if he was observing the proceedings from somewhere outside his body.

And then, as he instinctively reached for his nose and felt its distinctive bump, all of these sensations dramatically disappeared. There he was, back in the Cheese Hall, fully present on the evening of 20 February 1969 — Mr Edward Trencom of Trencoms in London, standing next to a certain Mr Papadrianos and introducing him to his wife.

"Elizabeth," he said. "Meet Mr Papadrianos. He's here from . . ."

"Salonika," said Mr Papadrianos.

"Ah," said Elizabeth, who was staring at Edward in concern. "Are you all right, Edward? You've turned as pale as a ghost."

"I was just telling your husband about our situation in Greece," interrupted Mr Papadrianos. "It's enough to make anyone blanch."

"Ah," replied Elizabeth, who had no idea about the current situation in Greece. "Yes — I hear things have taken a turn for the worse. Well, if you'll excuse us," she said firmly, "I'm going to have to reclaim my husband for a while. There are a few important people he needs to meet."

She laid rather too much stress on the word "important" than was strictly necessary, for it gave the distinct impression that she felt Mr Papadrianos was not all that important. And this was exactly what she had intended to do. For although Mrs Trencom appeared shy and often quite reserved, she had an uncanny knack of letting people know where she stood on matters.

She led Edward over to Gregory Wareham, vice-president of the Worshipful Company of Cheese Connoisseurs, who greeted his old friend with a hearty handshake and Elizabeth with an almost too familiar kiss on her cheek.

"Edward, old chap," he said. "What in the devil's name have you brought along this time? Smells of old goats."

"Well it *is* — in a manner of speaking — old goats," replied Edward. "Touloumotyri. The best ones come from a single peninsula in Greece — Mount Athos. I can tell you, it's very popular with the Greeks."

"Well," said Gregory, "it's all Greek to me." He responded to his own joke with a bellyful of laughs before adding, "Anyway, methinks it's time to start proceedings. Shall we get the tasting underway?"

"Yes, yes," said Edward, and he stood on a chair and called for a general silence in order to announce the event. As he did so, he noticed the figure of Mr Papadrianos slip silently out of the door.

The cheeses to be tasted were all goat's cheeses from the Loire Valley. A different country and area was selected for each gathering of the Worshipful Company of Cheese Connoisseurs and five or six representative cheeses from that area were prepared for tasting. This was to be one of the most challenging competitions for many a year, since the selected cheeses were extremely similar in colour, texture and flavour. Five members of the Company had elected to take part in the blind tasting, trusting that their noses and taste buds would not let them down.

Edward had always been the first among equals at such contests. He had taken part on every occasion for the last seventeen years and had so far never failed to correctly identify a cheese. Running a close second was Maître d'Autun, whose expertise almost rivalled that of Edward. Yet there had been several occasions when Henri-Roland had made foolish errors that cost him the chance of sharing the prize with Edward. This year he was quietly confident. He was extremely knowledgeable about the cheeses of the Loire and entertained high hopes of snatching the prize from under the nose, so to speak, of his old rival.

Edward was unusually concerned about this year's tasting and had confided his fears to Elizabeth. "Three times, darling, in the last week, my nose has failed me," he whispered. "Three times I've lost my sense of smell. What shall I do if it happens again tonight, of all nights?"

"But you've been OK so far," said Elizabeth in a most reassuring voice. "Haven't you?"

Edward said nothing for a moment before looking at his wife. "Well — yes and no," he admitted nervously. "I must confess, well, a moment or two ago, I clean lost all sense of smell. It's come back now, but . . ."

"You'll be fine," said Elizabeth, taking advantage of the short pause. "It's nerves and worry that are getting to you. Just think of all your past successes. You'll be able to do it again this year." Yet even as she said these words, she was struck by the realization that Edward — her Edward — might not be fine.

The contestants made their way up to the top table, where a thin sheet of muslin covered the cheeses. A screen had been erected in order that everyone in the hall would be able to see the cheese, save for those taking part in the tasting. When the contestants were all lined up and ready, Gregory Wareham rapped on the table and called for everyone's attention. Then, as a silence spread through the hall, he made a short speech in which he announced, among other things, that all six cheeses came from the Loire. "And that's all I'm giving away," he said, before whipping off the muslin cover so that the audience could see what was to be tasted. There was a murmur in the room as the assembled cheese-makers and mongers tried to identify the specimens. As the noise grew in volume, Gregory called for complete silence lest any of the contestants might overhear the names being whispered.

"I shall now present our guinea pigs with the first cheese," he declared, cutting the pouligny-saint-pierre into five equal parts. The first piece was handed to Edward, the second to Henri-Roland, and so on, until each of the contestants had a piece of the cheese.

"Now, let me just remind you of the rules," said the vicepresident. "No conferring — and no discussion. When you think you have the answer, write it down. At the end of the tasting, when you've tried all the cheeses, we'll collect your papers and announce your results. Any questions? Yes, Monsieur — sorry, *Maître* — d'Autun."

Henri-Roland wished to object to something. "Oui. It is so verrry difficult to smell anything — anything at all — when the room is imprégné with the toulou . . ."

". . . motyri," said Edward.

"Oui — *merci* — all we can smell is touloumotyri. And it gets worse an worse. You 'av an expression for dis. The more you stir it, the worse it sticks."

"Well, I fear there's not much we can do about that," replied Gregory, "except, perhaps, to thank Mr Trencom for introducing us to a cheese that, well" — he paused to smile — "sticks of old goats."

As he said these words, Edward was suddenly seized by panic. He inhaled slowly through his nostrils in order to test whether or not the touloumotyri really was overpowering the room. And as he did so, he realized that he could smell absolutely nothing. It was so strange — just moments before, he could identify more than twenty different varieties of cheese in the room, over and above the general cocktail of smells. And now — nothing.

"Now, gentlemen and lady — the first cheese."

Each of the five contestants held the cheese to their noses, having first examined its texture and colour. Most of the guests in the hall already knew it to be a pouligny-saintpierre, for they had seen its distinctive cone shape and its orangey-blue mould. But the mould had been removed before it was handed to the contestants, who had only the thick, creamy innards with which to identify the cheese.

Edward held the cheese to his nose and breathed in. "Oh — please, please," he said to himself, "let there be something." But his wish was not to be granted. As the air filled his nostrils and then penetrated deep into his nasal cavity, he realized that he could smell absolutely nothing.

Maître d'Autun was not so handicapped. He sniffed at the cheese and instantly recognized the sweet smell of straw and the sour odour of goats. "*Infiniment plus distingué que le touloumotyri,*" he muttered to himself. "Ah, oui — the distinctive mould, the exquisite balance of salt and sweetness. Ah, *la belle France.*

"Well — *alors* — dat's obvious," he said to Edward with a confident smile. "The tree is known by its fruit, *n'est-ce pas?*"

"Quite — quite," said Edward, who was thinking on his feet. "What am I to do? What *am* I to do?" He noticed Elizabeth out of the corner of his eye. She was staring at him anxiously, aware that his nose was unable to identify the cheese.

"This is going to be a disaster," she thought. "If he can't identify the cheese, where does that leave Trencoms?" And for the first time in her life, she foresaw the possibility that Edward would lose his crown as the undisputed authority on the world's great cheeses.

As the other four contestants reached for their pads and scribbled down the words pouligny-saint-pierre, Edward was asking himself what he should do. "Perhaps I can identify it from its pate," he thought. "It's very pale, soft, looks like a chabichou — but — no." He paused for a moment. This was hopeless. It could be one of more than two dozen goat's cheeses from the Loire. And then, out of the blue, he was struck by a rather brilliant idea. As the other contestants put down their notepads, Edward picked up his and scribbled something next to the first box. Elizabeth

200

looked at her husband and let out a relieved sigh. "Oh, thank heavens," she thought, "he's managed to identify it."

The second cheese, a chavignol, caused the contestants more difficulty. It had been aged for more than four months, to the point at which the cheese's belly was almost crumbling and it resembled scores of other cheeses from the upper reaches of the Loire. Henri-Roland was the first to write in his notepad. Next was Mr Charles Storeford of Storefords in Lancashire, followed by Lady Anshelm of Durham, producer of the famous durham weald. Edward had been hoping that his nose would bounce back after its momentary loss of smell but he now realized that this was not to be — he was unable to smell anything. Robbed of his sense of taste, he popped the piece of cheese into his mouth and chewed and squelched it around his tongue. Then, reaching for his pad and, with a conscious display of confidence, he wrote a single word beside box number two.

And so the proceedings continued until each of the cheeses had been consumed. Maître d'Autun was smiling to himself, for he was *convaincu* that he had got each and every one right, in spite of the touloumotyri. The other contestants were rather less confident. Lady Anshelm had been unsure of the fourth and fifth cheeses, while Paul Austin (of the Dorset Cheese Company) declared himself completely stumped by the final cheese.

"So," said Henri-Roland to Edward, "how do we think we 'av done? A piece ov cake?"

"A piece of cheese," joked Edward, who closed his notepad and folded his arms. "It was too easy this year, don't you think? Even Elizabeth would have managed to identify these."

Gregory Wareham declared the contest to be at an end and asked the five contestants to hand in their notepads. "There will now be a short pause," he announced to the hall, "while we examine the results. So, please — bear with us for just a few moments longer."

As the three judges flicked through the entries, Elizabeth signalled to Edward from the far side of the room and mouthed the words, "How — did — you — do?"

Edward smiled and mouthed back, "Fine — fine."

Elizabeth let out a huge sigh of relief. "Oh, thank heavens," she thought. "He managed to get through after all — I just hope and pray he's got them right."

It took longer than expected for the panel to pick over the answers. At one point, they called over to Gregory and it looked to everyone in the hall as if they were asking him for advice. The assembled crowd fell silent as it became clear that the judges were perplexed by something written in one of the notepads.

There were whispered exchanges between the judges and then Gregory said something that made them all laugh. Although two of them gave him a quizzical look, as if to ask him if he was really sure of his decision, they all eventually agreed on the same course of action.

"Silence — silence," called Gregory Wareham to the hall after more than five minutes of discussion. "Pray, silence for the results."

Silence slowly spread across the room until even the noisy little group in the corner realized that it was time to pipe down.

"Thank you. Now, as you can imagine, this was a very difficult contest. All the cheeses selected were made from goat's milk and all of them came from the Loire Valley. Yes — not an easy contest. Now, let me tell you what those cheeses were, in the order in which they were tasted. One, pouligny-saint-pierre; two, chavignol; three, sainte-maure de touraine; four, chabichou; five, selles-sur-cher; and, last of all, a particularly fine valençay."

As he named the cheeses, Henri-Roland clenched his fist in his pocket. "*Oui — oui — oui*," he said to himself, ticking each one off in his head. "All correct. Many a mickle makes a muckle." He cast a glance at the other contestants. Lady Anshelm and Charles Storeford were shaking their heads. So, too, was Paul Austin. And Edward?

Henri-Roland turned towards his rival and was disappointed to see him grinning. "Did you get dem?" he asked. "All ov dem?"

"Yes — in a manner of speaking," said Edward, who couldn't help himself from letting out a low chuckle.

"Now," said Gregory Wareham. "We find ourselves confronted with a most unusual situation this year." He broke off and started to grin. "One that has put our judges in a spot of difficulty. If we were to have one prize for *correct* answers and one prize for whimsical ones, well, we would have no problems at all. But, alas, we don't. So, ladies and gentlemen, after much conferring among the judges, we have decided that this year's prize will be awarded jointly to Monsieur Henri-Roland d'Autun, who accurately identified each of the six cheeses, and to Mr Edward Trencom of Trencoms, who has — how shall we say? — caused us a great deal of mirth."

A hundred or more expectant faces looked first at Gregory Wareham and then at Edward Trencom.

"Yes — yes. For if we are to believe Mr Trencom, each and every one of these Loire Valley cheeses, which have their own individual flavours and characteristics, goes by the name of — touloumotyri."

As he said this word, the assembled company erupted into laughter.

"Marvellous — brilliant," said Sir George to Elizabeth. "I'm glad to see your husband hasn't lost his sense of humour."

"Well, we've always known he's a wag," said Charles Storeford to Lady Anshelm. "I guess he must have known them all immediately."

Edward looked at the sea of faces in the hall and also began to laugh. And, as his face crumpled with humour, everyone began to applaud.

"Now *I* think," said Gregory Wareham as he motioned for the hall to fall silent, "that this is one of the more shameful attempts to promote a new cheese. But I must hand it to Mr Trencom, he's certainly made an impression tonight on our little gathering. I don't think many of us will forget touloumotyri in a hurry. Now, if I could ask him and Monsieur — sorry, *Maître* — d'Autun to step forward, I will jointly present them with the prize, which is . . ."

"A cheese knife," called someone from the room.

"A cheese knife indeed," repeated Gregory Wareham, before adding, "I'm beginning to think that some of you are getting a little too familiar with this gathering."

As Edward and Henri-Roland stepped forward, the Frenchman whispered into his rival's ear. "In my 'umble opinion," he said, "you did not know dose cheeses. I'm not so sure you could identify any ov dem."

Edward lifted his finger to his nose and gently tapped the dome over the bridge. "A king of noses," he said quietly, "Yes, a veritable king among noses."

CHAPTER
ELEVEN

25 February 1824

It has been raining for almost twenty hours — raining so hard that the two figures at the prow of the ship are drenched to the marrow. Their capes hang heavy and water-logged; their felt-brimmed toppers are drip-drip-dripping. Yet neither man shows the remotest concern about the inclement weather, for both are preoccupied with staring at the misty, opaque-grey horizon. They are looking for land — hoping that soon they will reach their goal.

The taller of the two men leans forward on the ship's rail and extinguishes the feeble lanthorn. "Yes, yes — I think, by God's grace, that I see the cherished land. O Greece!" he declaims with great theatricality. "O ye land of the gods! Our mission, our destiny, now awaits us. We must perform our duties with the courage, with the heroism, of the Ancients."

The man who has uttered these words is none other than George Gordon Noel, the sixth Lord Byron, who declared just two days earlier that he would end his life on Greek soil. He intends to offer himself as a sacrifice to the cause of the Greeks and his resolution seems to have given a new purpose to his existence.

The person to whom he is speaking is a rather less imposing figure, yet one who has nevertheless a most arresting and distinguishing feature. Charles Trencom (of Trencoms in London) has a nose that even his lordship has conceded to be extraordinarily noble. Long and aquiline, it is marked by a curiously shaped bump over the bridge.

Charles can scarcely believe that he is standing on board the *Hercules*, next to *the* Lord Byron, the dilettante, the debauched, the most famous poet of the age. "Pom-pom!" he thinks. "What a strange twist of fate!"

Just a few months earlier, Charles had been working behind the marble counters of Trencoms, selling cheeses to the tavern owners and grocers of Georgian London. The exact date — which he would never forget — was 7 November. He had just sold an exceptionally fine round of laguiole when two men with unfamiliar faces entered the shop and asked if, begging his pardon, they could have a word. A perplexed Charles had agreed and within a few minutes he found that his life was about to be transformed in a most unexpected way. The men introduced themselves as Sir Francis Burdett and John Hobhouse, founder members of the Greek Committee, which had been established just a few weeks earlier in order to promote the cause of Greek independence. They were helping to finance Byron's military expedition to the Peloponnese and had already sent munitions to help further his cause.

"But," they told Charles, "we have our fears about his noble lordship. He is so . . ." The two men glanced towards each other, unsure as to how indiscreet they could be. Hobhouse stared intently at his walking cane (as if that held some answers) while Sir Francis pressed on with the unfinished sentence.

"The fact is," he said, dropping his voice to a whisper, in spite of the fact that there was no one in the shop, "the fact is, we do not know if we can trust his lordship. He is so — unpredictable. At times so — irrational. He tells us he wishes to attack the Turkish fortresses of Lepanto and Patras — which has the full support of the committee — but what then? In short, we want to know whom he intends to establish as the ruler of Greece — presupposing that he manages to overcome the Turks."

Charles was utterly bewildered as to why these two strangers were confiding such matters to him. He shrugged his shoulders, not knowing if he was supposed to answer their question or take it as one of those rhetorical turns of phrase that had become so fashionable of late. He was, if the truth be known, quite taken aback by the forwardness of his two visitors, both of whom were unknown to him even though they had introduced themselves. Why, he wondered, were they confessing such matters to him? Of course, he had his suspicions — oh yes, he had his ideas as to why. But how, in heaven's name, had they come to know about *him*? How had they found their way to *his* particular door?

As he thought these thoughts, he noticed that Boy Cowper, the street-lighter, was in the process of sparking the gas lamps outside. "Great heavens," he said to himself, "is it really that late? I should be packing up, closing for the evening."

"The question is this," said the second man, John Hobhouse, interrupting Charles's train of thought, "will Lord Byron try to establish himself as ruler of Greece? That's what we want to know. You see, Trencom, there are three pretenders to the Greek throne — perhaps you have read about them in the pages of *The Times*? There is Prince Alexander Mavrocordato — yes — a friend of His Lordship, who is currently in control of the western Peloponnese. There is the despot, Koloktronis — a veritable satyr — who rules the Morea. And there is the most untrustworthy Odysseus, who controls much of eastern Greece. But is any of these men fit to rule an independent Greece?"

Charles shrugged his shoulders for a second time. He did not take *The Times* and knew nothing whatsoever about the three men of whom they spoke.

"No, sirrah, they are not at all fit to rule," thundered Hobhouse. "They are most certainly not worthy heirs of the land that brought us Freedom and Democracy." He paused for a moment to gather his breath and ponder the weighty matters of which he had just spoken. In the silence that followed, Charles offered the man a thin slice of milky tarentais, which his interlocutor graciously accepted and popped into his mouth.

"And that leaves only Lord Byron," continued Sir Francis, "who is, we fear, not worthy either. You see, sirrah, he suits our purpose very well *for the moment*. He garners attention to our cause — yes, you only have to regard the news-sheets to see that. But Lord Byron as ruler of Greece? No, sirrah!"

At this point in their conversation, the two men's voices dropped in volume. "Does the science of genealogy interest you?" asked one of them in an inquisitorial manner. "Do you care much for bloodlines and the like?"

"I must confess," responded an increasingly perplexed Charles Trencom, "it's not something that has preyed heavily on my mind. Us Trencoms are of west country stock. Yes, sir. Pure Dorset."

"The science of genealogy," interrupted Hobhouse, who had scarcely listened to a word that Trencom said, "has been known to offer surprises of import and magnitude. Consider, sir, your great-great-great-grandmother, Zoe Trencom —"

"Why — what — how?" Charles was so taken aback by the fact that these two strangers should know the name of his great-great-great-grandmother — someone he knew absolutely nothing about — that he involuntarily spluttered into the cheeses arrayed before him.

"I have to admit," he said when he had collected his thoughts, "that I have never considered her."

"Well, consider her you should," rejoined Hobhouse and Burdett. "And you should most particularly consider her nose. Yes, indeed. For she had a nose every bit as extraordinary as yours."

Both men moved closer to Charles and spoke so low that he had some difficulty in hearing them. But he listened carefully and attentively — and grasped at

Over the weeks that followed, Humphrey would explore every nook and cranny of his Turkey-bird, poking fingers into places where fingers ought not really to go. He stroked and caressed her, licked her and sucked her. "I shall drink deep and hard at this particular well of pleasure," he said to himself with a greedy grunt.

Humphrey's English compatriots observed his behaviour with some bemusement and not a little curiosity. He would spend his daylight hours in his quarters poring over hand-drawn maps, then leave the factory at strange times of the night. He arranged clandestine assignations with Feneriot merchants living in the Christian quarter of the city and had even been seen loitering in the streets around the Selim I mosque. The Levant Company factors quizzed him about his activities but he remained tight-lipped. "I'm roomaging for antiquytees," was his only reply. "Roomaging for antiquytees."

It was after returning from one of his strange noctural excursions that something rather odd happened to Humphrey Trencom. He had arranged to meet Hafise at the English factory in the hour before dawn, in order that he could indulge in his early morning sport. "My morning stroll in the country," he joshed. "Up with the cock-a-doodle-doo."

Hafise arrived at the English factory as agreed and followed Humphrey up to his chamber. She removed her saffron-coloured jubbah, pulled off her underclothes and — quite naked — spread herself on Humphrey's divan. Humphrey also stripped, with characteristic speed, and laid his much-diminished bulk next to hers.

One of his greatest pleasures was to lie beside her and allow his nose to explore the secretive nooks of her body. She had her own peculiar scent, altogether different from that of Agnes. The rouge on her cheeks smelled of safflower; the powder in her hair smelled of civet. And there were other more seductive scents — scents that pricked Humphrey's loins. Her armpits — oh, for her delectable armpits. Washed but never perfumed, they held the tangible tinge of exertion — the first stirrings of odour caused by her brisk, pre-dawn walk. Humphrey would always inhale deeply — two or three times — before moving to more fertile meadows.

He would allow his nose to travel southwards, down, down, until he reached his empory of delight. "My souk of pleasure," he would dribble. "My Orient of the flesh."

He would rest awhile as he allowed his nostrils to explore the miniature hills and gullies of her flesh. Bewitched and enchanted, his nose would always twitch uncontrollably.

But on this particular morning, for the very first time, something went strangely awry. Humphrey tweaked his nose as was his custom and pressed himself close to Hafise's arms. He took a deep inward breath, drawing the air up through the nostrils and down into the lungs. And then he paused, waited and scratched himself nervously. "Funny," he said, "and strange." The every word they said. And as he listened, he found himself involuntarily reaching for his nose. Yes, he began rubbing it with his thumb and index finger, as if he was trying to polish it to a sheen. After a hushed conversation that lasted upwards of twenty minutes, perhaps more, Charles found himself standing straight-backed, looking at the two men directly in the eyes and saying in the most imperious voice he could muster, "Yes, good sirs, yes! By God, the answer is yes!" And within a week of uttering these words, Charles Trencom of Trencoms in London found himself sailing for Leghorn and Argostoli, in order to join the irascible and untrustworthy Lord Byron.

As a weak dawn struggles to break through the drizzle, it slowly becomes apparent that the faint smudge on the horizon is indeed the coastline of Greece. Charles watches with some bemusement as His Lordship spreads his arms wide, as if to embrace the wind and rain, and declaims to the elements:

> "The sword, the banner, and the field
> Glory and Greece, around me see!
> The Spartan, borne upon his shield,
> Was not more free."

He pauses for a moment. "Did you catch those lines?" he asks Charles. "Did you note them down?"

"No, Your Lordship, my most sincere apologies. Could you repeat them for me?"

"Write, you fool, write. It is my poem in honour of this noble, this illustrious land:

> Awake (not Greece — she is awake!)
> Awake, my spirit! Think through whom
> Thy life-blood tracks its parent lake,
> And then strike home!"

"Very fine words indeed," says Charles. "Very fine. Do you have a title for your poem?"

"I shall call it," roars Byron, who is once again addressing the elements, "I shall call it, 'On This Day I Complete My Thirty-Sixth Year'."

"Why, is it your birthday, sir?" asks Charles.

"Not yet — not yet. But today, I feel as if I have been reborn. Ah, Greece! How dost thou fill our souls with youthful dreams!"

"Begging your pardon, but what *exactly* does that mean?"

Lord Byron looks suddenly sheepish. "Er, well, it's Sophocles. *Oedipus Tyrannus*. Or is it *Medea*?"

He furrows his brow as he tries to remember. No, it has gone clean from his mind. Indeed, he wonders if he's even got the right tenses.

"Forgive me," says a pensive Charles. "But I thought Your Lordship was one of England's greatest classical scholars. I thought Your Lordship had attained a remarkable level of fluency in the Ancients. Didn't you say you had translated . . ."

Byron coughs and emits what can only be described as a nervous noble giggle. "Well — I had some help, of course. Only a little, you understand. The gilded guinea can buy half a lifetime of knowledge. And — you see — I forget so easily these days. It's the laudanum. But it will all come back to me soon enough."

He stops for a second and, in the pause, realizes that the coastline is drawing close. "Quick — quick! We must change our vestments. Away with this cloak. Off with these nankeen trousers. Away with my befrogged jacket. The crowds must see us as heroes worthy of the cause and of our lineage. Come, come with me! I have created costumes for us both."

The two men descend into the cabin at the fore of the ship, where two uniforms designed by His Lordship lie spread out on the portmanteau. Charles takes one look at them and blanches. "You — you *really* expect us to wear these?"

"Oh, indeed," says Byron. "Impression is everything. Let us never forget that the Souliots who will greet us are a most ignorant and foolhardy people. More than that, they are liars, Trencom, yes, damned liars. Never was there such a capacity for inveracity since Eve lived in Paradise."

"Yes," interrupts Charles, "but that still doesn't explain the costumes, sirrah."

"Ah," says Byron, "the Souliots, this burglarious and larcenous people, are impressed by the smallest trifles. Yes, they are awed by pomp and spectacle. So we must create a little circumstance on landing to show them, well, that we are worthy of their devotion."

The costumes of which his lordship is speaking are extravagant in design, cut and cost. Byron himself is to wear a hussar's scarlet jacket that is fringed with gold lace and jewel drops. Charles has a camlet-caped surtout with an ox-fur collar — it makes him look quite the dandy. Both men are to wear huge plumed helmets made of beaten bronze. Byron's is adorned with his family crest while Charles's is topped by an antique Greek crucifix.

"They will fall at our feet," says Byron, "they will follow us to the furthest corners of Greece."

It is almost noon by the time the *Hercules* drops anchor in the dilapidated harbour of Missolonghi. It is still raining — although the rain has by now turned to drizzle — and a dirt-coloured mist is rising from the surrounding marshes. This half-abandoned port, built on rotten piles and mudbanks, resembles a squalid slum.

"Good grief," thinks Charles as he sniffs at the air. "The very place stinks of death." The odours that his nose has detected are most unpleasant: marsh gas, foetid water and putrifying bodies. A pestilence has only recently drifted across Missolonghi and scores of dead remain to be buried.

"Have I really left Trencoms for this?" thinks Charles. "Is it for this that I left my lovely Caroline and my eldest son, Henry?"

The harbour front is lined with Souliot irregulars who fire their guns in salute as the two men land. This fearsome band have heard much about the "General Veeron" who has come to save them, but they are unfamiliar with the figure that accompanies him.

214

Charles Trencom's role in Byron's schema — or rather the schema of the Greek Committee in London — has yet to be revealed to the Greeks themselves.

The enthusiastic crowd sweeps Byron and Trencom to the only imposing villa in town, the residence of Prince Alexander Mavrocordato. He embraces Byron with warmth and affection and encourages the Souliots to let off another salvo into the air. He appears rather less enthusiastic about receiving Charles Trencom, whom Byron introduces (rather begrudgingly) as "Greece's friend".

"Let us hope," says Mavrocordato, "that on this occasion, Greece's 'friends' do not betray her."

A week passes. And then another. And Byron begins to realize that his magnificent campaign has started to go spectacularly wrong. His Souliot mercenaries are lawless and argumentative — "an unreliable band of avaricious rogues", is how His Lordship describes them. Their only concern is to relieve him of as many gold coins as possible.

Byron discovers that his European mercenaries are no less troublesome. Of a force of sixty who landed with him, all but a handful have refused to join the artillery attack on the Turkish-held port of Lepanto. Nor is the Greek navy willing to join the fight, claiming that their vessels are no longer sea-worthy. To cap it all, both Byron and Charles are seriously, debilitatingly ill.

It started with a severe chill and lumbago in their loins and back. Next, both men were violently sick, vomiting a mixture of bile and blood. Byron's physician, the knavish Dr Milligen, gave both men fifteen grains of antimony powders before applying leeches to their temples. But this only served to weaken them still further.

Now, on the evening of 16 April, Charles has taken a dramatic turn for the worse. His frame seems to have shrunk in on itself; his face is deathly pale; his eyes are languid and fixed on the ceiling. Even his nose seems to have shrunk in stature. Pallid and clammy, it has been twitching uncontrollably for more than an hour. He moans and screams as he is seized by violent spasms in the stomach and liver. His brain is so excited that he shouts wild imprecations at both the physician and Byron himself. "Leave me! Go from here! Friends, bring me release from this hell! Help me — I am poisoned. Help me! Save me!"

Charles's downward turn seems to cause Byron to rally somewhat. He claims to be much recovered and even rouses himself from his portmanteau bed and struggles outside into the enclosed courtyard. He calls for a wench and, when a local village girl finally arrives with a curtsey, he charms her with sweet ditties, all in his abominable Greek. He wishes to endear himself to her by calling her "my frog", but he forgets the word and calls her "my wart" instead.

"My wart, my darling little wart," he soothes. "Sing of love to your own George Gordon."

His little wart is clearly unsure how to respond to such extraordinary behaviour but she's already been informed of what she is expected to do. She gurgles with delight (earning one gold coin), wipes the sweat from His Lordship's forehead (another gold coin) and then earns the rest of the bagful by performing a Greek speciality of hers that takes even his lord-ship by surprise.

"Goodness," he thinks. "Not even my sister would consider such an act."

Twenty minutes of wartish pleasure are followed by an attack of coughing. All the exertion has caused a relapse and leads to a renewed bout of vomiting and spasms. Charles, too, is feeling even worse and languishing in his own private hell. Dr Milligen applies leeches to both men for a second time, yet this seems to weaken them still further.

Unbeknown to anyone in the household — least of all Byron — is this secret fact: Milligen is in the pay of the Turks. No one knows that his orders are coming directly from Sultan Mahmut II. No one is aware that he is under the strictest instructions to kill both men. With an air of clinical efficiency, Milligen goes about his business quietly but ruthlessly, administering poisonous cocktails and bleeding both men when he knows it will do them most harm.

"He is killing me," shouts Trencom in a deranged and dislocated tone. "He is the source of my misfortune." But before he can say anything more — or even lift himself up from his couch — he falls back into a semi-conscious state. Byron, too, has been growing weaker with every day that passes and Dr Milligen knows that the end is very near.

On Easter Sunday, at a little after noon, Milligen feels both men's pulses. "Thank God," he mutters. "Today — today will be the day."

He administers leeches to their temples and is pleased to note that when he finally removes them, their blood is no longer coagulating. "It's at long last working," he thinks. "The poison is doing its job."

At a little after six o'clock in the evening, both Byron and Trencom suffer a violent, excruciatingly painful spasm.

"Oh, for my wart!" shouts Byron in his dying breath.

"Oh, for my cheese!" cries Charles.

"What poetry," thinks Milligen. "Better than anything *he* has ever written — and my most perfect deaths to date." A few minutes later, the chests of both men cease to rise and fall.

"Our Greek heroes are dead," announces Milligen to Prince Mavrocordato, "and Greece's noble cause has suffered its greatest setback."

Mavrocordato nods slowly as he turns his gaze on Dr Milligen. "It's most strange," he says. "Do you think, Doctor, that they could have been poisoned?"

CHAPTER
THREE

21 February 1969

At ten minutes before noon on the third Friday in February, Richard Barcley picked up his overcoat and flung it over his shoulders. Then, turning towards the mirror in the hallway outside his office, he placed his bowler firmly on his balding head and shifted it slightly until it was straight. There was something immensely pleasing about wearing a bowler, he thought. It made him feel, well, dressed.

"Now then, Mrs Clarke," he said, as he walked past the reception desk. "I'm popping out — I'll be back later."

"Have you any idea when?" asked Mrs Clarke, who appeared to be in the process of counting paper clips. "Just in case anyone calls for you."

"As a matter of fact," replied Richard nonchalantly, "I've no idea. I'm meeting someone in the City and I'm not at all sure how long it's going to take."

"Well, I'll be right at my desk," said Mrs Clarke. "I'm not going anywhere. Unless, of course, Nature calls —"

"Thank you, Mrs Clarke," interrupted Barcley.

There was a moment's pause as Mrs Clarke mentally replayed the last few sentences that Richard Barcley

219

had spoken. "You're being unusually mysterious," she said with a knowing smile. She was horrified to realize that as she said this, her left eye let slip an involuntary wink. In order to disguise her embarrassment, she teased him with motherly good humour.

"A *secret* assignation, then. That's what I'll say to anyone who calls."

"Thank you, Mrs Clarke," responded Barcley for a second time in as many minutes. He felt that her tone and manner had overstepped the boundary between professionalism and friendship. "I shall be back when I'm back," he said. "You just keep counting the paper clips."

And with that he walked out of the door.

He shivered as he set off down Queen Street and pulled up the collar of his coat. As he did so, he glanced across the road towards Number 14 and noticed that the curtains were still drawn. He had spent much of the morning watching the building in order to see if there was any sign of activity. As far as he was aware, no one had entered or left since he had arrived for work at 9a.m.

He glanced at his watch. It was nearly noon. Concerned that he would be late for his appointment, he increased his pace as he turned into Cheapside, walking briskly past the Royal Exchange and on into Threadneedle Street. When he came to Old Broad Street, he paused for a moment. "I'll be there any moment," he thought. "I wonder if he's already waiting."

It was almost lunchtime and secretaries and bankers were emerging from their offices. But although the street was crowded with people, Barcley could see quite clearly, some thirty yards in the distance, a tall figure clutching a sheaf of papers.

"That's him," he said to himself. "That is *definitely* him." He was dressed in a suit and tie and wore an elegant trilby at a jaunty angle.

The man spun around as he approached. "Ah, Mr Barcley," he said in a refined English accent. "I'm delighted to meet you at long last. I'm so sorry I couldn't make it earlier. I'm Mr Makarezos — we work in the same street."

Barcley couldn't help but smile when he heard this. "We do indeed," he said. "You could almost say we're neighbours."

Mr Makarezos smiled in turn then made a careful scan of the crowded street. "I've booked a table at the Hand in Glove," he said. "There's a private room upstairs. Does that suit you?"

"Fine," replied Barcley, before adding in a good-humoured tone, "so long as you're not intending to kidnap me."

Makarezos frowned. "No one is going be kidnapped," he said, dropping his voice. "But someone is in danger of being killed — and that is precisely why we need to talk. In secret."

Over a lunch of jellied eels and steak and kidney pudding, Mr Makarezos revealed a great deal about who he was and why he had been following Edward.

"What I am about to tell you must be treated in the strictest confidence," he began. "I hope that you, as a lawyer, can appreciate the importance of keeping this secret. If our meeting should be discovered — well, all our lives will be in danger."

"Mum's the word," said Barcley, before realizing that his luncheon partner did not understand this particular turn of phrase. "Don't worry," he said. "I won't say a thing."

Mr Makarezos began by telling Barcley that he was indeed the person who had been following Edward. "I needed to find out how much he knew," he said, "and how much danger I was in."

"How much danger *you* were in?" repeated an incredulous Barcley.

"Yes, indeed — Mr Trencom has become a pawn in a very dangerous game," said Makarezos. "And he could well destroy us all. There are many people who view him as their saviour — and there are many people who would dearly love to see him, and me, and perhaps you, dead."

"You talk in riddles," said a frustrated Barcley. "And I'm afraid you've completely lost me. Can we begin again — from the beginning? Tell me — in which particular camp do you belong?"

Makarezos let out a little laugh. "As a matter of fact — neither," he said. "Or, more correctly, I am choosing to abstain. You see, I find myself in a most delicate situation."

He leaned over the table and explained to Barcley that he had been hired by forces in Greece who wished to dispose of Edward Trencom. "I cannot tell you why — at least, not at the moment," he said. "You'll just have to accept, in good faith, that many people wish to see him dead."

Makarezos explained how he was under instructions to trail Edward, discover how much he knew about himself and his family history, and then — ultimately — get rid of him.

"Get rid of him?" said Barcley.

"Kill him," whispered Makarezos. "Do away with him."

Barcely gasped when he heard this. "And?"

"And I find myself unable to carry out my orders," continued Makarezos. "In the first place, I've discovered that Mr Trencom knows very little about his family history. I don't think he is remotely aware of the fact that his family were courted by half the dynasties in Europe before they finally ended up in Piddletrenthide. And I also know that, without outside help, he is unlikely to progress much further.

"In the second place, well . . ." Makarezos let out a long, low sigh. "I'm not sure how to explain this," he said, "for you, perhaps, will not believe me."

"Try me", said Barcley. "I'm a solicitor. I can be made to believe anything."

"Do you ever listen to music and find that it has penetrated into the very depths of your soul? Do you ever read a book that stirs you from within? Makes you shiver? Is it not true that you then wish to meet the creator? You feel instinctively that there must be something extraordinary about them — something that places them apart from the world. Something that, well, touches the soul."

Barcley nodded in agreement, although he had to confess he had never in his life felt such sentiments. Indeed the murder-mystery he was currently reading had left him desperately annoyed, since he had known from page thirty-two that Dr McLachlan had committed the crime.

"Well — this may sound ridiculous," continued Mr Makarezos, "but it is like that with Edward Trencom. It was about two weeks ago when someone — his identity is neither here nor there — brought me one of Mr Trencom's touloumotyris. And you know what? It was the finest, most delicate, most exquisite touloumotyri that I have ever tasted. It took me right back to my childhood — to my village in Greece — where my uncle used to make that self-same cheese. And no sooner had I tasted it, and discovered that Mr Trencom himself had selected that cheese, than I realized that I could no longer carry out my orders. You see, Mr Barcley, there are many hundreds of locally produced touloumotyri cheeses. Yet he had chosen the very finest one in Greece. A cheese that was nothing short of perfection. And I knew there and then that I could not kill somebody with such a divinely inspired nose. It would be — against nature. And God."

Barcley wiped the gravy that was dribbling down his chin and tried to imprint in his brain the exact words that Makarezos had used. "Edward is going to want to know everything," he thought. "Every little detail."

"I see," said Barcley, when it was apparent that Makarezos had finished speaking. "And that is why, perhaps, you were threatened the other day, in the upstairs room of your offices? It was at about five-thirty on the fifth, if I remember correctly. I was witness to it all."

"They have begun to suspect," said Makarezos. "They suspect that I have changed sides. Which is why I had to break into the shop. I had to search for the thing they most wanted."

"Which is?"

"Which is something I cannot tell you," said Mr Makarezos, strumming his fingers on the table. "You see, I cannot tell you because it will place Mr Trencom's life in even greater danger. Besides, it is no longer an issue. It was most fortunate for him that the document is no longer in the hands of the Trencom family. It is almost certainly in Greece."

Richard Barcley took a deep draught of his beer and sat back in his chair.

"Who *are* you?" he said at length. "Forgive me for asking, but are you by any chance related to Nikolaos Makarezos?"

There was a long silence as Barcley's lunch partner weighed up the pros and cons of telling the truth.

"Yes", he said with great deliberation. "I am. He is my cousin. But that is something that you must keep firmly under your belt. I repeat — firmly under your belt."

"Humph", said an increasingly impatient Barcley. "So what happens now? Where do we go from here?"

"We need to buy time," said Makarezos. "Events are changing rapidly in Greece. They will soon reach crisis point and whoever is the winner will decide upon Mr Trencom's fate. Until then, we must proceed with extreme caution. Your friend must continue his life as normal. I will still be following him, for I am under orders to follow him, but he must never try to make contact with me. And he must never come to our offices in Queen Street. So long as he does nothing untoward, he will be safe — for the time being.

"And one other thing, Mr Barcley. Could you please remind him that it is of the utmost importance that he stops all further research into his genealogy. For that is the surest and fastest way to get himself killed."

"Well, well, well," said a troubled Edward later that evening. "I don't know what to think. I really don't. On the one hand, I have people who apparently want to kill me. And on the other, I have people who see me as their saviour. And as for me, well, you know what, Richard? I just want to sort out my family tree and, well, return to my old quiet way of life."

Barcley took a sip of wine and offered his friend a sympathetic shake of his head. He had dropped in on Edward after work in order to tell him all the details of his lunch with Mr Makarezos. But no sooner had he repeated everything he'd been told than he realized that he had discovered very few answers.

"The only thing that *does* seem clear," he said, "is that you must stop your family research. As from today. Now. This evening. They're watching everything you do, Edward. Absolutely everything. You won't be able to hide it from them. And while we know that, for the moment, Mr Makarezos is on our side — or should I say, on *your* side — who's to say he won't change his mind again? After all, he's personally connected to the very men who are ruling Greece. They are one and the same family."

Edward looked at Barcley as if he was mad. "Out of the question," he said bluntly. "That is absolutely out of the question. If anything has persuaded me that I need to discover *more* about my family then it's what you've just told me. You're quite wrong, Richard. I have to get to the bottom of this mystery — urgently — and it's quite clear that I'm not going to get help from anyone else. Consider — I've now had contact with both of the men who are involved in this . . . this plot. And yet I've managed to learn almost nothing."

Richard scratched his head, took another glug of wine and noticed out of the corner of his left eye that an unseasonal daddy long-legs had settled on his shoulder. Slowly and with as little movement as possible, he lifted his right hand higher — higher — higher, preparing to smash the unfortunate creature. But something caused him momentarily to pause. The daddy long-legs cocked two of its longest legs, rubbed them together with apparent glee — and then launched itself into the cheesy air. Just as it did so — at that very split second — Richard propelled his hand downwards, and it forcefully connected with his now-vacated shoulder. "Ouch!" he cried, watching the creature fly away. "Damn things." He shook his head, as if distracted by a new train of thought. "By the way," he said, "what *did* you discover about old Charles Trencom? You never did tell me."

"It's not so much what I've discovered," said Edward, "as what I haven't discovered. And what intrigues me more than anything is why this Greek Committee chose Charles Trencom, of *all* people, to go to Greece — it's strange. And even more puzzling is the fact that he said yes."

Richard reached for a file of documents and reflected on why Charles Trencom might have gone to Greece. "There's always a logical way to approach such matters," he advised. "Never underestimate logic, Edward — it's kept me in business for more than a decade. Now — let's have another look at all the evidence."

Barcley sifted through the small pile of papers that Edward had laid out on the altar. "Let me see. Two, no, *three* letters. Several references to this Greek Committee and — heavens, old chap — this letter's signed by Byron himself. I'd say that must be worth a bob or two. Mind you, I never cared for Byron's poems:

"The mountains look on Marathon —
And Marathon looks on the sea;
And musing there an hour alone,
I dream'd that Greece might still be free."

"*Don Juan*, wasn't it? Remember studying it at school. Dreadful stuff. More of a Betjeman man myself."

Edward cleared his throat. "This, Richard," he said, clutching the little packet of Byron letters, "is one of the most exciting things I've found so far. Imagine, an ancestor of mine — a direct relation — was friends with Lord Byron. Isn't that exciting?"

"Reasonably," replied Barcley with his predictable lack of passion.

"*Reasonably!*" interjected Edward. "That very letter, the one you're holding, was written by Byron himself. He sat down one day with *that* sheet of paper in front of him. He took out his quill. He wrote those words. That is actually *his* handwriting. I can tell you one thing, Richard. This is better than coin collecting."

"Hmm — not sure we quite see eye to eye," said Richard. "In fact, I'm not even sure I'd want my family to be linked to Byron. Black sheep and all that."

"Well, I'm more than happy to be linked to Byron," said Edward. "And I'm even happier that one of the letters refers to Charles by name. Listen to this, Richard, listen to what Byron writes to Sir Francis Burdett. Hang on a minute — where is it? Ah, here we go. 'I do not consider Mr Charles Trencom to be quite the Greek hero that I need at this current time and nor, indeed, do I find him quite the hero that you profess him to be. My Greece, sir, is the Greece of the Ancients! The Noble Greece of Sophocles! The Sagacious Greece of Plato! O Socrates, where art thou now? O Aristophanes, where is thy wit? An independent Greece, Sir, must seek the highest born, not the debased.' "

Barcley let out a low whistle. "That's unnecessarily unpleasant," he said with a stifled laugh. "Not kind at all. Well, one thing is sure, Edward. Your lot certainly knew how to upset Lord Byron."

"We did," admitted Edward. "But what does it mean? And what about this?" He reached for another folded letter. "This," he said, "is no less puzzling. It's Charles's letter to his wife, Caroline. Take a look — read it carefully. You'll see that there's something not quite right — something sinister."

Richard unfolded the letter and read it from beginning to end. It was written in a spidery copperplate hand that was set neatly on the page. "*Sinister?*" he said in a tone of surprise. "I'm not so sure it's *sinister*. You've already told me that Charles was ill — some sort of fever, wasn't it? And you also said that Missol . . ."

". . . onghi . . ."

"Yes, onghi, was infamous for its fevers."

"Yes, Richard, it was. But you've read what Charles says — he claims that he's being poisoned. Poisoned by the very physician who's meant to be healing him."

"The delusions of a crazy mind," said Barcley. "I've seen it happen to one of my own clients. Can't say which — professional code and all that. But the dying often think themselves into a state of complete delusion. It's a well-known fact. There's even a name for it."

"I simply don't accept that Charles was deluded." Edward had become increasingly animated and he grabbed at the letter in order to read aloud the

230

pertinent sentence. "Come on, Richard. Logic, logic. You said so yourself. Do you not consider it strange that both men — Byron and Charles — died on the *same* day at the *same* time and of the *same* symptoms?"

Edward fell silent for a moment while he glanced through another file. "And let's not forget that my *father* was killed in strange circumstances, hmm? As was my *grandfather*. And, Richard, it now transpires that my great-grandfather was murdered. And as for my great-great-grandfather, Henry — he was shot dead by the Turkish sultan's bodyguards. It could almost be an Ealing comedy, were it not for the fact that it's so sinister. So, in my opinion, it would not seem to stretch *logic* too far to suggest that, perhaps, Charles Trencom was also done away with. Despatched."

"You have a point," conceded Barcley as he reflected on what Mr Makarezos had told him over lunch. He helped himself to another glass of wine and swirled it around in the glass. "Mmm — that's good. And if you don't mind, I might just have another slice of this tou . . ."

". . . loumotyri."

"Yes, Makarezos was right about one thing. It really is delicious. D'you know what, Edward? You can almost taste the goat."

He held a piece to his nostrils and Edward followed suit. But just as he did so . . .

"Richard," he said slowly, "there's another thing — and this is the strangest thing of all. Something happened to me today — something most peculiar. All

231

day long I've been holding cheeses to my nose and, well, there's nothing. I can't smell a thing."

Richard let out a low, drawn-out whistle. "Really! Not even this stinking old goat? How long has it been going on? Did it just start today?"

"No," replied Edward. "If I remember rightly, it first happened just a couple of days after I found these papers. And, well, it's been occurring ever since." His voice trailed for a moment as he wondered whether or not to continue. "The thing is — this may well sound ridiculous, but it's almost as if the two things are linked. These documents and my sense of smell. I can't help feeling that my nose is trying to warn me of something — only what it's trying to warn me of is not at all clear."

"What!" chortled Richard. "Oh, Edward! Now you're away with the fairies."

"No, Richard. No jokes. I'm being serious. It's as if these characters from the past — my own ancestors — are somehow playing games with my nose. Take this touloumotyri, for example. I know it smells of goat, stinks even, and yet, right now, I can't smell a thing."

Richard was on the point of chortling but the nascent laugh was involuntarily stifled by a lump of touloumotyri that had glued itself to his windpipe. The shock of choking brought him to his senses. "Well, well," he said gravely, "I hardly like to admit this, but you have a point after all. Remember what you told me about your grandfather — George, was it? You said that he, too, complained of losing his sense of smell?"

"Yes, he did," confirmed Edward. "And so did Emmanuel, my great-grandfather."

Richard took a few more glugs of wine to wash away the last residue of touloumotyri then tapped his fingers on the altar. "Perhaps this is the wrong moment to broach this," he said, "and perhaps it's not. I'm not quite sure how to say this, old chap, but, well, there's something I've been wanting to say to you for a couple of weeks. But I wasn't sure how."

Edward gave his friend a most quizzical look.

"Well — it's like this. If I'm completely frank, you don't seem quite yourself at the moment. If you don't mind me saying, as an old friend, of course, you've been behaving — how shall we put this? — a little strangely of late."

It was at this precise moment, just as Barcley uttered these words, that there was a shuddering groan from somewhere far beneath the building. It was the eeriest of noises — to Edward's ears it sounded like a cross between a low sigh and a yawn — that was so deep in register that it seemed to cause the stone floor to vibrate slightly.

"Jesus, Edward!" exclaimed Barcley. "What the hell was that?"

Edward shook his head. He had suddenly paled and he noticed that his hands were shaking uncontrollably. "I've no idea, he said. "No idea at all. But I'm glad you're here. You're my witness. It's almost as if — as if something deep below the building is stirring from its slumber."

The two men stood in absolute silence, half-hoping to hear the noise again. But it never came. All was apparently as normal in the medieval cellars of Trencoms.

When an interval of several minutes had passed without a repeat of the sound, both men began to relax.

"I don't know," said Barcley with a prolonged sigh. "Sometimes I think *I'm* the one who's out of touch. Logic, logic. Maybe I spend too much time on logic. The problem is, Edward, that it's ingrained. We've been solicitors for as long as I can remember. And logic has been in my family for generations. For us, one plus one has always equalled two, whereas in your family, I suspect, it has often equalled three, four or five as well."

He sat himself down on a carton of cheeses and tried to erase logic from his thoughts. "Now then — let's think long and hard about this. Could it be that some part of your brain is leading your nose astray? Or is it your nose that's leading your brain astray? Or is it both? Or neither? We need to examine it from different points of view before we can arrive at any sort of conclusion."

"The truth is," said Edward, "I'm just not feeling myself at the moment. You see, ever since this discovery — ever since I began to investigate my family — well, I haven't felt myself at all."

Edward arrived home rather later than usual. His cheeks were flushed from the wine he had drunk with Richard Barcley and he had a chirpy spring in his step. On previous days, his walk home from the station had filled him with anxiety. He never knew if he was being followed — if someone was watching him. Now, for some unknown reason, he suddenly felt in an inexplicably good mood. He had walked back from Streatham Hill with the growing sense that his life had become altogether more exciting of late. It was true that a number of extraordinarily untoward things had happened to him. It was true, too, that he was clearly in considerable danger. And yet life was infinitely more exciting when full of surprises.

"Evening, Mr Trencom. Why, you look cheerful tonight."

It was Mrs Salmon from Number 36. "And a very good evening to you, Mrs Salmon — yes, indeed, I *feel* cheerful."

Edward offered her a cheery wave and continued walking. He was almost home and could already see a rectangle of light beaming from his living-room window. "Nearly home, nearly home. Now, let me think — shall I mention to Elizabeth the fact that I know she's been chatting with Richard? No, perhaps not. Let's let sleeping dogs lie, at least for the time being."

Edward put his key into the lock and gave it a sharp turn.

"Hello," called Elizabeth. "Is that you?" She emerged from the kitchen and offered Edward a kiss on his left cheek and then another one on his lips. "Everything OK? You look happier than I've seen you in a long time."

"Everything is just tickety-boo," said Edward. "Sorry I'm a bit late home but . . ." He looked his wife up and down and, as he did so, he felt a sudden and quite uncontrollable tingle in his veins.

"I'm not quite sure how to put this, darling, but — I suggest that — unless you have strong reasons to the contrary, we should — within the next three minutes — give or take a second or two — find ourselves upstairs — in bed. Or, better still — yes, why not? Right here — now — will do."

Elizabeth let out a little laugh that contained more than a hint of complicity. "Goodness — I'm not sure how to respond to such a suggestion," she said in a tone of mock seriousness. There was a side of the new Edward that she found distinctly exciting. "But, well, if you insist, Mr Cheese, just give me a few moments."

"Quite out of the question," he replied. "I only have a few minutes. You see, Mrs Trencom, this is a case of extreme urgency — and there's no time to go upstairs."

With this said and done, Edward proceeded to unfasten and remove his wife's blouse and skirt — the first time in his entire life that he had so much as attempted to undress his wife. He would have proceeded on to her undergarments if he'd had the time. But Elizabeth beat him to it. She unhitched her bra, slipped out of her panties and turned towards him completely naked.

"Well, happy Christmas!" she said.

Edward gulped inwardly and then removed his own clothes as well. Neither he nor Elizabeth stopped to consider that the curtains were open. Nor did it seem to bother either of them that all the lights were burning brightly. Before you could say as much as a by-your-leave, an animated Mr Trencom and an excited Mrs Trencom were in the throes of a full twelve rounds of calorie-burning love-making.

"Good gracious!" exclaimed Mrs Hanson from Number 47 across the road, who was at that very moment looking down into their living room from her upstairs bedroom. "What *are* they doing?"

"Lucky man," murmured Mr Clarkson of Number 43, who was peeking at them from behind his curtains. "Wouldn't mind being in his position."

"And nor," added Mr Waller, from Number 39, "would I. He's a very fortunate man, that Mr Trencom."

And that much was true.

CHAPTER
FOUR

24 February 1969

Three days after this most enjoyable of encounters, Mrs Trencom took the train into town. As lunchtime beckoned, she found herself in the vicinity of Trencoms and decided to pay a surprise visit on Edward.

"It's been weeks since I've been into the shop," she thought. "I shall pop in to say hello." She walked down the length of Trump Street and then turned right into Lawrence Lane, the narrow thoroughfare on which Trencoms was situated. It was one of those glorious spring days that to Elizabeth's mind were reminiscent of childhood. She noticed that sunlight was streaming onto the facade of the building, picking out all of the irregularities in the window glass — the bubbles, bumps and ripples. The cheeses displayed in the window were distorted by the glass and looked as if they had been heated to the point at which their surfaces were molten and runny. Elizabeth lingered outside and peered in through one of the puckered panes. She could see her husband's head quite clearly and thought it strange how the irregularities in the glass had picked out his nose and warped it into the strangest shape. She moved her head a fraction and the nose was back to normal. But now the back of his head was distorted. It had been lengthened and elongated by the glass.

"Enough silly games," she thought as she opened the shop door and heard the bell ring with its familiar ding-a-ding-ting.

"Afternoon, afternoon," said Mr Trencom as he glanced up nervously from his notepad. "Ah — hello, darling! What a lovely surprise. I'd quite forgotten you were coming into town."

"Oh, Edward," said Elizabeth in a mock-scolding voice. "You *are* a clot. Don't you remember anything? I told you this morning that I had to come in — you know? — to pick up the curtains."

"Ah, yes," replied Edward. "Well, it's very nice of you to stop by to say hello. Come — let's go downstairs."

He called down to Mr George, who was filling out order forms in the cellars, and asked him to serve customers for a few minutes while he took a break.

Elizabeth cast her eyes around the shop and was somewhat alarmed by the sight that greeted her. Even a cursory glance at the display of cheeses was enough to convince her that all was not right at Trencoms. It had always been the custom in the shop to have the most popular cheeses laid out on the marble counters. Yet she noticed that less than half the normal number were on display and that many of the favourites were missing. There was neither epoisses nor emmental. And where was the gouda? Elizabeth also realized that many of the cheeses that *were* on display were in short supply. There were only three Belgian remoudous on the counter and the Californian monterey jack was almost finished.

"Edward, darling," she said as her husband reappeared, "why have you run out of so many cheeses? I get the distinct impression that Monsieur d'Autun was right after all — there *are* lots of the usual cheeses missing."

"Ah — no, no, no," responded Edward. "Just need to get some more up from the cellars. As a matter of fact, I was intending to do it later this afternoon."

He popped an oatmeal biscuit into his mouth and gave it a vigorous crunch; the sort of crunch that was designed to put an end to any more questions. "Don't you worry. It's true that we've been having problems with some of our deliveries — but who isn't at the moment? These blasted unions. Still, we've been going strong for three hundred and seven years and" — two more crunches — "I confidently predict that we'll be around for a few years more."

He put his arm around Elizabeth's waist and scooped her over to the stepladder. "Come on — let's escape the shop and go down into the cellars. There are a few family papers I wouldn't mind showing you — and a couple of cheeses that I want you to try."

As Edward went off in search of some Pyrenean moulis, Elizabeth took the opportunity to meander through the cellars, something she had not done for many months. As she wandered down through Burgundy and the Jura, and passed into the Alpine meadows of the Swiss Valais, she felt a growing sense of disquiet. Something was not right — something was not right at all.

"Edward?" she said, spotting her husband's head poking out between two stacks of Slovakian oschtjepek. "It feels damp down here — really damp."

"Nonsense," he said as he searched through some crates for the Serbian katschkawalj. "No damper than usual. Besides, darling, cheeses like the damp." His voice became muffled as he bent down to pick up a Transylvanian monostorer. "Oh, yes — eighty-five per cent humidity. That's what they like."

"Hmm," said Elizabeth, who was far from convinced. "Where do you keep the old humidity reader? It used to be by the ladder. I'm sure it's damper than it should be."

"The humidity reader — the humidity reader," repeated Edward, who was halfway between the Dolomites and the Apennines. "Ah — yes — it broke a couple of weeks ago. Blast — you've reminded me. I keep meaning to get it fixed."

Elizabeth made her way deeper into the cellars, passing the Ticino pioras and the Bernese saanen. Then, finding it much less damp in the side crypts, she headed back towards eastern France, picking up a bleu du haut-jura that had been left on top of a half-opened crate. She sniffed at it and then rubbed the smooth surface with her finger. Funny. When she looked at it closely, she noticed that both her finger and the cheese were covered in a dusty coating of mould.

"Edward," she called, telling him what she'd found. "Are you sure this is right? Is it meant to be like this?"

"Oh, do stop fretting, darling," replied Edward, who was flicking through some papers that were lying on the altar. "It's fine. A bleu du haut-jura, you said? Well, yes, of course it's meant to be mouldy — Penicillium glaucum, if you want to get specific."

"I know, Edward, but this mould is on the rind, not a part of the rind. And I may be no expert but I'm sure that's not right."

Edward was scarcely listening. "If there were problems with our cheeses, dear, I think I'd be the first to know. You remember Mrs Burrows? She always complains if there's something not right with a cheese."

He paused for a moment before turning to Elizabeth with an eager smile. "And now, if you'd be so kind as to follow me to northern Spain — yes, here, among the cheeses of the Asturias — there's spot of business I'd like to conclude with you, Mrs Trencom."

"Oh, Edward! Not here," said Elizabeth. "We can't possibly do it here!"

"Why ever not?" replied her husband. "It's not every day you get to make love in the mountains of northern Spain."

"I never thought," whispered Elizabeth some five or six minutes later, "never in a million years, that I'd find myself agreeing to that. Now, Mr Trencom," she said as she straightened her skirt and brushed out the creases, "you've got some work to do — and I've got some curtains to pick up. I shall see you tonight."

She blew Edward a kiss and headed back up the ladder. "And don't forget," she said, "to get that humidity machine mended."

CHAPTER
FIVE

16 August 1774

Joshua Trencom is in a most irascible mood. His periwig has been itching all morning (he suspects that it's riddled with fleas) and his lumbago has spread to his thighs. And now, to top it all, Dorothea, his wife, is squawking at him like a fishwife.

"Nah, nah, nah, Josh Trencom — fancy's a fine thing — you did not lead me up t'aisle only to lee' me a London widow. Dorothea says nah — ye shall not go abroad."

Joshua slides his hand under his wig and scratches vigorously. There's a fine layer of stubble which is aggravating the weals and spots on his scalp. Mites or fleas? He's not sure but he is most perturbed to see that his fingers are smeared with blood.

"D — n things", he says, "and d — n you, madam. I shall not allow meeself to be spaken to like that."

After scratching his head once again, he storms to the rear of the shop and descends the old stepladder that leads to the cellars.

Joshua Trencom cuts a comical, well-nigh preposterous figure. This is due, in part, to the curvature of his midriff which is as round and firm as a Suffolk rumple.

The expanse of his belly is exacerbated by his habit of waddling when he walks, for it is forced outwards rather than downwards, in apparent defiance of gravity. After a hearty luncheon (which he always takes at the Fox and Grapes), the buttons on his waistcoat are stretched to the limits of their endurance. One can almost hear them squeaking in pain as they attempt to stand firm against the gently swaying gut of their voluminous owner.

Joshua in motion is like a ship in a buffeting wind. His undercarriage holds steady, his belly sways gently and his jowls swing freely in the stiff upper breeze. "He walks," according to Mr Swithen, the nightwatchman, "as if he 'as a cork up 'is fundament." And although this is a cruel jibe — and the source of much laughter among the clientele of the Fox and Grapes — it is undeniably true. Joshua Trencom has the air of someone who has been plugged.

Yet there is a single feature to his person that confers upon him a certain nobility and charm. His nose! Yea! His nose! Long and aquiline, it is marked by a prominent bump over the bridge. "Ah, my nose," he says to the customers who frequent his shop. "It's my heritage and my fortune."

Joshua's clothes are scarcely less comic than his girth. Antiquated in style and polished to a sheen with wear, they belong rather to the age of the previous George, the Second, than to the current occupant of the throne. On this particular day — in defiance of the summer heat — Joshua is wearing an embroidered waistcoat and taffeta bow; knee-length breeches and boots with spurs. Most outlandish of all — indeed, positively rakish — is his tricorn, which has the appearance of having come under sustained attack from a battalion of famished moths.

Joshua Trencom is not easily upstaged, but there is one person in his immediate vicinity who is able to do precisely that. Dorothea Trencom, née Roudle, is larger by far than her conjugal Joshua. She is also (as a consequence of allowing herself no more than one bath a month) rather more pungent than her graveolant husband. Notwithstanding these defects — for even her most sympathetic contemporaries consider her size and smell to be beyond the norm — Dorothea has managed to bring no fewer than thirteen Trencom babes to maturity, of whom Charles (aged fourteen) is her firstborn favourite.

Large people do not necessarily make for loud people, but in Dorothea Trencom size and volume are as interdependent as a chunk of cheddar and a beaker of negus. Rare indeed is the day on which she does not lose her temper with Joshua and raise her voice to a pitch and volume which the king's household trumpeters would burst their spleens trying to imitate.

We must not necessarily conclude from this that Joshua and Dorothea Trencom are ergo unhappy in wedlock. Not at all. It is just that Dorothea likes to ensure (by brawn if not by brain) that she is the indisputable ruler of the roost. And herein lay the makings of a tragicomedy that was to reach its fifth and final act on 16 August 1774.

246

Joshua Trencom has, it would seem, been in correspondence with Vasilios Hypsilantis, a rebellious Greek chieftain whose forces have been launching spectacular raids on Turkish troops in the Morea. The letters received by Joshua have convinced him that Vasilios is indeed a power to be reckoned with, and he now announces to Dorothea Trencom that he is planning to "make an excursion" to the land of the Greeks.

Dorothea's initial reaction is to scoff at the notion that her husband might consider himself of such elevated birth that he could undertake a grand tour of the sort so fashionable among the upper classes of Chelsea and Kensington. But when he explains further, she grows genuinely alarmed. Had not someone once said that there was a plague and a curse on the family?

"Nah, Josh, nah," she says. "It kill'd yur farrther and it'll kill ye. Never, never shall ye leave Trencoms."

The above exchange is merely the prelude to a marital set-piece battle that will be on a scale not witnessed since the first Duke of Marlborough's victory over King Louis XIV at Blenheim. Consider: in the rear, right-hand corner of Trencoms stands Mr Joshua Trencom, who is politely informing his wife that whatsoever she might say to the contrary, he intends to sail for the land of Greece. And in the front, left-hand corner (waving her marital banners and standards) stands the burly Dorothea, who fully intends to use her weight, muscle and expansive cleavage in her bid to stop her husband's crazed project.

Tempers flare. The volume increases. Joshua is as flushed as a glass of claret and wobbling with rage. Dorothea is steaming and has started to hector her husband. "You're a selfish clod, Josh Trencom. A rotten crab — a good-for-nothing turnip."

He bids her to button up — to fasten her tongue. "I'll fasten me tongue," she screeches, "if you'll fasten yur feet. You'll leave me a widow, ye will, aye, with thirteen little uns, aye, just like Pa Alexander did fur yur ma."

When Joshua fails to rise to the bait, Dorothea finally snaps. In a tidal surge of fury, she reaches for the nearest cheese — a leaden wilstermarschkäse from Schleswig-Holstein — and hurls its across the shop. It catches Joshua on his nose — just above the bridge — and causes him to reel. He staggers backwards and catches his breath. And then, quite suddenly, a strange transformation comes over his face. His florid cheeks turn deep purple. He gasps for air. And, seemingly knocked off balance by the wilstermarschkäse, his huge frame crashes to the ground.

"Ow, gawd!" screams Dorothea. "Ow, gawd." She rushes over to her Josh but there is nothing she can now do to make amends.

"I must go to Greece," he cries in a desperate, rasping voice. His pulse has weakened and his heart is losing its rhythm.

"Yes, my darling," says Dorothea, who has suddenly come over all weepy. "You shall go — I promise you that — you shall go."

CHAPTER
SIX

11p.m., 2 March 1969

Elizabeth Trencom's concern about the damp in Trencoms' cheese shop was to prove all too prescient. For more than a week, one of the water pipes that supplied Lawrence Lane and Trump Street had been leaking water into the clay subsoil that entombed the limestone walls of Trencoms' cellars. Now, on the night of 2 March, the Victorian pipe spectacularly ruptured, gushing more than a thousand gallons a minute into the surrounding clay. The pressure was such that the water soon found cracks and faultlines in the subsoil, punching through air pockets and forcing new channels. Within a few minutes, the first squirts and trickles were leaching their way into the cellars of Trencoms, flowing freely down the limestone walls and forming a small puddle on the flagstone floor.

The immediate cause of the disaster was to be the source of much contention in the weeks that were to follow. But it is not stretching credulity too far to suggest that the deep groaning noise that Edward and Richard had heard in the cellar was in some way connected to the rupturing of the pipe.

249

It was most unfortunate that the water found a ready passage in the downwards direction of the Trencom cellars. No sooner had it established the easiest escape route from the cracked pipe than it channelled all its energies into widening the gullies and creating its own underground river system. Before long, the single stream of water flowing down the cellar wall was joined by many more rillets and springs. A second puddle formed on the floor of the cellar. And then a third. And just a few minutes later, the first puddle conjoined itself with the other two and made a much larger pool of water.

There was something fascinating about the way in which the water sought to spread itself across the floor of the cellars. It sped rapidly along the cracks and grooves in the flagstones, seeking thirstily those places which were already damp. In following the mortar lines in the flagstones, it flowed in patterns that water does not normally flow, turning abrupt corners, sneaking around right-angles and creating miniature pools in the dents and hollows of the old stone.

The water had first entered in the furthest corner of the smallest chapel — home to the salty goat's cheeses of the western Sahara. The floor here was several inches lower than elsewhere in the cellar, a happy coincidence for it meant that the water was for some little while contained in one small area. It rippled merrily along the cracks and gulleys until it was halted by the shallow up-step — a cataract in reverse — that led from the side chapel into the principal crypt and from thence into the other five chapels.

Within ten minutes of the pipe bursting, there were more than thirty streams of water spurtling from the walls of the chapel. These were soon joined by fine jets of misty spray which hissed from cracks and faultlines in the old stone. It was not long before the fluvial pools that had collected in the hollows were linked and conjoined by means of the cracks and gulleys. The floor of the chapel was soon more than an inch deep in water.

The backlog of pipe-water was such that it created enormous pressure behind the cellar walls. It was as if five or six strong men were pushing with all their might against the interlocking stone blocks. The medieval masons who had built these walls were skilful in their work. The arched ceiling rested its shoulders upon the solid body of the walls, exerting sufficient downwards force to have kept the structure in position for more than eight centuries. But now, for the first time since their construction, those same walls were facing a competing challenge from the high pressure of the water. It began to percolate and bubble, eddy and whirl, scooping out the wet clay and turning it into liquid soup before disgorging it through the cracks between the stones. Slowly but surely, large pockets of water were being created behind the cellar walls.

Walls built of hewn stone do not collapse in the same way as a dry stone wall. Remove a stone from the latter and — kerplunk — a whole section is likely to collapse. But the masons of medieval England constructed their walls with far greater attention to detail. It has been calculated that one in every five stones could be

251

removed from most cathedral walls and still the building would stand. In the case of Trencoms, the arched ceiling provided such a forceful downward thrust that it is quite conceivable that one in four stones could be dislodged without the wall collapsing.

But water is a more invidious destroyer than the hand of man. It did not seek to tear down the fabric of the cellar and nor did it wish to undermine the foundations. Its sole intent and need was to find an outlet for its every-growing frustration at being trapped behind blocks of stone.

Its time came soon enough. It began to swirl itself into a froth that scoured and scraped at the loosening clay. Soon, several of the wall stones found themselves deprived of support. And at exactly this moment, a sudden torrent of water tore through the clay and hit the wall with such force that two hewn stones were rent clean. At the very same moment, and contiguous with this disaster, a thick jet of yellow-brown water gushed into the once-dry deserts of the western Sahara.

The first cheeses to suffer were the okra-flavoured cheeses of Mauritania. The water hit the wooden crates with the force of a hydrant and the entire stack collapsed to the ground, landing into the water with an ominous splash. As it fell, one of the crates nudged into a stack of Egyptian domiati, causing it to wobble. It might yet have remained standing, were it not for the fact that the bottom crate, made of flimsy wood, had been weakened by the water. That one little nudge was enough to cause the stack to join the Mauritanian cheeses in the ever-deepening deluge.

The flood was increasing at an alarming rate. Within minutes, it had brimmed over the step and was leaching across the rest of the cellars, creeping its way across the principal crypt and thence into the rest of the side altars. It sent chutes and runnels through Poitou-Charentes and Languedoc-Roussillon, then streamed backwards into the fertile pastures of Burgundy. Here, it collected into a little lagoon in a stony hollow before regaining momentum and heading for the meadows of the Rhone Valley. The lowlands of Lombardy were the next to feel its plashy waters; then, just a few minutes later, the whole of eastern Europe found itself under an inch or two of water.

The floodwaters in the principal crypt followed a similar pattern to those in the side chapel. Pools formed. Then fjords. And within minutes the individual gulfs and firths formed themselves into one huge expanse of water. The Iberian Peninsula was already three or four inches deep. Eastern Europe was by now an aqueous marshland. And then, quite spectacularly, these two marish littorals found their confluence somewhere close to the cheeses of Ticino, forming one giant ocean of water.

Boing! The clock upstairs struck one o'clock. Water had been flushing into Trencoms for almost two hours, creating a scene of absolute desolation. In the chapel where it first entered, stacks, crates and piles had all crashed to the ground, spilling their contents into the filthy water. A couple of towers had been left high and dry. The Saharan goat's cheeses of the Hoggar Mountains were holding out against the billow and surge. So, too, were the ewes' milk cheeses of Qasr Bint Bayyah in the Libyan Wadi Bashir. But these were lone survivors in this balneal wasteland — fortified cheese castles standing indomitably against the incoming tide.

There was no logic to the way in which the cheese stacks collapsed or remained standing. One might have expected the Danish samsoes to have kept their sea legs for longer than the chevrotins of the Loire. Yet they were some of the first to crash into the water. As the water deepened to more than two feet, the rate of damage increased exponentially. Hitherto, individual stacks had fallen apart, but this had not signalled a widespread collapse. Now, with the bottom cases waterlogged and the rapids sweeping through with increasing speed, entire sections began to fall in on themselves.

One of the most spectacular examples was the cheeses of Aquitaine, which were under attack from waters sloshing from two directions. A ferocious current washing down from the Pyrenees was joined by a second flow of water cascading off the Massif Central. Suddenly, the entire western Pyrenees subsided and then collapsed. More than 400 individual cheeses burst from their crates and plopped into the water.

A similar scene of devastation was being played out elsewhere, right across Europe and Asia. The whole of Scandinavia was under three feet of water. Central Europe was in full flood. Australasia was under a rising tide. North America managed to hold out longest against the waters, for it was separated from western Europe by a large step. But it was not long before the cheeses of the Mississippi found themselves underwater, along with the cornhuskers from Nebraska and poonas of New York.

Eight and a half miles to the south of Trencoms, in the London borough of Streatham, Edward Trencom was having a most troubled night. He had fallen asleep as soon as he tucked himself into bed and — on any normal night — would not have woken until 6.30 a.m. But on this particular evening he woke after about two or three hours and could not for the life of him get back to sleep. "What *is* the matter with me?" he asked himself. "Why can I not sleep?" When he did finally fall back into a slumber, he was troubled by such vivid and disturbing dreams that his pyjamas were sodden with sweat when he awoke for a second time.

Just two days earlier Edward had brought home all of the family papers and laid them out on the large table in the living room. Now, after tossing and turning for the second time that night, he took the unusual step of climbing out of bed and going downstairs. "No point in lying there sweating," he thought. "Might as well use my time profitably." He flicked through the few papers pertaining to Joshua Trencom, searching for clues as to why he might have wished to go abroad. Again it was Greece. And again it involved fighting against the Turks. But why?

He had also discovered to his complete amazement a most intriguing reference to one of Joshua's sisters, Anne Trencom. In the year 1769, she had been visited in London by an emissary of no lesser personage than

Catherine the Great of Russia, who was apparently in search of a wife for her eldest son, the Tsarevitch Paul. Quite why the Russian tsarina had alighted on Anne Trencom, of all people, was a complete mystery. She was a mere fifteen years of age, in poor health and had worked in Trencoms cheese shop since the age of six. Edward thought it unlikely that she could read or write, let alone know how to converse with one of Europe's greatest monarchs. So why? Why? Why?

He could only assume that Anne had turned down Catherine's offer, since she had died in London just a few years later. Yet this was an extraordinary twist to the riddle — and one that was no less beguiling than all the others. Greece, Turkey, and now Russia. It made no sense at all.

Edward went into the kitchen and made a cup of tea. Funny. Still no sense of smell. He scratched his head and wondered whether or not he should go to the doctor. "But no — what's the doctor going to say? I'll discover what's wrong soon enough."

He let out a giant yawn and suddenly felt uncommonly tired. "Thank heavens tomorrow is . . ." He scratched his nose wearily. "What day *is* it?" he asked himself sleepily as he let slip another yawn. "Almost Monday. Oh, dear. I'm not sure I've got the energy to go to work. Perhaps I should call Mr George . . ."

And with that thought in his mind, Edward made his way back upstairs to bed and fell asleep almost immediately. Within seconds, he was transported back into the same disturbing dreamscape.

256

CHAPTER
SEVEN

3 March 1969

It was shortly after dawn when Mr Cooper, owner of the Fox and Grapes on the corner of Trump Street and Lawrence Lane, went to the bathroom and turned on the tap. Nothing. There was no water. "Strange," he thought, and headed downstairs to try the taps in the kitchen. These, too, were running dry, although they did emit a slight discharge of orange-brown water. "Oh, blast," said Cooper. "'Ow're we expected t'do business without water?" And he picked up the phone to call the Water Board.

To his surprise, someone answered the phone. He was even more amazed to learn that they already knew of the problem. Yes, the water had been turned off. No, it wouldn't be on again for several hours — maybe not until tomorrow. But not to worry, the Water Board would be setting up a standpipe in the street.

"Oh, great," thought Cooper, with customary sarcasm. His day had taken a dramatic downwards turn before it was even completely light.

He gazed out of the window towards the building opposite. His eye was involuntarily drawn to the door of Trencoms. "Uh?" he thought. "What'n earth's that?"

He noticed that water was flowing freely from the little crack underneath the door of the shop.

"Darling," he called. "Darling — quick — come an' look at this." Mrs Cooper yawned and asked what was going on. "No, come down — now. Come and look."

Mrs Cooper threw on her dressing gown, ran her fingers through her hair and made her way downstairs. "Oh, my gawd!" she said. "It's water! Quick, Albert, call the fire brigade." Albert dialled the number and within eight or nine minutes, a fire engine drew up outside.

By this time, Albert and Samantha Cooper were dressed and peering in through the window of Trencoms. The sight that greeted them was alarming, although they had not yet realized the extent of the disaster. They could see water flowing through the shop, but neither of them had considered the inevitable fact that the ancient cellars of Trencoms must — to have created such a flood — be totally submerged in water.

"Have you got their home number?" asked one of the firemen as he prepared to force the shop door. "Tell 'im — Mr Trencom, did you say? — to come over immediately. This has all the markings of" — he cleared his throat with a gravelly cough — "a disaster."

He and his colleague forced the door of Trencoms and splashed their way through the shop. When they realized that the water was welling up from the cellars, they both let out a low whistle. "*Jees!* Is this where they store their cheeses?" asked one.

Mr Cooper nodded. "Shh! I wouldn't wanna to be in 'is shoes. We can bring in pumps but, well, it's goin' t'be ruined down there. We need to get the owner to come."

More than an hour passed before Edward and Elizabeth Trencom arrived in Lawrence Lane. Mr Cooper had already prepared them for the scale of the disaster but it was only when they saw the fire engine — and the stream of water flowing down the street — that the enormity of what had happened actually dawned on them.

"Oh, Edward," said Mrs Trencom as she clutched onto his arm. Tears were streaming down her cheeks and she was dabbing her eyes with a small handkerchief. "We're ruined, darling — everything is lost."

He turned to her with the saddest expression, placed his arm round her waist and said, "Yes, I'm afraid it is. A lifetime's work — gone. Ten generations of experience. It's as if . . ." In the dreamy silence that followed, he stared at the water that was still flowing from the shop. "It's as if, well, it's just as Uncle Harry said. There really is a curse — yes. And it's latched itself onto me."

"If you don't mind, Mr Trencom," said the chief fireman, interrupting Edward, "it ain't no curse, I can tell you that much for nothing. It's a bust water main, that's what it is. And you can screw that bloody Water Board — excuse my French, Mrs Trencom —

but you can screw them for every last farthing they have."

And with that said and done, he and his team began to install pumps into the cellars of Trencoms.

CHAPTER
EIGHT

12 April 1769

It is long past dawn when the sun finally pierces the inner courtyard of the Topkapi Sarayi. The slim tower of the divan scores the flagstones with a diagonal shadow and the walls of the imperial treasury leave one side of the courtyard in pale grey shade. In an hour or so, the sun will hang directly above the palace and this enclosed pleasure ground, which has been laid out with beds of flowering tulips, will be awash with sun.

In one corner of the courtyard, close to the Gate of Felicity, a small team of workmen are preparing three large crucifixes, bolting the arm-beams to the uprights and digging holes in the dry earth. Sultan Mustafa III has ordered an execution by crucifixion and is looking forward to watching the spectacle from the comfort of the divan. "My order," he tells his vizier, "is that the prisoners must suffer. Crucify them. That is what these dogs deserve."

It is almost noon when the three convicts are led into the courtyard by the chief executioner. A select group of courtiers has been invited to watch the proceedings and are seating themselves under the decorative canopy of the divan. The sultan is beside himself with excitement and would not have missed such an execution for anything in the world. He sips at his sherbet and peers through the gilded grille. "Ah — here they come, here they come." He claps his hands with childish enthusiasm and emits a peculiar, high-pitched laugh. "Let's see how they will go to their deaths."

Two of the men are common thieves, Christians from the Fener district of the city, who have been convicted of stealing a rowing boat. The third is a foreigner, although he, too, is clearly Christian. With his distinctive nose and rotund belly, he looks almost familiar. Why, isn't it Samuel Trencom of Trencoms in London? Isn't it the self-same Samuel who discovered the crypts and cellars that lie below the floor of the shop? How on earth did he come to be a prisoner of Sultan Mustafa III? After all, just a few months ago, he was in the process of enlarging and rebuilding the busiest cheese shop in London.

"It's a good question," he says, "and one to which —"

He looks at the crucifixes laid out on the ground and almost faints. "I — I should never have left home. But I was drawn here — drawn by some . . ." His voice trails into silence as the executioners manhandle him towards the cross.

"Lie down," growls the chief executioner, "or you'll feel the force of these." He shows the three men his bolt-cutters and then points to an array of other instruments hanging around his midriff. All three lie on their crosses and await their doom.

The sight of a crucifixion is not for the weak of stomach yet the sultan and his courtiers watch and listen intently as the grisly proceedings unfold. There's the hammering of nails. The screeching of the men. The erection of the crucifixes, which slide down into their prepared holes with a sickening thud. All three men are groaning in agony and they are condemned to a slow and painful end. It will be five hours before Samuel Trencom is finally pronounced dead.

CHAPTER
NINE

5 March 1969

"'Allo, Mr Trencom," said a grim-faced Mr Cooper, the publican from across the road. 'Ow's you this morning? I don't envy you — they "ad the pumps goin' for two whole days now, motors going around the clock. There was enough water, well, to fill a reservoir."

Edward looked at him with a hangdog expression. He was on the point of tears. "Well," he said, "I'm very grateful to you, Mr Cooper, for everything you've done. I'm just sorry if those motors kept you awake."

"Oh, dun thank me," said the publican. "I dun what anyone would 'ave dun — I'm only sorry I couldn't 'ave called the brigade out a few 'ours earlier."

As the two men stood in the street chatting, Mrs Tolworth walked past.

"Good morning, Mr Trencom," she said. "I am so sorry to hear what's happened. How's Mrs Trencom taking the news?"

"Oh, she's bearing up, Mrs Tolworth," replied Edward. "We're all trying to bear up."

"Well, if there's anything I can do for you," said Mrs Tolworth. "You can always rely upon me for a nice cup of tea. And if you need a shoulder to cry on —" She stopped in midsentence and blushed. She suddenly realized that she was being rather too familiar with someone that she scarcely knew from Adam.

"Thank you, Mrs Tolworth," said Edward. "I might just take you up on that cup of tea — I might need it after this." He pointed towards the shop and then made as if to leave.

"Oh, well. Can't postpone it for any longer." And with that, he disappeared into the shop. This time, there was to be no — sniff, sniff — pleasant odour of cheese when Edward descended into the cellars. The Great Flood had wreaked a terrible destruction — the greatest and most devastating catastrophe in Trencom's three-hundred-and-seven-year history.

"So?" asked Elizabeth later that evening.

"So," replied Edward. "I don't know where to begin. It's terrible — terrible."

The destruction wrought by the flood was indeed inestimable. The entire stock of Trencoms — more than 3,000 types of cheeses — had been destroyed by the filthy water that erupted from the pipe. Many of the cheeses came from remote and inaccessible villages and would take weeks or months to replace.

"And some of them," said Edward, "may be irreplaceable." He was thinking of the fragrant goat's cheeses of Al Bint, the soggy remnants of which he had held in his hand just a few hours earlier. These were only made in the hill village of Bi'r Ibn Sarrar in southern Arabia. They were transported by camel to

Bani Thawr and thence by car to the Red Sea port of Jeddah. From here, they were flown to London's Heathrow Airport and finally, after a voyage of sixteen days — and often many more — they were delivered (*Inshallah*) to Trencoms cheese shop.

It was a similar story with all the other cheeses — from Transylvania, from the Douro region in Portugal and the mountain farms of central Sardinia. "And what upsets me the most," said Edward, "is I've lost all of the touloumotyri. It took me three months to get hold of that supply."

He found it impossible to calculate precisely how many individual cheeses had been lost, but guessed that it must have been in the region of twenty thousand. "I've been trying to add it up," he said to Elizabeth. "We were supplying more than fifty restaurants in London and a further one hundred and twenty elsewhere in the country. We've got at least eight hundred private clients who account for more than half our sales. You know, darling, it might even be as many as forty thousand cheeses."

"So what happens now?" asked Elizabeth. There was a long pause before Edward replied.

"The shop," he said, "or rather the wreckage. I shall put it into the hands of Mr George — just for the time being. He's more able than me to deal with this disaster at the current time. I've never seen him work with such energy. He was at the shop before me this morning and already working in the cellars."

"But Edward . . ."

"I've decided — I've no option but to devote all my time to *them*." He pointed towards his family papers. "Find out what's really going on."

"Oh, no," said a distraught Elizabeth. "No, Edward, not at a time like this. Have you lost your mind? What's wrong with you?"

"You can't understand, darling. I *have* to know more about them — discover what lies at the bottom of all this. Can't you see? It's so obvious. All these things — all these strange things that have happened — they're interlinked. Yes, in some way they're all part of a bigger story. Each and every one of my ancestors is caught up in this — yes — and very soon it's going to catch up with me. I can't stop it — it's got a life of its own, and it's completely beyond my control. But I've got to get to the bottom of it, Elizabeth. I *must* — even if it's the last thing I do."

CHAPTER
TEN

More than two weeks had passed since Edward's fleeting conversation with Mr Papadrianos at the cheese dinner yet still he had mentioned scarcely a thing to Elizabeth. He'd debated long and hard over whether or not to tell her about all the subsequent events but could not convince himself that it was the right thing to do. "It'll cause her no end of worry," he thought, "and it won't help to solve anything."

But after another week of anxiety, the strain began to tell on Edward. He was still being followed through the streets — at least, he thought he was — and he was also certain that his home was under surveillance. What particularly alarmed him was that it was no longer just Mr Makarezos who was following him. On several occasions, he'd noticed that a second man was also monitoring his movements — someone who was easily recognizable by the fact that he wore eau de cologne from Laughtons of Jermyn Street. "The finest eau de cologne in London," thought Edward to himself, "but a most foolish choice if you're trying to remain anonymous."

One evening, after a particularly energetic bout of love-making, Edward decided to confess everything.

"Darling," he began, "there's something I should have told you long ago."

Elizabeth felt a surge of panic spread through her veins. It was most unlike Edward to speak like this. But, well, he'd been so strange of late. She wondered if she could be surprised by anything that he might tell her. "Just let him speak," she said to herself. "And for heaven's sake, don't interrupt."

Edward began by revealing how he'd been followed through the streets by Mr Makarezos. He told her about Mr Papadrianos and then admitted that Richard Barcley already knew everything that had happened to him. He even recounted the story of how Richard and Makarezos had met in a pub just a couple of weeks earlier — and how Makarezos had spoken of the danger they were in. The only detail he omitted was the fact that he was still being followed.

Elizabeth's initial reaction was strange. She seemed less concerned that her husband was under surveillance than by the fact that she — of all people — was the last one to be told. Even Barcley knew before her.

"Why didn't you say anything to me before?" she asked Edward. "Why didn't you feel you could confide in me? It doesn't do any good to keep things bottled up."

She stopped herself in mid-flow, annoyed that she had interrupted Edward. That was exactly what she hadn't wanted to do.

"It's not because I didn't feel able to confide in you," responded Edward. "I promise you that. I was concerned for you. I didn't want you to worry — I didn't want to alarm you. You see, I could be in very great danger — and the last thing I want to do is drag you into it."

"But you were able to tell *him*," said Elizabeth, pointedly refusing to give Barcley a name. "Why him and not me?"

"I'm sorry, I'm sorry," said Edward, placing a comforting arm around Elizabeth's shoulder. "I really am. I don't know what else I can say."

"You're very English," said Elizabeth after a pause. She looked at Edward and forced a faint but well-meaning smile. "Only an Englishman would confide in a male friend before confiding in his wife."

Edward nodded — it was easier than speaking — and waited for Elizabeth to say something else.

"So where do we go from here?" she asked at length. "Personally, I think we should call the police. In fact, that's the very first thing we must do."

"No!" exclaimed a horrified Edward. "That's absolutely the last thing we must do. Can't you see, Elizabeth? That's the one way to guarantee trouble. Makarezos has told me to do nothing — keep a low profile — and that's what I intend to do. Meanwhile, I must continue researching my family. It's now abundantly clear that my genealogy holds the key to everything."

"Oh, no," groaned Elizabeth. "Surely not? It'll do you no good at all. Take a look at yourself, Edward. Look what's happening to you. You're changing before my very eyes. You're worn out. Close to breaking point.

This has all got to come to a stop. And come to a stop very soon. Otherwise, Edward, you're in danger of going off the rails."

CHAPTER
ELEVEN

Tuesday 12 July 1728

The London Chronicle

At approximately 8.20p.m. last evening, Mr. Alexander Trencom, the owner and proprietor of Trencoms Cheese Store on Lawrence Lane, was killed by a single blow to the head.

There were no witnesses to the incident, which occurred outside the Fox and Grapes on the junction of Trump Street and King Street.

Mr. Trencom was found by Mr. Josiah Glasse, an Officer of the Watch in St Paul's Ward. It is not yet clear as to the reason for the attack: the killer escaped unnoticed.

Mr. Trencom's death is likely to be a subject of debate in the House of Parliament, especially as Secretary of State, Mr. Isaac Cummins, is seeking to augment the number of parish constables in the capital.

Mr. Trencom is succeeded by his son, Samuel, who will take over as proprietor of Trencoms Cheese Store. The store will remain closed until Monday, July 18th.

CHAPTER
TWELVE

April 1969

In the three hundred and seven years since Trencoms had first opened its doors, the shop had never been closed for more than a week. The longest period it had remained shut was back in 1728, following the suspicious death of old Alexander Trencom. But even then it had reopened after just six days. Now, after the disaster of the Great Flood, it had closed definitively. Edward Trencom showed no interest in restoring the damage. He spent most of his time at Southwark library and only rarely made his way to Lawrence Lane to survey the still-dripping ruins of his once profitable livelihood.

Mr George had taken control of the situation almost from the moment he learned of the disaster. No sooner had the flood-waters been pumped out than he ventured back into the cellars and began single-handedly clearing away the thousands of sodden crates and boxes. It took him more than a week to remove the stinking cheeses from the cavernous cellars. The ones which were not too filthy he took back to his house, where they were enthusiastically gobbled by Dubonnet — the only living being that actually profited from the flood. Mr George spent a further ten days cleaning up the deposits of clay and silt left behind by the flood-water. Many an employee would have baulked at such work, but Mr George actually derived some sort of pleasure out of creating order from chaos. It was like working one's way through a mountain of washing up, only on a truly grand scale.

"Slowly getting back to normal," he said to himself when the first of the side chapels was cleared of debris. "We'll be there in another week or so."

He was used to being on his own, yet he did at times feel lonely in the damp and dripping cellars. On one or two occasions he brought Dubonnet into Trencoms — a treat for the both of them — and there were also days when he had the company of the engineers who were repairing the ruptured walls of the chapel.

"You Mr Trencom?" asked one of them.

"No, no, thank goodness," said Mr George. "Wouldn't want to be in his shoes."

"Not your shop then?" asked another.

Mr George laughed and tut-tutted at the same time. "Couldn't take the responsibility of it," he said. "Not for me. Like to be able to walk away from it in the evening."

The engineers made a careful examination of all the walls and ceilings and informed him that there was no lasting structural damage. "But it'll take at least three months for the damp to dry out sufficiently," they said. "Especially if you're going to have cheese back down here."

274

Mr George conveyed all this information to Edward and suggested that they should start reordering cheeses — especially the ones that took many months to get delivered.

"Could you make a start?" asked Edward. "It would be a huge weight off my mind."

"Consider it done," said Mr George, "Incidentally, I've managed to save some of the order books. Got them all drying on the radiators. But I have a sneaking feeling that four or five are beyond repair. The Spanish and Portuguese ones are almost impossible to read."

"Well, call me if you need help," said Edward. "You know where to find me."

"That I do," muttered Mr George under his breath. "Probably in Southwark public library."

It was a comment that could just as easily have come from the mouth of Elizabeth Trencom.

"Your problem is no longer your nose," she told Edward one evening. "It's the fact that you've lost all sense of reality. This business with your family — I'm sorry, but it terrifies me. You need to step back from it for a moment and look at what's happening to you. People are following you. People are threatening you. You've been told that under no circumstances should you continue to delve into your past. And what do you do? The exact opposite."

She folded her arms decisively, as if to underscore what she had just said. But she hadn't finished quite yet.

"I strongly suggest you forget your family for a while — let the matter rest. And I also suggest that you go to the doctor about your nose — find out what's *really* wrong. Let's get back to some old-fashioned common sense. There's not nearly enough of it around here these days. You said yourself that the same thing had happened to your father. It's probably hereditary — something that can be cured."

"Spot on!" said Edward, who sprang into life for the first time in days. "You're right, darling, it *is* hereditary. That's what I've known all along. Everything that has happened — absolutely everything — is somehow linked to my nose."

Richard Barcley looked around his office and then back at Edward. His friend really was behaving in a most peculiar fashion and he could now see that the strain was beginning to take its toll.

"I must confess, you've lost me," said Barcley after a long silence. "I'm not quite sure what you mean. You're trying to tell me that this disaster — the flood — is in some way linked to your nose?"

"Not everything can be explained by logic," said an exasperated Edward. "Take one pot of milk, add a starter culture and within days you've got cheese. Now tell me — where's the logic in that? And what about roquefort? It's filled with greeny-blue mould and yet it tastes quite delicious. You've said so yourself. Is there any logic in that? You're quite wrong to rely upon logic, Richard. Quite wrong. It can't explain everything."

"Well, all I can say," responded Barcley, "is that I'm very glad my clients aren't all like you. I'd be out of business in no time."

"I thought you, of all people, would understand," said Edward wistfully.

"No — I'm afraid that on this occasion you've lost me," replied Richard. "And I'm afraid you're in danger of losing yourself as well."

Edward caught a reflection of himself in the window of Barcley's office. How strange, he thought, that the sun was shining directly onto his nose.

"Everything is working towards a conclusion," he said. "I don't have much longer to wait. There's only one Trencom left to investigate: old Humphrey, the founder of Trencoms. And I'm sure that he holds the key to us all."

PART FOUR

CHAPTER
ONE

10 September 1666

Three days after the last of the flames were finally extinguished, Humphrey Trencom returned to the site of Trencoms cheese shop. It took him more than an hour to make his way from the river to Cheapside and he marvelled at the destruction wrought by the fire. Not a single building was left standing. Where once there had been taverns, stores and busy markets, now there was a mass of charred debris.

Foster Lane had ceased to exist. The Olde Bear was a smouldering pile of masonry. The Olde Supply Store had collapsed in on itself. And Trencoms itself . . . "Oh, Lord," said Humphrey to himself as he picked through the slough of smouldering rubble that had until recently represented his livelihood. He clambered over the pile of broken bricks, stone, mortar and tile, pausing only to sniff at the air. Little wisps of smoke were still filtering out of the debris and the bricks were hot underfoot. Humphrey sniffed again. Funny, he thought. Amid the overpowering smell of charred timber and masonry, he was sure he could detect a more familiar scent. "Ah — yes," he said to himself. "I do believe it is." And as he took a long and deep inhalation of breath, he allowed himself a vague smile of recognition. "Mmn — yes — even here, where there's such desolation, the noble charworth can make itself known."

He fell to his knees and put his nose right up close to the rubble. As he breathed deeply for a second time, he began to smell other familiar scents as well. "Oh, caerphilly, my beauty, — and my fragrant neufchatel. My beloved cheeses! Papa Humphrey will miss you all." And as he thought these thoughts, two large tears welled in his eyes then rolled down his bulbous cheeks.

In the days since the destruction of his shop, Humphrey Trencom had taken a most momentous decision. He had not the heart to rebuild the shop — not after all the hard work he had put in the first time round. The new shop could be opened under the auspices of brother John, who was a bright young lad and full of promise. It would be a challenge for him, thought Humphrey, something to spur him on in life.

There was another reason why Humphrey had no wish to spend the next few years rebuilding his shop — one that was rather harder to fathom. He had come to believe that the fire was some sort of portentous sign from on high. The heavens, yes, the very heavens were calling Humphrey to his destiny. Had his mother not told him as much? What were her exact words? A "signal from the heavens . . . a welter of fire and flame".

Well, surely to God this was a welter of fire and flame. And therefore, this was the moment that he must seize. It was now — right now — or it was never.

And so it was that Humphrey Trencom returned to the Dorset village from whence he had come just four years earlier. It was his first port of call in a voyage that was to lead him into treacherous and treasonable waters.

The Trencom farmhouse stood in the Dorset village of Piddletrenthide — a cob and timber affair that had been in the possession of the family for at least eight generations. Humphrey's parents had lived in the farm before him, and so had their parents and grandparents. Indeed, ever since the house was built, in the turbulent reign of King Henry IV, it had been occupied by one or another of the Trencom family.

It was surrounded by flower-strewn meadows on the banks of the River Piddle. It was a peaceful spot, especially in midsummer when the meadow was waist-high in grasses and wild flowers — yellow tansies, wild camomile and the rare purple larkspur. On autumn mornings, when the mists hung low over the river, Humphrey was in the habit of poking his nose out of the window and sniffing the odoriferous air. "Ah," he would say to himself with a sigh, "the sweet smell of the Piddle — what scent could be more delightful?"

Humphrey's forebears had been remarkable only for their ordinariness — they farmed, they milked cows, they made cheese. But he differed from them in almost every respect — in temperament, intellect and in body mass. "I am," he admitted to himself wearily each morning, "of ample girth — of large belly — and fat." And as he said these words, he would rub his smooth white hands over his smooth white belly and ponder, misty-eyed, on when he had last seen his fleshy undercarriage.

The extent of his rotundity was never so apparent as when he relaxed in his favourite oak settle. There was a clear two feet and six inches between the arms of the chair — making it rather larger than average — yet it was only with considerable difficulty that Humphrey managed to squeeze himself into position. There would be a dreadful squeaking noise as the wooden arms were forced outwards from the perpendicular. The dovetail joints would groan. The mortise joints would gasp. As the full force of Humphrey's posterior neared the seat of the chair, the rivets and wedges which held the settle together would brace themselves for an all-out assault.

The clock's pendulum would tock six times before Humphrey was settled comfortably into his chair and it would be a further three tocks before gravity allowed the ripples of body fat to slide themselves into place. It was as if every wobbly bulge — every pinguid roll and droop — needed a few moments of catching breath before allowing itself to subside into the rigid parameters of the chair.

Humphrey was in every sense a man of the flesh. He could not begin the day — at least, not in good humour — unless he had spilled his seed into Mrs Trencom, his wife. And thus it was that every morning, just as soon as the cock crowed, Humphrey's privy parts started to stir. He would heave himself onto the long-suffering Agnes Trencom, who was scarcely awake, and proceed to pummel his way into her with great gusto. Agnes did not exactly enjoy the experience and once remarked that it was like having a large wardrobe falling on top of her. Indeed, during coitus, she would often turn her gaze to the vast oak chest in the corner of her chamber and wonder, idly, which was the heavier — it, or her husband. "Probably my Humphrey," she concluded, "who at least has no blunt edges."

Agnes had come to accept that this morning ritual was just one of her husband's foibles. She knew from weary experience that there was little she could do to change him, for the Trencoms were incapable of overriding their passions. There was a disturbing sense in which they allowed their obsessions to take control of their personalities.

Humphrey had displayed a talent for studying at a very tender age. Whether or not his precocious skills came from his mother — a newcomer to the Piddle Valley — remains unclear. But she certainly nurtured his genius, registering him at Briantspuddle Grammar School at the age of seven. Humphrey soon mastered Latin and went on to excel himself at Greek. Indeed, he displayed such a faculty for this latter language that it was as if he'd been born with it already installed in his head. By the time he was fifteen, he was able to read the three books he had inherited from his maternal grandmother: George Sphrantzes's *Chron. maius.*, Michael Eugenikos's *Cosmographia* and John Doukas's *Ekthesis Chronicle*.

Humphrey was almost certainly the first Trencom to be literate. He was also the first to display an interest in the near Orient and the expanding empire of the

Ottomans. By the time he was twenty-seven, he had amassed a considerable library of books about the history of Constantinople. His purchases had been greatly aided by his move to London in the spring of 1662. No sooner had he begun to earn a living from the sale of cheese than he began to spend his money on books, almost all of which were about the history and topography of the city of Constantinople. His fascination with the Ottoman capital rapidly turned into an obsession and he developed a desperate urge to visit the city. He even told Agnes his wife of his wish to set sail, and said that a voyage to the east would be the making of him.

"Aye," she said in her weary tone. "But I know ye, Humphrey Trencom. Ye'll catch ye pox there yonder, from some Orient whore."

Humphrey would never have fulfilled his desire to travel to Constantinople had it not been for a most fortuitous set of circumstances. First of all there was the Great Fire, which forced him to return temporarily to the village that he left just four years earlier. Then there was the unexpected upsurge in demand for the trencom round, the hard cows' cheese that had, for centuries, been made in the Piddle Valley. The interest in this cheese had waxed so sharp over the previous months that Humphrey was obliged to buy milk from neighbouring farms — one of which lay on the estate of the Duke of Athelhampton.

When the two men met, the duke was most interested to learn of Humphrey's urgent yearning to visit Constantinople. Only a few weeks earlier, His

Grace had been informed that Byzantine antiquities were being sold for a song in the city souks. And since he had a keen interest in the exotic (he had recently acquired a mummified pygmy from the highlands of Borneo), he decided to despatch Humphrey to the city of cities with orders to buy whatever took his fancy.

Mrs Trencom was most unhappy about her husband's voyage, although she did look forward to rising from her slumber without the marital wardrobe falling on her. She knew that Humphrey would not survive months away without "sheathing his pinis" (her expression) and sanctioned him to enjoy whatever pleasures that the Orient might offer. "Find yourself a Turkey whore," she said, "and don't bring back the pox." With these words ringing in his ears, and after one final bout in the bedroom, Humphrey bid a tearful farewell to his patient Agnes.

Thus it was that a rather apprehensive Mr H.T. found himself standing on the cobb at Lyme Regis on a blustery October afternoon, preparing to sail on the *Hector*, an 800-ton leviathan owned by the merchants of the Levant Company.

"I dranke verrie moche," he wrote about the eve of his departure, "and was in a most miserable, squaimish and puking condition." Yet he managed to carry aboard his sea chest, books, bedding and a pair of virginals before collapsing into the bed-sized cabin he had rented from Captain John Davys.

It is hard to comprehend Humphrey's horror when he awoke to the vile stench of the good ship *Hector*. He was blessed with an extraordinarily sensitive nose —

the first of the Trencom family to have been granted this beneficent curse — and he was now introducing it to a strange new world where smell was the most powerful sensation. The first and most overwhelming odour on this particular morning was that of his own vomit. It was sickly sweet — the overripe smell of malmsey mingled with the sour contents of his guts. Beyond this and emanating from the bowels of the ship was an altogether more pervasive stink. It was hard, even for Humphrey, to detect the individual components. There was the stench of meat — several barrels of which were already putrid. There was the vinegary stink of sour beer; the smell of tar and sweat, rank pork and stale cheese. Even the water — barrelled just three days earlier — carried a worrying pungency. To Humphrey's nose, it smelled like the stagnant millponds of Piddletrenthide.

"Oh fie," he said. "To think that we haven't even left port. Nothing good will come of this."

Humphrey had always had a big appetite. But every week of his sea voyage to Constantinople would see him diminish slightly in stature. His belly, once as rotund as an inflated pig's bladder, soon collapsed into airless ripples. His lardaceous under-chin — in times past the size of a large gourd — soon hung empty and withered. Even his cheeks, which held their own for six long weeks, eventually fell victim to hunger and thence to gravity. They hung from his face like a pair of heavy flesh drapes, with only the ruptured capillaries serving to remind Humphrey of the shadow that he had become. His nose alone, with its peculiar dome, remained immutable in the face of hunger. As Humphrey slowly collapsed in on himself, his imperious nose seemed determined to retain its shapeliness — a beacon of defiance on a storm-tossed and rapidly crumbling promontory.

It was not just the foetid food that led to Humphrey's decline. Seasickness, too, took its dreadful toll. "I evacuated all the humours that wished to overflowe," he wrote, "yet still I puked." Not until the *Hector* reached the Straits of Gibraltar — by which time even the ship's tack was riddled with weevils — did Humphrey's guts accept the roll and swell of the sea.

On Tuesday, 15 January 1667, some two hours into the second watch, Humphrey went out on deck. He sniffed the air, as was his fashion, drinking deeply at the salty sea breeze. And almost immediately he detected an unutterably blissful fragrance on the wind.

"Land", he shouted. "I smell land."

And sure enough, some six and a half hours later, the broken coastline of Asia was sighted. The *Hector* — and its contingent of hungry sailors, merchants and one cheese-farmer-turned-antiquarian — was approaching the straits that led towards Constantinople.

"When I went to land my books," wrote Humphrey, "the customs ript open my trunks and chests and rifled every thing." They confiscated his copy of Rycaut's *The Present State of the Ottoman Empire*; they "filch't" his edition of Lane's *The Negotiations of Sir T.L. in his Embassy to the Sublime Porte*. But they left untouched the rest of his travelling library and Humphrey had the good sense not to lodge an official complaint.

He had been offered lodgings at the factory of the Levant Company, which stood on the waterfront at Galata. He made his way there in the company of the other merchants and settled into his comfortable but modest living quarters. His first and most immediate task was to secure himself a Turkey whore. This was easier said than done, for he discovered that Sultan Mehmet IV had recently passed a decree forbidding sexual relations between Muslims and Christians. But Humphrey eventually found himself a young strumpet called Hafise, who offered to service his needs for a mere 1s 2d per session.

She smelled of the East — a fresh, newly washed aroma of attar and bergamot, orris and eau de cologne. "If only my Agnes . . ." thought Humphrey wistfully, before checking himself. "Humphrey Trencom," he added, "you're an ungrateful wretch."

Hafise had been plying her fleshy trade for many years. She had provided entertainment for pashas, merchants, a lapsed dervish and three European traders. Yet even she was taken aback by the gusto with which the rumbustious Humphrey performed his lovemaking. With a low growl, he stripped off his hose and breeches, unbuttoned his chemise and kicked away his boots. Then, when he was entirely naked (and "prick at noon", as he wrote in his journal), he made his move on Hafise. "Come on, my little Turkey," he purred. "Come to Humphrey."

explosion of odours that he was expecting, well, it never came. Humphrey Trencom smelled absolutely nothing.

He moved himself down the gully of her cleavage, pausing for a moment at her delectable belly button. This was a veritable whirlpool of odours on any normal day. But once again — nothing. Humphrey was by now truly disconcerted. He continued on his journey downwards into the souk of pleasure. He emptied all the air from his lungs in one noisy evacuation and then took a long, deep breath. But where, oh where, was the familiar odour of love?

"Why, my beauty, have you lost your scent?" But in his heart of hearts, Humphrey knew that Hafise had not lost her scent. It was his nose that was at fault. Something had gone terribly wrong. For no obvious cause, and with absolutely no warning, his olfactory receptacles had betrayed him.

With a heavy sigh, and a loud groan, Humphrey heaved himself atop his lovely Hafise and girded himself for action. The sun rose. The cock crowed. And in Humphrey's little chamber, a silk-covered divan received the battering of its life.

Humphrey managed to track down many oddities for the Duke of Athelhampton and had soon acquired a fine collection of gospels and manuscripts. His choicest item was an imperial crystobull bearing the seal of John Palaiologos, which he intended to keep for himself. He bought it from the monks of Heybeli Island for a mere £2 3s 12d — a tidy sum — but a mere cornflower in the meadow for the Duke of Athelhampton. "A verytable bargayne," wrote Humphrey in his journal. And so it was.

The focus of Humphrey's attentions, aside from the privy parts of Hafise, was the Porta Aurea. Almost every day since his arrival in the city, he had made his way to this city gate and spent hours here sketching its facade and measuring its structure. He knew more than most people about the Porta Aurea, for he had studied it for much of his adult life. "It was the scene of the greatest triumphs of the Byzantine Empire," he would tell the English merchants with whom he shared his lodgings. "It was where Basil I celebrated his victory over the Bulgars. It was where Michael III feted his rout of the Arabs." He would pause at this point in order to reflect on past glories. "And it was through this gate that the Emperor Michael VIII Palaiologos rode on a white charger in the summer of 1261 after recovering his city from the crusaders. And then" — he would let out a low sigh — "it was the end." It was at this very gateway that the once mighty Byzantine Empire finally expired. And this was a subject about which Mr Humphrey Trencom knew a great deal.

A large crowd has gathered in the shade of the gateway. There are pedlars and beggars, soothsayers and fakirs. An apothecary is selling musked sherberts; an imam is reciting his prayers. Watch out for the shoemaker, with his oval platter of slippers. Look sharp! Watch your backs! "*Allah, yanssur es-sultan,*" cries a water-seller. "God render the sultan victorious." And the crowd replies, "*Allah, Allah*".

294

In the far corner of the makeshift souk, next to the great gateway, Humphrey Trencom is nosing around. He seems to have found something that has caught his attention.

Some time after midnight, when the only visitors to the Porta Aurea are scrawny cats and pot-bellied rats, Humphrey Trencom can be seen slipping through the shadows. He is dressed in a black turban, a dark worsted cloak and soft slippers. It is clear that he's trying to reach the Golden Gate unobserved.

There is only a thin shard of moon in the sky and the streets are locked in shadow. The great land walls reveal themselves as a black block against a veiled backdrop. The other buildings are nothing more than caliginous silhouettes.

Just before Humphrey reaches the gate, he scurries down a side alley. About twenty yards further — just past the Osman Camii — there's a small passage leading to a tiny courtyard. Humphrey darts down this passageway and feels his way into the yard. There is no light whatsoever so he has to rely on other senses — his nose and his hands. He feels for a door. It's locked. He feels for another. It's also locked. But the third doorway is slightly ajar. And his nose, which is now fully recovered, has detected an unusual scent that is filtering through the gap.

He pushes the door and it creaks. A cat miaows. A shutter bangs. "Tum-tum," whispers Humphrey to himself. "Keep silent, Humph, keep silent."

There is a flight of steps behind the door — shallow steps that are worn with age. "Careful, old boy," he says to himself. "Wouldn't want to take a tumble in this place."

The smell grows stronger with every step — the odour of spice and balm. "Thuriferous, thuriferous, thuriferous," whispers Humphrey as he sniffs the air. "From the highlands of Arabia."

He reaches the bottom of the stairs and feels for the walls. The floor is sandy and the rock is damp. The passageway is narrow, just two feet wide, and Humphrey can only just squeeze through. If he had come here six months earlier — before his long sea voyage — he would not have got through. "Thank God for putrid food," he thinks.

He can smell lichen beneath the layer of incense. "Nearly there, Humpers," he says under his breath. "Another twelve steps."

Humphrey is now directly underneath the Porta Aurea, in a low, round room that is cut from the rock. He can see nothing — not even the slippers on his feet. But he knows something about this room that is so secret, so dangerous, that if it was ever discovered, it would lead to his instant despatch. He takes two steps forward, reaches out his hands, and feels for the bundle.

"The patriarch was right," he whispers under his breath. "The patriarch was right."

There it is, just as he is expecting. A thick layer of sackcloth enclosing a most precious object. Humphrey takes it in his arms, holds it to his nose briefly, and then stuffs it under his cloak.

CHAPTER
TWO

3 April 1969

Streatham Police Station. Streatham Police Station. Streatham Police Station. Elizabeth was running her finger down a long list of Streathams in the telephone directory in search of the non-emergency number. Streatham Animal Welfare Group. Streatham Chiropodists. Streatham Genealogical Society. She emitted a little groan when she saw that particular entry. "The very last thing we need," she thought. "Ah — here we go. Streatham Police Station, General Enquiries."

She made a note of the number and took it over to the phone. But when she came to pick up the receiver, she hesitated and then sat down again. "What on earth am I going to say?" she thought. "It's going to sound ridiculous." She also recalled how she'd sworn blind to Edward that she wouldn't contact the police. "I don't want to start deceiving him now, not at the very time when he's told me about everything that's happened."

Yet despite deciding to hold fire for the time being, she remained beside herself with worry and couldn't help turning things over and over in her mind. The man at the cheese festival, the man following Edward, the flood. None of it made any sense whatsoever.

She had yet to sight anyone trailing her husband —
although she was constantly on the look-out — and this
only increased her sense of frustration. "It's the fact
that one never knows what's around the corner," she
admitted to Edward one evening. "If only I could see
what he looks like — somehow that would make
everything seem more real."

Edward had not told Elizabeth every detail of what
had happened to him because he hadn't wished to
alarm her more than was necessary. But he did describe
how he'd followed the Greek man back to Queen Street
and he also told her about the various strange scenes
that he and Richard had witnessed from the first-floor
window of Barcley's office.

One morning, not long after Edward had left to go
shopping, Elizabeth suddenly put down her mug of
coffee, folded her arms and announced to herself that
enough was enough. "I can't stand this waiting around
any longer," she said with characteristic resolve. "It's
time to take control of the situation." And she decided,
there and then, to visit Mr Makarezos in Queen Street.

If Edward had been at home at the time, he would
have done his utmost to dissuade his wife. He would
have told Elizabeth that such a move would only
increase the danger he was in. He would have implored
her not to make such a foolhardy move. But with no
one to temper her indignation and anger, she was able
to follow her own course of action.

It was shortly after 11 a.m. when she turned the
corner into Queen Street. She was not in the slightest
bit nervous; indeed, she gave every indication of

looking forward to her forthcoming confrontation with Mr Makarezos. "I'll listen to what he has to say," she thought. "But I'll also give him a piece of my mind. I really will. What right has he to do this to Edward? And for what?"

She slowed her pace slightly as she approached Number 14 and looked up at the brass plaque. "Well — here goes." After taking a sharp intake of breath and exhaling slowly through her nose, she gave the knocker a loud rap on the door.

There was a long pause before footsteps could be heard approaching from inside the building. A chain was drawn back and a key was turned in the lock. And then, after what seemed like an eternity, the door opened to reveal a small, slight and rather elderly Greek lady.

"Yes?" she said in a questioning tone of voice.

"I've come to see Mr Makarezos," said Elizabeth Trencom boldly. "I need to speak with him."

"Could you repeat that, dear?" said the lady as she leaned towards Mrs Trencom. "I'm a little hard of hearing."

"Mr Makarezos," said Elizabeth. "I've come to see him."

"Ah yes," said the lady. "Well, I'm afraid he's in a meeting. Could you come back in" — she looked at her watch — "an hour or so?"

"No," said Mrs Trencom firmly. "No, I wish to see him now, thank you very much. Could you please get him?"

"I'm afraid you'll have to speak up, dear, speak a little louder."

"Could you get him? Please. I need to see him urgently."

"Well, if you insist. I shall see if he's available. Your name?"

"It's Mrs Trencom."

"Mrs Trondheim?" repeated the lady.

"No — Trencom."

"Good, dear," said the lady. And she disappeared along the corridor and up the stairs.

Elizabeth waited on the doorstep for two or three minutes, trying to work out in her head exactly what she would say to Mr Makarezos. The door had been left ajar and she peered inside the hallway. There was a poorly lit corridor which led to a flight of stairs. Beyond the stairs, a door provided access to the ground-floor rooms. But apart from that, the hall was completely empty. There was nothing on the walls, which looked to Mrs Trencom's eyes as if they hadn't seen a lick of paint for many a year.

It was while she was standing on the doorstep that she suddenly heard her name being called.

"Elizabeth — Elizabeth."

She looked up and down the street to see where the voice was coming from.

"Elizabeth — up here."

She turned round, glimpsed up and saw Richard Barcley leaning out of the first-floor window of the building opposite.

"Elizabeth! No! No! Quick! Come over here."

Elizabeth was torn between staying where she was, in order to give Mr Makarezos a piece of her mind, or doing as instructed by her husband's oldest friend.

"I beg you," shouted Barcley. "You mustn't."

With great reluctance, Elizabeth stepped back from the doorstep and made her way across the street. She had scarcely reached Number 11 when the door was flung open and an anxious Richard Barcley pulled her in by the arm.

"What *are* you doing?" he said, speaking in a tone of voice that he had never before used when talking to Elizabeth. "Are you mad? Don't you realize? Your husband, Edward, is in great danger. His life is under threat. Really, to go knocking on the door and confronting Mr Makarezos is" — he searched for the appropriate word — "insane."

Barcley's words deflated Elizabeth, yet she still retained a flash of defiance. "Well, if that man" — she pointed at Number 14 — "is going to ruin our marriage, then he's jolly well going to get a piece of my mind."

And with that, the stress of everything that had just happened got the better of her and she broke down in tears.

"Mrs Clarke," said Richard, calling to his secretary. "Could you make Mrs Trencom a nice cup of tea. And I don't mind if I have one too.

"Actually," he added as an afterthought, "make mine a coffee."

★ ★ ★

On the other side of the street, the elderly Greek lady was knocking on the door of the boardroom.

"Enter," said a voice from within.

As she opened the door, four men looked up.

"There's someone for you, Mr Makarezos," she said. "Someone who seems very anxious to see you. A lady."

"Who is she?" snapped Makarezos. "What's her name?"

"Mrs Trondheim. Says it's urgent."

"Never heard of her," he said. "Tell her to come back another time."

CHAPTER
THREE

April 1969

More than four weeks had passed since the night of the flood yet still Edward showed no signs of returning to Trencoms. He had left Mr George in charge of preparing for the eventual reopening of the shop, phoning him occasionally to enquire as to how he was getting along. He, meanwhile, spent most of his time working on the first chapters of *Dynasty*. He found himself inspired by Harry Barnsley's *Ten Chimes to Midnight* and was considering writing *Dynasty* in the same style. "In some ways it's a detective story," he thought, "and in others it's a tale of history and dark intrigue."

Elizabeth was pleased to have Edward at home and did everything she could to encourage him. She was delighted when he told her that he'd resumed work on his *History of Cheese* and looked forward to the day when he showed a similar enthusiasm for Trencoms. Yet she remained extremely anxious about the way in which her husband's personality was mutating before her very eyes. He seemed more detached than ever — so listless and changeable. One minute he was full of fire — and the next? Why, he didn't even seem to know who he was. He ate his meals at increasingly strange hours and slept erratically at night. In the past, he'd eaten large quantities of cheese in the evenings and never been troubled by disturbing dreams. Yet now that he had almost given up snacking on cheese, he claimed to be having more vivid dreams than ever. And as for his lovemaking. Elizabeth gulped. That was becoming more extravagant and uninhibited with every day that passed.

She smiled as she remembered how, twelve years earlier, she had lain nervously in bed awaiting her husband's approach. "To think that not long ago we only made love once a week, on Sundays. And now — gracious . . ." She paused to count on her fingers. "We've made love five times in the last two days." It was as if Edward was being invigorated by some internal spirit — a spirit that was at the same time acting like a leech, sapping away at his lifeblood.

Just an hour or so after Elizabeth had had these thoughts, she was dusting the writing bureau that stood beside the window. This was where Edward usually worked when he was at home and the top of the desk was almost lost under a patchwork of notebooks, cuttings and scraps of paper. The topmost folder was marked "Humphrey Trencom" and Elizabeth could see that it was bulging with Edward's jottings about the original founder of the shop. Intrigued, she opened the file and idly flicked through the papers.

"Goodness, Edward *has* done a lot of research," was her first thought. "There's enough here to write a book about Humphrey Trencom alone." The folder contained hand-copied extracts from Pepys's diary (all referring to the Fire of London) and a map of the city in 1666. There were two pamphlets about Piddletrenthide, the Dorset village from which Humphrey and his antecedents had come, and a short monograph on Sultan Mehmet IV. "*He* looks rather grim," thought Elizabeth as she picked up a copy of his portrait. "Wouldn't want to meet *him* on a dark night."

As she replaced the picture in the folder, her eye was drawn to a largish sheet of paper folded into four quarters. It was old — even Elizabeth could tell that — and felt satisfyingly weighty to the touch. Taking care not to tear it, she opened out the folds and spread the sheet on the writing desk. It was completely covered in handwriting — a slanting italic hand that was as clipped as a toparian box-tree. Elizabeth noticed the date at the top — "Lord's Day, Septb'r 10th, 1666" and then saw that it had been written by Humphrey Trencom. "I'm surprised Edward hasn't shown me this," she thought. "I didn't know he had any of Humphrey's papers."

The letter, written in the aftermath of the Great Fire, described how Humphrey had lost all enthusiasm for reopening Trencoms. He explained how he had spent the previous four years amassing the finest assemblage of cheeses ever known to the city of London. And now, everything — cheeses, shop and garret — had gone up in smoke. "My deare mother once tolde me to expect a signe," he wrote to the unknown recipient of the letter. "Now, it has come. This is the signal for which I have beene wayting all these yeeres. And it is this which propells me on my voyage — it is this that carries me to ye Orient."

Elizabeth read the letter with a growing feeling of disquiet. "And you must also knowe," it said, "that my nose, the tool and instrumente of all my joye, has become a curse and an hindrance. Sometimes I can smelle and at other tymes I am lost."

It was as she read these words that Elizabeth found herself taking a sharp intake of breath. "Huh! How extraordinary."

She read them again, to double check that she had not invented them. But no. There they were, written in plain, clear English. "Sometimes I can smelle and at other tymes I am lost." She refolded the paper and looked over her shoulder, as if to ensure that no one had been spying on her. She felt as if she had just done something illicit — something she shouldn't have done. "Well, well," she said at length. "I think this calls for a cup of tea." And with that she disappeared into the kitchen.

As the kettle approached a rolling boil, Elizabeth turned the words in the letter round and round in her head. She was puzzled. No, she was more than puzzled. She was completely taken aback by her discovery. "Is Edward in some way mimicking Humphrey Trencom?" she asked herself. "Or is he suffering from the same strange condition as his ancestors? Is it all in his head? Or is he incapable of helping himself?"

As Elizabeth splashed milk into a cup, she had an even more disquieting thought. Was it conceivable that all of the Trencom men — generations of them — had

306

suffered from the same terrible affliction? She now regretted not paying more attention to Edward when he'd spoken about his ancestors. But she was certainly familiar with the story of his father and grandfather and remembered that they, like Humphrey, had abandoned Trencoms in order to go overseas in pursuit of some strange obsession.

She pulled the tea-strainer from the teapot and banged it on the side of the bin.

"At least Edward shows no signs of leaving London," she said to herself. "I suppose we can be grateful for small mercies."

Edward had spent the morning seated at desk twelve in Southwark's municipal public library. It was his custom to flick through *The Times* before beginning his research and that is precisely what he did on this particular morning. There was news of a forthcoming documentary about the royal family and an interesting article about an upcoming auction of Napoleon's memoirs. But it was an item at the bottom of page seventeen — the court circular page — that particularly caught Edward's attention. It was only short, just five or six lines, but it caused Edward's heart momentarily to freeze. "D'Autun's Cheese Shop to be Honoured by Queen," read the heading, and the lines underneath reported that d'Autun's of St James's had become the second cheese merchant in the capital to be honoured with a "by royal appointment". The article touched briefly on the rivalry between d'Autun's and Trencoms and claimed that this news "will be unwelcome to Mr.

Edward Trencom, owner and proprietor of London's oldest cheese shop, Trencoms, which recently suffered extensive damage from floodwater. Trencoms remains closed until further notice."

Edward read the article through for a second time. "Unwelcome news —" he said. "Hmm." He put down the newspaper and sat back in his chair. "*Is* it unwelcome?" he thought. "Am I *that* bothered?" And he realized, somewhat to his surprise, that he was not.

"Good luck to him," he thought. "He deserves it — besides, some of us have got rather bigger fish to fry."

Edward got up from his chair and walked across the library to replace the newspaper on its rack. Then, as he returned to his desk, he opened an oft-thumbed antiquarian book and started to read.

The book in question was by Humphrey Trencom and was entitled *Ad Portum Constantinopolum*, which Edward would have translated as *To the Gates of Constantinople*, had he not felt the ghostly presence of his old Latin teacher leering over his shoulder.

"Of course not," he thought. "It's singular." And he wrote *To the Gate* (singular) *of Constantinople* at the top of his notepad.

The title page of Humphrey's book gave the impression that readers should expect a conventional travelogue in the manner of Sir Japhet Browne's *Tales and Travailes* (published in the same year) or Asheby's *Manners and Customs of Æthiope*. But Edward quickly discovered that Humphrey's work was not quite as it first seemed. From the opening sentence of page one to the last line of page 243, it was filled with histrionics and cryptic clues, digressions and verbal perambulations. It was as if the author was playing an elaborate hoax on the reader, flipping betwixt subjects with scarcely a care in the world. The book was made even more confusing by his tendency to withhold any information that might have helped to clarify the narrative.

Edward was surprised to discover that Humphrey, unlike his voyaging contemporaries, had recorded his long sea voyage with scant reference to ports, maritime hazards and wind directions. He dwelt instead on the fantastical monsters he had seen — hippogriffs and jelloid octopuses, mermaids and clams the size of cartwheels. It was apparent to Edward that most of these were figments of the author's imagination — or plagiarized from Herodotus — and yet Humphrey assured his readers that he had seen all with his own eyes.

His description of Constantinople was even more cryptic, though to Edward rather more pleasing. Humphrey led his readers on a nasal tour of the city, depicting each quarter in terms of its smell. Interspersed with this were panegyrics written in Byzantine Greek — descriptions of Constantinople as it had been before the siege of 1453.

"Hmm," said Edward to himself as he scratched his head for the eighteenth time that morning. "It's quite the most peculiar book I've ever read." And he wondered how he was to fathom such a tale.

The book was preceded by an engraved frontispiece — a portrait of the author that had been commissioned by Mr H.T. himself. It depicted a lean and undisputedly handsome man with a romanesque jaw and chiselled cheeks.

"A man who took care of himself," thought Edward. "A man who kept one eye on the mirror."

The most eye-catching element of the portrait was the author's peculiar nose. Long, thin and aquiline, it was marked by a prominent yet perfectly formed bump over the bridge. Edward instinctively moved his hand to his nose as he studied the engraving once again. "It is indisputably my nose." He noted this with satisfaction. "We're both Trencoms, that much is certain."

Mr H.T. had written a great deal about himself in the preface to his book and came across as a studious and rather serious individual. While the English merchants in Constantinople spent their time drinking and whoring, Humphrey seemed to have preferred studying Byzantine manuscripts. He had also included a number of sentimental references to Agnes, whom Edward already knew to be his wife. "He must have missed her," he thought, "but then I miss Elizabeth when I'm away."

The main section of the book was a great deal more challenging than the preface. The principal difficulty for Edward was the author's tendency to defer to Latin or Greek whenever he had something important to say. It was so infuriating. Every time Humphrey looked set to shed some insight into the mystery goal he was pursuing in Constantinople, he would switch into Byzantine Greek. The more Edward studied the book, the more he realized that his ancestor had an obsession with the Porta Aurea. He described it in meticulous detail and provided diagrams of its western and eastern facades. Edward began to think it entirely possible that Humphrey's sole purpose in going to Constantinople was to explore this historic gateway.

"Ah — good," he thought as he looked up from his desk. "Here's Herbert — the very person I need."

Herbert Potinger had been kept in the dark about Mr Makarezos and the strange things that had happened to Edward over the last two months. Edward had not told him that he was being followed, since he wished as few people as possible to know. But Herbert was familiar with every last detail about Edward's family papers and promised his friend that he would help solve the mystery of what had happened to Edward's forefathers. Now, catching sight of Humphrey Trencom's book, he smiled and whispered, "Now that reminds me. I've got some information for you — and I think it might prove of some interest."

He pushed his fingers into the dense bush of ginger on top of his head (a nervous twitch) and vigorously scratched his scalp. As he did so, a snow-shower of dandruff fell lightly through the air, dusting his shoulders and sleeves. Edward watched it fall, remembering that he had once read that household dust was 75 per cent human skin. "In dear old Herbert's house," he mused, "it must be nearer ninety per cent."

Edward was pleased to see that Herbert was clutching a file marked "Trencom". A few days earlier, he had copied many of the Greek passages in

Humphrey Trencom's book and dropped them round to Herbert's house. Now, he was about to discover what they all meant.

"Where shall we begin?" whispered Herbert. "Ah, yes — now — if you look in chapter twenty-two of the fourteenth volume of Agallianos's *Chronicle*, you'll find an important cross-reference to the third section of Eugenikos's four-volume *Address*."

Edward did exactly as requested and discovered that he needed to check volume fourteen of *The Patristic and Byzantine Review*. This had a footnote that hinted at an interesting passage in the second volume of John Kantakouzenos's *Historiae*. Edward returned to the card index, excited to be at long last on Humphrey's trail, only to discover that he should have been looking in Papadopallos's *Versuch einer Genealogie der Palaiologen* (Munich, 1938). But this important reference work had somehow escaped Herbert's acquisition and was only to be found in the London Library. Moreover, it was in German, which neither Edward nor Herbert could understand.

Some people enjoy research and others do not. Edward and Herbert belonged in the former category and they spent the next three days attempting to unravel the mystery of Humphrey's book. It was clear to both men that he was engaged on some sort of clandestine assignment, searching for something of the greatest importance. But what this thing was, and what he intended to do with it, was not at all clear.

Edward called at Herbert's house each evening after work and both men redoubled their efforts to discover why Humphrey was so obsessed with the Porta Aurea. On each occasion, Edward stayed until long after midnight. He spent an entire Saturday researching in Herbert's front room. And on the seventh day, at about the time when everyone else in Heythrop Avenue, Streatham, was awaiting their Sunday beef, Edward and Herbert had a minor breakthrough.

"*Eureka!*" said Herbert. "Got it — got it — got it."

He had just finished translating a Byzantine riddle that Humphrey had inserted at an important point in his book. He read back through his translation to ensure it was correct, then allowed himself a self-satisfied smile. He had cracked a part of the mystery.

"So?" asked an excited and impatient Edward. "Tell me, for heaven's sake, tell me."

But he was to suffer a few minutes of agony before his friend could inform him of his discovery. For whenever Herbert Potinger found himself in moments of stress or high excitement, he developed a most excruciating and crippling stutter.

"Spe- spe- spe- spe-"

Edward tried to encourage his friend, raising his eyebrows up and down in an effort to coax out the word.

"Spe- spe- spe- spe-"

He didn't like to stare at Herbert so he looked down at the floor, hoping that this would alleviate the stress and dampen the stutter. But it was all to no avail.

"Spe- spe- spe- spe-"

Next he tried another tack, attempting to guess at the word. "Spectacle? Speciality? Specimen?"

Herbert did not respond — he merely pressed on with his valiant effort to cough, spit or splutter out the all-important word. It was most fortunate that at the very moment when he found himself in the greatest difficulty, the back door of the house slammed shut with a violent bang. The noise seemed to penetrate deep into Herbert's body, forcing the offending stammer out of his system. Unexpectedly, and quite without warning, Herbert's handicap was suddenly overcome. A single Latin word popped from his mouth.

"Spelaeum," he said, before slumping back exhausted into his chair.

"Spelaeum," repeated Edward. "And what does it mean?"

"C- C- C- C- C- C-"

"Oh, no," groaned Edward. "I don't think I can stand this."

But this time the stammer didn't last.

"C-C-C-Cave," said Herbert. "It's a cave. Don't you see? There was once a cave underneath the Porta Aurea."

And both he and Edward smiled. They realized that they were at long last on to something. They had sniffed out Humphrey's trail.

CHAPTER
FOUR

18 April 1969

Two fishing skiffs had been drawn up onto the pebble beach, just beyond reach of the waves. They were still dripping water onto the bleached stones, creating a ring of light grey around each boat. But with every minute that passed, the dripping slowed and the ring grew lighter. The sun was screaming in the sky — a light so piercing that it caused a sharp ache behind the eyes. The sea was an infinitely more restful sight; a near-motionless slab of blue, flecked with tinsel.

In one of the boats, the owner lay snoozing in a tiny patch of shade. He had moved his hat from the top of his head to the side, in order to provide a sunscreen for his eyes. To anyone looking on from afar, the effect was decidedly peculiar. It was as if his neck had been trussed into an impossible, spine-breaking angle.

In the other boat, a man was slicing sea urchins with a broken knife and sucking the salty sea-juice into his mouth. He swilled it around once or twice to savour the taste then poked a dirty finger between his teeth in order to remove a rogue spine. His movements were slow and deliberate. It was as if he was working at half speed — a metronome on its slowest beat. He looked at his watch and yawned for the third time in as many minutes. It was far too hot for April.

Not for the first time, these two "captains" had spent their morning ferrying eight men to a disused fisherman's shack somewhere on the western coast of Mount Athos. It was an unlikely place for a meeting. The only window had lost all but a jagged isosceles of glass and the exposed woodwork was the colour of old whalebone. The roof, too, had seen better days. The orange-ochre tiles were as ruptured as a furrowed field and slowly slipping earthwards under the inexorable draw of gravity.

But these features were the very reasons why the building had been chosen. No one would have ever suspected that it had, for the last four months, provided the meeting place for underground agents plotting against the Greek government. Nor would anyone have suspected — not in a million years — that the subject of their conversation was (more often than not) one Edward Trencom of Trencoms cheese shop in London.

On this particular day, the assembled men included three priests, four agents and Andreas Papadrianos. The latter was doing much of the talking, urging the rest of the men to awaken to the fact that the moment must not be missed. "If we don't act now," he said, "we may well find that we have lost our chance for another generation — perhaps for ever. I urge you all to say yes."

One of the priests nodded in agreement. "I concur with Andreas. Just look at the gravity of the situation we're in. Riots, protests, resistance growing with every

316

day. All we lack is a figurehead and *he* alone' — he laid a special emphasis on the word "he" — "can bring us that. He will unify the nation behind us. He will be our rallying cry."

"But, friends, I must object." The speaker was Father Iannis, the eldest of the assembled company. "As far as we know, he doesn't speak a single word of Greek. Surely — can't you see? — this presents a problem."

"That's been taken care of," interjected Andreas. "We will use him as an image — we will use his nose — and we will have someone to speak on his behalf if and when the need arises."

"And let us not forget," added one of the agents, "that he merits and deserves it. His family have been persecuted for generations. Nine, if my memory's correct. And look how much they have given to Greece. We — this great nation — have come so close to our dream, thanks to the Trencoms. Now, in our more desperate hour, we need them more than ever."

There was a long pause while everyone helped themselves to salted almonds from the bowl in the centre of the table. Andreas took a sip of water in the hope of dislodging a piece of nut that was caught in his throat and then spoke once again. "Then I ask you all — shall I now send this letter? Is the time right?"

He held up the envelope, on which was neatly handwritten the words, Edward Trencom, 22 Sunnyhill Road, London.

"Yes," said one of the priests, followed by a chorus of "Yes — Yes — Yes — Yes — Yes."

"Then the time really has come," said a now-smiling Andreas, bringing the meeting to a conclusion. "Friends, our lives are now in the hands of Edward Trencom."

CHAPTER
FIVE

January 1667

Humphrey Trencom is blithely unaware that, ever since his arrival in Constantinople, his movements have been noted and studied in great detail. No fewer than three people have been on his trail — following him, tracking his footsteps and compiling three separate dossiers of information about his untoward behaviour.

One of the three is Ralph Pryor, chief merchant of the English factory and a man who is of a naturally suspicious bent. He has mistrusted Humphrey from the minute he clapped eyes on him. "I don't like the cut of his nose," he recorded in his diary.

Ralph Pryor had been informed of Humphrey's arrival in a letter from the Duke of Athelhampton. The duke had begged "my lovinge servant, Mister Pryor" to do everything in his power to facilitate Humphrey's acquisition of "antiquytees". He had also asked him to introduce Humphrey to any Ottoman official whom he considered might prove useful. Ralph had read the duke's letter with a chill disdain. "I would sooner give my cat a dish of roast'd viands than aid Your Lordship," he had thought.

One cause of his hostility is the fact that he fought against the duke's forces in the Civil War. But it is equally a result of his upbringing. Ralph Pryor is what the better sort like to call "a man mayd goode". Born into poverty in Limehouse, and taken on as an apprentice to the Levant Company, he has slavered his way up through the ranks. Now forty-two years of age and factory chief in the company's most profitable trading post, he has managed to form an instinctive dislike towards anyone and everyone for whom life is "a dish of oysters".

Pryor's position pays him a substantial income and he never goes short of victuals, yet he retains the hereditary leanness that is characteristic of all the stick-thin Pryors. His cheeks are pinched and his belly is hollow. It is as if the bloody flux has taken up permanent abode in Ralph Pryor's guts, sucking and disgorging every last globule of fat and marrow.

It has taken many centuries of gristle and gruel for Ralph to reach the state where every rickety component, every sinew, ligament and ossicle is distorted from the state which Nature might have originally intended. Immensely tall and gangly to boot, he has the sloping gait and posture that afflict so many very tall people. It is as if he has grown tired of breathing the rarified air of the upper stratosphere and wishes to rejoin the breezier altitudes of his fellow mortals. In short, he stoops — stoops badly — and this has caused his joints, bones and shoulder blades to slowly collapse in on themselves over the four decades since he first struggled onto his pins. He suffers from tennis elbow and housemaid's knee, a touch of sciatica and occasional lumbago. In winter, he has spasms. In summer, he has slipped discs. And the patrilineal gout, which afflicts his left toe, has been known to keep him horizontal for days.

To counter this extreme skinniness, Pryor has bought himself one of those concave mirrors that have recently become all the rage in Constantinople. They put flesh on bones in a way that only decades of indulgence could hope to replicate. Yet even the artifice of anamorphosis is unable to puff out Ralph's cheeks and lard his jowl.

When Ralph Pryor had first met Humphrey, he had greeted him with perfunctory courtesy. From that point on — and with very little effort — he has managed to dislike him intensely. When he learns that the factory staff have been whispering about Humphrey's unorthodox behaviour, his suspicions are immediately awakened. "A conspiracy is surely afoot," he says to himself, "and Humphrey must certainly be guilty."

A knock at the door causes Pryor to look up from his rosewood desk. "No time — no time," he snaps, but the door opens anyway and in walks James Nealson, the factory's clerk.

"Ah, Mr Nealson — for you, I have always got time."

"You summoned me, sirrah," says Nealson. "Nothing amiss, I pray?"

"Something is very much amiss," replies Pryor. "There's something rotten in the state of —"

"Denmark?" ventures Nealson, eager to show off his learning.

"No, you fool. Are we in Denmark, you joskin? Is this the land of the Danes?"

Nealson coughs nervously as Pryor spells out what he believes to be blindingly obvious. "There's something rotten, sirrah, in the state of our factory."

"And what, exactly, might you mean by that?" queries Nealson.

"Humphrey Trencom," replies Pryor. "I don't like him — I don't like his face, I don't like the way he speaks. In short, I find him obnoxious, cantankerous and dangerous. He is a snake, and a venomous one at that. If we don't watch him, he will poison us all."

"Agreed," says Nealson, who is not entirely sure as to what he is agreeing with.

There's a moment's silence. A hush descends. Pryor picks up his gold-framed oval hand-mirror and admires the curvature of his chin.

"We live in dangerous times," he says, picking at a scabrous red pimple. "Dangerous times."

"In what way do you mean, sirrah? I'm not sure I quite follow you." Nealson is perplexed by his superior. Mr Pryor always speaks in riddles.

"I want you to follow Humphrey Trencom," he says. "I want you to track him — hunt him down — note his movements. He's up to something — up to no good. And I want to know what."

Pryor puts down his mirror and looks Nealson sharply in the eye. "Deliver me Humphrey," he says, "and I will deliver you the world."

322

"Why, thank you, sirrah," says Nealson, who is still no nearer to discovering what Mr Pryor means. "That's very kind."

"And remember — I want a full report by the end of the week."

Nealson turns to leave and Ralph gets up from his desk. "I'm coming out," he says. "I need to piss."

Ralph Pryor is not alone in having suspicions about Humphrey Trencom. In the innermost quarters of the Topkapi Sarayi, the chief vizier, Ishak Bey, is briefing the divan, the muftis and his most trustworthy agents.

"Our wise, noble, beloved ruler, the ineffable, the effulgent Sultan Mehmet (may Allah preserve him!) is in danger." He clears his throat, as if to emphasize this danger. "Outside forces are at work — and they must be stopped.

"We have yet to discover from whence this danger comes. It may be spies from Vienna. It may even be forces from within. As the poet Al-Mutanabbi once wrote, 'even the flower can have poison in her heart'. Whatever it is, we must act — act now — before it is too late."

The imperial divan gives a collective nod. They let out a collective murmur. And then the officials, judges and men of religion debate the danger. After just a few minutes, they agree that their suspicions fall upon one man. The newly arrived Humphrey Trencom of Piddletrenthide in Dorset is behaving most strangely. He presents a grave threat to the throne of Sultan Mehmet IV (may Allah preserve him).

It is unanimously decided that he must be followed, tracked, hunted down. The man chosen for this task is Hamed Efendi, the vizier's most dependable agent. But the vizier also selects a second person to monitor Humphrey Trencom — someone he has found to be most reliable on previous occasions. Her real name is Huma, but to the vizier, as to her clients, she is known as Hafise.

Humphrey Trencom is unaware of the disquiet he is causing. He wakes, yawns and listens for the cock-crow. Cock-a-doodle-doo. Still half asleep, he pulls up Hafise's nightshift and enters her from behind. "Oh yes — ," he grunts. "And a good morning to you, madam."

In the room below, James Nealson is standing on a chest with his ear to a goblet and the goblet to the ceiling. He is trying to eavesdrop on the recently arrived Humphrey. He need not have bothered, for the floor is soon vibrating vigorously and Nealson's eyes are filled with plaster and dust.

"Mr H.T. performs coitus," he notes in his journal. "Duration, four minutes. Activity level, high." He lays aside his quill and reads over the first entry in his book. Then, picking up his pen while the ink is still fresh, he adds, "Woman, Turkish whore."

Nealson soon deduces that coitus is over and Humphrey is getting dressed. "Track him, follow him, monitor him," he mutters to himself as Humphrey pulls on his breeches. "He's up to no good."

Outside in the street, but concealed in a passageway, is Hamed Efendi, agent extraordinaire. He has been waiting there since dusk, studying the left-hand window on the upper floor. Shortly after cockcrow, he notices activity. Hafise comes to the window and flashes a pre-arranged signal. Humphrey is in the process of stepping outside.

Hamed Efendi is a shrewd operator who made his name with the capture of al-Sahif the Betrayer. But on this occasion he makes one foolish slip. He does not consider, not for one moment, that someone else might be stalking his quarry. As Humphrey leaves the factory — and Hamed turns to follow him — he bumps headlong into James Nealson.

"Ouch," cries Nealson, who gives Hamed a shove in his ribs. Humphrey hears the kerfuffle and looks around. He is most anxious not to be seen.

"What in devil's name is *he* doing out and about at such an early hour," he thinks, spying Nealson from the corner of his eye. "Hmm — no good will come of this." And he quickens his pace, turning left and right, and then right and left, in his effort to shake off Nealson.

Hamed knows every alley and back-lane of Constantinople and is fairly certain as to where Humphrey Trencom is going. "The waterfront," he says to himself. "He'll cross the Golden Horn." He overtakes the huffing-puffing Humphrey, makes a dash to the shoreline, and is already seated in the soon-to-depart ferryboat when Trencom arrives at the wharf. He steps into the same skiff and hands his coin to the ferryman.

By the time the third of the trio, James Nealson, reaches the water, the ferryboat is already halfway across the Golden Horn, heading towards the Fener district of the city on the far side of the water.

Nealson clambers into the next ferryboat to depart. There's one other person already seated in the stern — a Turkish lady veiled from head to foot in black.

"I'll never understand these blasted women," ponders Nealson, whose mind is still focused on the antics he had heard taking place earlier. "I wonder if Trencom's whore dresses like this when she goes out in public . . ."

Almost two hours are to pass before James Nealson returns to the English factory in Galata. He has a blister on his left foot, a welt on his cheek (resulting from his collision with Hamed) and a notebook filled with scribbles. He is feeling decidedly pleased with himself. "Why," he thinks, "I'd make a first-class detectionist."

He taps on the door to Ralph Pryor's study, anxious to report back on the untoward events he has witnessed.

"No time — no time," comes a voice from within.

"But it's me, sirrah, Nealson. I need to talk."

"Enter," is the immediate response, and Nealson opens the door.

He is greeted by a most extraordinary sight. Ralph Pryor is standing on his desk, on one leg, and is in the process of fixing a small convex mirror to the ceiling. In one hand he holds a mallet and some nails; in the other, some sort of measuring device.

"Excuse me, sirrah," ventures a sheepish Nealson, "but could I be so bold as to ask what *exactly* you are doing?"

"Dangerous times," says Pryor. "Need to keep an eye on one another."

"Sirrah?" says Nealson in a tone that clearly suggests he is angling for an explanation.

"This mirror here," says Pryor, "is aligned with the mirror in that tree." He points to the flowering maple in the courtyard garden. "And that one reflects with a third that is up there, on the eaves."

"And?" asks Nealson.

"And," responds Pryor, "it means that I can see directly into Trencom's chamber. Yes, I'll catch that rat if it's the last thing I do."

"Perhaps *I* can help?" suggests Nealson. "You see, I've been on his tracks since dawn."

"Ah-ha — so, prithee, tell me."

Nealson recounts how Humphrey Trencom had headed for the Fener district of the city, on the far side of the Golden Horn. Once there, he had hot-footed his way to the Greek patriarchate, the focal point for the city's large Christian community.

"I was unable to enter the patriarch's quarters," explains Nealson. "It's under guard. But I did see something that may prove of interest."

Nealson informs Pryor of how he had climbed the disused Byzantine watchtower that stands directly opposite the patriarchate. From here, with the aid of a chair and his spyglass, he was able to see directly into the patriarch's quarters.

"And who should be there, talking to the patriarch?"

"That rat," snaps Pryor, "that scoundrel, that codpiece of the duke's."

"Correct", says Nealson. "Mr Humphrey Trencom."

"So what, zounds, was he doing there?" asks Pryor, whose impatience was writ large in the frown lines of his forehead. "Come on, spit it out."

"I don't know," admits Nealson. "I've already told you, I wasn't in the room."

"Well, what did you *see?*" says an exasperated Pryor. He bangs his fists on the table, causing his quill to leapfrog out of its inkstand. A drop of dark sepia ink attaches itself to his chemise, then licks its way rapidly along the thin hatchwork of serge.

"Quite a lot," says Nealson. "The patriarch — Bartholomeus — handed Trencom something, a scroll of parchment. At least, I think it was a scroll. And then, well, he gave him a blessing and showed him to the door."

"That's all?"

"That's all — except — well, there's one other thing. On two occasions this morning I bumped into the same man — a Turk. You know what, sirrah? I can't help thinking that he, too, is watching Trencom."

Hamed Efendi has been rather more successful in his quest to discover more about Humphrey Trencom. No sooner had his quarry left the patriarchate than Hamet sent in three Ottoman janissaries, who arrested the patriarch's dragoman on a trumped-up charge of treason. This unfortunate individual was then marched to the Topkapi Sarayi, where he was handed over to Abdul Ali, the court's chief executioner.

Within the hour, the dragoman has confessed all he knows. Yes, Patriarch Bartholomeus gave the Englishman a parchment. No, he doesn't know what it said.

The thumb wrench is given another twist.

"Aaaagh — I *really* don't know."

Another two turns.

"I — don't — know — aagh — I promise — I swear — I — don't — know."

A spiked clamp is bolted onto his head.

"In the name of God — I — don't — know."

"Then I will roast you alive," roars the executioner as he pauses to survey the trussed and bleeding dragoman. The only other information he gleans is this: Humphrey Trencom has come to the city to collect some sort of package.

"And what was in the package?" asks Abdul Ali the executioner, as he heats an iron bolt over a flame.

"I don't know — in God's name, I don't know."

Hafise, the perfumed, fragrant, delectable Hafise — Hafise who can stir the hardest men's hearts — is proving rather more successful in discovering Humphrey's movements and motives. She bides her time; waits until her paramour is at his most vulnerable.

Cock-a-doodle-doo. The morning cock crows.

"Come, my Turkey," purrs Humphrey, "come to Humphrey."

He prepares to roll himself onto his Turkey bird but, just as he does so, she shifts herself to the other side of the divan.

"Oh, no," he says in a tone of disappointment. "Oh, you *can't* do that — you *can't* let down your Humphrey."

Hafise smiles inwardly. Men are so easy, and this particular Nazarene is proving to be a walkover.

"Come, my sweet thing — it's dawn. My prick's at noon. Let me spill my seed."

Hafise, who has begun to move closer and closer, now rolls away for a second time.

Humphrey is twitching with frustration and no longer in the mood for frivolity. He is angry with Hafise. More than that, he is getting desperate.

"Now you come over here, girl, come back to Humphrey, I need you — I need you right now."

Still Hafise doesn't move.

This proves more than Humphrey can bear. His blood is up, his pulse is on fire, his heart is thumping and his loins are aflame.

"What?" he roars. "*You* — a slut, a common whore — are spurning the seed of Humphrey Trencom. The seed of noble lineage; the seed that once ruled an empire." He clutches at his privy parts and displays them to Hafise. "The seed inside these sacks," he fumes, "helped build this queen of cities."

Scarcely has he spoken these words than Hafise smiles to herself, sidles over towards Humphrey and clambers astride his white fleshy thighs.

330

"Why didn't you tell me before?" she says softly. "That's everything I wanted to know."

"Eh?" says Humphrey as he primes himself for action. And before the cock crows for a second time, the divan in Humphrey's chamber is getting the first instalment of its twice-daily exercise.

"Good God," says Ralph Pryor, who has just at that moment glanced into his contraption of mirrors. "Zounds and great heavens!" He has rigged up his device in order to spy on Humphrey's chamber, but he never for the life of him expected this.

"What, in heaven's name, *is* she doing to him?"

He peers more closely into the mirror.

"But that's not possible. No, that's — that's . . ." He searches for the appropriate word. "Revolting — abhorrent."

Pryor, it should be explained, has studiously avoided the city's stews and whores. A puritan in thought and deed, he has neither the time nor inclination for such abominations of the flesh. "No time for pleasure," he says. "Got to keep up the books."

And now he finds himself watching an explicit display being performed before his very eyes. He recoils in horror as he catches sight of Humphrey's bare fundament in the mirror. "I'm a peeping Tom," he mutters in considerable distress. "I've become a voyeur."

As he prepares to tear down the spy contraption, Humphrey Trencom — who is fast approaching the moment he likes to call "voidance" — turns to the mirror that he has seen attached to the eaves of the building and gives it a saucy wink. The wink winks at the mirror in the maple tree, which winks at the mirror attached to Pryor's ceiling. This, in turn, transmits the wink to Ralph Pryor himself.

He shudders. "I'll destroy him," he hisses, "if it's the last thing I do."

Later that day, Hamed Efendi and a veiled Hafise can be seen passing through the Gate of Salutation. They are reporting to the Grand Vizier on what they have seen and heard. They are joined by a third person, Abdul Ali the executioner, whose tunic is stained with human blood.

"It is clear," says the vizier in a voice of disquiet, "that we have found our man. He represents a threat to the stability of our empire. He represents a threat to the life of our most wise, most noble and most magnanimous sultan, the incomparable, the effulgent, the ineffable Mehmet (may Allah preserve him)."

"His privities should be severed from his body," counsels Hamed Efendi, "and his seed should be flung into the Bosphorus."

The vizier acknowledges this remark with a gracious nod. "And what did *you* learn?" he asks, turning to Abdul Ali and noting with distaste the blood on his jerkin.

"Well," replies Abdul in a studied voice, "the patriarch handed the Englishman an imperial crystobull — yes — a decree signed by Constantine XI Palaiologos, the last Byzantine emperor." He allows himself a theatrical pause and takes the opportunity to roll his eyes. "But what this decree said, alas, we do not know. Our witness expired before we could find out more."

"A pity," says the vizier as he plays with his beard. "Your methods do not always speak of finesse."

"If I may be allowed," says Hafise. "It means this: Humphrey Trencom is not Humphrey Trencom at all — he is Humphrey Palaiologos, a descendant of the infidel Emperor Constantine. He is here, I believe, in search of his throne."

The three men lean forward as her words take effect.

"But why is he awaiting a signal from the patriarch?" asks the vizier. "And what does he hope to find at the Porta Aurea?"

"I don't know," says Hafise.

"And nor do I," says Abdul Ali the executioner.

"And nor do I," says Hamed Efendi.

"And nor, for that matter, do I," added a frustrated Edward Trencom, some 302 years after the above meeting took place. All he knew for sure — and he knew it from the journal of Ralph Pryor — was that two days after Humphrey Trencom fled Constantinople aboard a vessel bound for Salonika, agents of the Grand Vizier discovered a small, stone-lined cave underneath the Porta Aurea.

It was empty. There was nothing there.

CHAPTER
SIX

25 April 1969

On Friday, 25 April 1969, the postman delivered a long-awaited letter to Number 22, Sunnyhill Road. It was addressed to Mr Edward Trencom and bore the postmark of Salonika in Greece. Edward picked it off the mat with great excitement and noticed that his hands were shaking. "This is it," he thought. "This is really it." After checking that Elizabeth was still busy in the kitchen, he took the letter into the living room, leaving the rest of the post on the mat.

"Anything interesting?" called Elizabeth. "Anything for me?"

"Nothing that'll change the world," replied Edward. "I'll bring them in a minute."

He opened the letter with such haste that he tore the envelope all down one side. "It must be from Papadrianos," he thought. "It can only be from him." As he unfolded the paper, he realized that it was indeed from Andreas Papadrianos.

Although the contents were exactly as Edward had been led to expect, he was so taken aback to have at long last received the letter that he twice dropped it onto the floor. And when he picked it up for the second time, he noticed that his hands were trembling so uncontrollably that he was unable to keep the paper still.

"You will fly to Athens on May 10th," read the letter. "You will then change onto flight AH240 to Salonika. Here you will be met and taken to the rendezvous. Everything will then be revealed."

Edward pulled the tickets out of the envelope and checked them. "Everything's been arranged," he murmured under his breath. "And now I must go. I *have* to go. I can at last solve everything."

"Were there any bills?" called Elizabeth from the kitchen. "They said they'd resend the electricity bill."

"Hmm?" said Edward. "No bills, darling. I'll bring them to you in a minute."

"*And* I was expecting that catalogue," she added. "The new needlepoint catalogue."

"Ah-ha," said Edward, who was so lost in his thoughts that although he could hear Elizabeth talking to him, he did not register a word. He read the letter for a second time, and then a third, as if to confirm that his eyes were not flashing false messages to his brain. And then, with a troubled smile, he folded the letter in two and placed it in the inside pocket of his jacket.

CHAPTER
SEVEN

2 May 1969

It was just after 6.30p.m. on a glorious spring evening. Edward and Elizabeth had been driving for the best part of three hours, chasing the sun as it scored a line through the sky. It was fast approaching that time of day — Edward's favourite — when the meadows would turn yellow and the sky royal blue.

"Just look at the shadows," said Edward as they drove past a field that was lined with poplars. "You could play giant chess in there." The trees had been stretched into impossible shapes by the low sun and cast a hatchwork of slanting stripes that reached towards the furthest boundary.

Edward and Elizabeth turned off the A357 and onto the submerged country lanes, following the signs for Mappowder, Melcombe and Plush. From here, it was another twenty minutes to their destination, the little village of Piddletrenthide.

Their visit to the Piddle Valley had been Edward's idea — one that Elizabeth had at first resisted. She wanted him to spend less time on his family history — not more — and didn't want to feel that she was aiding and abetting him. "And what about Mr George?" she asked. "He's been slaving away in the shop for weeks now. Isn't it about time you started to help him restock the shop?"

"I will — I promise. When we come back from Dorset. It's just that, well, I must first find out what happened to Humphrey Trencom. I need to know whether or not he died in his native Dorset. If I could find out that then I'd be happy. You see, I need to discover where he was buried. I need to know what happened to him."

Elizabeth slept on what Edward had said and eventually decided that a trip to the Piddle Valley might be just the tonic they needed. "And if it really *will* get him back to Trencoms," she said to herself with a heavy sigh, "then I suppose it's worth it. But . . ." She folded her arms and watched a squirrel race across the garden. It paused as it approached the bird bath, looked her directly in the eye and then dipped its feet into the water.

"Oh dear," thought Elizabeth, lost in her own world. "Where *will* it all end?"

They had booked two nights in the Coach and Horses in Piddletrenthide, an oak-framed building whose painted sign declared that it had been a hostelry since the reign of King James I. It was owned by Mr and Mrs Singleton, a husband and wife team in their late fifties who had a most unhealthy vice, one shared by many a middle-aged couple in this part of Dorset. And while their collective behaviour did not contravene any law laid down by parliament, it most certainly transgressed the boundaries of what might justifiably be considered good taste.

Their vice was this: Clive and Clarissa Singleton had a "thing" for all things floral. The walls of their bed and breakfast were lined with floral wallpaper. The beds were covered in floral drapes. There were buttercups on the curtains and cornflowers on the carpet. And when you laid down your weary head at night, you found yourself sinking into a fuschia-patterned pillowcase.

This passion for flowers was not uncommon in the rural bed and breakfasts of England in the late 1960s. From Abberly to Zennor, one could find coaching inns and hostelries whose crumbling plasterwork was held together with swathes of floriferous paper. It was as if every surface and every bed had been sprinkled liberally with plant feed and then sprung spontaneously into bloom. Yet the Coach and Horses took this floriculture to new extremes. Under the horticultural tutelage of Mr and Mrs Singleton, the guest bedrooms gave the impression of a flower garden gone to seed.

Only one item of furniture in Edward and Elizabeth's bedroom was devoid of flowers: a sturdy four-poster whose upper deck was carved with the date 1616. It was not a large bed — Edward could rub the wooden footboard with the soles of his feet — but it was certainly beautiful. That night, as Mr and Mrs Trencom tucked themselves into their flowery bower, Elizabeth admired the gleaming corkscrew pillars and the wonky oak headboard.

"Imagine all the people who have slept in this bed," she said. "Darling, think how many generations of people have, well . . ." She placed her arm over her husband's chest and her right leg over his left knee. She was playing with her thoughts, daring herself to say aloud the idea that was currently running through her mind. "Think," she said in a whisper, "of all the children that must have been conceived in this bed."

She sensed that Edward was miles away. "Mmm?" he said as he stared blankly at a particularly garish spray of carnations. "Yes, perhaps even Humphrey himself slept here — in this very bed."

Elizabeth let out a disappointed sigh. "Yes," she said, "perhaps he did. And perhaps he didn't." She moved onto her side, pressing herself even closer to Edward with the intention of getting her husband to think rather less about Humphrey and rather more about her. Yet she feared that the moment had already passed.

"I wonder," yawned Edward, "if he ever did get back to Dorset. What do you think, darling?" And, without even waiting for a reply, he clicked off the light and curled up his legs. Elizabeth knew that this was his sleeping position and that she'd have to act fast. She sat up in bed, leaned right across him and planted a kiss on the end of his nose.

"Are you really so tired, Mr Cheese?" she said. "I'm sure your friend Humphrey would have played ball."

There was a moment's pause before Edward turned over, kissed Elizabeth's left ear and then affectionately nibbled her elbow — an action that was so ticklish she squeaked.

"Beware," he said with a low growl, "it's not only the bed-bugs that bite." And with that, he slipped out of his pyjamas.

The couple came down early for breakfast and tucked into poached eggs, grilled tomatoes and a great slab of fried back bacon. "Just what the doctor ordered," said Elizabeth as she wiped her mouth with a floral-patterned napkin. "That's well and truly set me up for the day. Even I can face Humphrey now."

They had arranged to visit Piddletrenthide church later that afternoon, in order to check the register of deaths in the church archives. But first they were going to see the source of the River Piddle, which lay some two miles to the north of the village. It was Elizabeth's idea. For some reason that Edward failed to understand, she was keen to see where it bubbled out of the ground.

"I simply can't see why you're so interested," remarked Edward. "I'm sure there won't be much to see."

"Oh, Edward," she replied, "you can be so unromantic at times. And you of *all* people. I'd have thought you'd love to visit the source of the river, see where it actually springs from."

"Eh?" said Edward, whose mind was immediately transported back to the flood at Trencoms. "Well — I think I've had quite enough of water recently."

There were many people living in this valley — including scores of long-dead Trencoms — who considered the Piddle to be one of the great rivers on earth. It was not, of course, on quite the same scale as the Amazon or Nile. No Victorian adventurer had ever hacked his way upstream in search of its elusive source; no army of panners had trudged across the flood meadows in the hope of striking gold. But the Piddle was one of the more enchanting rivers in this part of the world. Twenty-two and a half miles in length, and replenished by scores of becks and rills, it had bestowed its name on more than half a dozen mellifluous-sounding villages.

Edward and Elizabeth drove to Highton Farm, parked their car at the edge of the lower meadow and clambered over a low stile that had clearly seen better days. As Elizabeth took her first step, she discovered that terra firma lay some five or six inches below the surface. "Ayeee — wet feet."

She was disappointed to find that it was not possible to locate the exact point from which the river sprang to the surface, for there was no single source. Rather, the water leached from the ground in more than a dozen places, forming a squelchy sponge that was studded with sedge and marsh-grass.

"Don't you think it's exciting to come to a river's source?" said Elizabeth suddenly. "To think that this is where it all begins." She was staring at the ground, watching the water ooze and swell to the surface. In places it blew itself into translucent little air-filled bubbles as it broke the surface. They puffed themselves up, wobbled precariously in the breeze and then popped into nothingness.

"It's joined by other branches, of course," continued Elizabeth, "other streams which add water, which change it. And yet it always remains the same."

Her mind was half on the River Piddle and half on the family tree that Edward had been showing her over breakfast. Yes. A river *was* like a tree — an upturned one — with each little rill and stream contributing something to the principal trunk.

"Well — yes and no," said Edward after a long pause. He had not been listening to Elizabeth at first but now that he was, well, he was not at all convinced by what she was saying. "You see, darling, the tributaries add water — and they change the flow of the river. Remember the stream we saw at Puddleton Down? The one that joins the Piddle? It completely altered the river's character. It looked different afterwards — it became wider, slower, more sluggish."

"Yes, I know, but it was still the same old Piddle. Can't you see? It's still one river." Edward could be so infuriating and Elizabeth was determined to stand her ground. "It's the Piddle here," she said, pointing to the marshy earth, "and it's the same Piddle when it reaches the sea."

Edward kept his silence. His wife was wrong. She was very wrong. One branch — one seemingly insignificant little branch — could utterly change the main stream.

Edward had made two previous trips to the Piddle Valley and visited the parishes of Puddletown, Briantspuddle, Tolpuddle and Piddlehinton. He had searched through the records of baptisms and deaths and combed the lists of Trencom marriages. In so doing, he had managed to build up quite an archive about the early Trencoms. This was the first time he had been able to contact the archivist at Piddletrenthide and he was most excited at the prospect of searching for a record of Humphrey's death.

"If I can discover whether or not he made it home from Constantinople," he said to Elizabeth, "then I might be able to find out what he was bringing home — what was inside the package — and where it is now."

"Assuming it still exists," cut in Elizabeth.

"Yes, assuming it still exists."

The church of All Saints was situated on the west bank of the river, a Norman building that had been remodelled in the fourteenth century. According to A. G. Smithers's *History of the Piddle Valley*, it was the most interesting of all the Piddle churches. "With its Norman porch, Elizabethan chancel and its array of funerary monuments," wrote the author, "it must surely rank as the architecturally richest parish of the valley."

Edward pushed open the lychgate, entered the churchyard and sniffed at the branches of the overhanging yew tree. Elizabeth followed him, noticing that the ground was sprinkled with little red berries.

"I'd have thought it was most unlikely the actual headstone will still be here," she said, as Edward began studying the upright slabs of stone. "Even if it was, it must be faded by now. I doubt that you'd be able to read the inscription."

"I don't know," said Edward as he worked his way methodically through the churchyard. "There's one here from 1723." He found a John Trencom, an Emilie Trencom and two Martin Trencoms; there was also a Katherine Trencom and an infant Job Trencom. "You know what, darling? There was a Job Trencom in the Piddlehinton churchyard," he observed. "And I think there was a Katherine as well."

Soon he had checked every stone in the churchyard without finding a single Humphrey. "I think you must be right," he said. "The oldest headstone was the one from 1723 — that must be at least thirty years after he died."

He pushed open the west door of the church and stepped down into the nave. Edward held his nose for a second and then took a long, deep inhalation of breath. "How strange," he thought. "How very strange." His nose, which had failed him on at least five occasions in the last two days, was suddenly back on form. The church smelled of watercress. Yes, water-cress and mushrooms. It was the same smell that Edward had detected in the pages of Humphrey's book.

"You know what?" he said to Elizabeth. "If history has a smell, it's this."

The two of them looked around the church for a couple of minutes, examining the funerary monuments and old brasses. Then, just as Edward began reading a short pamphlet about the building, there was a squeaking of hinges and the door opened. "Ah-ha — you must be Mr and Mrs Trencom," said a jovial lady who bounded up to Edward and Elizabeth and shook them heartily by the hand. "I'm Joyce Woolley, the curator. Reverend Bailey told me you'd be coming."

"Yes," said Edward, "thank you — thank you. You see, I'm trying to find an ancestor of mine," he said. "A chap called Humphrey Trencom."

"Ah-ha," replied Mrs Woolley. "Well, let's see what we can find."

She trotted off to the sacristy and returned with a heavy folio that was embossed with the words, *All Saints: Register of Deaths 1680–1691*.

"Now," she said, "tell me. When do you think Hubert died?"

"Humphrey," said Edward, politely correcting her.

"Sorry, sorry — did I say Humphrey?" she said.

Edward looked at Elizabeth, who signalled a smile with her eyes. "He died in 1685," said Edward, "or at least I *think* he did. That's really what I need to check. And I'm presuming he was buried here, but I'm not certain."

The register was difficult to decipher. It was written in an ungainly, cursive hand that had turned every twirl and letter into a spirograph of squiggles and loops. In places it looked as if an ink-toed spider had danced a quadrille across the page.

"No, no — nothing for 1685," said Mrs Woolley. "Let's try 1686."

The three of them scanned the page, looking for any entry that looked like a Humphrey. There was a surprising number of mortalities in 1685; Edward counted them and found that no fewer than sixteen people had died that year, including four members of one family.

"Ah, look, look — now, here we go," said Mrs Woolley. "Here he is — isn't this your chappie? Humphrey Trencom?"

Edward and Elizabeth peered closer at the handwriting to check that she hadn't made a mistake. But no — she hadn't. Humphrey Trencom's name was clearly marked in the register.

"Well," said Elizabeth with a relieved smile. "That's good news, isn't it? You've found him at last. And in less than five minutes."

"Oh — oh — oh. But what have we here?" said Mrs Woolley, sounding a little disconcerted. "Hello, hello — what does this say?"

There was a faint sepia scrawl in the margin of the register — a note that had been added at a later date.

"Well, that *is* strange," she said. "Well, I'll be blowed."

"What does it say?" said Edward, who was straining to read the writing.

"Your Humphrey Trencom," said Mrs Woolley. "He was indeed buried here in Piddletrenthide — yes — buried here in this very churchyard. But look what it says underneath — right here. Apparently, his body was disinterred less than a week after his funeral."

"*What!*" exclaimed Edward. "Disinterred?"

"Apparently so — at least, according to this. Look — his corpse was stolen. Dug up and taken away. Your Humphrey Trencom was never seen again."

Mrs Trencom glanced at Edward. Her heart sank. "Oh, no," she said. "That's all we need."

346

CHAPTER
EIGHT

At approximately the same time as Edward and Elizabeth were investigating the source of the River Piddle, Herbert Potinger was to be found sitting on the top deck of a Number 12 bus. The bus was almost empty and Herbert was most annoyed when a tall, foreign-looking man — who had been waiting at the same bus stop — sat down next to him. "Two dozen seats," sighed Herbert, "and he chooses the one next to me."

Herbert was heading to work (rather later than was usual) and normally spent twenty minutes on the bus making a checklist of all the things he needed to do during the day. But on this particular occasion, he had rather more pressing matters on his mind. As the bus crawled along Denmark Hill, passing Ruskin Park and Camberwell Green, Herbert found himself drawn into his own private world.

The person who so occupied his thoughts was none other than the chimerical Humphrey Trencom. Herbert had spent the previous night in bed with Humphrey, trying to piece together Mr H.T.'s whereabouts in the days that followed his sudden departure from Constantinople. It soon became clear to Herbert that

Humphrey's written account was not nearly as straightforward as it first appeared, and in places seemed to be deliberately misleading. The ship on which he had made his escape was bound for Salonika (or so he claimed) but if this was to be believed, then it had by no means taken the most direct route. The captain had first sailed to the little island of Ayios Evstratios, where the vessel had made its first port of call. "We rested five dayes," wrote Humphrey, "and the agha did rommage my possesyons."

Humphrey spent much of his time trying to get passage to the nearby island of Lesbos, although he gave no inkling of what he wished to do there. "I can't understand why a man like Humphrey Trencom would be so keen to go to Lesbos," said Herbert as he scratched his scalp. "After all — Lesbos, Lesbos — no, I can't think of any obvious attraction on the island."

After a week on Ayios Evstratios, Humphrey and the crew set sail again, this time heading due north. It was not long before they found themselves in serious trouble. On their third day at sea the vessel was struck by a tremendous storm.

"It did bellowe and puff into an exceading tempest," wrote Humphrey, "and we did most sorely fear that we would be drowned." The storm raged for a day and two nights, tossing the ship into cavernous troughs and plucking its cladding from the frame. Twice it almost capsized. Twice the crew managed to right it. "And the rayne did come down in torrents," wrote Humphrey, "sluicing the decks and flooding the hold."

The men lost their bearings and feared they would be drowned. "And each and every one of our companye did make his peece with God, knowying that every wave myght be our last." Not until the second day did the storm finally abate. The wind dropped to a breeze and the sea calmed. And when the sun finally rose to burn off the sea mist, the men found themselves in sight of a coastline that was unfamiliar to everyone on board.

"And we came," wrote Humphrey, "unto a fayre enchanted isle with a mountain that touch'd the heavens." He claimed that there were twenty bejewelled cities in this uncharted realm and each was inhabited only by princes and men. "And these men do reproduce by themselves," he wrote in typically cryptic fashion, "like unto the twin-sexed hermaphrodyte."

Humphrey left his readers in little doubt that this was the place he had been searching for all along. "This was the realm I had hoped to discover," he wrote. "This was my Promised Land." He added, "It was with the greateste solemnity that I offered over my parcel and was greeted with prostrations by all the princes of that isle."

It was this mysterious and quite possibly fantastical island that preoccupied Herbert's thoughts as he sat atop the Number 12 bus. At the exact moment the driver swung into Walworth Road, a reversing van collided with a roadside vegetable stall, spilling half a hundredweight of parsnips across the street. Yet Herbert was so distracted by his thoughts that he failed to register the sight of buses, cars and taxis swerving violently in order to avoid colliding with a thick carpet of root vegetables.

It was with a start that he realized he had missed his stop. The vague awareness that he was crossing Southwark Bridge triggered something in his brain. It clicked him back to the here and now and told him (quite unconsciously) to push the "stop" button. By the time Herbert finally got off the bus, he was more than six hundred yards from where he wanted to be. He noticed that the man sitting next to him got off at the same place. "I seem to have made a new friend," mused Herbert with an inward chuckle.

When he at long last reached the library, he headed straight into his office and pulled down an atlas of the Mediterranean. If Humphrey was to be believed, then the island to which he referred must lie within a few days' sailing of the coast of Asia Minor. Herbert located Ayios Evstratios on his map — Humphrey's last known port of call before the storm — then allowed his finger to trace an arc of ever widening circles.

He quickly realized that there were only three possible contenders to be the "fayre enchanted isle". There was Limnos, a large and once-wooded island that Herbert knew to have been the home of the god Hephaestus, patron of metalworkers. "A most unlikely destination," he thought. "After all, its population was largely Turkish in Humphrey's day."

The second possible island was Thasos, which lay some eighty miles to the north. This was famous for its wine in the seventeenth century but — like Limnos — it, too, had a large Turkish population.

The only other possibility was Samothraki, a much less populous island that lay to the north-east of Limnos. Herbert knew little about Samothraki and looked it up in his copy of *Islands of the Eastern Mediterranean*. "Ah, yes, yes," he said as he scanned the page. "This sounds *much* more like Humphrey's goal."

It certainly had a mountain that "touch'd the heavens" — Mount Fengari stood more than five thousand feet above sea level and its peak was often shrouded in cloud. Moreover, although the island was not inhabited exclusively by "princes and men" — and certainly not by hermaphrodites — it did have a reputation as the male island. For centuries in antiquity it had been the home of the cult of the Cobeiri, a Phoenician fertility god whose symbol was a large phallus.

The most cryptic detail in Humphrey's account was his description of the island's capital. "I walked to the chief citadel of this fayre isle," he wrote, "which was perched on the edge of a cliff. It was called A+9VATPD70+O."

What could Humphrey have possibly meant by that? Herbert checked the principal settlements of Samothraki. There was Samothraki itself. There was Palaiopolis, the ancient capital. And there were the two towns of Kamariotissa and Chira. And that was it. None of these bore any resemblance to the code-word in Humphrey's journal.

Herbert returned to his account to see if there was any more information, but Humphrey was frustratingly circumspect. "In A+9VATPD70+O I had the good fortune to meet Anathasius, Antonius and Nicholas," he wrote, "who were each more than seven hundred yeers of age."

"Is it all fantasy?" Herbert asked himself. "Perhaps Edward is right — perhaps the answers lie in Piddletrenthide."

He knew little about codes and ciphers and, since Saturday was one of the quieter days of the week, he devoted much of the morning to reading the three books that Southwark municipal public library possessed on the subject. It soon became apparent that unravelling Humphrey's code would not be easy. According to Hartwell's *Secret Ciphers*, codes that mixed letters, numbers and symbols were the most difficult to solve. "The greatest achievement in the Guy Fawkes' conspiracy," wrote Hartwell, "was the deciphering of his encrypted letters. It took the genius of Sir Howell Stokes to crack the code."

Herbert was disheartened when he read this. "If it were written in letters alone," he thought, "I'd only need to work out the substituted letters. But *this* . . ."

He scratched his head with unusual vigour. The one thing of which he was reasonably certain was that Humphrey's code-word seemed unlikely to refer to any of the towns on the island of Samothraki. Herbert was left with the impression that Humphrey's "fayre enchanted isle" was not an isle at all.

"He's playing games," thought Herbert to himself. "And I've always been good at games."

He looked at his watch and then glanced around the room. He was most surprised to see that the man who had sat next to him on the bus was now sitting in the library, less than twenty feet from Herbert's desk.

"Surely he's not following . . ." thought Herbert, before dismissing the thought with a shake of his head. "No, no, Herbert. You've been reading about too many mysteries lately."

He was about to start answering the pile of letters on his desk when he had one last thought about Humphrey Trencom. It was a thought that, with hindsight, struck him as rather brilliant. He reached for volume seven of the *Oxford English Dictionary* and looked up the word hermaphrodite. "An animal in which the male and female sexual organs are (normally) present in the same individual," read the entry. "Some hermaphrodites are self-impregnating."

"Of course!" thought Herbert. "I should have guessed. A r-r-r-red herring — yes, indeed — a whopping, Humphrey-style red herring. But not an out and out lie."

CHAPTER
NINE

2 September 1671

It is a stifling autumnal day and the crowds are strolling aimlessly down Seething Lane in the city of London, trying to cool themselves in the faint Thames breeze. The lane is just close enough to the riverside wharves to catch the scent of Oriental merchandise that is stored in the nearby docks of Wapping. It is also one of the only areas of the city to have escaped the devastation of the Great Fire. Little has changed since medieval times and, bordered on its southern side by the Tower of London, this network of streets and alleys has long been home to a sizeable population of foreigners. According to Tobias Smythe's *Wards of London (1670)*, there are more than half a dozen nationalities living in an area not much larger than St James's: Swedes and Russians, Balts and Venetians, Genoese, Turks and Greeks.

It is this latter community that is of particular interest to Mr Humphrey Trencom. Greek merchants and mariners have lived in the area around Seething Lane since the reign of Queen Elizabeth I and the focus of the community is the little church of Aghia Sophia which stands out from the surrounding buildings because of its tiled Byzantine dome. The Greeks who worship here will tell you that the church was built in the early Middle Ages. This is not, in fact, correct. It was actually constructed within a few months of the 1654 Act of Tolerance and, ever since, the Greeks have been celebrating their liturgies, feasts and festivals under its cuspidated dome.

At the far end of Seething Lane, a familiar figure can be seen struggling through the crowds. He has put on weight in recent weeks — plumped out his skeletal frame with a hearty diet of soused herrings and venison pie. His belly is once again as smooth as a porpoise; his under-chin has regained its drapes of pendulous flesh. There is no mistaking Humphrey Trencom and he looks to be in fine fettle.

He must be in something of a hurry, for he is walking much faster than usual. The physical exertion has left him gasping for breath. As he charges down this narrow thoroughfare, jostling traders and passers-by, he can be heard grunting and steaming like a warthog. "Damn this waistcoat," he mutters to himself as he struggles to undo the top button. "I'm too hot." This is self-evident. His armpits are wet and his cheeks are flushed. His head is a hairy watershed that is drenched and dripping with sweat.

Humphrey reaches the church of Aghia Sophia and pauses to sniff the air. Then, after polishing his nose on a purple kerchief, he climbs the two steps to the entrance and pushes open the door.

As he enters the church, he blinks several times in the hope of adjusting his eyes to the darkness. His nose twitches as it detects the thick scent of frankincense. "Ah, yes," he says to himself. "Thuriferous — thuriferous. It's good to be home." Candles are flickering before icons and an oil lamp adds its reflective glow. Humphrey is still looking around when the following scene is played out before his very eyes. A priest and two monks appear from the altar, emerging into the body of the church from the doors of a carved and gilded iconostasis. They catch sight of Humphrey's figure, which looms large in the gloom, and shoot nervous glances at one another.

Suddenly, and with choreographic precision, all three drop to the floor and prostrate themselves before Humphrey. Their behaviour might be taken as unusual — unorthodox, even — but what makes it all the stranger is Humphrey's reaction. He seems to see nothing untoward in their manner; indeed, it is almost as if he expects them to prostrate before him. After a pause of at least a minute, perhaps longer, Humphrey summons them to their feet. "You may arise now," he commands in a tone that is marvellously grandiloquent. "Come now — get up."

"Basileus," begins Father Panteleimon, addressing Humphrey with the title that custom and tradition reserved for the holy emperors of Byzantium. "We have been expecting you, *Kyrie eleison*. News of your visit to the holy city has reached us from Patriarch Bartholomeus, may God bless him, and we have also been informed of the success of your mission."

The father then embraces Humphrey and, in a rather more familiar tone, enquires as to his health. "Better," replies Humphrey as he slaps his belly. "Much, much improved." He inadvertently lets slip a loud belch, the result of too many oysters in the Three Choughs. He coughs slightly to mask the noise, hoping that his little audience has not noticed. But they have, and they recoil slightly as they catch the unpleasant whiff of old seafood.

"Yes," continues Humphrey, swiftly changing the subject. "It was just as I'd been led to expect. Below the Porta Aurea — and it's now in safe hands. Never in a thousand years will the Turks recover it."

In the pause that follows, he takes the opportunity to rub his belly. Come to think of it, he has a slight ache in his gut. Yes, and a bitter-sour taste in his mouth. "I hope that the oysters weren't bad," he thinks. "They certainly tasted rather stronger than usual."

"But the timing," he continues aloud, "well, it was not good. No, the time was not and is not right."

"No," chime the two monks who flank Father Panteleimon, "the time is most definitely not right." One of them, warming to his theme, adds a few more thoughts. "The sultan is too powerful — see how he's planning an assault on Vienna. If we make an error now — if we slip — the future of everything will be compromised. The empire will be doomed for eternity."

Father Panteleimon takes Humphrey by the arm and moves closer, only to move back again when he catches that same whiff of seafood. "But did you bring the imperial crystobull?" he asks in a low voice. "We were told you'd have it with you."

"Yes," says Humphrey. "I have." He reaches into his breeches and, after loosening a couple of notches on his belt, pulls out a small scroll of parchment. It is tied up with a frayed purple ribbon which Father Panteleimon (after seeking Humphrey's permission) deftly unties with the fingers of one hand. He then unrolls the document and smooths it flat in order that he can read it more easily.

"Ah, yes," he says as he scans each line. "Exactly as we thought."

"Yes," says Humphrey, "and it's exactly as I'd been led to believe by my late mother. Read it aloud — read it aloud."

"The Palaiologi are the rulers in perpetuity of our most glorious and sacred city of Constantine," begins Father Panteleimon, reading from the scroll. "Blessed by God and sanctified by the Church, they shall remain so until the end of time."

Humphrey listens enraptured as Father Panteleimon speaks, but then lets out a low sigh. "It's one thing to be an emperor," he says, "and quite another to have an empire."

"Patience," says the Father, "is one of the virtues. Remember, our city is under the protection of the ever-virgin, most holy Mother of God. Our time will come."

Humphrey nods and reaches into the inner pocket of his jacket. "Here," he says. "I wanted to show you this." He produces a small bronze coin that bears the portrait of the Emperor Constantine XI Palaiologos.

358

"Look carefully," says Humphrey. "It is most interesting. Can you see? The basileus and I — we share something in common."

Father Panteleimon has never been a man to smile without just cause, but on this occasion his lips take a brief upwards turn.

"Yes," he says slowly as he studies the nose more closely. "It could almost be said that you carry the seal of the Palaiologi wherever you go."

Four years have passed and the seasons have turned. It is a shiveringly chill February day and the sky is so pale it has drained the landscape of any residual colour. Snow is blowing off Eggedon Hill, banking into drifts along the hedgerows and sheep-folds of the river meadows. The brilliant greens of nascent spring have leached back into the earth; now, there is only a monotone of white and grey.

In Piddletrenthide churchyard, a small group of villagers can be seen standing in the driving snow — the parson, Mr Jolyan the tavern-owner and a handful of others. As the wind increases in velocity and the snow's trajectory changes from the vertical to the horizontal, they find themselves blending into the surrounding landscape. Jupes, kirtles and worsted coifs — all are turned to white by the relentless onslaught.

The furrowed hillsides are as smooth as an ice-shelf; the branches of the churchyard yew tree hang pendulous, as if their outermost tips are attached to the ground by invisible threads. In such a uniform winter-scape, only the River Piddle stands out — a thick black ribbon that has left a score of ice along the rim of the frozen banks.

Among the mourners is Agnes Trencom, widow of the dead Humphrey. Her freely flowing tears are genuine enough. Despite her husband's failings; despite his insatiable sexual appetite; despite his trysts and infidelities, she has always treasured her Humphrey. And now his huge, towering presence has been snuffed out. No longer will he regale his friends with tall tales. No longer will his guffawing laughter be heard from across the fields. Humphrey lies dead — a rigid, frozen corpse that is as white and waxy as alabaster.

Shortly before his coffin was sealed, one of the mourners remarked that his nose remained as immutable as ever. His cheeks had hollowed, his jowls had collapsed, but his nose stood defiant in death. So, too (though this escaped the notice of the mourners), did his magnificent penis. This fine organ, which had brought him such pleasure throughout the course of his life, had stiffened for the last time. Even in death, Humphrey Trencom would be ready for action when the cock crowed. But there was no longer any comely maiden to straddle his frozen loins.

"Man that is born of a woman," intones Pastor John as the coffin is borne to the graveside, "hath but a short time to live, and is full of misery. He cometh up, and is cut down, like a flower; he fleeth as it were a shadow, and never continueth in one stay."

A violent gust of wind whips snow off the gable of the church, drowning the funeral prayers. "In the midst of life we are in death: of whom may we seek for

360

succour, but of thee, O Lord, who for our sins art justly displeased . . ."

Humprey's coffin is lowered into a hole that is rapidly filling with snow. "Farewell," whispers Agnes as she takes one final glance at the bier. "Farewell, my emperor."

It is long past midnight and the villagers of Piddletrenthide are at rest. The parson is snoring in his bed; in the Coach and Horses, the last of the candles have guttered and died. There is neither moon nor stars in the sky yet the landscape is washed with a curious luminosity. The snow seems to have retained the pale half-light of the previous day, lending a dull glow to the night.

In the churchyard of All Saints, there are grave-robbers at work. Three men dressed in black are digging up the newly filled grave of Humphrey Trencom. They speak in whispers — so low that it is impossible to hear a word. But they seem to have reached their goal. A mattock strikes wood; a hollow boom emerges from the grave.

Two of the men jump into the hole and heave at the wooden coffin. It is covered in wet earth and its smooth oak surface is slippery in their hands. But they succeed in raising it to the perpendicular and the third man leans down from above and starts to pull. In a matter of seconds, the coffin emerges onto the snow.

What are they doing? Why are they stealing it? All that can be said with certainty is that they are last seen riding eastwards, bearing off the corpse of Humphrey Trencom on a low wooden sled.

Humphrey's lifetime voyages may have come to an end, but in death he is to experience one final adventure.

CHAPTER
TEN

6 May 1969

Edward vowed to follow the summons to Greece within a few seconds of receiving Papadrianos's letter. Yet he waited more than ten days before broaching the subject with Elizabeth and, when he did eventually tell her, he found that he was uncommonly nervous. He knew that she would be unhappy with his decision, yet he had made up his mind that, come what may, he would go to Salonika.

"I have to — I have no alternative," he thought. "It's my only hope of finding answers."

He finally summoned the courage to speak to Elizabeth, one evening after they had finished eating. They were sitting in the living room and Elizabeth had just picked up her book.

"Darling," he said.

"Mmm?"

"Darling, there's something I need to tell you — something important." Edward looked out of the window and saw Mrs Hanson from Number 47 washing her car with a large yellow sponge. "What a strange time to be washing her car," thought Edward.

"And why does she keep staring at me? She really is a most peculiar woman."

"What did you say?" said Elizabeth, who had just come to the end of the paragraph she was reading.

"Well," replied Edward. "I have to go away, darling. Just for a short while. I need to go abroad."

There was a moment's pause.

"*Abroad*? But why, Edward? Whatever for?"

"Well," he said slowly, thinking carefully about his answer. "I've decided — you see — I've decided, darling, that it's time I started preparing for the reopening of Trencoms. You know, until recently, I just haven't had the energy. I don't know why but it's all seemed too daunting. But the other day I suddenly thought to myself: 'Come on, Edward. Pull your socks up. You've got three centuries of history to live up to.'

"And also, well, I also realize I've not been fair on Mr George. He's been working around the clock for weeks, clearing up, ordering cheeses, getting everything ready. I think it's high time he had some help. So, well, the long and the short of it is that I've decided it's time to start afresh."

Elizabeth looked intently at Edward. She was so amazed by what she was hearing that she was momentarily transfixed. Then, when she realized that he'd finished speaking, she got up from her chair and made her way over to the window, where he was standing. She wrapped her arms around his waist and gave him an affectionate kiss on the nape of his neck.

"Oh, darling," she said, squeezing him tightly. "I can't tell you how happy you've just made me. I've been praying for this moment for a long time. Maybe we need a few more little breaks in Dorset. It *was* the tonic we needed."

She kissed Edward again, this time on the lips, and as she did so Mrs Hanson happened to cast her gaze over to the Trencom house. "Good Lord," she muttered to herself. "They're at it again — whatever are they going to do this time?"

Elizabeth asked Edward where he was intending to go. "Can't you order the cheeses from England? That's what Mr George has been doing. And that's what you've done in the past."

"Some, yes," he replied. "But I want to start everything afresh. Start from scratch. I want to meet the producers and farmers again. Let them see that we're back in business."

"So you'll go to France?" said Elizabeth.

Edward nodded. "A whistle-stop tour. A flying visit. Quick as a flash."

Elizabeth smoothed her hands over his back and kneaded his shoulders. "Do you think . . ." she asked tentatively. "Would there be any possibility of us going together?"

Edward's face displayed a momentary flicker of alarm. Hell. He hadn't expected that.

"Well, I'd love to, darling — I really would. But, you see, I'm going to be chasing around from one place to the next. And, besides, you really need to be here — we can't leave Mr George entirely on his own."

Elizabeth was not convinced by this last line of argument. Mr George had more than proved himself over the past weeks and could certainly be trusted to take the right decisions. But she decided not to push the issue. Edward had always gone alone on his cheese expeditions and perhaps that's how he preferred it.

"I suppose you're right," she said. "But I will miss you. I'll miss you more than ever. How long will you go for?"

"Ah, not long. I was thinking of a fortnight. That'll give me time to visit —" He stopped for a moment and ran with his thoughts. He was shocked at how easy it was to lie. And how natural. He realized with a start that he had almost convinced himself that he was going to France.

"Where was I?" he said. "Ah, yes — that'll given me time to visit the whole of eastern France. I'm sure that word will soon spread to producers elsewhere."

CHAPTER
ELEVEN

10 May 1969

In the cool and ill-lit interior of the parliament building in Athens, three men were seated around a small conference table. Two were dressed in khaki fatigues and adorned with such a preponderance of medals and colours that one suspects they had been awarded less for heroism on the battlefield than for services to corruption and nepotism. The third was wearing civilian dress and was more rotund in the belly than his compatriots. He wore the same grave expression of the other two men and seemed to have locked his eyebrows into a permanent frown. The names of these men, once familiar to every householder in Greece, were George Papadopoulos, Nikolaos Makarezos and Stylianos Pattakos.

These three men — the junta — had awoken to discover that they had a crisis on their hands. "A crisis, a crisis," muttered Papadopoulos. He tapped his silver-topped pencil on the leather writing mat then scratched his ear. "And, gentlemen, I'm not at all sure how we should solve this particular crisis."

The crisis to which he was referring was to tax the leading brains of virtually every government in the democratic world. But since these events occurred many decades ago — and all the leading players have long since shuffled off their mortal coils (along with their khaki uniforms and shiny medals) — it is worth remembering that Greece, in the spring of 1969, was in something of a stew; a mixed-up, mushed-up plate of luke-warm greasy moussaka. Parliamentary democracy had collapsed. The king had abdicated and fled. And the government had been seized by a junta of army colonels. None of this had been popular with the people of Greece and their anger was rapidly approaching the sort of temperature that even Syntagma Square only experiences once in a blue August. The students were rioting, the priests were incensed, the shopkeepers were up in arms. Mothers feared for their sons. Their sons clashed with the police. And everyone else — except for Messrs Papadopoulos, Makarezos and Pattakos — was decidedly unhappy with the spiralling downturn of events. Which is precisely why, on this very day in May, 1969, the three aforementioned men had gathered in a conference room of the parliament building in order to discuss how best to react to a crisis that was spreading out of control.

All three shook their heads and stared vacantly into the room. Pattakos picked out a large chunk of loukoum from the dish in the centre of the table. It was dusted with sugar and he could already imagine it melting on his tongue. Mmm — delicious. He savoured the flavour of pistachios and thought of his ripe-breasted Eleni. How he would like to be in the little vixen's arms right now.

"Strikes and rioting," growled Papadopoulos, disrupting Pattakos's reverie and transporting him rapidly back to the here and now. "The students are demonstrating, the bishops are protesting."

"Hang 'em," interjected Makarezos. "Hang the lot of 'em."

"And the royalists are growing stronger by the day."

"Hang 'em as well," added Makarezos. "And hang the king." He spat on the floor.

The king in question — and who aroused such passion in Nikolaos Makarezos — was none other than Constantine II, king of the Hellenes. A tall, angular individual, of Danish stock, he had fled into exile in Italy after the failure of his counter-coup. In the cool splendour of his Roman palace, he twiddled his thumbs, chatted with advisers and wondered if his regal posterior would ever again grace the throne of Greece.

In the event, His Majesty's fundament would never again renew contact with the plush purple cushions of the throne. Nor were Papadopoulos, Makarezos and Pattakos unduly bothered by the man they referred to as "the Danish bacon". They were more concerned about another individual — a rather more English bacon — whom they believed to represent a far graver threat to their power.

"I urge caution," said Pattakos, speaking very slowly. "I urge the utmost caution. Forces in the Church are still actively plotting a return to monarchy. Yes, indeed. They have many agents working on their behalf. And

369

my informers tell me that these agents, who include bishops and priests, represent a very real danger for us."

In the pause that followed, Papadopoulos slid his cup of coffee towards him and plopped three cubes of sugar into the unguent black liquid. He had a sweet tooth — a very sweet tooth — and could never have too much sugar. He stirred his coffee, lifting, as he did so, the thick grainy sludge that kept sinking to the bottom. Then, sliding his spoon back into the liquid, he watched as the coffee grains slipped back into the murky depths.

"And is there any news of Andreas Papadrianos?" he asked. "I presume you bring us news of him?"

Pattakos opened his file and took out a few sheets of paper. "Indeed I do. And it is not good. We are watching him — for he is a danger to us all. In the last week, gentlemen, he has made three visits to Mount Athos. He has had meetings with the abbots of at least five monasteries and has been seen consulting with Bishop Anastasius of Salonika and Archbishop Gregorius of the Morea. Yes, he has been consulting with all the troublemakers."

In the ensuing silence, a large bluebottle left its perch on the window and began buzzing around the room. After performing a few circuits of the three men's heads, it came to rest on the sickly-sweet rim of Pattakos's coffee cup. All three men watched intently as it sat there cleaning its front legs.

When, after more than twenty seconds, it showed no signs of moving, Makarezos thumped the table with his clenched fist. The coffee cup jingled in its saucer, the fly propelled itself upwards into the thick air and the three men resumed their conversation.

"And another thing," he said. "Our mission in London appears to have failed. Your cousin, Nikolaos, has proved most unsatisfactory. He has not done what was asked of him. Indeed, worse than that — we have reason to believe that he has changed sides."

"No," roared Makarezos. "Impossible. Nothing but lies."

"I only wish that were true," said Pattakos. "But he failed to act when he should have acted. And now it is too late." He paused for a moment and stared at Makarezos. "We have reason to believe — no — we know for certain, that Andreas Papadrianos has been able to make contact with *him*."

He did not specify who *him* was, for he had no need. All three men clearly knew the name and identity of *him*, for no sooner had Pattakos uttered the word than both Makarezos and Papadopoulos spat on the floor.

"He should be strung up and hanged," snarled Makarezos.

"He *should* be," said Pattakos. "Indeed, he should have *been* strung up and hanged. But unfortunately he wasn't. And now it is too late. For we do not know exactly where he is."

At the precise moment that these words were being spoken, Mr Edward Trencom of Trencoms Cheese Shop in London was passing through customs and security at Salonika Airport.

That he had got this far without being arrested was surprising; that he managed to be waved through Customs with little more than a scant glance from the border guards was little short of miraculous. For an order had been issued to all officials working at Greece's airports that anyone bearing the name Edward Trencom — and in possession of an extraordinary nose — should be arrested immediately. Greece is Greece, however, and this order had not been circulated to every airport and had most certainly not been passed down through all the ranks. Although everyone working at Athens Airport was familiar with the directive, along with the duty guards at Piraeus and Heraklion, those at Salonika remained in blissful ignorance of the dangers posed by a middle-aged Englishman with a strange-shaped nose. And thus it was that Mr Edward Trencom, holder of passport number NZ0206830, managed to slip into the country unnoticed and unheeded.

He was met in the arrivals hall by Andreas Papadrianos, whom he had not seen since the annual dinner of the Most Worshipful Company of Cheese Connoisseurs.

"I cannot tell you how happy I am to see you here," said Papadrianos. "And nor can I tell you how Greece herself will rejoice when she is told of your presence."

Edward looked alarmed; he motioned Papadrianos to stop. Then, catching his breath, he whispered, "Please, please, please, you must tell me what you have discovered. Your letter said nothing — I'm still not sure why I'm here. What am I to do? What do you expect of me?"

"All will be revealed in good time," replied Papadrianos. "The abbot will explain everything."

"The abbot?" asked Edward. "Who? Where? Where are you taking me?"

"Tomorrow, before dawn, we shall head to Mount Athos, the Holy Mountain. There Father Seraphim will reveal everything."

CHAPTER
TWELVE

11 May 1969

Edward had been gone for just over twenty-four hours when Mrs Trencom learned that he had not headed to France. Her discovery came quite by accident. The airline telephoned on the morning after he left to explain that there was a problem with his return flight and the ticket would need to be changed.

"Ticket?" said Elizabeth. "Flight?"

And then, as frosty icicles pricked her heart, she realized that her husband — her Edward — had lied.

"Ah, yes," she said, desperately trying to compose herself. "Ticket — to . . ."

"Well, the flight from Salonika to Athens is fine," said the voice at the other end of the phone. "But it's the return from Athens that is the problem."

Elizabeth nodded silently, forgetting that the person on the phone could not see her.

"Hello?" said the voice. "Are you still there?"

Elizabeth let out a slight murmur.

"You see, what with all the troubles in Greece at the moment, all our flights are subject to change. And we are in the process of reducing our schedule to just three flights a week."

374

"Right," said Elizabeth. "Well . . ."

"I presume you can contact your . . ."

"Husband."

"Yes, you see, he left us no address or number in Greece. The home number was the only one we had."

Elizabeth felt giddy and leaned against the kitchen cupboard for support.

"Yes, well, thank you," she said. "I'll make sure the message gets through." And with that she replaced the receiver on the phone.

"His father," she whispered to herself, "and his grandfather — and *all* of them. And now him." And she had the sudden realization, as she thought these thoughts, that her husband's life was in the gravest danger.

CHAPTER
THIRTEEN

12 May 1969

When God created man, he singled out Father Seraphim for special treatment. He provided him with a broad grin, a quirky dimple on his left cheek and a pair of mischievous eyes that invited one to step into his company and share a little private joke. In another age he might have been a wag or a courtly fool, for his wisdom was always dispensed with a light-hearted jest. Instead, he had been anointed Abbot of Vatopedi Monastery on Mount Athos and had spent half a lifetime infusing the monastic corridors with his felicific charms.

Father Seraphim was rarely to be found unaccompanied by a smile. He smiled when he hoed the courgettes. He smiled when he fished for octopus. But rarely did he have more occasion to smile than on the morning of 12 May 1969. For three decades he had wished, hoped and prayed to set eyes on Edward Trencom. Now, at long last, those prayers were going to be answered.

"Ah — yes. Now, let me have a look at you," he said, as Edward was ushered into the room. "Exactly — exactly as I thought. You're the very picture of your father." He reached out towards Edward's chin and gently rotated his head side-ways in order to examine the profile of his nose.

"It is he — the very image of Peregrine."

The abbot took three dwarf-sized glasses from the cupboard and poured a drop of distilled liqueur into each. "Now let's drink," he said. "We must drink to your health." After welcoming Edward to Mount Athos and making a short toast, he drained his glass and encouraged Edward and Papadrianos to do the same.

When both men had performed this pleasurable duty, Father Seraphim motioned to the door. "And now, before we do anything else, you must see around our monastery. For it holds something — several things — that I think will interest you greatly."

"But wait," interrupted Edward. "Wait — wait. This monastery — it's called Vatopedi?"

"Precisely," said the abbot. "Vatopedi."

Edward reached into his pocket and pulled out a folded sheet of paper bearing the code-word A+9VATPD70+O.

"Then this," he said, "this word in Humphrey's book, is connected with here — with this monastery?"

Father Seraphim nodded and draped his arm across Edward's shoulders. "Come," he said with a smile. "You've been kept in suspense for too long. But you won't have to wait much longer."

He ushered Edward out of the back door of the monastic gatehouse and into a large paved courtyard surrounded by half-derelict buildings. On one side of the courtyard was the monastery's principal church, a

Byzantine edifice built of worn red brick. On the other side, opposite the church, was the refectory, whose exterior walls were adorned with frescoes by St Theodore the Cretan.

"We shall look at these later," said Father Seraphim. "All in good time. First we must visit the church. It is the church that I wish you to see."

He led Edward across the courtyard and pushed open the door. Edward took a deep intake of breath as he entered the little church. "Ah, yes," he said under his breath. "At long last it's returned."

The abbot cast him a quizzical smile and asked if he could share in the secret.

"My nose," explained Edward. "For more than three months it's been failing me — it hasn't been working well. But now . . ." He sniffed again at the pungent air. "Now, it's detecting everything."

"Just as it always was," said the abbot. "It was thus with your father, and it was thus with the others."

"My father? The others?"

"Come," replied Father Seraphim, "let's descend into the crypt."

At the same time as the two men made their way towards the crypt, Mount Athos was to find itself welcoming another English visitor on that warm spring morning. For more than thirteen hundred years, no woman had set foot on this holy peninsula. No female guests had ever visited the monasteries; no female animal was permitted to graze on the flower-strewn slopes of the mountain. This rocky finger of land was dedicated to the Mother of God — the only woman whose name was ever mentioned in the hushed chapels of the monastic foundations.

But all that was to change on the morning of 12 May 1969. At shortly after 11 a.m., an attractive and rather prim-looking English lady could be seen stepping off a fishing boat, aided by two elderly and unkempt Greek men.

"Mercy," said one to the other as he made the sign of the cross. "May the Mother of God have mercy on us."

The other man nodded in agreement. "She knows what she is doing," said the other.

"Who? The Mother of God?"

"No — this lady here."

Mrs Trencom thanked the fishermen, paid them their fare and strode off along the pebble beach. As she made her way towards Vatopedi Monastery, which was set back from the shoreline, she reflected on the extraordinary events of the last forty-eight hours. What a topsy-turvy time she'd had. No sooner had she learned about her husband's voyage than she'd decided to track him down and rescue him. She bought herself a ticket to Athens with a connecting flight to Salonika and headed for the airport — the first time she had ever made a plane journey by herself.

It was evening by the time she'd arrived in the city and she spent more than an hour trying to find accommodation. Scarcely had she settled into her room in the Olympus Hotel than there had been a knock on her door. After briefly debating whether or not to open it, she turned the latch and found herself face to face with a tall, impeccably dressed Greek man.

"I'm Mr Makarezos," he said, putting out his hand. "I think you've heard of me. Can we talk?"

Mrs Trencom was quite taken aback at being visited by a strange man in an unfamiliar hotel, yet she betrayed no sign of surprise or fear. She had been awaiting a confrontation with Mr Makarezos for many weeks and was so relieved that the moment had finally arrived that she did not even consider it strange that he had followed her to Salonika.

"Come in," she said with extraordinary calmness. "I've been wanting to speak with you for some time."

"Before you say anything," he replied, "you must allow me to speak. I bring you news that they know you're here — yes, the junta. They're watching you, and they're hoping that you'll lead them to your husband. You must not contact him. You *must not*. You will place his life in the greatest danger."

"Oh, come now, Mr Makarezos," said Mrs Trencom in a voice that sounded unnaturally composed. "I hardly think that I can place my husband's life in even greater danger. He is far more likely to be in harm's way if I *don't* find him. Can't you see? Nine generations of Trencoms have died because of their obsession with their nose. They can't help themselves. It's their noses that lead them astray."

There was a long silence as Mr Makarezos considered how best to deal with this stubborn and most inflexible woman. He'd never warmed to English women and Mrs Trencom was about as English as they came.

"But do you know where he is?" he asked. "Would you know where to find him?"

"Oh yes," said Mrs Trencom with a note of triumph. "I know exactly where he is. You see, his old friend, Herbert Potinger, managed to unravel all of Humphrey Trencom's riddles and red herrings. He told me exactly where I'd find my husband. And I've no reason to doubt that that's precisely where I *will* find him."

"But surely you won't go — you can't possibly. It is absolutely forbidden for women to set foot on Mount Athos. Don't you understand? It's preserved for the Mother of God."

"Well," said Mrs Trencom, folding her arms. "That's all about to change. I am going to Mount Athos, Mother of God or no Mother of God. I thank you for your advice, Mr Makarezos, I really do. But I assure you that Mrs Trencom is quite capable of looking after herself. If there's anyone in danger, I'd suggest that it might well be you."

In spite of these bold words, Mrs Trencom experienced a sudden flutter of nerves as she approached the stout walls of Vatopedi Monastery. She stared at the stonework for several minutes before making any move towards the gatehouse. The walls stood more than thirty feet in height and encircled all the buildings within — a great stone rampart that had been built to protect the monastic treasures from the Barbary pirates who had once raided these shores.

"Well, well — here we go," said Elizabeth to herself as she walked up to the main gate. "I only hope that Herbert was right."

The gatehouse was empty and Mrs Trencom was able to enter the enclosed courtyard without being seen. Dressed in a lilac cotton dress and wearing a large straw sun hat, she looked the very picture of Englishness. She made no attempt to conceal her presence in the courtyard. Indeed, for several minutes she wandered around, admiring the climbing roses and pulling together her thoughts. She saw no sign of anyone in the monastery and was beginning to wonder if everyone was at work in the nearby fields.

When she was at long last spotted, there was considerable confusion. Two monks entered the courtyard from the refectory and looked on with absolute incredulity at what appeared to be a woman — or the vision of a woman — sniffing at the roses that surrounded the porch of the church.

"What in the name of God!" exclaimed one.

"Merciful Father!" said the other.

The two monks remained rooted to the spot for more than a minute, wondering whether or not they were beholding the Mother of God.

"Is it She?" said one, who was on the point of falling to the floor in obeisance.

"I — don't — think — so," said the other in a faltering voice. "She looks too — English."

As they debated what to do next, Mrs Trencom looked up, saw the two monks staring at her and walked briskly over to them. She asked if they spoke English, but both looked at her blankly.

"I've come for my husband," she said, speaking loudly and rather more slowly than usual. "Edward Trencom — that's his name."

When still this elected no response, she pointed at her wedding ring.

"Ah!" said one of the monks, who proceeded to converse with his fellow monk at a rapid pace. As the identity of this mystery woman slowly dawned on them, and they realized why she might have come, they both pointed towards the monastery's church.

"There," they said. "He's in there."

"Thank you very much indeed," said Mrs Trencom with customary politeness. And after giving the two monks a little bow, she entered the narthex of the church.

Father Seraphim was blithely unaware of Mrs Trencom's unorthodox arrival at Vatopedi Monastery. He was still celebrating the fact that Mr Papadrianos had managed to coerce Edward into coming to Mount Athos and could scarcely conceal his contentment as he led his English guest towards the crypt staircase, passing blackened frescoes and icons lit by candlelight.

"Can you see those?" he said, pointing to three reliquaries. "St Athanasius, St Antonius and St Nicholas, the founders of this monastery. They've been here for nine hundred years."

The air inside the church smelled of frankincense and floor wax, but Edward noticed that every time he

383

passed an icon lamp he caught a whiff of burned vegetable oil. He wondered why they didn't use olive oil. "It would smell much nicer," he thought. "And it wouldn't be *that* expensive."

"Now, do be careful on the steps," warned the abbot. "We wouldn't want you to — how do you say in English? — come a cropper."

He disappeared round a sharp corner and Edward followed, clutching tightly at the thin metal banister. The steps were smooth as pebbles and the only light came from a single bulb at the top of the stairs.

Down they went, around three more twists in the staircase, until Edward noticed that the darkness was at last being softened by a low pale gleam of light. He followed the abbot down two larger steps and suddenly found himself in a large chapel lit by dozens of oil lamps. As he scanned the room with his eyes, he was most startled by what he saw. An open stone sarcophagus stood before him, and at its furthest end there was an icon of someone who had exactly the same nose as his own. It was long, thin and aquiline with a prominent dome over the bridge.

Edward's eyes switched to the sarcophagus itself and was horrified to see that it contained a complete human skeleton. He gulped and swallowed hard.

"My God", he said. "Who is it?"

The abbot made the sign of the cross and stooped down to venerate the icon. He then walked back to Edward and led him to the side of the tomb.

"Tell me," said the abbot, "tell me what you know about Humphrey Trencom."

"Humphrey Trencom?" repeated Edward in a whisper. "Well, he left Constantinople with a parcel — some precious object. And he came, well, it's clear that he must have come here."

"Yes," said the abbot. "You see, his code was not so difficult after all. Come, show me your paper."

Edward pulled out the sheet for a second time and unfolded it.

"The 'A' and 'O'," said the abbot, "well, they stand for Agion Oros. The Holy Mountain. Mount Athos. And the numbers, well, 970 was the year in which our monastery was founded."

Edward took a sharp intake of breath. "Of course," he thought, harking back to his previous conversation with Herbert Potinger. "And as for the hermaphrodites — why, he must have meant monks. Monks have lived here for generation upon generation, but, in the manner of hermaphrodites, they seem able to reproduce themselves."

"You're right," said the abbot. "Humphrey Trencom came here, to Vatopedi. He came here with the package that he had found in Constantinople."

"But what on earth did it contain?" asked Edward. "That's what I've been trying to discover all along."

"Bones," said the abbot.

"Bones?" repeated Edward. "Is that all?"

"*Is that all!*" exclaimed the abbot as he pointed towards the sarcophagus. "He brought these very bones. These relics — these holiest of holies. They are holier, even, than the relics in the church above."

385

"But whose bones are they?" said Edward. But even before he had completed his sentence, he realized that he knew the answer.

"They are the mortal remains of the last Byzantine emperor, Constantine XI Palaiologos. He was killed during the siege of the city in 1453. Cut down by the infidel as he was valiantly defending the Porta Aurea. His death marked the end of an era. It brought about the demise of the most noble, most glorious, most Christian empire the world has ever known."

There was a long silence as Edward digested everything that Father Seraphim had told him. But it still didn't quite make sense.

"But why Humphrey?" he asked. "And why me? I still don't know why I'm here."

"I think you do," said the abbot. "But first, let me explain something else. Something important. Once the Turks had captured Constantinople, they began a desperate search for the emperor's body. You see, many people believed he was not dead; that he would rise again; that he was immortal and would return to crush the Turks. The Turks themselves believed these prophecies. It was said that Sultan Mehmet the Conqueror could not sleep for fear that his lifelong enemy was regrouping his forces."

The abbot cleared his throat and started to sing in a low clear voice:

"King, I shall arise from my enmarbled sleep,
And from my mystic tomb I shall come forth
To open wide the bricked-up Golden Gate;

And, victor over the Caliphs and the Tsars,
Hunting them beyond Red Apple Tree,
I shall seek rest upon my ancient bounds."

"What's that?" asked Edward, when he had finished. "What are you singing?"

"It's by Palamas. One of our most famous Greek poets. He's speaking of Emperor Constantine. You see, many in Greece also believed that the emperor would come again, and stories of his resurrection eventually entered our folklore."

"So why were his bones brought here?" asked Edward.

"Well," said Father Seraphim, "the monks in Constantinople were no fools. They realized the importance of keeping the emperor's death a secret — of safeguarding his body and perpetuating the stories of his impending return. They knew it would help them keep alive the dream of recapturing Constantinople. So they buried Constantine's body for seven years, as is our custom, and then disinterred his bones. They were kept for more than two centuries in a secret chapel under the Porta Aurea."

"And then Humphrey brought them here?"

"Yes, he did. But you're jumping ahead," said the abbot. "There is one more thing that you need to know. Emperor Constantine died without an heir and the succession passed to his brother, Thomas. *He* had a son called Andreas, who in turn became the lawful heir to the Byzantine throne. The family no longer lived in Constantinople, of course. The entire clan had fled when the city fell to the Turks. Some took refuge in the Morea, where they were welcomed by the local nobility. Others went much further afield — to Florence, Sweden, Bavaria and Russia.

"The eldest sons were courted by all the greatest crowned heads of Europe, since they were the legitimate and lawful heirs to the Byzantine throne. Even daughters, cousins and nephews found a welcoming hand throughout Europe, such was the fame of the Palaiologue name. For the three generations that followed Andreas, children and grandchildren produced sons to perpetuate the lineage. But when it came to Ioannes, Andrew's great, great-grandson, well, there was a problem. For Ioannes only had daughters, of whom the firstborn was given the name of Zoe."

"Zoe," repeated Edward, whose brain was now racing to keep up. "I think I know where this is leading."

"You should do," continued the abbot, "for this is where you enter the story. By the time Zoe was born, the Palaiologue family was scattered across Europe. The principal line had settled in France, but Zoe's father had crossed over to England, where he hoped to find sanctuary at the court of King Charles I. But the English king was far too preoccupied with his own troubles to help Ioannes Palaiologos. The poor Ioannes, in ill health and beset with financial difficulties, went first to Bognor and then to the west country. And it was here that Zoe, hereditary heir to the Byzantine throne, met and married —"

388

"Alexander Trencom," interjected Edward, with a note of triumph.

"Precisely," replied the abbot. "And when they produced a son, whom they called Humphrey, he became the legitimate heir and sole claimant to the Byzantine throne. You see, Emperor Constantine XI Palaiologos had signed an imperial decree to this effect. 'Blessed by God and sanctified by the Church, they shall remain rulers of the empire until the end of time.' The document was brought to our monastery by your father. We have it to this day — I'll show it to you later. This, indeed, was the document that Mr Makarezos was hoping to find in the cellars of your shop."

Edward asked the abbot to pause for a second as he took stock of everything he'd been told. "Then that means," he said slowly, "that I, too, am . . ."

"Yes," said the abbot. "As was your father. And your grandfather. All of them were linear descendants of the last Byzantine emperor."

Edward pursed his lips and let out a low murmur. "Is that why Humphrey went to Constantinople?"

"It was indeed. Humphrey was convinced that he had been given a sign. His mother, Zoe, had told him as much. It was a family tradition — nothing more. But Humphrey thought that the destruction of his shop really was a sign from God — a sign that he should travel to Constantinople to reclaim his throne.

"When he arrived in the city, he found that the monks were anxious to support him. Oh yes, the Church was desperate to restore him to the throne. But the time was not right, for the sultan was far too powerful. Although there were thousands of Greeks still living in the city — it was their home — there was no support for a general uprising."

"But why did he bring the bones to Mount Athos?" asked Edward. "Surely they could have stayed in Constantinople?"

"No," said Father Seraphim. "You see, the sultan fully understood the power of relics. And he also understood the power of folklore. He suspected that Constantine's bones were hidden in the city and he ordered that they be found. I think he knew that if he could prove that the emperor had died, then he could demolish the myth that Constantinople would one day be returned to the Greeks. In the summer of 1667, shortly after Humphrey arrived in the city, the sultan's officers came within a whisker of finding the bones. And this was why the patriarch entrusted Humphrey with bringing them to the safety of Mount Athos. He could be sure that no one would ever find them here.

Edward let out another low murmur. He was staggered by what the abbot had just told him and could not quite take in the fact that his own family were descendants of the Emperor Constantine. Never for one moment had he imagined that his story would have such a fabulous ending.

"So whatever happened to Humphrey?" he asked. "What happened to *his* body?"

"Come," said the abbot. "Follow me."

He led Edward into what appeared to be a much larger room that adjoined the little crypt. It was completely dark inside and the abbot reached into his cassock for a box of matches. He struck a match and held it to the wick of a candle, waiting for the flame to latch hold. No sooner had a low light spread across the room that Edward found himself gasping at the sight that greeted his eyes.

"Oh, God!" he said, leaning against the wall for support. His legs felt weak and his head was spinning. "My God. Tell me it's true — tell me I'm awake."

"You *are* awake — and it *is* true," said the abbot. "I've waited much of my life to show you this."

Laid out in front of the two men were nine open tombs, and each one contained a perfect human skeleton.

"It's my family," gasped Edward. "My ancestors."

He peered into each of the tombs before switching his gaze back to Father Seraphim.

"Humphrey, Alexander and Samuel," said the abbot, pointing at the first three skeletons. "Joshua, Charles and Henry. Emmanuel, George and — yes — these are the bones of your own father, Peregrine, who died on this very mountain."

"And they all lost their lives . . ." began Edward.

". . . in the cause of Greece. Yes, all of them hoped — desired — to re-establish themselves as leader of the Greek people, of our heroic nation."

Father Seraphim walked over to the tomb that contained the bones of Charles Trencom. "It was Charles who came closest to realizing this dream," he said. "If Lord Byron had been successful, and if Charles had not been murdered, then he might have been established on the throne of Greece."

"And Henry?"

"A brave man — brave indeed. He tried to assassinate the sultan. But, alas, he was killed in the process."

"And George?"

"Ah, yes, your grandfather. He also came close to receiving his crown. If it had not been for Ataturk, that scoundrel, George might even have been crowned in Constantinople. But it was not to be."

Edward wandered between the sarcophagi, trying to comprehend everything that he had just been told. All his life he had wondered what had happened to his father. Now, he found himself standing in front of his skeleton.

"But how on earth did they come to be here?" he asked. "How did you get them all?"

"It was not easy," admitted the abbot. "And it required a great deal of effort. But we *had* to get them. These bones are holy relics. The Trencom family is one and the same as the Palaiologos family and sacred to all who call themselves Greeks."

Edward sat down on the edge of one of the stone sarcophagi. Of all the extraordinary things that had happened to him over the previous weeks, nothing, but nothing, could compare with this. Papadrianos had assured him that he would be given answers and now — little by little — everything was indeed falling into place. He now knew why Humphrey's body was disinterred from Piddletrenthide cemetery. It was so that his mortal remains could be brought here, to Greece, to their final resting place.

After reflecting on what he had been told, Edward turned to Father Seraphim with a question that remained unanswered in his head.

"But in what way," he asked, "is our nose connected to all this? Has its shape really been passed down through the ages?"

Father Seraphim had been awaiting this very question and reached deep into the pocket of his cassock. After fumbling for a few seconds, he pulled out a small copper coin depicting the profile portrait of an emperor.

"It can't be," gasped Edward as he studied the emperor's strange-shaped nose. "It's really him? I've spent years looking for a coin bearing his portrait."

"Well, here he is," said the abbot. "The Emperor Constantine XI Palaiologos. Your ancestor. Take it — it's for you."

"For me? But — it's so rare. Are you sure?"

"Yes," replied the abbot. "One could even argue that you are its rightful owner."

Edward shook his head in bewilderment as he once again admired the profile of the emperor. His nose was remarkably similar to Edward's own — long, thin and aquiline and marked by a prominent bump over the bridge.

"And the nose has been passed down from generation to generation?" he said. "For more than seven hundred years? Down through the family?"

"Yes," said the abbot. "It must have been. Indeed, the Emperor Constantine was by no means the first to have your nose. You only have to look at the portraits of the first Palaiologos emperor, Michael, to see that he also had an extraordinary nose."

"But it's not just the shape," interjected Edward, who had switched his gaze back to the skeletons of his ancestors. "That's only a part of it. It's the strange ability of our nose to detect the merest hint of a smell — its astonishing power. That is something that I don't understand at all."

"Well, that power has also been in the family since the beginning of time," said the abbot. "The Emperor Michael VIII Palaiologos records how he could smell victory in the air on the morning that he recovered Constantinople from the crusaders. He describes the 'incense of thanksgiving' floating on the breeze.

"And the nose has given many signals of impending doom. Consider the Emperor Manuel II Palaiologos. He lost all sense of smell shortly before being imprisoned in the Tower of Anemas. And Constantine's nose failed him just hours before the siege of Constantinople. It was as if it were presaging his coming defeat."

Edward instinctively lifted his hand to his nose and rubbed his forefinger up and down the ridge.

"And you, Edward, have also inherited this extraordinary sixth sense. Many say that you have the most powerful nose in generations."

Father Seraphim fell silent for a moment and once again made the sign of the cross. "You asked me why you have this ability. And you asked me how. My personal view is that memory, the treasure-house of the human mind, can store the experience of smell. I believe that different odours, sensations, are passed from father to son. Just think — you can smell a crocus in spring and recall it months later, in the depths of winter. You can smell a goat's cheese in Greece and remember it when you're back in England. In that same way, but on a far grander scale, the power of smell can be transmitted across the generations.

"But I fear that you ask too many questions. It is the vice of the West. There are many things — wonderful things — that cannot be explained. They will never be explained, for they are in the hands of God. There are depths that cannot be fathomed — that will never be fathomed. You see, Edward, science can make no sense of mystery."

It was as the abbot said these concluding words that Edward felt a tingling chill surge upwards through his body, from his feet to his scalp and thence to the tip of his nose. He felt giddy, light-headed, and felt himself reeling with fear. It was all proving too much to take in.

"And why am *I* here?" he said at length. "What do you want of me?"

There was a long silence before the abbot turned to look him in the eye. But just as he did so, he found himself receiving the greatest shock of his life. He caught sight of a woman descending the last few steps of the staircase that led into the crypt. And although he had never set eyes on her before, he had no doubts as to her identity.

"What in the name of God! How did you —?"

"Elizabeth Trencom," said the dimly lit figure as she held out her hand. "And I've come to reclaim my husband."

"But how in the devil's name did you get here?" roared the abbot, who seemed suddenly infused with energy. "Don't you know that women are banned from Mount Athos? It is sacred ground. It is blessed."

"Yes, yes," said Mrs Trencom in her most businesslike voice. "I know all that. And I will make my apologies later. But let's move swiftly to the matter in hand, before it's too late. I believe that you were about to say something to my husband. He wanted to know why he's been brought here. Why you need him so much. But before you explain, allow me to say one thing."

Elizabeth smiled nervously as she collected her thoughts. She could scarcely believe that she was standing here in the monastery of Vatopedi, in front of her bemused and confused husband.

"As you know," she said, "Edward has the finest nose in generations of Trencoms. He also has the finest cheese shop in the whole of Britain. For months he has been pursuing some unknown goal — some ridiculous goal. He has been watched and followed. We have both been spied on. Our shop has suffered a terrible catastrophe. Our lives have been in danger. Now, it all has to end. Enough is enough. I will not allow you to ruin our marriage. I will not allow you to destroy Trencoms. Edward's nose is needed in London."

Elizabeth was so animated and angry that two red blotches had appeared on her cheeks. She was about to continue when she found herself interrupted by the abbot.

"No, no," he said. "I command you to stop. His nose is needed here."

"Well, in that case," said Elizabeth angrily, "let his nose be the judge. Let us put it to the test. And let us trust its judgement. But first, please, put him out of his misery. Tell him what you want of him."

Father Seraphim weighed up what Mrs Trencom had said and realized that he had little option but to continue. She clearly had no intention of leaving the crypt; besides, the abbot now knew that he could no longer pressurize Edward into staying. His nose — and his nose alone — would indeed have to make the choice.

"Edward Palaiologos," he began, pointedly turning his back on Elizabeth. "Our country is in crisis. We have come to a turning point. The king, our *Danish* king, has fled. He has abdicated. He will never return. Forces of evil are ruling this land — the junta are destroying our country. But good is at long last fighting back. There are riots in Athens. There is a general strike. The students are rebelling in the streets. And the Church, too, has spoken out against the junta. Now, with all our force, power and prayers, we shall resist this band of common criminals."

"And me?" whimpered Edward. "What do you want from me?"

"You, Edward, shall be our figurehead — our rallying cry. You are the only rightful and legitimate heir to the Greek throne. You have the blood of Greece coursing through your bones. You are the chosen one — the one who shall lead us to victory. We anticipate a long struggle. We shall have to fight the colonels who are ruining our sacred land and then we shall take our fight to the very gates of the holy city. There will be much slaughter and death, but victory, Edward, will ultimately be yours. Yes, yes — victory will be yours."

Edward looked at the abbot with an empty feeling of terror. His nose began to twitch violently, as if it was reacting to every word that the abbot spoke. His nostrils seemed to be expanding, reaching outwards as they grasped the full meaning of Father Seraphim's words. Edward could no longer smell the incense of the church, nor the candles, nor the oil lamps. Now, his nose was picking up the stench of the battles to come: gangrene and cordite and foetid corpses. He could smell guts and vomit, caustic smoke and putrid flesh. For hundreds of years, the Trencoms had been blessed with the most extraordinary sense of smell. For generation upon generation, they had sniffed at life and death and stored the odours of mortality in the inner recesses of their minds. Now, in their time of direst need, the inherited memory of these smells returned to fill the sensitive nostrils of Edward Trencom. He felt sick in his stomach and the room spun before his eyes. His nose had transported him to the battlefield, where the forces of royalty were butchering the forces of the junta. And he found the smell of conflict as repugnant as a glass of milk that has curdled and soured.

Was this *really* his mission in life? Was this why he had been blessed with such an extraordinary nose? The stench grew stronger and more pungent — a relentless wave of terrible, freakish odours. But just as Edward felt that he was about to swoon, a very different scent began to permeate his nostrils; one that was sweeter and more fragrant than any he had smelled for a long time. A procession of cheeses seemed to be marching through his nose — a stately procession that grew in strength with every second that passed. At first they were as mild as the creamy chevrotin. Edward could detect the lemony tang of a Prussian tilsiterkase and the ambrosial fragrance of a rollot. These were followed by the muscadine septmoncel and the pigsty pong of a cabreiro. And then came the venerable generals of the cheese-board — the noble roquefort and the piquant epoisses! As Edward revelled in this inherited nosegay, he realized that all the scents were starting to mingle into one heady cocktail that infused its way into every pore of his receptive nostrils. It was as if he was standing under the slowly spinning fans of Trencoms.

"What should I do?" he murmured to himself in a low voice. "Of all my ancestors, I am surely the one who can be the saviour of Greece. My father, my grandfather, Emmanuel, Henry, Charles, Samuel and Alexander. All gave up their lives for this moment. What should I do, Elizabeth? What choice should I make?"

Elizabeth said nothing. She looked intently at her husband's nose and could see that it was still twitching violently. His face had turned a deathly pale and a cold sweat was trickling down his forehead. Seeing that he was close to collapse, she realized that now was the moment to act. Without further ado, she reached into her handbag and pulled out a small Tupperware box.

"What is it?" whispered Edward. "What have you brought?"

"Stop her!" shouted Father Seraphim in a voice that was loud enough to wake the dead. "You must not open that box. In the name of all that is holy, I command you to keep it closed."

"It is too late," said Elizabeth, who had already positioned her fingernails under the rim of the lid. "There's no going back. I only hope that the nose will at long last give us an answer."

There was a snapping noise as the lid popped off and fell to the floor. And at precisely the same moment, a new and extremely pungent smell seeped through the crypt.

"Oh, my God!" exclaimed Edward. "Can it really be?"

And as he inhaled deeply, the thick, goaty scent of touloumotyri filled his nostrils. He sniffed again and allowed the odoriferous smell to work its way deep into the inner recesses of his nose.

"Ah, yes," he said with a dreamy smile. "Just as it should be. A spring cheese, of that there's no doubt. You can smell the wild meadows. And I do believe it's" — sniff, sniff — "from the village of Dhimitsana, in the Peloponnese." He was lost now — half in a trance. In his mind's eye, he saw goats and hill villages and fields of red wild poppies.

"How did you get it? Where did you buy it? Oh, Elizabeth, I want this cheese for Trencoms. I want it more than anything in the world."

As Edward's thoughts hot-footed themselves back to the family shop, he felt a renewed wave of giddiness wash through his head. His eyes filled with mist and his knees shook uncontrollably. And before he had time to clutch onto a pillar for support, or even sit himself down, he swooned, fainted and collapsed to the floor. Unconscious but deliriously happy, his nose seemed to twitch a few more times before a radiant smile could be seen spreading across his face.

"I think," said Elizabeth to Father Seraphim, "that my husband's nose has made up its mind. Now, if you'll excuse us, we ought to be heading for home."

ISIS publish a wide range of books in large print, from fiction to biography. Any suggestions for books you would like to see in large print or audio are always welcome. Please send to the Editorial Department at:

ISIS Publishing Limited
7 Centremead
Osney Mead
Oxford OX2 0ES

A full list of titles is available free of charge from:

Ulverscroft Large Print Books Limited

(UK)
The Green
Bradgate Road, Anstey
Leicester LE7 7FU
Tel: (0116) 236 4325

(USA)
P.O. Box 1230
West Seneca
N.Y. 14224-1230
Tel: (716) 674 4270

(Australia)
P.O. Box 314
St Leonards
NSW 1590
Tel: (02) 9436 2622

(Canada)
P.O. Box 80038
Burlington
Ontario L7L 6B1
Tel: (905) 637 8734

(New Zealand)
P.O. Box 456
Feilding
Tel: (06) 323 6828

Details of **ISIS** complete and unabridged audio books are also available from these offices. Alternatively, contact your local library for details of their collection of **ISIS** large print and unabridged audio books.

White Gold

Giles Milton

The Extraordinary Story of Thomas Pellow and North Africa's One Million European Slaves. Giles Milton vividly reconstructs a disturbing, little known chapter of history.

This is the forgotten story of the million white Europeans enslaved by North African barbarians into a life of harsh servitude. Ignored by their own governments, very few lived to tell the tale. Giles Milton has written a gripping and brilliantly realised and researched account of this particular time in history, using the first-hand testimony of a Cornish cabin boy named Thomas Pellow.

ISBN 978-0-7531-5647-6 (hb)

ISBN 978-0-7531-5648-3 (pb)

Sex and Other Changes

David Nobbs

A funny and compassionate study of what being a man and a woman really means

a highly readable and strangely affecting comedy of embarrassment, resentment, grief and love

The Sunday Times

Meet the Divots. They seem a happy married couple, in their cosy suburban home in a cosy suburban town. Then, one day, everything begins to change. Nick drops his bombshell. He wants to become Nicola.

Alison is extremely upset, naturally. But she has more reason than most to be upset, because she has a secret too. She wants to become Alan. Nick has pulled the rug from under her. However, she's always been the supportive type and she'll wait her turn.

Will Nick become Nicola? Can Alison become Alan? Can both partners in a marriage change sex and save their marriage? What effect will this have on their children, the sexy Emma and the hi-tech loner Graham? There are dramatic changes in store for them too — and for Alison's father, Bernie.

ISBN 978-0-7531-7469-2 (hb)
ISBN 978-0-7531-7470-8 (pb)

May Contain Nuts

John O'Farrell

a wonderful satire on the all-consuming madness of modern parenthood

"The other day there was a feature on the radio about the dangers of asteroids falling from outer space. When David came home he wanted to know why the children were splashing around in the paddling pool wearing their cycle helmets."

Alice never imagined that she would end up like this. Is she the only mother who feels so permanently panic-stricken at the terrors of the modern world — or is it normal to sit up in bed all night popping bubble wrap? She worries that too much gluten and dairy may be hindering her children's mental maths. She frets that there are too many cars on the road to let them out of the 4x4. Finally she resolves to take control and tackle her biggest worry of all: her daughter is definitely not going to fail that crucial secondary school entrance exam. Because Alice has decided to take the test in her child's place . . .

ISBN 978-0-7531-7513-2 (hb)
ISBN 978-0-7531-7514-9 (pb)

The Sunny Side

A. A. Milne

The Sunny Side is a long-forgotten collection of short stories and poems by A. A. Milne. Though Milne is best known for his classic children's books, these tales for adults shine just as brightly, full of wit and wisdom. From summer days to wartime, from dogs to gardens and card games, these stories are perfect reading in the hammock or by the fire.

ISBN 978-0-7531-7608-5 (hb)
ISBN 978-0-7531-7609-2 (pb)

The Act of Roger Murgatroyd
Gilbert Adair

A wonderfully witty novel that plays with the Golden Age crime genre

Boxing Day, 1935. A snowed-in manor on the very edge of Dartmoor. A Christmas house party. And overhead, in the attic, the dead body of Raymond Gentry, gossip columnist and blackmailer, shot through the heart. But the attic door is locked from the inside, its sole window is traversed by thick iron bars and naturally, there is no sign of a murderer or a murder weapon.

Fortunately (though not for the murderer), one of the guests is the formidable Evadne Mount, the bestselling author of countless classic whodunits. In fact, were she not its presiding sleuth, The Act of Roger Murgatroyd is exactly the type of whodunit she herself might have written.

ISBN 978-0-7531-7740-2 (hb)
ISBN 978-0-7531-7741-9 (pb)